Nektaria Anastasiadou's writing has appeared in *The Huffington Post, Al-Monitor, Daily Sabah, Mashallah News, Panoply, East of the Web, Sixfold, The Shanghai Literary Review, Eclectica,* and *The Eastern Iowa Review*. In 2019, one of her short stories was included in the *American Fiction Anthology* and she won the Zografeios Agon, a prestigious Greek-language literary award established in Constantinople during the late Ottoman Empire. She also received an honorable mention in *Glimmer Train*'s Spring 2017 New Writer Contest and in *Ruminate*'s 2015 Short Fiction Contest.

She lives in Istanbul and *A Recipe for Daphne* is her debut novel.

D0036329

A Recipe for Daphne

Nektaria Anastasiadou

hoopoe

AN IMPRINT OF AUC PRESS

First published in 2020 by
Hoopoe
113 Sharia Kasr el Aini, Cairo, Egypt
One Rockefeller Plaza, New York, NY 10020
www.hoopoefiction.com

Hoopoe is an imprint of the American University in Cairo Press
www.aucpress.com

Dar el Kutub No. 22298/19
ISBN 978 977 416 979 3

Dar el Kutub Cataloging-in-Publication Data

Anastasiadou, Nektaria
        A Recipe for Daphne / Nektaria Anastasiadou.—Cairo: The American
    University in Cairo Press, 2019.
        p. cm.
        ISBN 978 977 416 979 3
        1. English Fiction
        823

1 2 3 4 5   24 23 22 21 20

Designed by Adam el-Schemy
Printed in the United States of America

1

Preparation for an Encounter

WHAT THE MAN IN WHITE called cerebral arteriosclerosis and vascular dementia, Fanis called preparation for an encounter with divinity.

"You're just a little confused," said the man. He withdrew the icy metal thing he'd been holding to Fanis's chest. "That's common after a syncope. You're going to be okay."

Fanis took a deep breath: the place smelled of iodoform and humiliation. He could hear restrained murmurs, offensive beeping, and somebody emptying his insides. It wasn't what he expected of Hades. His vision was still blurry, but he was able to make out a golden caduceus on the man's lapel. "My God," he said. "Is it you? And why are you speaking Turkish?"

"I'm sorry," said the man. He had the deep bass voice that Fanis had always wanted. "I forgot to introduce myself. I'm Dr. Aydemir."

"A doctor? But that staff belongs to Hermes, not to doctors. Asclepius's staff—with just *one* snake—is the symbol of medicine. Which makes you an impostor, sir."

Dr. Aydemir glanced at his watch. "Do you know where you are?"

"Of course I do. I'm in the City."

"Which city?"

"There's only one. Istanbul."

"And just where in Istanbul are you?"

Fanis looked around. He saw a nurse's foot—in an ugly white shoe—peeking out from beneath the flimsy yellow privacy curtains. "The German Hospital," he said.

"Good," said Dr. Aydemir. "Do you know what day it is?"

"June 4, 2011. The day I was supposed to meet a god."

The doctor smiled. "It's true that some people think of me that way. But I'm human after all."

"That's not what I meant," said Fanis, suddenly aware that they had dressed him in one of those awful paper gowns.

"Did you mean," said the doctor, "that you thought you would die today? It's not time to worry about that yet. Medications can treat your condition."

Fanis, however, did not believe that multicolored pills could cure anything. Apart from sporadic aggravations such as erectile dysfunction, that was.

The doctor took out his mobile phone. "Perhaps I misunderstood. Maybe you'd like me to send for a priest?"

Fanis rolled his eyes. He knew the fellow was only trying to be considerate, but the question irritated him. Everyone had noticed the Greek name on Fanis's chart and the religious classification on his identity card: Christian. Those were his minority tags, his marks of non-Turkishness. And so, when he had mentioned an encounter with divinity, the doctor had assumed that he was referring either to death or to churches. Yet Fanis had seen the cause of the illness in his dreams, and he knew what it meant: it was time to unbind knots, loosen tongues, and release what had been kept hidden. The divinity who would help him was neither Christian nor Muslim, but Hermes, the god of transitions and boundaries and the patron of shamans, travelers, thieves, storytellers, and liars.

Still, Fanis realized that this young pup would never understand. So he said, "That's not necessary. Just give me your side of the story."

"Excuse me?"

"The prognosis, the treatment, and all that ho-hum."

"Right." The doctor sat on a rolling air-lift stool and crossed his long legs. "Let's start with the arteriosclerosis. The risks are ischemic or hemorrhagic stroke—"

"Death, you mean."

"Yes, as well as vascular dementia. Thank God, you've managed to avoid a stroke so far, but from the symptoms—confusion, difficulty making decisions, restlessness, agitation, memory issues—it seems you're already in the early stages of vascular dementia."

"So it's all over?"

"Not necessarily. I suggest you reduce your fat intake—"

"Impossible."

"Then you'll at least have to take these medications." Dr. Aydemir tore five prescriptions from his pad.

Fanis was unable to read the snake-track writing. "What are these?" he asked.

"Just a few things to lower your cholesterol and blood pressure, and help prevent cognitive decline and a potentially fatal stroke."

"Can I take them with Viagra?"

"You take Viagra?"

"Didn't they tell you? That's why I came. I want a prescription."

"At seventy-six?"

"Why not?"

"You mean you still—?"

"Of course."

"Shouldn't you be spending time with your grandchildren?"

"I don't have any. My late wife—may God give her rest—couldn't conceive. But I'm going to remarry as soon as I find a beautiful woman of my own kind. Rum, that is."

The doctor stared at Fanis. He probably didn't even know that the word *Rum* was a Turkified version of the Greek word *Romios*, which meant Roman. At best, Dr. Aydemir thought

3

of Fanis in the terms of the rest of the world, as an "Istanbul Greek," which implied that his forebears hailed from Greece and not from Istanbul. Aydemir surely didn't know—because almost no one did nowadays—that many of Istanbul's Greek-speaking Rums were descendants of a native population that had lived in the City since well before AD 330, the year in which Constantinople became the capital of the Eastern Roman Empire.

Fanis explained, "The Patriarch says we should all have three kids to perpetuate our race. I probably won't manage so many. I'd be happy with just one son to carry on the Paleologos name. It's Byzantine, you know."

"I'm sorry, sir, but I don't think it's a good idea. You've got more important things to worry about now."

"What could be more important than that?"

"Listen. It's imperative that you begin taking these medications today. Not tomorrow, today. Otherwise your condition could worsen rapidly. You're still a vibrant man. I don't want to see you lose your independence."

"And the Viagra?"

The doctor sighed. "We'll revisit the subject at your next appointment. Two weeks from today, okay?"

The doctor shook his hand, lifted the yellow curtain, and disappeared. A male nurse handed Fanis the clothing and accessories that had been neatly stored in a cabinet at the foot of the examination table: a crisp shirt, creased pants, a gold-buckled belt, and well-polished shoes. Thank God no one had stolen his watch. It was still on his left wrist, and his wedding ring—along with that of his dead wife—was safe on his right ring finger. After tying his silk handkerchief around his neck, Fanis thanked the nurse and left the hospital through the back entrance in order to reduce the chance of being seen by acquaintances.

Once outside, Fanis turned right into Turnacıbaşı Street. While walking beneath the grapevines that crawled over electric lines and drooped like pearls on a woman's chest, he tried to decide whether he should follow the doctor's advice. Fanis wasn't against sleeping pills, necessary antibiotics, or romantic helpers. After all, those weren't things you took every day. But chronic medication was another thing altogether. Once you go down that road, he had always said, there's no coming back. You're on the fast track to more and more disease. But if the alternative was a stroke that could put him in Baloukli Nursing Home, where he would spend his days staring at the ceiling, muttering incoherently, and doing his business in a bedpan? Then what?

He entered the Turnacıbaşı Pharmacy, whose floor-to-ceiling wood and glass cabinets were filled with sinister little boxes. "Is anyone here?" he asked.

"Be out in two minutes!" shouted the pharmacist from the back room.

Fanis went outside and petted the two homeless Kangal-mix dogs that lived nearby. They lifted their dirty heads, sniffed his air, and leaned into his caresses. Fanis's neighbors were stingy on love, but at least they kept the beasts fed and watered. Everywhere you saw the bottoms of five-liter plastic bottles that had been cut to make water dishes for dogs and cats. Across from the pharmacy, an artist had made a cat bed from an old pink suitcase and a green pillow, and she had placed a pot of carnations beside it so that the cat would imagine he was lounging in his own private garden.

"How I would love to be that cat," said Fanis in Greek.

"Me too," replied a voice, in the same language. Fanis looked up. A full-figured woman with black hair so curly it was almost horizontal gave him a quick smile and a flash of her dark eyes and scampered off.

"Madame," he called out, but she didn't turn back.

Fanis looked through the open door. The pharmacist still hadn't appeared. Fanis stuffed the prescriptions into his pocket and took off toward the narrow pedestrian byway into which the woman had turned, but he made it all the way to Çukurcuma Street without another glimpse of her. He sighed and glanced down the hill toward the Galata Tower, rising like a party hat above the peninsula. The view was especially touching at that time of day, when the orange light of sunset zigzagged over the tile-roofed buildings of Pera.

Suddenly a beat-up black sports car came whizzing around a curve in the road. Fanis was obliged to jump backward in order to avoid being flattened. The car skidded to a stop.

The buff young driver opened his window and said, "Sorry, Uncle."

Fanis kicked a tire. "You're going to kill someone!" he shouted.

"It's not my fault they made these streets for mule carts and carriages!"

The car sped off. Miffed that he had lost the curly-haired vixen and also afraid of falling prey to the next rapscallion on wheels, Fanis hurried into the crook of the side street embracing the local mosque. Before him was Çukurcuma Antiques, the shop he had owned and operated for thirty-eight years and sold in 1996.

He popped his head inside, scanned the fifties retro furniture that was now passed off as "antique," and said in Turkish, "Attila! Good evening, son, how are you?"

Attila put one hand on his hip and waved with the other. "Mr. Fanis!" he called. "Come in for a tea."

"Thanks, but I don't have time right now. Did a woman with black curls come this way?"

"Skirt-chasing again, Mr. Fanis?"

"Never. Have you seen her?"

"Maybe. She climbed the hill toward Firuzağa Mosque, but you'll never catch up. Why don't you come in? I'd like to get your opinion on some carpets."

"Another time, son." Fanis hurried toward the next shop, which specialized in antique kitchen counters and basins. Ten or twelve heavy marble pieces leaned against the wall, like uninscribed tombstones. Fanis wondered how many of the meals he had eaten at departed friends' houses had been prepared beside those very sinks. Such a macabre thought. He drove it from his mind, scurried past the graveyard of oblong kitchen vestiges, and hung a left up a steep hill. Before continuing up Ağa Hamamı Street, where red flags and election placards waved from the lampposts, he caught sight of a nest of crazy black curls behind the great jars of preserved onions, cucumbers, tomatoes, carrots, and lemons on the shelves of the pickle-shop vitrine. He crossed the street and stepped inside the aquarium-like store, but the curly hair he had spotted from afar turned out to belong to a chubby teenage clerk.

"Good afternoon, dear," he said. "A small jar of pickled sea herb, please."

"I probably shouldn't tell you this," said the girl, "but the greengrocer next door has fresh sea herb. Why would you want to buy pickled when you can get fresh?"

"So true," said Fanis. "But cleaning fresh sea herb is a woman's job."

"You don't have a wife?"

"No. Do you know anybody who might be interested?"

The girl stared at him for a moment, then put the jar of sea herb in a blue plastic bag, rang up the purchase, and wished him a good day. Fanis stepped out into Ağa Hamamı Street grinning: the girl was far from attractive, but it had been fun to tease her a little. He looked this way and that, but the dark woman had disappeared. His little flirtation in the pickle shop had cost him the chase. Oh, well. He probably ought to return to the pharmacy, anyway. Fanis continued on his way, now in such a good mood that he forgot to avert his eyes when he passed the cul-de-sac where Kalypso, his lost fiancée, had lived. As much as Fanis loved his neighborhood, he hated the hill leading to that dead end of deserted and now reoccupied houses. Especially the one that had belonged to Kalypso. For a second he thought he heard the Roza Eskenazi record that Kalypso used to play when her mother wasn't home. Fanis stopped dead in the middle of the sidewalk. No, he hadn't heard Roza. The music was just something similar coming from the barbershop. He took another few steps toward the pharmacy and stopped again, this time grasping a streetlamp for support. He wondered why he should prolong his life with pills when Kalypso was—*perhaps*—waiting for him in the next world. Besides, he couldn't come to terms with having to buy one of those plastic pill boxes with a separate compartment for each day of the week, and he was sure that all doctors were liars. Thinking things over for just one more day couldn't possibly cause any harm.

He did an about-face and walked straight to the trendy bakery and tea garden that had recently reopened, after an extensive renovation, behind Firuzağa Mosque. He went inside and scanned the glass cases of lira-sized cookies in dozens of flavors—apple, coffee-filled-chocolate, pistachio, cherry-jam surprise, almond, fig-and-walnut, apricot-and-hazelnut, and orange-vanilla. The decision was easy. Cherry jam had always been his favorite. While waiting in line, he examined the tea garden's décor. Its walls were done in tastefully modern white brick. Its counters, tables, and signs were faced in a material that resembled golden oak or pine. He applauded the decorator: there was hardly any plastic in sight.

Having placed his order, Fanis collected his tray of tea and cookies, stepped onto the patio that stretched between the north wall of the bakery and an abandoned Ottoman cemetery, and settled down at a small wooden table shaded by a great linden tree and an awning with the shop's name— Neighbor's House—printed in whimsical brown letters.

While nibbling a cherry-jam surprise, Fanis overheard a woman's voice speaking the pure City Greek of the mid-twentieth century. He took a short breath of the linden-flower-scented air. Could it be her? He looked toward the other side of the crowded patio. The woman with curly hair was nowhere in sight. Again he heard Greek, this time coming from a balding, stubble-faced fellow in a pocketed fishing vest. Fanis felt the visceral attraction of a foreigner to his own kind and to a home that had vanished despite his never having left it.

The fellow in the fishing vest was his friend Julien Chevalier, of course, a retired music teacher descended from one of the old French Levantine families. Beside him sat Aliki Marouli, a sweet but unsightly Rum widow, whom Fanis had known forever. He waved.

"Come join us," Julien shouted. "Unless you're waiting for a lady friend, that is."

Fanis picked up his tray and set out for the other side of the patio. On the way, a gray cat tangled itself within his legs and caused him to trip on the slate pavement. He caught himself, but his tea spilled all over the tray.

"Damn cat," said Julien. "Someday it's going to kill someone."

"Ungrateful beast," said Aliki. She pressed the knuckle of her index finger to the bottom of her nose so that the rest of her hand covered her mouth—a nervous vestige from the days when one could be reprimanded for speaking Greek in the street. "That cat's already made me trip twice. Next time I'll probably end up in the hospital."

"Speaking of hospitals," said Julien, "how did it go?"

"Not so well," said Fanis. "I had a little episode while I was there."

"Episode?"

"I blacked out. Briefly."

"Is something wrong?" asked Aliki.

"No, the tests were fine. It was just nerves. The doctor says I'm as healthy as can be."

Aliki scrunched both eyes into a joyous double wink. "You always were."

9

"Anyway," said Fanis, momentarily disturbed by the crinkle of the prescriptions in his pocket, "the doctor gave me another good twenty years at least."

"More tea?" asked a waitress.

"Yes, please, Emine," said Julien. When the young lady had gone back inside, he said, "See her? Another girl gone religious. The baseball cap is only for work: she'll leave here in a headscarf."

"As if the secular girls were dressed any better," said Fanis. "Look at them in their rag-tag outfits, going about with mobile phones glued to their ears and speaking with the drawling accent that's become fashionable lately. I hardly understand them."

"Don't say any more, brother. Have you seen the transvestites in Tarlabaşı?"

"At least their hair is nicely done. Remember when women used to go to the hairdresser twice a week and come out looking like movie stars? Just like our friend Aliki here." Fanis patted Aliki's arm. She blushed.

"Ach," said Julien, "and the worst part is that even when a nice one comes along we're too slow to catch her."

"Don't put so much stock in speed, friend," said Fanis. "Skill has always been more important. We still have that. Apropos"—Fanis lowered his voice—"do you know a Greek-speaking woman who lives in the area, dark, attractive, full-figured, with black hair as curly as an Arab's?"

"Can't say I do. And I'd remember if she's attractive."

"Just my luck," said Fanis.

Aliki fluttered her blue-powdered eyelids. "Don't worry. There are plenty of other ladies who would—"

"Three days ago it was pouring chair legs," said Fanis, fanning himself. "Now I'm sweating like a sausage." Aliki and Julien looked perfectly comfortable, but he was burning up. Could this overheating be a sign of more trouble? Aliki offered him a handkerchief embroidered with a single violet.

Fanis thanked her and dabbed his forehead. When Emine served their teas, he said, "Could you raise the awning, dear? It's blocking the cool breezes coming up from the Bosporus."

Emine side-nodded. "Of course."

Fanis looked toward the street. Rea Xenidou, supporting herself on the arm of her son, Kosmas, was shuffling onto the patio. Rea's ankles and knees were unnaturally swollen. She winced at each step and progressed at a turtle pace, but her middle-aged son Kosmas showed no sign of haste or annoyance.

"Almost there, Mother," he said.

Fanis offered his canvas chair. He had always appreciated Rea's elegant French twist, the barely there shade of her lipstick, and the fact that she still donned all her gold jewelry for teatime, just as everybody had done half a century ago. Ladies like her deserved special treatment.

Rea's son, on the other hand, was a real piece of work. It was obvious that his mother still dressed him because he wore hideous, horizontally striped polo shirts in which Fanis would not have been caught dead. Kosmas had the brush-cut of a soldier, which, in combination with his tasteless outfits, led one to suppose that he was some sort of computer geek rather than an award-winning pastry chef.

"Ach, that feels good," said Rea, as she eased herself into Fanis's chair.

Aliki leaned against the low wall of the Ottoman cemetery and covered her mouth. "What are you talking about? These chairs are awful. They sag in the middle."

"Don't do that," snapped Julien.

"What?" said Aliki.

"The cemetery shakes at night from the unrest of its souls. It's bad luck to touch that wall. Unless you're in a hurry to join its inhabitants, that is."

"God forbid," said Aliki.

"Come on," said Fanis. "We aren't superstitious. Stop trying to frighten poor Aliki."

Just then, a seventyish woman wearing a gold necklace that disappeared beneath her blouse—an obvious sign, to the trained eye, that she was a Christian or Jew who preferred to keep her religion private—approached arm in arm with a young woman who walked with the rod-straight posture of a ballerina and the curious gaze of a foreigner.

"Good evening," said Aliki in Greek.

Gavriela Theodorou, a remarried divorcée from the hill-top neighborhood of Tatavla, kissed her friends and said, "This is my niece. Just arrived from America."

Fanis suddenly understood the workings of destiny: the curly-haired woman was not *the one*, but rather the rabbit who had led him down the hole to the wonderland in which Gavriela Theodorou's niece was waiting for him. Then again, Gavriela had never made any mention of an American niece. That was rather strange. Suspicious, almost.

Julien stood and pulled out his chair with a gallant sweep, a bow, and a chivalric triple turn of the wrist that ended in an upturned palm pointed at the chair. Kosmas also stood and offered his seat, but without any embellishments. Fanis tried do the same, but the skinny gray cat, which had apparently resettled beneath his chair, screeched so loudly that it startled him, and he fell back down.

"Stay where you are, sir," said the niece. "We only need two."

Annoyed that he had been surpassed in gentlemanly con-duct, Fanis waited until Julien and Kosmas had gone inside for more chairs. He took advantage of their absence to pull his seat over to the young lady's and ask, "What's your name, dear?"

"Daphne." She gathered her loose hair, which undulated like the curls of a Minoan princess, and let it tumble down her back. Although Daphne was not as voluptuous as the curly-haired siren, Fanis was excited by the way her black shirt exposed one of her pale shoulders. It was as if she was only half dressed.

"The most beautiful name there is," said Fanis. "Where are you from?"

"Miami."

He held out his hand. "Fanis."

"Pleased to meet you," said Daphne. Her voice was nasal and her accent in Greek strange: something between Istanbul and Athens, with a tinge of American.

He grasped her fingertips as gently as he would an old tapestry. "What beautiful, natural nails you have. It takes pluck not to hide behind polish. I suspect you have quite a lot of fire in you. What's your sign?"

Daphne tried to pull away her hand, but Fanis held it firmly. "Scorpio," she said.

"I knew it! Didn't I say you were fiery?" He kissed her chapped knuckles.

"What's your sign, Mr. Fanis?"

The 'Mr.' nettled Fanis, but he let it slide. "Guess," he said.

"Leo."

"Not far off. But I'm neither cruel nor bossy. Guess again."

"Gemini," said Daphne.

"That's an air sign. Do you really think I have an air sign?"

"Aries, then."

He released her hand. "I knew you'd get it. After all, it's the sign of energy and ardor. I'm Aries through and through. Did you know that Aries men and Scorpio women can be a perfect match?"

Daphne clicked her tongue. "I don't believe in that stuff."

Fanis continued: "It's because Scorpio women are so difficult to satisfy. Aries is the only sign that can handle it. His passion is raw, whereas Scorpio passion is—"

"Cut it out or you'll scare her away," said Julien, just returned with Kosmas and the extra chairs. "Now, tell me, Daphne, what brings you to the City?"

"A Turkish class." She twisted a tendril of hair around her finger.

"*Turkish?*" said Rea.

"I'm thinking about a PhD. In oral history."

"How interesting," said Fanis. "Do you know, my dear Daphne, that you have the heavy eyelids of the last Ottoman sultans? But that's not surprising because most of the sultans' mothers were Rum."

"For how long will you be in the City, Daphne?" asked Julien.

Gavriela removed her dark glasses and announced triumphantly, "Five weeks."

Everyone hummed in satisfaction: it was long enough.

"How old are you, dear?" asked Aliki. Fanis could have kissed Aliki's bristly cheeks. It was just what he wanted to know, but he made a point of never asking a man's salary, or a woman's age.

"Thirty-two," said Daphne.

Slightly young for Fanis, but he was sure he could win her. Instead of taking part in the usual chitchat, he sat back in his chair and listened while each of his friends put forward what they considered the most important subjects.

"Do you work, sweetie?" asked Rea.

"I'm a teacher."

"Oh, that's the very best profession for a woman," said Aliki.

Rea smiled sweetly at her son, turned back to Daphne, and asked, "Do you love children?"

"Yes, but I don't always love their parents."

"Are you married?"

"Not yet."

Fanis felt a secret tickle of delight, but he kept his hands folded across his belly, as if these details held no importance for him. He watched the flexing and curling of Daphne's unpainted toes, and he suspected—despite her confident replies—that her fidgeting was an indication of a certain discomfort.

"Good for you," said Julien. "Marriage destroys romance. Stay single if you want to have a good love life."

"Still," said Aliki, "one gets lonely."

"Don't worry, little mama," said Gavriela to her niece. "We'll find you a groom."

"But you haven't told us," said Rea. "Whose child are you?"

"My aunt's sister's," said Daphne. Everyone laughed.

Meanwhile, like any expert hunter, Fanis was completing the essential task of reconnaissance: the girl prickled at their questions, and her replies, although proper, were evasive. How he loved a mysterious woman. More than that, however, he admired her trim dancer's torso, the round posterior that he had glimpsed just before she sat down, and the child-thin wrists on which she wore silver cuff bracelets. Fanis knew, just as he could estimate the quality of an antique ring or some other fine thing, that Daphne was a find.

Of course, sitting as they were in a group, he couldn't use the infallible strategy he had developed and refined throughout his decades of amorous adventures. That would require him to gaze directly into the eyes of his intended and say, "I find you *incredibly* beautiful." So he thought for a moment and, with his instinctive acumen, adjusted the line both to his age and to the current situation by looking into Daphne's eyes and saying, "Every young man in our City must find you *incredibly* beautiful."

"Why don't you ask them?" said Daphne.

Delighted by her riposte, Fanis said, "What an original idea. Kosmas, don't you agree, as a young man, that Daphne is *incredibly* beautiful?"

Everyone fell silent. Kosmas scratched his brush-cut hair, stood, and asked, "Would anyone like more tea?"

"You haven't answered the question," said Fanis.

"Of course she is," Kosmas mumbled.

2

A Baker's Son Awakens

As a result of Fanis's puckishness, Kosmas found himself inside the narrow shop, standing at the unattended counter and waiting to order tea that no one wanted. He looked through the windows and beheld his mother's friends laughing and chatting, and then his eyes settled on *her*, the American who resembled the actress Semra Sar in the 1960s films of which Rea was so fond. She had the same ribbon brows, the same downcast glance, and the same tentative smile as that heartbreaking Turkish actress. Wearing only a plain dress and orthopedic sandals, without any makeup as far as he could tell, the American was indeed *incredibly* beautiful.

Kosmas leaned on the high counter with folded arms, lowered his forehead onto them, and sighed. All he had ever wanted was to become a pâtissier, restore his family business to its former glory, marry a lovely Rum girl, and live a normal life. The first dream he had realized by completing pastry school in Vienna. Since then his mille-feuille had become so famous that he had been asked to give lectures on its preparation at the Istanbul Culinary Institute. Moreover, he was well on the way to doubling the original size of his father's pastry shop. But he still had not found a bride, and now that a diaspora Rum had appeared in his life, like a golden coin in a Saint Basil's cake, he didn't even have the mettle to pay her a compliment.

A Greek voice recalled him from his sulk: "Those look tasty."

Kosmas raised his head from the counter and saw the American peering into the cookie case. "You've got to be joking," he said.

She cocked her head to one side.

Instinctively switching into culinary-professor mode, he explained: "It's just pre-prepared frozen stuff that they bring in and bake here. The City has much better to offer. Come by the Lily sometime and you'll see." He presented his card.

She stuffed it into the pocket of her cross-body bag. "Is that where you work? At the Lily?"

"It's our family business."

"I guess that explains the flour on your pants."

He looked down and saw the white dusting on his left thigh. Damn it. "Confectioner's sugar," he said, brushing it off. "From the mille-feuille."

She pulled her hair to the nape of her neck, twisted it, and let it fall over her chest in a long coil. "If you've got a bakery," she said, "then why are we here?"

Kosmas straightened his shoulders. "The Lily is a serious pâtisserie. Not a bakery, and definitely not a tea garden."

"I see. Anyway, I just came in for some napkins. My aunt spilled her tea."

Kosmas grabbed a stack from the counter and gave them to her. "I'll have somebody come out and wipe it up."

"It's not necessary." She smiled and held up the wad of napkins. "These are enough."

He watched her long dress sway as she crossed the patio. When she bent over to clean the table, her buttocks separated. The soft fabric of her skirt draped between. From behind she was almost obscenely beautiful.

As if reading his thoughts, a woman said in Turkish, "*Güzeller güzeli.*" A beauty of beauties. Kosmas turned back toward the counter and saw his old flame Emine, a Muslim girl who had worked at Neighbor's House a few years ago, quit, and—apparently—returned. Although civil marriage

18

between Muslims, Jews, and Christians was perfectly legal in Turkey, Kosmas had no desire to marry without the blessing of the Church. Still, he had been unable to prevent himself from being seduced when, one evening after a particularly hard day at the Lily, Emine had insisted on making him Turkish coffee instead of tea. She had carried it with great care so that the foam wouldn't break and set it gently on the table before him. As she retreated, with the subservience of an odalisque, her arm had brushed his shoulder. A good Turkish girl would never have let that happen by accident. Later that same evening, she'd left Neighbor's House wearing, instead of her short-sleeved uniform top, a headscarf and raincoat: the creative compromise between secular and religious dress. Kosmas, who had always had a weakness for hijabi women, had been instantly hooked. Nevertheless, it had taken him three months to work up the courage to ask her out, and by that time she was already engaged. Julien had tried to assuage Kosmas's disappointment. "Don't worry, my boy," he'd said. "When one woman leaves your life, ten arrive to take her place." But the promised ten never came.

"What can I get for you?" said Emine. She had gained a few kilos.

"Nothing," said Kosmas. "I mean, may I have seven teas, please?"

"Right away." As Emine arranged the tulip-shaped glasses on a tray, Kosmas discreetly observed her from behind. He visually caressed the wisps of hair escaping the full bun at the nape of her neck; by ten o'clock that evening, they would all be covered with a titillating headscarf.

"Haven't seen her before," said Emine, still with her back to him.

"American," said Kosmas.

Emine dropped two sugar cubes onto each saucer. Without looking up from her work, she said, "You'd better be quick. The men here are going to be all over her."

"I gave her my card."

"Did you get hers?"

Kosmas tapped his fingers on the counter. "No."

Emine sighed. "You have to get hers. She won't call you."

"I've never been good at these things," said Kosmas.

"I know." Emine filled the bottoms of the tulip-shaped glasses with dark-brewed tea. Before topping them off with hot water, she paused. Something had caught her eye. "Are you sure you want seven?"

Kosmas looked out the window. The American lifted an arm as thin as a swan's neck, waved him goodbye, and left the tea garden with her aunt.

"The extras are for you," said Kosmas. "My treat."

"Always such a gentleman," said Emine, with a fond smile.

"Yeah, for all the good it does me."

The next morning—Sunday—Kosmas rose early. A few days before, Madame Eva, his mother's best friend, had offered to arrange a meeting with a Levantine Catholic girl named Rita Tereza. Since the Ecumenical Patriarchate of Constantinople allowed marriage with Catholics and Armenian Apostolics— provided they signed a triplicate affidavit saying they would baptize their children Rum Orthodox—Kosmas had agreed to the matchmaking.

As he showered, images of Daphne arranging her long hair flooded his still sleepy mind. So he turned the tap to cold, gave himself a good shock, and said out loud, "She's a high-class salon type. She'll never fancy you."

He shaved with care, all the while fantasizing about Rita Tereza's blue eyes, which Madame Eva had described as "very sweet." He imagined that they would go for a walk along the Bosporus after church and stop for tea and sweet *börek*. The afternoon might end with a tender kiss at her door-step, which meant that he had to eliminate every last bristle so that it wouldn't scratch her rose-petal lips. After rinsing and drying, he reached for his Davidoff Cool Water, but it wasn't in its place on the clothes washer. His mother had probably tossed it somewhere during one of the obsessive ceiling-to-floor bleach-downs she performed at least twice per week with the help of her cleaning lady. He rummaged through Rea's bin of nail polish, her lipstick drawer, and her hairclip basket, where he finally found the blue–black bottle. He spritzed himself generously. As with pastries, scent was just as important as appearance.

Kosmas dressed in gray pants and a polite white shirt, with the sleeves turned up to the elbows. After pulling his socks as high as they would go—a fixation he had developed as the result of Rea's distaste for socks pooling at ankles—he slipped on his brown bit loafers, took a quick glance at the cloudy morning sky, grabbed an umbrella, and was out the door.

He climbed Yeni Çarşı Street, turned into the sleepy Grand Avenue, and hurried into a cobbled byway leading to the Panagia church. The rain began just as he was entering the gate. He greeted the two gruff Antiochians serving as guards and waited until he was inside to cross himself because his mother had taught him never to do so in the street. In the night-sky-painted narthex, he lit three candles: one for himself, one for his dead father, and a third for the blue-eyed beauty whom he was about to meet.

Kosmas had never seen the Rum Orthodox churches so full that "there was no room for a pin to drop," as his elders fondly described the golden days before the 1955 pogrom. On that Sunday, the church contained no more than twenty warm bodies: a dozen old women with flowers and barrettes in their hair; a handful of fifty-something dames in short skirts; a few men in suits; and a couple of Greek tourists in shorts and athletic shoes. A headscarved Russian woman was venerating an icon in the ornate gold-painted iconostasis wall that separated the nave from the sanctuary. Fanis was chanting away at the cantor's stand and—judging from the way he dragged out the syllables—enjoying his own voice. The well-dressed Rum women congregated near the bishop's throne, where they could see and be seen. The Rum men had taken positions near the door, through which they could easily escape for a cigarette. Tourists were strolling up and down the aisles, looking at the ceiling and snapping photos as if they were in a museum.

Madame Eva entered, brushed Kosmas's back, and whispered, "Today's the big day."

"Where is she?" he asked.

Just then the priest appeared in the Beautiful Gate of the iconostasis and blessed the congregation. Kosmas and Eva crossed their right hands over their chests and bowed in reply. A lady wearing old-fashioned lace gloves and a wide-brimmed hat emerged from behind the left-side stasidia, the wooden stalls with high arms that helped the Orthodox remain standing during long services. Kosmas wondered if the lady was Rita Tereza. Only Levantine women wore hats in churches. But as the woman traversed the red runner stretching from the Beautiful Gate to the entrance, Kosmas noticed that she had albino white skin, wore bottle-cap glasses, and walked with a pronounced hobble. Obviously not Rita Tereza.

As soon as the priest had withdrawn into the sanctuary, Madame Eva said, "Be patient." She squeezed Kosmas's arm and settled into one of the right-aisle stasidia that still retained the name plates of formerly privileged—and now dead—parishioners.

Kosmas lingered by the entrance with the other men. Every time the heavy narthex door squeaked open, he listened to the footsteps. At first he thought he was listening for Rita Tereza, and then he realized he was also hoping for Madame Gavriela's niece. Every time he was disappointed, for he could tell from the lazy shuffle that the entrant was just another old person. The American had either stayed home that morning or gone to Holy Trinity. As for Rita Tereza, perhaps she had slipped in before him and hidden behind one of the faux-marble basilica columns, freshly painted green during the church's recent restoration.

Finally the grizzly priest chanted an unmelodious benediction. Kosmas lined up with the others to receive his square of blessed antidoron bread. As soon as he had taken it, Fanis stepped down from the cantor's stand, grabbed Kosmas's arm, and nodded toward the albino, who was praying before the iconostasis icon of the Holy Mother. "Watch out for that one," Fanis whispered. "She's been after me for months. I'll have to disappear as soon as we're done . . . or she'll eat me alive."

"Sure, Mr. Fanis," said Kosmas.

After venerating almost every icon in the church, Madame Eva led Kosmas across the courtyard.

"She didn't come, did she?" he said.

"Be patient," Madame Eva repeated. They entered the bright tea room, whose shelves were full of community antiques, including leather-bound codices, a desk clock, and donation boxes that resembled old clothes irons with wooden handles. There was a box for the church's lighting, another for the soup kitchen, another for the long-closed orphanage, and yet another for the Zografeion Lyceum, Kosmas's alma mater.

"Let my tea be light, please," said Madame Eva, to the guardian, as they took their seats. "The doctor says that too much caffeine doesn't combine well with my medications."

"Same for us," said an octogenarian with a purple lily in her chignon.

The lame woman with eyes of ice limped into the tea room and dropped herself into the free chair next to Kosmas.

"Rita Tereza," said Madame Eva, still speaking Greek, "I'd like you to meet Kosmas. Kosmas, Rita Tereza, a graduate of the Liceo Italiano and the University of Rome. She's also a brilliant watercolor painter, aren't you, dear?"

Kosmas wanted to protest. *She* could not possibly be *his* Rita Tereza. Then he recalled his passing years, his awkwardness, his lack of luck with women, and a rhyme that his father had coined about their lame but pretty neighbor Madame Aglaia, who always had difficulty climbing their hilly street: "She huffs and puffs, but she's still got a muff." So Kosmas made up his mind to be sociable and give Rita Tereza a chance.

"Pleased to meet you," said Kosmas in Turkish. "I've always thought that multicultural people are the wealthiest of all."

She smiled and bashfully lowered her eyes—or at least so he thought. It was difficult to see what was happening behind her thick glasses.

"Is this your first time at an Orthodox church?" he asked.

"My grandmother was Rum," Rita Tereza replied in Greek. "She taught me the language. And all churches are the same to me."

It was a pleasant answer, and Rita Tereza's Greek was impeccable. Up close—and in a seated position—there was indeed something sweet about her, just as Madame Eva had said. "Are you a professional painter then?" he asked.

Rita Tereza pushed up her glasses with a gloved finger. "I'm a speech therapist. For special-needs children."

A caring profession, thought Kosmas. She would probably make a good mother.

"Kosmas, dear," said Madame Eva, rising slightly and then reseating herself, "what was the prestigious prize you won a few months ago?"

"The Pfeifenberger. For my wedding cakes."

"He's very talented. Rita Tereza, what's your favorite pastry? I'm sure he makes it."

"I'm diabetic," she said.

"*Üf!*" said Madame Eva, blowing through pursed lips. "Never mind that, then. Kosmas, your mother never told me if you have any hobbies. I always hear about your awards and distinctions, but do you do anything else?"

"I've never had time. Except for reading history, especially architectural, and studying Ottoman Turkish. But I've always wanted to learn ballroom dance. What about you, Rita Tereza, have you ever thought of taking dance lessons?"

Madame Eva elbowed Kosmas and whispered, "She can't!"

At that moment, the old lady with the purple lily in her hair said, "Smile for Facebook!"

Rita Tereza adjusted her glasses, leaned in toward Kosmas, and pulled a smile. As soon as the flash had gone off, she directed her attention toward the other end of the table.

In an attempt to make amends, Kosmas grabbed Rita Tereza's empty tea glass and took it into the church office, which doubled as a coffee- and tea-making station. While filling it, he noticed an almost empty coffee cup resting on the desk of the decrepit, nearly deaf priest. It was obvious from the way the fine grounds were spilled into the saucer that someone had been reading his future in their designs.

The priest came in and took a drag on the cigarette smoking in the desk ashtray.

"Father," said Kosmas, "isn't coffee-reading forbidden by the Church?"

The priest blew smoke toward the ceiling. "Pardon?"

Kosmas pointed to the overturned cup and raised his voice as much as he could without sounding disrespectful: "Is coffee-reading allowed? I mean, can clerics do that?"

The father righted the cup, covered it with a napkin, and winked. "You're still a bachelor, aren't you, Kosmaki?" he said. "Are you aware that no one in Pera gets married without my authorization?"

"Of course, Father," said Kosmas. "If you'll excuse me."

Kosmas returned to the tea room hoping that Rita Tereza might have forgotten his faux pas. But she frowned when he delivered her tea, turned her back when he sat down, and resumed a heated debate with the lily-adorned old lady about the nutritional value of white flour. Another bride lost.

Kosmas was the first to depart. Halfway down the hill, at the point where Yeni Çarşı becomes Boğazkesen Street, he stopped and looked up at the birds sweeping through the stratified glow around the dome of Kılıç Ali Paşa Mosque. Now *that* was architecture: a mosque built on the model of Hagia Sophia for Ali Paşa, a sixteenth-century Italian corsair who had converted to Islam and later become an Ottoman admiral. The complex was designed by Mimar Sinan, a converted Rum and the chief architect to three Ottoman sultans, including Suleiman the Magnificent. For a second, Kosmas thought that maybe he, too, should stop wasting his energy and convert, like Ali Paşa and Mimar Sinan. Then he lowered his head beneath his umbrella and walked on.

He didn't want to return home to his mother, yet on a rainy Sunday morning there were few places to go. Without any particular destination in mind, he trudged down to the Bosporus, wandered through the muddy seaside park where working-class families picnicked on sunny days, and took a seat at one of the tea gardens. What he really wanted was to see Gavriela's niece, but she was probably still in bed.

He ordered a toasted cheese sandwich and settled down to watch the boats gliding between the Asian and European shores within the strait and across the mouth of the Sea of Marmara. Waves crashed against the quay and sprang up like fountains, leaving pools of saltwater on the rough cement. On the other side of the inland sea, the mountains of Anatolia rose into low gray clouds. Kosmas wondered, as he always did while watching Istanbul's waters and the smooth movement of the ferries, why he still lived in the City of his isolation, where he didn't seem to have the slightest chance of ever finding a Rum wife. Perhaps he should have left long ago for America, Canada, Australia, or Greece, like everybody else. But now he had his pâtisserie and an aging mother on his head. It was too late.

A waiter with a full tray of tea glasses made his way through the tables. Kosmas raised a finger. The man set a glass before him. The seagulls, which seemed to have more of a right to the City than anyone, uttered murderous cries when a hobby fisherman emptied a plastic bucket of fish heads onto the quay. Within minutes, nothing but a water-blood trail remained. As Kosmas watched the poor Sunday fishermen casting their lines into the gray Bosporus, he wished to God that he could be like Fanis, who knew the names of all the female cashiers at the local supermarket, never exited without saying hello to each, and sat in the tea garden like a pasha while women of all ages came to kiss his cheeks and forehead. Kosmas, on the other hand, had never even worked up the courage to ask for Emine's phone number.

Kosmas was sick of the moldy angels of love who worked in Tarlabaşı's derelict Rum houses: the last prostitute he had visited had filed her nails while he toiled away and then charged him extra to touch her breasts. Kosmas had vowed to change on numerous occasions, yet he couldn't manage to assume the confident, carefree air that enabled Fanis to acquire the numbers of half the women of Pera. He had tried impressing the American with his new business card—complete with the gold-embossed Pfeifenberger symbol—but she hadn't even deemed it worthy of a glance. He realized that part of the problem was that he had a penchant for cultivated "salon girls," but look what had happened when he gave homely Rita Tereza a chance. If *she* had no interest in him, how could he possibly aspire to please Gavriela's niece?

"My God," he said out loud, "if only you had made me like Fanis."

And then he had it. He would go straight to the source, to Fanis, and ask the old rascal to become his mentor. He took his phone from his pocket, called Monsieur Julien, and scribbled Fanis Paleologos's phone number on a napkin.

3

The Lady of the Western Approaches

THE NIGHT BEFORE DAPHNE LEFT for Istanbul, Sultana Badem warned her daughter that she must not under any circumstances fall in love with a man still living in the Poli, which is the only word Istanbul Rums use for their homeland: the City.

"Why?" Daphne asked in Greek, her mother tongue.

Sultana pulled taut the floral-print sofa cover, sat down beside her, and lit a cigarette. "Because he'll only be using you as a ticket out. And his mother! There's nobody nastier than an Istanbul mother-in-law."

Daphne rolled her eyes. Sultana was sometimes strangely critical of other immigrants and overly admiring of natural-born citizens. This explained her particular affection for Daphne's boyfriend Paul, a white-toast American mutt with only a vague notion of his English, Polish, and Lithuanian heritage. Even Paul's surname—Winters—was a rootless, immigration-office switch for a long and difficult Polish name.

"And don't go about alone," Sultana continued. "At least until you've learned your way around. All you have to do is smile at a man and he'll think you want to jump into bed with him."

"Things have probably changed since 1969, Mom," said Daphne. She grabbed the embroidered pillow with which her mother had propped open the living-room window.

Sultana snatched the pillow from Daphne and stuffed it back between the glass and the frame. "You've been with Paul for four years now. He's gold. So polite, fixes everything in the house, encourages you to continue your studies. Don't you love him?"

Daphne nodded.

"Then when are you getting married?"

"Mom, please. He's all that you said but . . . he dances with other women."

"He'd been dancing for years when you met him! If that was going to bother you, why did you take up with him in the first place? And how did you become such a jealous East-erner? You were born here. You should be more American, more open-minded."

"He lied to me about that tango festival in Vegas. Why don't you get that?"

"*Seni taşımak kolay değil,*" said Sultana, peppering the other-wise Greek conversation with a bit of Turkish.

"What's that supposed to mean?"

"Putting up with you isn't easy. Look, Daphne, he went to a dance event. It doesn't mean he slept with anyone. He shouldn't have said it was a teacher's conference, true, but maybe *you* shouldn't be so possessive. . . . Yes, I'm going to say it: you shouldn't be so Turkish!"

"Then maybe *you* shouldn't have married a Turk."

Sultana scowled. "I'm just saying that American men don't like our kind of jealousy. It's insulting to them, not flat-tering. It shows a lack of trust."

"But what if he did sleep with someone?" said Daphne. She'd believed Paul when he tearfully swore that he'd never been unfaithful. But the possibility later returned to torment her, cause her nightmares, and make her feel painfully inse-cure every time she and Paul went tangoing.

"Look, Daphne, you can't prevent a man from going to another woman. All you can do is find one who respects you, treats you well, and fulfills his family duties. Paul is that sort of man."

"I'm not even married yet and you're saying I should put up with other women?"

"*Allah, Allah!*" said Sultana, in exasperation. "You're missing the point."

Daphne banged her cup onto the dining table. Coffee spilled onto the semi-transparent runner. Thank God her mother didn't notice. "You know," she said, "you can get windows that stay open by themselves."

"That's the way my grandmother kept the window open, and that's the way I do it. And if you're not going to follow my advice about Paul, you should at least listen to what I have to say about the City." Sultana drew an arch from one corner of her mouth to the other. "This needs a zipper. *Never* ever talk politics."

"Why not?"

"Because it's dangerous. Always has been, always will be. Things might seem fine over there right now, but don't be deceived: it's just a period of calm before the storm. And don't be too open with anyone about your personal life, including Gavriela's friends. They mustn't learn that your father isn't Rum."

"Is it so terrible?"

"If they find out your father's Muslim, they won't trust you. They won't consider you one of their own."

"Is that why you and Baba never took me there?"

"Maybe." Sultana inhaled deeply on her cigarette and blew a white cloud out the window, well over the propping cushion. She smoked "like an Arab," as Daphne's father was fond of saying. Even so, Sultana had an intense distaste for cigarette stench. She only smoked outdoors and by the window so that the slipcovers and curtains she washed regularly and ironed with rosewater wouldn't stink.

"Is that why Aunt Gavriela stopped visiting?" said Daphne.

"Listen, miss." Sultana pulled up the strap of the last sundress she had made for herself before she retired from Flora's

Fabrics. "When Gavriela came here for your high-school graduation, she asked me to send you to college in Istanbul. As your godmother, she insisted, she had a right to see you more often."

"And?"

"I knew what she was up to. She wanted you to move back there and marry a Rum. That way she could keep you all to herself. And that's why I never let her visit again."

"Don't you think that's a little extreme?"

"Your father and I didn't work all our lives to send you back there. The City is a magic place, like no other, but remember: you can't stay. There's no future for the Rums there. *Bitti.*" It's finished.

Daphne struggled not only with her mother's domineering ways, but also with her pessimism. On Facebook, Aunt Gavriela was always posting photos of renovated churches, tea parties with Rum friends, and cultural events at the Greek Consulate. Gavriela also shared hopeful articles about the future of the Rum community and the return of confiscated Rum property. It seemed that the current government wanted to make amends, yet Sultana clung to the mess of the past.

Daphne removed the coffee cup and sugar bowl from the soiled runner.

"What . . . ?" said Sultana. "Coffee on my favorite piece? Oh, don't bunch it up and make it worse. I'll take care of it."

"I'm leaving," said Daphne.

"One last thing. I don't want you listening too much to my older sister while you're staying with her. She's always giving advice, like she's better than everyone else."

"And you never give advice, do you, Mom?"

"*Üf!*" said Sultana, jamming her half-smoked cigarette into the silver ashtray. "It's an evil hour when you open your mouth! You're just like your aunt."

*

On Daphne's first Sunday in Istanbul, three days after her arrival, she lazed in bed, looking through the window at the dark, flat clouds covering the sky. She thought of the Sunday brunches that Paul always prepared while she enjoyed her last hour of sleep: omelets and quiches, crêpes, coffee cake, cappuccino, fresh orange juice. . . . There was nothing he didn't do. Perhaps going to Istanbul alone had been the wrong decision. Perhaps what they needed wasn't time apart, but time away together.

Aunt Gavriela knocked softly on the bedroom door, tiptoed inside, and kissed Daphne on the forehead. "How about I make a good Turkish breakfast?"

Daphne followed her aunt to the kitchen, which was really no more than a closet with an oven, a sink, and a small barred window that opened onto an air shaft. She inhaled its distinctive scent: Turkish coffee, cinnamon, garlic, and naphthalene. As much as Sultana and Gavriela pretended to be different from one another, their kitchens smelled exactly the same.

Gavriela took a pot from the squeaky cupboard and began pumping water into it from the nineteen-liter plastic demijohn that took up half the kitchen's narrow walking space: a necessity since Istanbul's tap water was "full of rust and chlorine," as Gavriela had explained when Daphne first arrived.

"Can I do anything?" said Daphne. She felt like she was moving through a thick gray cloud of semi-sleep, but her mother had taught her always to offer help in the kitchen.

"Go get the eggs from the refrigerator," said Gavriela. "Then we'll chat."

Daphne turned the corner of the L-shaped hallway and entered a small, dark room. In one corner was the household iconostasis with its holy images, photos of dead relatives, and an always-lit vigil lamp that seemed a rather risky thing to have in a country plagued by earthquakes. In the opposite corner was a large 1960s American refrigerator. Daphne took the eggs from the middle compartment and brought them to her aunt.

"I can't understand that room," she said. "What's the point?"

"The maid's room, from back when the apartment belonged to a Jewish family." Gavriela pointed to the red plastic stool in the kitchen doorway. "Now have a seat."

Daphne leaned her jet-lagged head on the kitchen door. Gavriela turned on one of the burners and pulled the trigger of the handheld gas igniter. The blue flame encircled the burner with a soft ripping sound. "A good house had everything," she said.

"Including a closet-sized kitchen? Why don't you knock down the wall and combine the two rooms?"

"What for? In those big American kitchens you have over there, nobody makes a damn thing worth eating, if they ever use them at all. It's not the space that matters. It's the hands. Didn't my little sister teach you anything?"

"She didn't have time. Not with working six days a week in the fabric shop."

Gavriela combined coffee, sugar, and water in a small bronze coffee pot and set it on the burner. "We can fix that," she said. "You drink Turkish coffee, don't you?"

"Only when Mom makes it. For me it's too much trouble."

Gavriela clicked her tongue in disapproval. "Because you're my niece, I'll tell you my secret, but you can't tell anyone, not even your mother." She ceased her relentless chewing of mastic gum and lowered her voice: "I mix Turkish Mehmet Efendi and Greek Loumidis. Mehmet's too dark and Loumidis too light, but together they're divine."

"Half and half," said Daphne. "Like me."

"That's why you're both so tasty," said Gavriela, pinching Daphne's cheek. "You have to hover over the pot while it's heating, always on low flame. The second you look away it will boil, and then you've got to dump it into the toilet. Look there it goes, foaming up." Gavriela whisked the pot from the flame, poured the contents into a demitasse cup, and handed it to Daphne. "Lots of bubbles. That means money. Or jealousy."

"Which one?"

"Whichever you want."

After waiting for the coffee to settle and cool, Daphne took a tiny sip and leaned her head back on the door. Although she didn't like the fuss, she had to admit that her aunt's brew was far smoother—friendlier, homier even—than the Cuban espresso she brewed at home in a moka pot.

"What's that ringing?" said Gavriela.

The muffled electronic tune was coming from the pay-as-you-go phone Daphne had bought at the airport. She set her coffee on the counter and rushed to the foyer, where she had left it. "Hello?"

"Hey, babe," said Paul. "How are you?"

Daphne felt the warmth of their first days together. Maybe the relationship crisis was all in her head. Maybe he did love her, after all. "Still jet-lagged," she said.

"You'll get over it soon."

"I was thinking, maybe you'd like to come here."

"Hmm . . . maybe. I changed all the pipes in the garage today. We'll never have to worry about the bathroom clogging up again. I installed special filters that are super-easy to change."

Daphne sank into the foyer armchair. Paul always made her feel so secure about the house and daily problems. If only he did the same on an emotional level. "Thanks. You're the best. But you didn't answer my question."

"The cat misses you."

"And you?"

"You only just left. How are things there? Are you having a good time?"

Daphne felt a surge of annoyance. "You were the one who wanted space. Are you having a good time?"

He sighed. "Needing space doesn't mean I don't want you."

"What does it mean?"

"I just enjoy my alone time. I can blast the music, do my house jobs, get back to my pottery."

Paul's second hobby, after tango, was potting. He'd made all their dinner ware, coffee mugs, and plenty of objets d'art, including the ceramic pomegranates on Gavriela's entryway coffee table. "My aunt says thank you for the pomegranates," she said.

"My pleasure. You know, I'm really glad you're going to do those Turkish classes. I want you to realize your goals—even if that means a few sacrifices for me. Go all the way, Daph. Apply for those PhD programs as soon as you get back."

"Thanks," said Daphne. Yet she was unable to strangle her irritation.

"You know, I missed dancing with you tonight."

For a moment Daphne allowed herself to remember Paul's clear and gentle lead, as well as his keen musicality, weaving itself into the song. He was one of the rare cavaliers who danced both rhythm and melody equally well. "Where did you go?" she asked.

"La Porteñita. Everybody was asking about you. They all say hello: Helena, Lillian, Steve, Luciana—"

"The Brazilian? Did you dance with her?"

"Just once."

"Just *once*?" Daphne tried to keep her voice down so that Gavriela wouldn't overhear. "You're ruining tango for me. It used to be our th—"

"Daph, please. If something was going on, would she be sending her regards?"

"You know how I feel about her."

"I *danced* with her. I didn't screw her."

Daphne took a deep breath and released it. "I have to go. I'm cooking with my aunt."

"You cook?"

"I do now."

"Call me tonight."

"If I can."

"Love you, babe."

Love you. Not *I* love you. She wasn't even worth a complete sentence.

"Me too." Daphne snapped the flip phone shut, replaced it in her purse, and noticed the business card Kosmas had given her the day before. In the upper left corner was the pâtisserie's logo, a flamboyant lily. Beneath the name was a list of degrees, followed by his culinary institute title, a German word she couldn't pronounce, and a gold symbol that looked like a falling cake, but which was probably an abstract chef's hat. Impressive. But why had he given it to her? He obviously wasn't interested in her or he would have asked for her number. Perhaps he was just overly enthusiastic about advertising his business. Daphne returned to the kitchen and stuffed the card into the tiny white plastic trash bin that her aunt kept on top of the counter.

"Who was that?" said Gavriela.

Daphne finished her coffee. "My boyfriend."

"You have a boyfriend?"

"Paul."

Gavriela turned down the flame beneath a pot of boiling eggs. "Rum?"

"American."

"American-American?"

"American-American. English only."

Gavriela grunted, took a bunch of parsley from the vase of cut herbs, and said, "You'd be better off with a Rum."

"Are you trying to reclaim me?"

"That's not what I meant. It's just better to find someone who shares your language and religion, that's all."

Daphne began washing her coffee cup. "And where would I find him? Most are in the Baloukli Nursing Home already."

"Don't be so sure," said Gavriela. She opened the oven and took out a baking tray covered with bright green papery things. "Celery-root leaf. You dry it in the oven and then grind it up to season your soups and stews. Did your mother teach you that?"

Daphne sat back down on the stool and toyed with the tiny icon of the Holy Mother dangling from a door handle. "No."

"Tell me more about this Paul." Gavriela tossed the celery leaves into a mini-blender. "What does he do?"

"He's a math teacher."

"A *teacher*? Now I know your mother didn't teach you anything."

"He's a nice guy. He takes care of everything in the house, cooks, brings me flowers—"

"*Flowers?* Flowers you can buy yourself. You need a man who puts both hands in his pockets for you, little mama, not just one. A teacher isn't going to do that."

Daphne suddenly felt defensive. She had always admired Paul's dedication to his students. Once he had stayed up half the night messaging with a boy who was having an anxiety crisis over a final English exam. "Money isn't everything," she said.

"It isn't everything, but it's a big thing." Gavriela emptied the blender contents into a jar. "Stinginess kills a woman."

"Paul isn't stingy."

Except when it came to their joint tango lessons. He insisted that Daphne pay half, even though his salary was twice hers. And he also expected her to pay for dinner every other time they went out. But Daphne thought it best not to confess this to her aunt.

"Fine, maybe he's not stingy," said Gavriela, "but is he a worker? What does he do in the summer? You don't want a man in the house all day, little mama. When your uncle retired, I thought I was going to go insane. Then he went out and got another accounting job. That's the kind of man you need. Does this Paul work with you?"

"No. I'd never date someone from the same school."

"At least you know not to shit in your own kitchen." Gavriela tucked the ends of her housedress into the bottom of her underwear so that they wouldn't catch on the plastic bags and cardboard boxes at the foot of the cupboards. "I hate it when my dress gets in my way," she said. "How does he treat you?"

"Very well. Most of the time."

"*Most of the time?*"

"He likes dancing with other women—"

Gavriela stored the celery-powder jar on a shelf. "You let him dance with other women? Are you crazy? You shouldn't even trust your best friend close to your man."

"I told him how I felt recently."

"Told him how you felt? Christ! A man should know you from here down, little mama"—Gavriela crossed her arm over her waist—"and from here up he shouldn't know a thing. Don't tell him how you feel."

"That's a strange philosophy."

"My grandmother's," said Gavriela. "Anyway, you know best." That was Greek for: I'm not going keep arguing with you, but you're still full of shit. She took the plates, napkins, and silverware from the crowded kitchen counter and handed them to Daphne. "Now go set the table." She followed her niece into the living room with the breakfast tray and shouted, "Ready!"

Uncle Andonis, still wearing his baby-blue pajamas, emerged from the master bedroom and joined Gavriela and Daphne at the table. "You always wake me from the best dreams," he grumbled.

Gavriela placed her mastic gum in a dainty ceramic dish and covered it with a lid. To save for later, apparently. "What did you see?" she asked her husband.

"Yüksek Kaldırım Street." Andonis poured Daphne's tea and then his own. "And the women's behinds jiggling as they went up and down those steps, just like they used to—"

"Andonis!" snapped Gavriela.

"What? You'd prefer I think of Cobblestone in 'fifty-five? Or after all our people left? When there are better things to remember about the place?"

"Life goes on," said Gavriela. "We don't have to talk about any of that."

The call to prayer buzzed from the local mosque. Andonis clicked his tongue. "The call to prayer was beautiful when the muezzin still had to climb up to the top of the minaret," he said to Daphne. "Now those damn loudspeakers make him sound as if his balls are being squeezed in a vise."

"Watch your mouth," said Gavriela. "You made me think of *back then*, and you know how much I hate it when you do that."

Andonis scratched his mustache. "Didn't you just say that life goes on?"

"It does, but in a way no one would have chosen. If all that hadn't happened, Daphne would have grown up near us. We could've been present at her baptism."

"Would she have been baptized at all? That's the question."

Gavriela glared at her husband. "Well, she could've served us sour-cherry liqueur on her birthdays, at least."

"I'm not entering into that discussion of lost opportunities, but what I would like to know"—he winked at Daphne—"is whether she's going to stay."

"Of course she is. We're going to find her a groom. One of our own."

"Did you decide that or did she?"

"Are you done?" Gavriela buttered a piece of bread and placed it on Daphne's plate. "At least let us see you as a bride," she said. "But not with some language-less American."

"You two need to get out more," said Andonis.

"For once he's right about something." Gavriela set her knife across her tea saucer with a rude clink. "This week, as soon as the weather improves, we'll have tea with the gang at Neighbor's House. After your classes, of course."

"You mean with the widows, the old Casanovas, and the baker?" said Daphne.

"Exactly. And the baker is a gentleman, by the way, a hard worker who wins international prizes and has his own business. In other words, a two-pocket man!"

Daphne thought of Kosmas's business card in the trash can and felt a tiny pinch of regret.

4

A Hero's Garb

FANIS WAS STANDING ON THE landing with his garbage bag in hand, about to knock on the neighbor lady's door. Her husband had recently passed away, and, although she was not the least bit attractive, Fanis had made a habit of taking out her garbage: one had to be courtly with widows. Just as he raised his fist, however, his phone rang. He quietly reentered his apartment and picked up.

"*Allo?*"

"Mr. Fanis? It's Kosmas. I wanted to ask if we could meet for coffee, just the two of us, outside the neighborhood. I wanted to discuss a private matter."

"What?" said Fanis, staring at Dr. Aydemir's crumpled prescriptions, which he had left on the sideboard. He opened a drawer and threw them inside.

"Women," said Kosmas.

Fear of past sins gripped Fanis. "Has your mother been talking to her friend, the one who lives on my street? Whatever she said isn't true. I never cheated on my wife as long as she lived. And certainly not with the woman with whom they say I did—"

Kosmas interrupted: "It's not that. It's about me. I need your advice."

"Why didn't you say so from the beginning?"

They made an appointment for five o'clock on Wednesday evening at a *muhallebici* pudding shop in Taksim where they wouldn't chance upon any of their acquaintances.

*

Fanis arrived first and chose a table upstairs. He glanced briefly at a newspaper someone had left on a nearby table: on the front page was a photo of the prime minister in shirt-sleeves and sunglasses, clapping his hands at a campaign rally somewhere on the other side of Istanbul. Fanis hated politics, but at election time he was obliged to take an interest. His views were aligned with those of the secular Republican People's Party, but it was a secularist party that had organized the pogrom of 1955. The prime minister and his Islamist party, on the other hand, had treated the Rum community and its churches with respect. Moreover, the economy was booming, and negotiations for full accession to the EU were under way. Still, everyone knew that the Rums got a knife in the back every ten years, regardless of which party was in office. Fanis didn't know whom he could trust. Which was why, he always said, it was better for Christians and Jews to keep their mouths sewn shut.

When Kosmas arrived—twenty-five minutes late—Fanis complained: "I've been waiting for years."

"I'm so sorry, Mr. Fanis. A sugar sculpture broke and I had to remake it. I would've called your mobile phone if you had one."

"Oh, never mind. What will you have? Coffee? Pudding?"

"Just coffee."

"Come on, now. Have a sweet." Fanis had been looking forward to a pudding, and he hated it when others didn't indulge with him.

"Mr. Fanis, I'm a pâtissier. I make that stuff all day."

Fanis curled his lip and ordered two coffees and a sweet chicken pudding without cinnamon, which, he insisted, was very bad for the liver. Again he asked Kosmas what else he would have, hoping that the added pressure of the waiter's presence might sway him, and again he was disappointed. The waiter displayed the compassionate smile that Turks reserve for idiosyncratic old folks—which rankled with Fanis even more—and sped off to fill the order.

First they talked about the rain and the latest gossip. When the shredded chicken pudding and coffee arrived, Fanis examined both cups for jealousy bubbles: Kosmas's had none, whereas his had a persistent bead near the edge of the glass. "An evil eye," he said, "and foam at the center. That's money. Probably the stipend I'll collect in a couple of weeks." He took a sip. "The eye still didn't break! It's obstinate jealousy, the worst kind." Fanis broke the jiggling white roll with his spoon and ate with childlike pleasure. A chicken thread dripped onto his chin. Wiping it with his napkin, he asked, "What did you want to talk about?"

Kosmas ate the chewy Turkish delight served with his coffee, summoned the waiter, and ordered a dried fruit pudding.

"Well?" said Fanis.

Kosmas folded his hands on the table. "I need help with the girl who looks like Semra Sar."

Fanis's mouth curled into a mischievous smile. "Daphne?"

"Daphne! I was so fucking nervous I forgot her name."

"I've never heard you speak like that before," said Fanis, with his spoon in midair.

"I don't speak like that when I'm around my mother."

Fanis snapped his tongue against the roof of his mouth in disapproval. "And what do you want with Daphne?"

The boy looked left and right to see who could be listening. Finally he said, "I'd like to marry her."

"You've seen her once."

"Monsieur Julien proposed to his wife the night he met her."

"And where is Julien's wife now? In Paris with another man." Fanis rolled his eyes. Kosmas's father, who had died when the boy was just a teenager, had obviously not had a chance to educate him about women. Fanis continued: "Listen, son, the first thing you have to learn is this. A man who is on the lookout for a woman must never—*never!*—permit himself any weakness in vocabulary. You have to cut the foul language. From this moment on, you must be a perfect gentleman both in speech and in demeanor. You won't do anything foolish. You won't kiss a woman on the first date, if you get one—"

"Why not?"

"Do you want my advice or do you just want to do things your way?"

"*Tamam, tamam.* But may I ask a question? Are the stories they tell about you true?"

"If they were, a gentleman would never admit it."

"Will you help me?"

Not even if it would guarantee me a place in Heaven, Fanis thought. Then he had an ingenious idea: perhaps playing the harmless grandfather and matchmaking confidant would provide him with a wedge into the life of that very woman who, on account of his advanced age, was just out of reach. So he said, "What do you want to know?"

"How do I get her to go out on a date with me?"

While Fanis considered what advice he should give—something useful enough to whet the girl's appetite, yet not so effective that it would get the boy what he wanted—the waiter delivered the dried fruit pudding. Kosmas stared at it.

"Does it smell bad?" asked Fanis.

Kosmas clicked his tongue no and began eating. "It's very sweet. And thick, which means they used starch." He took another bite. "No rosewater, too little clove, but otherwise it's not bad."

"Finish your coffee, chef," said Fanis. "Then cover the cup with the saucer, turn it over, and make a wish."

"You read coffee dregs?"

"Yes. What of it?"

"Nothing. It's just that I've never seen a man read coffee before. I thought fortune-telling was a female vice."

"Well, you're wrong. About that and a lot of things. Now do you want me to have a look or not? We might learn something about your chances with Daphne."

Kosmas took his last sip of coffee, flipped the cup, closed his eyes, and made a wish.

Fanis wiped his mouth. "The first thing is your clothes. I don't mean to offend, but those striped shirts . . . where did you get them?"

"My mother does our shopping."

"Well. Mothers are sacred. But if someone were to dress me in your clothes before sealing me in my coffin, I'd come back to life screaming. No woman wants a man who dresses like that. We'll have to change them."

Kosmas dropped his spoon and looked at his watch. "It's a quarter past six. Let's go now. I'd like to pass by the tea garden later to see if she's there, so we'd better hurry."

"Finish eating," said Fanis. "There's more, much more, and we haven't even looked at the coffee yet. Besides, you don't want to make the rookie mistake of stalking her. You have to let women cook for at least a week after you meet them." Fanis turned over his own cup, took out a pen, and wrote his barber's address on a clean napkin. The boy wasn't bad-looking: puppy brown eyes, mildly tanned skin, and features unworthy of note—except for a tiny scar on the forehead that made the right eyebrow seem permanently raised. If you didn't know Kosmas well, you'd think he was looking at you with a dose of disapproval or sarcasm. All things considered, you might call him a good-looking fellow. But that brush-cut was another subject altogether.

"Let your hair grow a bit and then go to Ali. You look like you're still in the army." Fanis pricked his ears like a dog and tuned into the conversation at a nearby table. "Did you hear Greek?"

"No."

"Yes. I think the girls over there are Greek. I have a nose for them. In the end, though, we aren't Greeks. We're Rums. Grandfather from grandfather, all the way from Byzantium, and we're better off with our own Rum women, most of whom don't care to get married because they have their retirement and their stipends. Why would they want a man over their heads? The rest have married Turks, and I don't respect them. They don't know how to choose. Who's left?"

"Daphne."

"Yes, Daphne. Let's look at the coffee." Fanis picked up Kosmas's cup. "I see a voyage. It will happen soon."

"Do you think it could be a trip to America to meet Daphne's parents?"

"The path loops and comes back to the beginning."

"That's good," said Kosmas. "I'd never have the courage to leave the City. And it's her home, too, isn't it? We'll come back here to live."

"There are obstacles."

"I know. That's why I wanted to talk to you."

"That's it," Fanis concluded. "The saucer is a plate of mud. I can't see anything in it."

Presently he picked up his own cup and beheld the clearest and most beautiful shapes that had ever appeared in coffee dregs. There was a thin woman with her arms crossed over her chest. A long, fanciful ponytail rose from her crown and undulated round the cup. The woman had to be the symbol of the solid good health that Fanis would enjoy with Daphne. Yet what was to be made of her crossed arms and ponytail? Presently he remembered the first time he'd seen Kalypso. Ponytail bouncing, she skipped into the Petridis Winehouse, her father's *meyhane*, where Fanis ate his lunch on Saturdays, his mother's reception day. Kalypso stopped in front of her father, crossed her arms over her chest, and said, "Well, Tasos, are you going to take me to the cinema or not?" Fanis was impressed by her sass: not many girls dared call their fathers by their first names. He was also impressed by Tasos, who grabbed his hat without a second thought and left with his beaming daughter. But what was Kalypso doing in Fanis's cup? Coffee dregs belonged to the realm of the future, not to the past.

"What do you see?" asked Kosmas.

"Never mind," said Fanis. "Let's hit a few stores."

It was raining again when they stepped out into the crowds of evening shoppers. Fanis took Kosmas's arm so that they could speak confidentially and nearly poked Kosmas in the eyes with the spokes of his plaid umbrella. They passed the Pearl, that old, wainscoted pastry shop where people lined up for a dish of profiteroles and fought for a seat at tiny marble-topped tables, if one was free, or ate standing up if there was no sitting room, so great was their addiction to the pâtisserie's chocolate-drenched specialty.

"The newcomers have no idea that the Pearl was Rum," said Fanis, stopping short. "They don't know that almost every shop on this street was Rum. After the pogrom, when the cloth from all these shops was shredded into strips and the stinking shoes of the criminals were left in the streets to fuse with dried fruits, cheeses, and smashed refrigerator parts, I passed by here and recognized the Pearl's pastries in the mess. That was where I used to take my sweetheart." Fanis took a deep breath, blinked away the tears that were stinging his eyes, and resumed walking. "Haven't you ever looked for a girl in Athens?"

"I can't get used to the people over there," said Kosmas, looking at his watch again.

Fanis sighed. "Foreigners here in our own place, foreigners there twice over. That's our lot." He pointed to a black shirt worn by a mannequin in the display window of a trendy shop. "Tomorrow you must come here by yourself and get some casual shirts for afternoon tea. Black, not striped, and Armani. I couldn't pull off Armani, but you can. And start going to a gym. Girls don't like tummies nowadays." Fanis quickened his pace. "Suits, however, are another matter. One must never buy a suit off the peg. Tailor-made is the only way to go, for a true gentleman, that is."

They turned into a dim side street and entered a shop marked with an overhanging sign: "Hüsnü Mirza's Custom-made Suits and Shirts." Bald Hüsnü set down the monstrous scissors with which he had been cutting a bolt of poplin. His thick gold wedding band flashed as he took a pen from his shirt pocket and said in Turkish, "*Hoş geldiniz, Fanis bey.*" Welcome, Mr. Fanis.

Fanis shifted gears into the language of the outside world: "Well we find you."

Hüsnü picked up the phone, ordered three teas from the local concession, and sat down with his clients on wooden stools at the center of the shop. Above the counter, next to the de rigueur image of Atatürk, were two midcentury photographs of a fair woman with a bouffant hairdo and an older man with thick glasses.

"Your parents?" asked Kosmas.

"Oh, no," said Hüsnü, "the original owner and his daughter. Both Greek citizens. I began working here when I was twelve and took over when they were deported. Pera was beautiful back then, wasn't it, Mr. Fanis? Now it's filled with outsiders and peasants. You can't even walk in Tarlabaşı without fear of being mugged."

The tea runner stepped into the shop and distributed full glasses with red and white thumbprint saucers.

"You haven't been in for some time, Mr. Fanis," said Hüsnü.

"I haven't had reason to. What's the use of a new shirt with no one to wear it for?"

Hüsnü peered over his wire-rimmed glasses. "I've missed you. You're my inspiration."

"I beg your pardon?"

50

"You used to eat in that cheap Circassian restaurant across the way with some very nice-looking ladies."

"What kind did you expect to see me with? Ugly ones? And those young ladies weren't dates. They were just friends."

"Of course, brother. I assumed so. Now, tell me, what can I do for you today?"

"We need a suit for the boy, but we don't want one of those shiny gray things with the stitching showing that all the young men without taste are wearing nowadays. We want something elegant. Not exactly the kind that *I* would wear, but along those lines. And he'll also need two shirts."

"Let's measure him," said Hüsnü, pulling the tape from his neck.

A minute later Kosmas was standing like an awkward giant with his arms raised while Hüsnü measured his hips, waist, chest, legs, shoulders, and arms. The tailor wrote down the measurements, removed his bifocals, and said, "I assume it will be a drape cut?"

"Of course," said Fanis. "Double-breasted."

"I'd prefer single," said Kosmas. "Double seems too 1980s."

Fanis glared at him. He himself had never worn a double-breasted suit. It was for exactly that reason that he had suggested the style for Kosmas: he wanted the boy to look good, but not too good. "But you're tall," he said. "Double is better for a tall man."

"With all due respect," said Hüsnü, "I have to agree with our young friend. I've always considered single classier. And it works very well for tall men if it has two buttons instead of three. What do you think about the color?"

"Navy," said Fanis. "But with some detail."

"What about brown?" said Kosmas.

The tailor replaced his bifocals and pulled a bolt of all-brown plaid from one of the upper shelves. "I have just the thing."

Fanis ran the edge between his fingers. "Very fine," he said. "But I don't know if it's right for him."

Hüsnü draped the ends of two fabric bolts over Kosmas's shoulders and turned him toward the mirror. "The subtle blue plaid of this beaver brown will add width while playing down your height. The navy is also a classy color, but, in my opinion, the brown suits you better."

Kosmas rotated one shoulder forward, then the other.

"Definitely the navy," said Fanis, knowing that it would make Kosmas look like an obelisk.

"The beaver brown plaid," said Kosmas.

Disobedient worm, thought Fanis. How dare he disregard my opinion?

"Right," said Hüsnü. "Brown plaid it is. Now for the shirts."

"I like the one you're wearing," said Kosmas. "Blue with a white collar and cuffs. What do you think, Mr. Fanis, would it go?"

"I suppose. But you must have a good all-white."

"And the price?" asked Kosmas.

"Shall I call for more tea?" asked the tailor.

"It's a quarter past seven," said Kosmas. "I think we'd better—"

"Thank you, we'd be happy to take another glass," said Fanis.

The tailor punched a few numbers into his calculator, wrote a figure on a piece of paper, and spun it toward his client. Kosmas took a sharp breath and said, "It's a lot."

"Did I tell you that Kosmas is my nephew?" said Fanis. A little white lie always facilitated negotiations.

The tailor immediately crossed out the first figure and wrote a new, significantly reduced number. "I'll add a couple of pocket squares on the house. I always recommend them for tall men."

Kosmas capitulated. "If I get the girl, it will be worth it."

"I'll have it ready by Saturday," said Hüsnü. "You can wear it to church on Sunday. It will be like you stepped back in time to the days when ladies went about in hats and pearls and men wouldn't dare be seen in the Grand Avenue if they weren't wearing their best suits and ties. I'm telling you, this suit will seduce any woman. Now, Mr. Fanis, are we making something for you as well?"

"Yes, two shirts. One for the courtship and one for my wedding. Nobody knows it yet, but I'm going to be married." Fanis turned to Kosmas, who was staring in surprise, and added in Greek, "You must keep it a secret, son, and not ask any questions."

By the time they left Hüsnü's shop, it was going on eight. Even if Daphne had gone to Neighbor's House, she would be leaving soon. Just to make sure that the boy missed her, he said, "Now for an important detail. The ties."

They headed toward the Galatasaray Lycée and ducked into a shop with a vitrine full of large silk scarves portraying Ottoman palace and market scenes. Fanis marched straight to the men's tie counter, put on his most charming smile for the well-dressed woman who offered to assist them, and displayed his index finger, around which he had tied a number of brown, white, and blue threads.

"May I have your advice, miss?" he said. "This is the color of the young man's suit, and these are the colors of our shirts. We just ordered them, tailor-made. I always take threads with me. It helps me match the ties."

"What an ingenious trick, sir. And what a discerning eye for color. Such a rich brown, such a beautiful gray-blue."

"Let's see what you've got. How about that one in the cabinet behind you? The brown on brown stripe high up in the corner?"

Fanis took a good look at the clerk's backside while she stretched to reach the tie. He decided that he would need to see a lot of ties from the upper cabinet, one by one.

After the thirteenth, Kosmas pointed to the clock and said, "Mr. Fanis, it's getting late."

"Young people," said Fanis. "Always in such a hurry. They don't realize that the finer things in life take time. Now, how about those over there—"

"Mr. Fanis, if you want to stay, perhaps I should pay for my ties."

A killjoy if ever there was one, Fanis thought. There's no way he'll get the girl.

Fanis turned to the saleswoman, smiled, and said, "I've tired you enough, miss. You've been most helpful. Let's wrap up those four. I don't want to be impolite by keeping my friend waiting."

They left the silk shop with two new ties each, shook hands, and separated. Kosmas proceeded up the Grand Avenue. Fanis turned down Yeni Çarşı Street and stopped abruptly when he spotted a mustachioed man of roughly his own age sitting on a stool and scattering seed for his three chickens and one rooster. Fanis plastered himself against the corner building and peered round into the byway. The man wore mirrored glasses and a smart hat with the brim turned up at the back. Fanis observed the way he slouched, his legs spread wide and his belly hanging between them. The abrupt motion of the wrist was familiar. The Panama hat with a blue band was familiar. The man looked over his shoulder and called through the open door in Turkish, "*Çay hazır mı?*" Is the tea ready? At that moment, Fanis was certain he had found the man responsible for his fiancée Kalypso's rape during the 1955 pogrom.

As soon as the troubles had started on September 6, 1955, Tasos Petridis, Kalypso's father, had ordered his employees to close the winehouse. He then went to the local police station to ask for protection. He was sure he would receive it because Captain Tayyip Aydın was one of his most regular customers. Furthermore, the Petridis Winehouse waiters had standing instructions never to allow him to pay.

But Aydın replied, "Tonight I'm not a policeman. Tonight I am a Turk. We have orders."

As soon as Petridis left the station, he was beaten senseless by a gang of thugs. His wife and daughters, who were visiting his mother on the other side of the Golden Horn, were thereby left without protection.

When the story about Captain Aydın reached Fanis's ears—about a week after the Petridis family immigrated to Canada—he said, "What kind of person could do that? Live with us, eat with us, drink with us, and then, overnight, become somebody else?"

The question obsessed him for decades. He had always considered his Turkish neighbors to be compassionate, honorable people. He didn't want to allow the pogrom to overturn this idea. He tried to concentrate on those who had protected the Rums, but still, Aydın and others like him existed.

So Fanis stalked the captain, learned where he drank tea, with whom he played backgammon, where he lived, which football team he supported, what he did on his days off, and how many children and later grandchildren he had, but he never had the courage to ask why he had done what he did. In the late eighties, Fanis came to realize that what had happened to his fiancée might have occurred even if her father had been present, but his questions goaded him on. In 1993, he lost the captain's tracks entirely. Some people said that Aydın had been hospitalized after suffering a heart attack in Ankara. Others said he had moved to Antalya.

Now here he was once again, scattering birdseed just a few hundred meters from Faik Paşa Street. He was at least ten kilos heavier than the last time Fanis had seen him and significantly more wrinkled, but there could be no doubt. Fanis's heart felt like it would beat out of his chest. For over half a century he had fantasized about confronting Aydın, showing him a photograph of Kalypso, and asking him why he had been so ungrateful to Petridis. But Fanis wasn't prepared to do it that afternoon. He opened his umbrella, even though it was no longer raining, shielded his face, and walked as quickly as he could past the byway.

5

Mother and Son

"SUCH A PERFECT SON," SAID Rea. "I knew I didn't have to remind you to stop by the cobbler's. How did they come out?"

Kosmas changed into his slippers and stepped into the musty living room. He kissed his mother's powdered forehead, nodded to Dimitris Pavlidis, the retired journalist who often came to their house for tea, and joined them at the dining-room table. "I'm so sorry, Mother," he said. "I completely forgot the shoes."

"You *forgot*?"

"I'll get your shoes tomorrow."

"But you've never forgotten my errands."

Dimitris, who was rolling candy foils into a ball on the shiny silver tablecloth, said with a slight stutter, "It's not a big deal. Tomorrow's another day."

Kosmas glanced at Dimitris's thick yellow fingernails. Half of the index claw had separated from the rest, popping up like a wire fence barb. A simple fungicide would cure the condition, but Dimitris refused to go to the doctor.

"For somebody else it wouldn't be a big deal," said Rea, "but it's not like my Kosmas to forget an errand."

Dimitris stood and held out a trembling hand. "Give me the ticket and I'll go get them right now."

"Please, Mr. Dimitris," said Kosmas, "the shoes can wait until tomorrow."

Rea removed a limp yellow leaf from the African violet serving as the table's centerpiece and dropped it onto the bed of cookie crumbs on her plate. "Have a seat, Dimitraki. He'll do it."

Dimitris tilted his head back and held up his hand in a gesture of refusal. "I'll have your shoes in twenty minutes, Ritsa." He took the cobbler's ticket from Kosmas, grabbed the canvas briefcase he still carried, even though he had retired from his politics beat at the *Tribune* over twenty years ago, and was out the door.

As soon as he had gone, Rea looked at the shopping bag still in Kosmas's hand. "What's that?" she asked.

"Never mind."

"I don't know what's gotten into you. You know how much I was looking forward to my new shoes."

She limped into their tiny box-like kitchen and turned on the wall-mounted television to a rerun episode of *The Foreign Bridegroom*, a soap opera about a Muslim girl in love with the son of a Christian shipowner. Neither she nor Kosmas had missed an episode during its first broadcast. She poured Kosmas's tea and turned up the volume so that they could listen while she chopped onions, threw them into the pan with olive oil, cut a cauliflower into large pieces, sliced a red pepper into thin rounds, and julienned a carrot.

Kosmas drank his tea at the two-seater linoleum table under which his legs hardly fit. How dare she snap at him? He took her shopping, to tea with friends, to the beauty parlor. He never argued about the visits to the dead, as his father had. Every Saturday he led Rea arm in arm up the cemetery's central path and kicked the round cypress cones out of her way so that she wouldn't trip. He enthroned her on a folding stool beside the family plot, in the shade of the cypress trees and laurel bushes, and then he scrubbed the tombstone with soap and water, and polished the inlaid photographs of his father, grandparents, great-grandparents, and great-great-grandparents, a few great-uncles, aunts, and distant cousins. All the while, she had nothing to do but tend the censor, pray, and watch. But it wasn't just the cemetery visits: he brought her footrest whenever he saw that her feet were aching, called the doctor at the first indication of indisposition, and only saw his friends at night, after he had put her to bed. Furthermore, he said that *her* cooking—not his grandmother's—was the best in Pera.

Rea took a casserole dish from the oven and served Kosmas a piece of the cheese pie that she had warmed as a snack. Kosmas picked at it with his fork. "Mother," he said, "I've been wanting to tell you this for a while. You know that we sell cheese pies in the Lily. Uncle Mustafa bakes them every morning. They're not as good as yours, but I really have no desire to eat cheese pie of any kind after work. You understand it has nothing to do with you, don't you?"

Rea looked at him like a scolded puppy. "But that cheese pie was your favorite when you were a boy."

"I'm forty-one."

"You've changed," she said, shaking a wooden spatula at him. "Something's changed you." She turned to the window and stared at the pink hydrangeas bowing in the rain that had just begun again. "Were you out with someone?"

"No." Kosmas flattened himself against the wall so that she could open the refrigerator door and take out the previous day's lentil and bulgur soup.

Rea set the pot on the stove, lit the gas burner beneath it, and loaded a tray with three sets of her mother's silverware and three water glasses. "You were out with a woman this afternoon," she said, turning down the flame on the cauliflower mixture. "She must have been Ottoman. Otherwise you'd tell me."

"You didn't mind when the Greek guy married the Turkish girl on *A Foreign Bridegroom*," said Kosmas.

"That's a soap opera!"

Rea stepped past Kosmas into the living room, collapsed into an armchair by the barred window, and rubbed her knees. "They always ache when it rains. And these bars! Whoever thought of putting bars on the inside of a window? You can't get even a breath of fresh air."

Kosmas leaned against the kitchen doorjamb, staring at her. "I'm not complaining to the landlord again. There's no point. He won't change them."

Rea took a bundled-cane crucifix from the doily-covered corner shelf that served as the household iconostasis. She crossed herself and kissed the crucifix. "On the black Tuesday night of the pogrom—"

"Not this again."

"—we were at our cottage on the island. It's always on a Tuesday that these things happen, just like in 1453."

"Mama, please. What do your shoes have to do with black Tuesdays and pogroms and the fall of Constantinople?"

"When the mob arrived by ferry, my mother and I hid in a shed behind the house. My father and brothers took refuge in the fig trees. The thugs threw the bell of Saint Nicholas into the sea and killed the monk who used to make these crucifixes. They tried to burn our house, too, but the fire extinguished itself. My mother said it was because of the crucifix. She'd fixed it to the inside of the door before we hid in the shed."

Kosmas crossed his arms over his chest. "I've heard this a thousand times."

"And you need to hear it again so you understand why it would kill me if you married an Ottoman. When my family returned to the City, my mother and I wore headscarves. We communicated with hand motions. If we spoke Greek, people would know we were Rum. If we spoke Turkish, they'd know from our accents. So we didn't speak at all, like animals. If you marry an Ottoman, your whole life will be like that. You'll forget your religion and your language because your wife won't share them. Where will that leave your children?"

Kosmas pulled a chair from the dining table, sat, and lowered his head to Rea's eye level. "I had coffee with Mr. Fanis, Mama, not with a woman."

"Whatever for?"

"I wanted a little fashion advice, that's all. He's a nice dresser."

"But I buy your clothes for you."

Kosmas leaned back, balancing the chair on its rear legs.

"You're going to ruin my furniture," said Rea. "I've told you a thousand times not to do that."

The chair's front legs crunched onto the wood floor.

Rea struggled to her feet, replaced the crucifix in the iconostasis, and hobbled over to the chipped walnut sideboard. She opened a drawer, shuffled through a pile of unframed black-and-white photographs, and set one in front of Kosmas. "This was taken in Halki when I was sixteen. The one pouring lemonade is Aliki when she still had teeth. Kalypso—cutting the cake—lived at the top of the cul-de-sac off Ağa Hamamı Street."

"And?"

"She was engaged to Fanis."

"I thought he didn't marry until he was in his forties."

"He didn't." Rea eased herself into her armchair and looked out the barred window, toward the little park across the street.

"And the girl in the picture?"

"You know what they did to girls during the pogrom." She puckered her face and drew her hand backward in an expression of disgust. "Kalypso was one of those. Her family decided to emigrate the following day, but she didn't want to go. Even after what they'd done to her, she didn't want to leave the City. Fanis didn't go to her afterwards. It was such a difficult time, so I try not to judge. But I think about Kalypso now and then, and I wonder . . ."

Kosmas stared at the fuzzy mold on the wall behind the television set. The previous week he had thought it was just dirt, but now it was forming rusty continents. He'd have to call a specialist.

"Are you listening?" Rea snapped.

"Of course I am. What happened to her?"

Rea grabbed her embroidery hoop from the side table and pulled out the needle. "Never mind. I'm just saying that you ought to know what sort of man Fanis is. If he's giving you romantic advice, you certainly don't want *that* from *him*. Everybody knows what a libertine he was. He even made a mistress of one of the French nuns living up his street."

A rattling and then a hissing came from the kitchen, but Kosmas was too angry to pay any attention. "And what makes you think my meeting with Fanis had anything to do with a woman?" he said, convinced that his mother couldn't have guessed his attraction to Daphne. "Rita Tereza and I didn't even exchange phone numbers."

There was more hissing, louder this time, accompanied by the faint odor of burned food. "The soup!" said Kosmas. He bolted to the kitchen and removed the pot of boiled-over, bottom-burned lentil and bulgur from the stove.

6

Teatime

IT WAS FRIDAY AFTERNOON, JUST before teatime and—Fanis
hoped—a propitious meeting with Daphne. The sun poked
through the acacia leaves and speckled the tables outside
Ismail's Home-cooked Food, the restaurant where Fanis
was grabbing a late lunch of eggplant stuffed with suspi-
cious-looking gray meat. Ismail's was not the type of place
to which Fanis would ever take a lady friend. It was a place
for being alone. The tables rocked on the uneven sidewalk
and the food was indifferent, but occasionally, when Fanis
couldn't be bothered to cook or walk far, he would go there
and chat with the pleasant waitress, who always wore hip-
pie-ish strings of beads and a pair of brightly colored pants.

A handsome thirty-something customer took a seat at
the next table. He set his mobile phone, a pack of Winston
cigarettes, and a Turkish copy of Arthur Miller's *Death of a
Salesman* on the grubby bamboo placemat and ordered two
plates of the day's special: schnitzel and salad. When a beautiful girl in a revealing tank top approached, bent over to kiss
the man, and sat down, Fanis growled, "Bastard." He hated
the envy that had been boiling in him for the past decade, and
he hated his failing exterior even more.

Fanis heard a French conversation at a neighboring table.
He was surprised he understood after not having used the language in years. A tour guide was telling a Parisian couple that
most of the City's residents had no awareness of Istanbul's

Hellenic past. Fanis knew that the guide was referring to Byzantium rather than to the history of his own lifetime, but he felt that his existence had been confirmed. He stole a glance at the French woman: her backpack rested on her lap as if she were impatient to leave. Fanis wanted to say to her, "I am one of them. One of the last Byzantines." As he practiced his French in silence, a van with an enormous picture of the prime minister drove by, blasting a campaign theme song— "One More Time"—on a loudspeaker. But Fanis wondered: would this be just one more term for the prime minister, or was he becoming a permanent fixture? By the time he had recovered from the interruption, the French tourists and their guide were almost out of sight.

The waitress in red pants collected Fanis's plates and delivered a tumbler of lemon juice and a tiny glass of tea. That was what Fanis liked about the place: they remembered that he always finished his meal with lemon juice for good digestion, and that he chased the lemon juice with tea. The brakes of cars and trucks coming down Sıraselviler Avenue squeaked as he stirred two sugar cubes into the tulip glass. He wasn't bothered by the car noise: it was mitigated by his deteriorating sense of hearing. What he really hated was the exhaust. It was too bad one couldn't choose which senses and abilities one lost. Had anyone bothered to ask Fanis, he would have chosen to forgo olfaction and retain erection.

After lunch Fanis went straight to Neighbor's House, where he hoped to chance upon Julien reading a newspaper or perhaps chatting up some unfortunate young lady. After finding his friend people-watching at a street-side table, Fanis ordered tea for both and pulled up a chair. The first oddball of the evening was a religious type with a black beard dyed red at the tips. He wore a long coat and a black hat wrapped in a green turban, the ends of which hung down his back as the symbol of a completed pilgrimage to Mecca. Was the great work of Atatürk, who had banned religious dress of any kind, unraveling? No. Fanis's vision was going. Visual impairment was, after all, a classic symptom of cerebral arteriosclerosis. Then the young secularists sitting nearby shook their heads and made clucking sounds of disapproval with their tongues. Fanis felt a measure of relief. His eyes were just fine.

When one of the handsome waiters delivered the teas and a complimentary plate of sesame rings made for the anniversary of the Prophet's Ascent to Heaven, Julien asked the young man to keep an eye out for a dark beauty. "You'll spot her immediately," he said. "If I have to step away for a moment, send her to my table."

Disregarding his friend's little show, Fanis looked across the street toward one of the old Rum houses confiscated by the government in the sixties. It had since been painted an obnoxious mauve, and air-conditioners had been installed in its oriels. On the first floor was a business sign that read, in edgy purple letters on a black background, "Coiffeur." When the proprietress opened her windows and leaned out with a cigarette, Julien shouted, "When are you coming down, my pretty one?"

"Later, later!" she returned.

"She has nice tits," Julien whispered.

"Not bad," said Fanis, "but too much of a peasant for my taste."

A fat boy of twelve pedaled his bicycle in their direction. Julien bellowed, "Yusuf!" The boy waved and pedaled past them. Julien called again, "Yusuf! When are you going to bring me what I need? The ladies are asking!"

"Who's he?" asked Fanis.

"The pharmacist's son."

"Is his father good? Accommodating, I mean. I need to get some medication—"

"I thought you were in perfect health."

"I am. That's why I asked the doctor for Viagra."

"I thought they were too good for that at the German Hospital. He gave it to you?"

"Well, no. Which leads me to my next question. Do you know a pharmacist who will sell it without a prescription?"

Julien grinned. "Plenty. But go to Serkan Sözbir on Yeni Yuva Street. Yusuf's father. Tell him you're a friend of mine and he'll set you up."

"Do you . . . ?"

Julien folded his hands behind his head and leaned back in the canvas chair. "Never needed it, friend."

Fanis took a miniature pen and pad from his breast pocket and noted the name. "Thanks for the tip. Not that I need it either, but just for the odd occasion when one is feeling out of sorts."

Ten minutes later Yusuf walked into the tea garden smirking like a fellow twice his age. He tossed a box of condoms into Julien's lap and strutted back up the street.

"Dirty old man," said Fanis. "Look at you, corrupting children."

"Educating children, sir! At least Yusuf won't knock up his girlfriend at fifteen, all because I set a good example." Julien shouted his thanks and stuffed the package into one of his Velcro pockets. "I'll have to buy him some candy."

"I suppose," said Fanis, "that you take your diabetes meds regularly, just as the doctor prescribed?"

"Of course," said Julien. "At our age, you've got to do what the doctors say. Otherwise you're in big trouble."

Presently Fanis heard the characteristic tic-tac of stilettos on cement. By instinct he knew that an exciting woman was approaching. He looked up. A pair of black eyes were fixed directly on him. Black curls bounced around the woman's head, like the rubber Afros on the dolls in the nearby toy shop. Hips, breasts, and just the right amount of belly fat jiggled beneath an A-line dress.

Hermes, help me.

The woman quickly transferred her gaze to Julien, kissed him on the cheek, and said in Turkish peppered with French,

"If you'd told me that parking was so difficult around here, Professeur, I'd have come by metro instead of borrowing my mom's car. *Mais vraiment*, you know I'm not supposed to tire myself."

"*Ma pauvre*," said Julien, offering his chair. He switched to Turkish: "Don't worry. I'm here now."

The woman looked remarkably like the siren who had spoken a few words to Fanis outside the Çukurcuma Pharmacy. But, Fanis reasoned, if she knew Greek, Julien would surely have addressed her in that language: speaking Greek was a point of pride with the *professeur de musique*. Moreover, Fanis had guessed that the woman in the street was in her late thirties. This one seemed more like early forties.

Julien ordered tea and made introductions: "Selin, this is my old friend Fanis. Fanis, the lovely Selin, a former pupil from Saint-Benoit, a graduate of the Conservatoire de Paris, and now a professional violinist. She recently gave up her job at the Vienna Philharmonic to play with the Borusan."

"Pleased to meet you," said Fanis, shaking Selin's hand. "I knew that the Borusan Corporation imported BMWs, but I didn't know that they also imported beautiful violinists."

Selin smiled. "A pleasure. So you've heard of the Borusan Orchestra?"

"I go at least once or twice per season," said Fanis. "I've always loved music. I'm a church cantor."

Selin took a paper handkerchief from her oversized handbag and wiped the perspiration from her forehead, neck, and chest. On the left side of her neck, just beneath her jaw line, was a purplish discoloration—a hickey, perhaps? Fanis's eyes wandered downward. On her left breast there was some sort of floral tattoo. Fanis felt his temperature rise: this one was definitely a fire sign. He realized he was staring, yet he couldn't look away. So he said, "What an interesting design."

"Oh, that. A lotus flower. I had it done when I was in college. I wish I could have it removed, but I'm afraid of the pain."

The skinny tea-garden cat, as if on cue, rubbed itself against Fanis's legs. He stood, pretended to shoo it away, and moved his chair a few inches closer to Selin's. "What does it represent?" he asked.

"The lotus has its roots in the mud of the world and rises through the waters of experience to bloom in enlightenment. Kids' stuff. My mother cried for days."

"So you ran out and got another?"

"Two more," said Selin, with a characteristic Turkish side-nod.

Fanis searched the exposed portion of her right breast, her supple arms, and the ankles around which dangled thin silver anklets. All bare. "Where are they?" he asked.

"Private," said Selin.

Aman. Mercy. *This one's going to eat me, finish me off.*

The bells of Saint Anthony of Padua began ringing for vespers. Aliki limped into the tea garden, piled her shopping bags on the table, and said in Greek, "At least there are still trees here, even if they aren't cypresses."

"You remember my pupil Selin, don't you, Aliki?" said Julien in Turkish. "She's looking for a place in the neighborhood. Is there anything for rent on your street?"

"Not that I know of," said Aliki, smiling to show off her new dental implants. "Where do you live now?"

"With my parents," said Selin. "In Levent."

Single, thought Fanis. But that hickey probably means she has a boyfriend. He said, "I've always considered attention to one's aging parents a great virtue. I lived with my mother and took care of her until she died."

Selin brushed from her lap a fuzzy linden flower just fallen from the tree. "That's admirable, Mr. Fanis, but I need my independence."

"You know," said Fanis, suddenly remembering having seen a For Rent sign in the building opposite his, "I think there's a garret available in Faik Paşa Street. Number thirty-two. You might want to check it out."

Selin noted the address on napkin. "Thanks for the tip."

"In my opinion," said Aliki, "you should stay with your parents until you marry. So men don't take advantage of you."

"I've already been married," said Selin. "That's the surest way to get a man to take advantage of you."

Aliki chuckled.

Fanis nodded toward a yellow house that a building crew had been renovating for the past few months. It had rounded oriels, sculpted white molding, a black iron door, and bars on the ground-floor window. "What about that one?" he said. "If you lived there, you could drink tea with us every day."

Julien clicked his tongue. "No way. The moans from the cemetery are terrible."

"There he goes again," said Fanis. "Those ghosts are a figment of your imagination, Professeur, stuff for superstitious old people. Nobody would even notice that tiny cemetery if you didn't keep bringing it up."

Once again Fanis heard tic-tacking on cement, but this time there was no emotional surge. He raised his gaze and beheld Rea trying out her sparkly new cane. Kosmas, wearing one of the low-end black Armanis they had seen during their shopping trip, was inching along beside her, like a faithful dog. At Rea's other side was Dimitris Pavlidis, the old politics reporter from the *Tribune* and one of Fanis's former schoolmates.

"That's it, Ritsa," Dimitris cooed in Greek. "Take it slowly."

"Were you hoping she'd be here to notice?" said Fanis to Kosmas, as soon as the boy was close enough to hear.

Rea turned sharply to her son and examined him for an instant. Then she took the seat offered by Julien and said, "So *that's* why you were so obsessed with the crease in your pants."

Kosmas dumped the slumbering gray cat from a chair and settled down beside his mother. "Nothing escapes you, Mama."

Rea switched to Turkish: "*Ben malımı bilirim*." I know my goods.

"Don't worry, son," said Aliki, scrunching both eyes at Kosmas. "Her aunt told me she's coming today."

"Are you dating her?" asked Rea.

"No." Kosmas held up two fingers and mouthed the word tea, but Emine, the waitress, ignored him.

"Well," said Rea, recovering a little, "at least Daphne's one of ours."

"I probably don't have a chance, Mama, ours or not," said Kosmas.

Aliki leaned back in her chair and swung her legs, like a child. "How could any girl not fancy a strong, handsome gentleman like you?"

Rea folded her freshly manicured hands on top of the table. "She'd have to be out of her mind."

"Selin," said Fanis, "let me introduce you to Rea, Dimitris, and Kosmas. Friends, I'd like you to meet our star violinist, Selin, who speaks French like a native. She is also an expert in *the lotus*." He looked Selin in the eye for a second, wondering if she would realize that he was referring neither to the flower nor to the tattoo, but to one of his favorite Kama Sutra positions. Alas, there was no sign of recognition. Fanis quickly changed tack: "Excuse me, Madame Emine! A second round of tea, please." Then to Selin, "Yours must be cold by now. A hot tea will cool you off. That's what the Arabs say, anyway."

Selin put her hand on Fanis's forearm for a split second, provoking a tingling sensation that shot all the way to Fanis's groin. "Thanks, Mr. Fanis," she said, "but my doctor said only one per day."

Julien explained, "She recently had an operation to close a hole in her heart."

"Now that's the operation I need," whispered Fanis.

Selin leaned sideways. He could smell a sweet, spicy perfume whose name he could not recall. Her curls brushed the tip of his ear. "I'm warning you," she said, in a seductive tone, "I'm dangerous. Before men came and went through the hole, but the next one will have to stay."

For a second Fanis wondered if he should leave Daphne to Kosmas and pursue this feisty one instead. In an attempt to determine her religion, he asked whether her name was the Turkish Selin or the French Céline, which were almost identical in pronunciation, and he received an answer he had not expected: she was not French at all, but a Turkish Jew. Fanis felt a sudden thrill, as if he were standing on the edge of a precipice, looking downward. He had always wanted to have an affair with a Jewish woman. He'd had plenty of Rums, a few Levantines and Armenians, one Turkish widow, and even a Sri Lankan waitress, but not one Jew. *At last.*

"How nice," he said. "I go to Neve Shalom Synagogue occasionally. I love the chant, so much like ours, but more refreshing."

"That's rather unusual, isn't it?" said Selin. "I mean, a Rum going to synagogue?"

"Certainly it is. But I passed by one Friday evening years ago and was enchanted by the melody. I've been hooked ever since."

"I'd like to hear you chant sometime," she said.

"Perhaps you will. I'm not sure if you're aware, but the roots of our ecclesiastical chant are Jewish. In the depth of history, our traditions meet. So why shouldn't they meet again in the present?"

"True," said Selin, looking into his eyes as if no one else were present. "I bet I'll even understand a little."

"You speak Greek?" said Fanis, unable to believe his luck.

"I learned from a Rum boyfriend."

"Are you still together?"

Selin giggled, like a mischievous jinn. "No, Mr. Fanis. I haven't seen him since I was eight. Our summer houses were next to each other on Prinkipos Island. He also taught me how to pee like a boy into a laundry drain so that I didn't have to go home to use the restroom."

"How *naughty*," said Fanis. The childhood boyfriend had been an unconventional type: just like Fanis.

"We got in trouble for rusting the drain, and I had to relearn how to pee like a girl, but I can still understand Greek."

"Could we have met in Turnacıbaşı Street recently? I thought it might have been you, but when you started speaking Turkish with the *professeur* I wasn't sure."

Before Selin had a chance to reply, Dimitris interposed, "Do you speak Ladino?"

"Yes," said Selin. "But none of my nieces and nephews can. They're all learning English instead. My generation is probably the last of the Spanish speakers."

"What a pity," said Aliki, covering her mouth. "It's the same for all of us. My daughter married a Muslim. Her children understand Greek, but they're too lazy to speak it. If you want my advice, marry one of your own. Otherwise, your traditions and identity will be lost."

The conversation about marriage and continuity dragged on, but Fanis found himself unable to concentrate on what Selin was saying. Her voice washed over him, pulling him inside its current, spinning him around, floating him on its crest. Was this the beginning of a second infatuation? Or was it a "declining ability to pay attention," yet another symptom of vascular dementia? Sometimes it was so difficult to know the difference between love and degeneration.

"Good evening, everyone!" said Gavriela, breaking the trance.

Daphne was standing beside her aunt in a straight day dress just like the ones that Fanis remembered from the sixties, when he was a comfort to women whose husbands had gone to Greece to find a job and a small apartment before sending for the family. *My God.* How could he have allowed himself to be distracted by the violinist? A woman like Daphne could raise the dead. Marriage with her would be a renaissance not only for him, but for their community as well.

In an expert hustle and bustle, Fanis grabbed a chair from a nearby table, offered it to Daphne, and squeezed himself between the two young women. Adjusting the silk scarf around his neck, he said, "Daphne, dear, with all that studying, I don't know if you've had a chance to see our City. I'd love to show you around. Would you like to join us, Selin? If you have some free time on Saturday, perhaps the three of us could meet at the Pearl for profiteroles and go from there. I can show you parts of the City that *nobody* knows."

"Why not start at the Lily?" said Rea.

"The Lily," repeated Fanis. "Well, yes, the Lily has quite a reputation, and I'm sure Kosmas does a superb job, but I was thinking of the Pearl more for the atmosphere." To show that he was *au courant* with current issues, Fanis added, "Besides, I don't know if anyone can make anything decent out of the genetically modified wheat we have now. What you do think, Kosmaki? Share your thoughts."

Kosmas set his elbows on the wooden armrests of the patio chair, folded his hands in the air, and said, "I'm not old enough to remember what wheat was like when *you* were young, Mr. Fanis."

Was the little brat trying to stick it to him? Well, it wasn't going to work. Because Fanis was not the least bit ashamed of the number on his identity card. "Such a pity!" he said. "I remember the Lily when it used to make a fabulous pastry called the Balkanik. Back in your grandfather's time. I bet you've never even heard of the Balkanik."

"I have, in fact," said Kosmas, "but it's not something I've ever made. Or tasted."

Fanis turned to Daphne. "The Balkanik, my dear, was a coiled éclair filled with strips of different flavored creams. One for each of the Balkan peoples. Despite recent conflicts, we lived in harmony for centuries."

"Do you know its origins?" said Daphne.

"No, but I do remember my mother saying that it was a very, very old recipe. Unfortunately, everybody stopped making it after the pogrom of 'fifty-five and the deportations of 'sixty-four. Harmony became a doubtful word back then. It's too bad because it was the most divine pastry ever created."

"The Balkanik was the reason I became a journalist," said Dimitris, with his characteristic stutter. "Fanis, do you remember Miss Evyenidou?"

Fanis served Daphne a few butter cookies despite her protests. "Of course," he said. "I used to try to touch her long hair when she wasn't looking."

Dimitris waved both of his shaking hands in excitement. "Miss Evyenidou failed me in first grade because I didn't pay any attention. The second time around she made sure I learned to write better than anyone. My mother felt sorry for her because she had to deal with me twice, so she sent me to school with a Balkanik as a gift, and Miss Evyenidou shared it with the class."

"Do you know its origins, Mr. Dimitris?" asked Daphne.

"Of course. Miss Evyenidou gave me a prize for an essay I wrote about it. The Balkanik was invented by the great Rum pâtissier Christakis Usta in the sixteenth century. He went to Florence to study with Pantarelli, the chef of Catherine de' Medici, but he missed Istanbul so much that he decided to invent a pastry to honor it. Christakis Usta mastered Pantarelli's pastry technique, then designed flavored creams that would represent the diversity of his homeland." Dimitris gazed dreamily upward at the linden tree, ruffling in the evening breeze. "Rose, cardamom, chocolate, vanilla, pistachio, and others that I don't remember—all distinct yet complementary.

You could pick the pastry apart and try to eat them one by one, or you could be lazy and stick your spoon in with your eyes closed and taste them all together."

"I'll ask Uncle Mustafa," said Kosmas.

Daphne took a sudden interest in Kosmas. "You have a Muslim uncle?"

"He was my late father's business partner. And now mine. But I've called him 'Uncle' for as long as I can remember."

Daphne leaned her elbows on the table and cradled her chin in ringless hands. "I love the symbolism of that pastry."

"Uncle Mustafa has an old Ottoman recipe book," said Kosmas. "The Balkanik has to be in it."

"You can read Ottoman script?"

"A little. I studied it a few years ago."

Daphne faced Kosmas squarely, turning her back to Fanis. "Really? Why?"

"I found it frustrating not to be able to read the inscriptions on mosques, fountains, and other monuments. Once I got past the Arabic script, I found it wasn't as difficult as I thought it would be."

Daphne nodded in respect. Fanis, however, was not so gullible. He would put the boy to the test. Pointing at a cemetery obelisk with ornate floral motifs, he said, "Can you read that tombstone over there, Kosmaki?"

Kosmas examined the obelisk. "It's the grave of a nineteen-year-old girl named Şükran, daughter of Ömer Efendi. She died in the Islamic year 1313, at the end of the nineteenth century, that is. The poem reads: 'I came into this world to become a blossoming vine, but I did not have the joy of raising a child, nor did I find medicine for my sorrow.'"

Bastard. It seemed that he really could read Ottoman, unless he was clever enough to fake it, which was doubtful. Fanis returned his attention to Daphne. He loved her smile, but not when it was directed at Kosmas. Feigning annoyance with some fallen leaves, he pulled his chair closer to hers. The tea-garden cat, which had apparently been lying beneath it, startled and yowled.

"There you are!" said Julien. He unwrapped a packet of raw minced meat and set it beneath a bush. "I've been waiting for this one. What can I do? I feel sorry for the poor things."

"And the pellet rifle you keep on your back balcony," blurted Aliki, "for the ones who do their business—"

"*Sus!*" he said. "That's for rats."

Selin stood. My, she was lovely. The kind that others might call plump, but to Fanis she was as voluptuous as Titian's *Sleeping Venus*. "It was a pleasure meeting you all," she said, "but I have to be going."

"It's so early," whined Julien. "Stay a bit longer."

"Do you have a rehearsal?" Fanis asked.

"No," said Selin. "My family always eats dinner together on Friday nights."

"Of course," said Fanis. "Shabbat. From my visits to the synagogue, I know exactly how important it is."

"We aren't religious. It's just a family tradition." Selin took a business card from her wallet. Unable to believe his good fortune, Fanis raised his hand to take it, but Selin reached straight past him and gave the card to Daphne. "In case you'd like to have coffee sometime," she said.

Fanis stood, grasped Selin's fingertips, and kissed her knuckle beneath the daisy-shaped bijou ring on her middle finger. He sighed as she hurried off. If only he'd met her twenty years before, but now he couldn't afford to be distracted. By the time he sat down again, Rea was already on to her favorite subject: the retirement stipends distributed to the Rums by the Greek Consulate in order to maintain the community and ensure the survival of the Ecumenical Patriarchate. Fanis couldn't imagine a more boring subject.

"Plenty of people take advantage," Rea said softly, in Greek. "Like the Bulgarians who immigrate to Turkey and obtain certificates from the Patriarchate saying that they're Rum Orthodox so they can get a stipend—"

"I don't get it," said Daphne.

"Well," said Rea, speaking more slowly, "the money should only go to *real* Rums—"

"What's a real Rum?" said Daphne.

"Whatever do you mean?" said Rea. Her spit landed on Fanis's hand.

Daphne pushed her movie-star sunglasses onto the top of her head, like a hairband. "I mean that in Byzantine and Ottoman times, the term was religious, not ethnic. So how can we make it the exclusive property of Greek speakers?"

"Because it *is*," said Rea. "If you don't speak Greek, you're not Rum. Somebody enlighten her!"

"Mama," said Kosmas quietly. "She's right about Byzantium."

Daphne sat tall in the sloping canvas chair. "Are Rums thoroughbred dogs? Do they have papers to prove it? Any Orthodox Christian is Rum, Madame Rea, regardless of his ethnicity."

"Amen," said Fanis, already fed up with the conversation. "Now let's talk about Saturday—"

"Are you saying, Daphne," Rea continued, "that the Antiochians and Bulgarians are Rums? If you are, you're misinformed. They're not part of the *homogeneia*."

"I despise that word," said Daphne. "*Homogeneia*—the same race. Which means it's a racist word."

"What's she talking about?" said Rea, looking from one friend to the next. "*Everybody* says *homogeneia*."

"I've always thought it was a dumb word," grumbled Julien.

"You're missing Rea's point," said Aliki. She planted both feet firmly on the ground.

"Madame Rea," said Daphne. "The ancestors of the Antiochians were Byzantines. That's what Rum means—Eastern

Roman, Byzantine. And you're saying that they're not Rum because they speak Arabic instead of Greek. That's racist."

"Ritsa, she has a point," said Dimitris, gently. He took a *Tribune* from his briefcase and fanned himself with it.

"I'm not having this conversation," Rea huffed.

Kosmas caressed the back of his mother's head. "Mama, please."

Rea slapped her hand onto the table. The tea-garden cat bolted toward the cemetery. "You're not *from here*, Daphne," she said. "You don't know what you're talking about."

The argument was a better gift than Fanis could ever have hoped for. Kosmas certainly would not pursue Daphne now, and Daphne, judging from the way she clenched her jaw, had already begun to hate Rea.

"Come, come, Rea," said Gavriela, nervously twisting a used antibacterial wipe. "Let's settle down."

"Daphne," said Kosmas, in a pathetic peacemaking effort, "don't you think there can be some good in preserving one's community? Don't you think that there can be good in wanting to keep together so that it's not all diluted and lost?"

"Of course there is. But cultural heritage and religion don't depend upon race."

"So well put," said Fanis. He clapped his hands. "She's right, you know."

"But I thought, Mr. Fanis," said Kosmas, "that you, too, wanted to marry a Rum. I thought our community was important to you."

"It is. But a Rum, as our lovely Daphne just said, is an Orthodox Christian, not a thoroughbred dog. Anyway, let's not give her a hard time. She has her views, and they happen to be quite intelligent, just like her."

The call to prayer resounded from the loudspeaker of the nearby mosque.

"Beautiful, isn't it?" said Fanis. "One doesn't need to understand the call to prayer's words in order to experience their meaning. Islamic chant also has a strong historical relationship with ours. We're all linked in some way."

Daphne smiled. Realizing that he had found her spot, Fanis pursued his advantage. "Which reminds me, the bishop will be at the Panagia church on Sunday—it's Pentecost, you know—and he always has good stories. Why don't you come, my dear Daphne?"

Daphne looked to her aunt.

"We'll see," said Gavriela, standing. "Now, if you'll excuse us, Daphne and I have to be going. You know how my husband hates a late dinner."

After the others had left, Fanis and Julien ordered their last tea. Fanis hated nothing more than solitude at the close of the day, yet there was nothing more certain than solitude for the last of the Levantine Christians and Rums.

"Selin's a good one," Fanis said. "Her hair is a bit—what's the word? Outrageous? But she's attractive nonetheless. Fetching, really. You're a lucky man."

"Don't be silly," said Julien. "Selin is way out of my league. We're too old for women like that."

"Apropos, how old is she?"

"Forty-three."

"That's well within your range, Prof," said Fanis. "You're only twenty-nine years older."

"Please. I'd be lucky if I could get Aliki."

"*Aliki?*" Fanis wrinkled his nose. "You've set your sights a little low, don't you think?"

"I'm not a crazy old bastard like you. I'm practical. If you want somebody to share your loneliness, you're going to have to start thinking about women your own age. Or at least closer to it."

"Speak for yourself," said Fanis, rising. "I'm off. Goodnight."

"Sweet and naughty dreams," said Julien.

Fanis plodded down the hill and stopped to peer through the open windows of the Çukurcuma mosque. The minarets and chandeliers were illuminated for the holiday of the Prophet's Ascent to Heaven. Shoeless men kneeled on the rugs of its sunken floor. It looked inviting.

Upon arriving at his building—a late-nineteenth-century rust-colored mansion with old-style oriels on each of its five floors—Fanis looked over his shoulder. Having reassured himself that no one was following, he fumbled in his pocket for his keys, unlocked the heavy iron door, and stepped inside. He shut the door gently so that its dull clang would not disturb his neighbors and took a deep breath while observing the faded entryway wall paintings, which had been designed to look as if they were alcove statues. Within a burgundy-bordered panel of yellow ochre, the tall figure of the goddess Athena stood to his left. Directly across from her was a male counterpart, the god Hermes. Fanis had always attributed the sparing of his house from the mob to their guardianship, rather than to a God he visited every Sunday in church and in whom he did not entirely believe.

"Friends," he said to the faceless paintings. "Lend a hand, will you? Daphne hasn't bitten yet, and that bewitching Selin is more than I can handle."

He ascended the staircase, pausing at each landing for a rest so that he wouldn't suffer the stroke predicted by Dr. Aydemir. He felt just as fit at seventy-six as he had at sixty, but his mouth was parched. He opened his water bottle and took a sip but had difficulty swallowing. Wasn't that a symptom of arteriosclerosis? If Fanis were not so attached to his apartment, he would have moved to the ground floor and saved himself the daily torture of ascending four and a half flights with a list of symptoms flashing like warning lights on a car dashboard. Damn that Aydemir.

Once inside, he double-bolted the door, closed the velvet curtains, checked that he had indeed locked the balcony window before going out to tea, and peered inside closets and behind doors to make sure that no one had entered while he was out. When he was certain all was secure, he disconnected the telephone—lest he be bothered by his habitual prank caller—and arranged his cutlery, a plate of leftover meatballs and pilaf, and glass of lemon juice on a nineteenth-century Qajar table tray. Then he turned on the television to *Magnificent Century*, a historical soap opera that was the subject of much current debate. The prime minister had criticized it for misrepresentation of the golden age of Ottoman history. He was right, of course. Women—and men—of that epoch did not wear so much makeup; neither did the sultan's wives and concubines expose their augmented breasts in such a fashion. Furthermore, uncastrated men did not enter the harem, as they had to in the soap opera in order to create a spicier plot. Even so, Fanis cringed whenever he heard talk of prohibiting certain representations of history.

Sitting down to dinner, he chased the controversy from his mind and lost himself in the palace intrigues. Halfway through his meal, the electricity went out. His terror of intruders made him freeze with a mouth full of pilaf. Perhaps *they* had done it. Perhaps *they* were waiting in the street, like a flow of molten evil, just as they had been on that September night, and perhaps this time they would succeed in breaking down his door. Or perhaps it was just another electricity outage like the one they'd had last Monday.

Fanis peeled back the curtains. The entire street was black. It was, after all, just a power cut. Swearing and stubbing his toes, he fumbled his way through the living room and located candles and matches in a sideboard drawer, beneath Dr. Aydemir's crumpled scripts. He was sure that Aydemir was nothing but a pharmaceutical salesman, even if his diagnosis had been correct. So what was the use in keeping those hateful papers? Besides, Fanis was going to get his Viagra after all, and who knew if erectile aids could be taken with that poison?

He lit a candle, snatched up the prescriptions, and carried them to the kitchen sink. Then, one by one, he set them on fire and watched the flames eat half-moons into the paper. A few wispy embers wafted up from the sink and settled down again. When the flames had gone out, Fanis surveyed the insignificant ashes, set the candle on the counter where his mother had rolled pastry, turned on the tap, and washed the death sentences down the drain.

He took the candle into the bedroom, put on his pajamas, and stretched out on the bed. Over the roofs of Pera, a flock of screaming seagulls surged and receded like an ocean wave. A cat howled, like a woman having an orgasm. Now that's a good sound, Fanis thought. He tried to picture Daphne's face on the ceiling. Nothing. He tried Selin's. Nothing. He tried again, and the result startled him, for he conjured his lost fiancée Kalypso instead. She was just as real as Daphne and Selin had been in the tea garden that afternoon, and she was not angry with him. He had always supposed that, if there was a heaven and if he met her in it, she would refuse to speak to him. Instead, smiling and laughing, she nibbled his ear. Then some idiot let the heavy iron building door slam shut, and she disappeared.

Fanis tried to bring her back but other sounds—motors, a catfight, and Anatolian music—kept breaking his concentration. The couple who lived beneath him began quarrelling. Fanis unlocked the balcony door and shouted, "Can't you argue during the day?" The couple fell silent. He extinguished the candle and lay down to wait for sleep or death, whichever came first. Not having gone to see Kalypso was the greatest regret of his life, the secret sorrow he had tried to numb with amorous adventures. He hadn't expected her to die as she had, without warning. He'd thought they had all the time in the world—a lifetime—to heal the wounds of that night. Wouldn't running to her bedside have made her feel dishonored twice over? Wait until she's up and about again, his mother had advised him. Wait and then tell her that none of it makes any difference.

7

Those Who Live in Hades

IT WAS PENTECOST SUNDAY, THE day on which the souls of the dead, which had been released from Hades during the Easter Resurrection liturgy, would be obliged to return to the underworld. Fanis thought of the old-fashioned country housewives who said that one should never trim trees or vines between Easter and Pentecost because wandering souls liked to rest upon them. His own mother had never left laundry hanging out past sunset lest the souls wrap themselves in the forgotten linens and leave nasty stains. As a modernist, Fanis did not give much credence to visions of ghosts on bedsheets and tree branches, but he wondered whether Kalypso might be walking beside him that morning and enjoying the tranquil emptiness of the Grand Avenue just as much as he did. Suddenly he felt a light caress on the back of his hand. He looked to his right, but no one was there. Nothing even nearby. He really was losing it.

He arrived at the Panagia before everyone but the custodian. He lit a solitary candle in the narthex, looked up at the starry-sky ceiling, and took a deep breath of church air. If he were a *parfumier*, he'd try to market that scent. Heaven, he'd call it: an Oriental classic with a stale wood and mold base, top notes of apple and rosewater, and a spicy heart of myrrh and cinnamon. Supplies not expected to last more than twenty years. Heaven: get it while you can.

"*Kalimera*." It was an ordinary Greek greeting—good morning—but since one hardly ever heard it in the street anymore, *kalimera* was balm to Fanis's ears.

He turned and saw the bishop standing beside him in the narthex. "Good morning, Your Eminence. You're here early."

The bishop lit two candles and placed them tightly together in the sand, like inseparable lovers. "Couldn't sleep. Probably from the fried zucchini I ate late last night. I should never, ever eat fried stuff at night, but what can I do? I've a weakness for it." The bishop pulled open the heavy door to the nave and held it for Fanis. "Anyway, let's not drag things out today. Pentecost liturgy is long enough as it is. Chant quickly and let's be done by half past twelve."

"I'll try," said Fanis, knowing he'd do just the opposite.

The bishop unbuttoned his suit jacket as they walked down the right aisle toward the sanctuary. "You're looking gloomy," he said.

"Just the usual stuff," said Fanis. "I try to be optimistic, but sometimes I think about how we'll all be gone soon, and how these churches will be deserted, and it gets me down."

The bishop gave the Archangel Michael's door a little push. "Maybe the prognostications are right," he said. "But, for some strange reason, I believe in resurrection."

Fanis followed the bishop through the iconostasis door and into the sanctuary, which was lit only by the flame of a vigil lamp. Switching on the lights, he said, "You have to. You're a bishop."

"I didn't mean *that*," said the bishop. "I meant the resurrection of the community. I feel it today especially. Our young people are going to return."

Fanis hung up his suit jacket and took his black, satin-edged polyester cantor's robe—a gift from the Patriarch—from the closet. "Dream on," he said, threading his arms through the sleeves. "My godson wouldn't come back if you paid him."

He returned to the nave and climbed the two creaky wooden steps to the first cantor's stand. He reviewed the Byzantine music notation, which looked remarkably similar to Arabic script, and distributed his weight evenly on both legs: correct posture would help him avoid foot pain over the next few hours.

Matins began, followed by the Great Litany. A few old peacocks gathered on the left side of the church, opposite the first cantor's stand. Fanis paid them no attention. Still, he couldn't prevent his eyes from wandering when a shapely Greek tourist venerated an icon at the front of the church and performed not one, not two, but *three* full hand-to-floor bows. Fanis continued chanting mechanically, but his mind inevitably traveled straight up the woman's skirt.

Kosmas entered just before the Holy Anaphora and settled into a stasidion opposite Fanis. As Fanis chanted his favorite part of the liturgy—"*Holy, holy, holy, Lord Sabaoth, heaven and earth are filled with Your glory*"—he couldn't help noticing that Kosmas looked infuriatingly good in the new brown suit.

Soon it was so hot that Fanis was obliged to dab his forehead with a handkerchief every few seconds. Wondering where Daphne was, he furtively observed the church. Cantoring was so much more enjoyable when you knew that a beautiful woman was listening. Yet Daphne and Gavriela were nowhere to be seen.

As always, the Great Vespers of Pentecost were tacked on to the end of the liturgy. During that service, the bishop read a long series of poetic supplications while kneeling on a pillow in the Beautiful Gate. The parishioners kneeled on walnut branches, whose bitterness represented the grief of the souls who, at that moment, were being forced to walk the hair-thin bridge back to Hades. Fanis closed his eyes so that he wouldn't see the sadness of the departing shades. After all, Kalypso was probably among them. When the bishop had finished the prayers, Fanis took a deep breath and let it all go. The souls had gone. They had taken their sorrow with them. The parishioners wiped their eyes and composed themselves. Fanis hid behind the cantor's stand and discreetly blew his nose. He silently repeated one word, the most important of all: Resurrection. Perhaps the bishop was right. Perhaps it was coming.

"Don't worry. Liturgy is not a train," Aunt Gavriela said, when Daphne woke up late. "Besides, it's Pentecost Sunday. We won't be out of the church before half past twelve, and the tea will drag on even longer."

They dressed, enjoyed a quick coffee and a leisurely walk, and slipped into the church just before eleven o'clock. After collecting bunches of walnut branches from a table in the narthex, they entered the nave and settled into the stasidia at the base of an arch. Daphne turned toward her left and had a good look at the ornate carved pulpit and its mahogany staircase, which wound tightly around a green faux-marble column. At the column's base a tall man in a russet suit stood with legs spread and one hand clasping the opposite wrist. Every so often he pulled his shoulders backward. *Could it be?* Daphne lowered her prescription sunglasses from the top of her head. Yes, it *was* Kosmas Xenidis, the mama's boy baker, looking surprisingly . . . *hot*. Before Daphne could take her eyes off him, he nodded in her direction like a *tanguero* delivering a subtle invitation to dance. She nodded back, then tried to refocus on the liturgy. Mr. Fanis had a deep, melodious voice. He drew out single syllables through various notes, as if he wanted to express a full range of human emotion: sadness, despair, hope, joy. What a relief from the cold, untraditional choirs and funereal-sounding organs that had become fashionable back home.

Gavriela dropped her bunch of walnut branches on the marble floor, spread a handkerchief over them, and knelt on top. Everyone else in the church did the same. The first set of Pentecostal prayers was only mildly uncomfortable, but by the second set, the veins of the walnut leaves were digging into Daphne's bare knees. During the third and final set of kneeling supplications, the bishop began choking up. "Because, Lord," the bishop prayed, "the dead will not glorify You and those who live in Hades dare not acknowledge You, but we the living praise and entreat You."

Daphne looked to her aunt, who was also weeping with closed eyes. "What's wrong?" she asked.

"The damn incense," said Gavriela, wiping her nose. "It always makes my eyes tear."

"You're weeping, Auntie, not tearing."

Gavriela sniffled. "It's the dead. They've become too many. And we don't have any children to replace them."

"You have me."

"Do I?"

Daphne squeezed her aunt's hand but said nothing.

At the close of the service, the bishop delivered a short sermon about the survival of the Rum community: "When Leonidas, King of the Spartans, went forth to battle the Persians at Thermopylae with a force of only three hundred men, someone asked how he planned to defeat an enemy so numerous with so few. Leonidas replied, 'If you think I am going to fight by numbers, then the whole of Greece would be insufficient to match the Persians, but if I am going to fight by courage, then even this number is sufficient.'"

"You see?" said Daphne to her aunt. "Even this number is sufficient."

"Time will tell," said Gavriela.

The bishop gave the dismissal. The congregation lined up at the foot of his throne to receive the blessed antidoron bread. Kosmas joined Daphne at the back of the line. "I wanted to apologize for my mother's bad behavior yesterday," he said. The sleeve of his silky suit jacket brushed against Daphne's wrist as they shook hands. "She also wanted to apologize, but—"

"Seriously?" said Daphne. She took a good look at Kosmas. His right eyebrow was raised, almost as if he was teasing her—or, worse, making fun. She'd noticed that expression at Neighbor's House but hadn't taken it personally. Now it puzzled her. Gavriela poked her in the back. Daphne changed the subject: "Mr. Fanis is a fabulous cantor, isn't he?"

Kosmas nodded yes and made a polite gesture for Daphne to precede him. "Ladies first," he said. But as soon as they'd received their antidoron, he resumed his apologies: "Mama's knees were hurting her. That's why she couldn't make it today. She sends her regards."

Daphne stopped chewing her dry, tasteless bread square, raised her own eyebrows, and said, "Hmm. Likewise."

A short blond in a hat waved a white glove. "Good morning, Kosmaki! What a fine suit!" The blond hobbled toward them as fast as she could and stood on tiptoe to kiss Kosmas. "And who have we here?"

"Daphne," said Kosmas. "From America, but one of ours."

The pale woman slipped one arm through the crook of Daphne's elbow and took Kosmas's forearm with her other hand. "I'm Rita Tereza. The bishop told me not to let you get away." Rita Tereza whisked Daphne and Kosmas across the courtyard as quickly as her unmatched legs would take her. Along the way, she rattled: "Daphne, did you know that Kosmas and I are great friends? I'm sure we'll become great friends too. One of the ladies told me you're a teacher. I'm a speech therapist! Which gives us lots to talk about." She ushered Daphne to a free chair in the tea room, next to Mr. Dimitris the journalist, and pulled her own chair close to Daphne's.

So. Kosmas had a girlfriend. That was why he had given Daphne the business card and not asked for her phone number. He'd only meant to be polite. And perhaps to gain a new customer.

"Have you two known each other for a long time?" said Daphne.

"Oh, yes," said Rita Tereza.

"Not quite," said Kosmas. He pulled out a chair near the head of the table. "Daphne will be cramped there in the corner. She'd better come over here."

"She's fine where she is. Come sit with us, Kosmaki." Rita Tereza patted the empty seat on her left. "Are you on Facebook, Daphne? If you are, look me up. There's a darling photo of me and Kosmas from last Sunday."

Kosmas leaned over the table and picked up Daphne's tea. "The bishop always wants guests to sit close to him," he said.

Was this a troubled relationship?

"If that's what the bishop wants," said Daphne, transferring herself to the chair that Kosmas held for her, "then I ought to move."

Before Rita Tereza had a chance to object, the bishop swept in, buttoning the collar of his blue cassock. He made his way around the table, stopped in front of Kosmas, and said in a low voice, "What a fine suit that is. Such elegant fabric, such precise tailoring. Italian?"

"Hüsnü Mirza," said Kosmas, pulling in his tummy and puffing out his chest. "On Balo Street."

The bishop winked. Fanis, now looking like a debonair Einstein in a sleek black suit, skipped into the tea room, grabbed the empty chair on Daphne's right side, and said, "What do you say, Daphne dear? Did I do a good job today?"

"It was a real treat, Mr. Fanis. You have a lovely voice."

"I do my best. The 'Kalofonikos Eirmos'—the piece I was chanting during the distribution of the antidoron—was for you. It's a very special hymn that we use only on holidays."

"What's that?" said the bishop.

"The chanting," said Fanis. "Our guest enjoyed it."

"Yes, but our feet didn't," said the bishop. "Anyway, you haven't introduced our guest."

"My niece Daphne," said Gavriela, from the other end of the oval table. "From Miami."

"*Miami*," repeated the bishop. "Now there's a city. I toured the whole country—New York, Chicago, Miami, San Francisco. We also went to a desert town with casinos, grandiose hotels, and dancing girls. What was the name of it?"

Daphne smiled at the thought of an Istanbul bishop playing the slots in Sin City. "Las Vegas?"

"Las Vegas! What a fun place that was! Now, Miss Daphne, tell me, are you married?"

Before Daphne had a chance to reply, Gavriela said, "Not yet."

"Have you moved back to the City?" said the bishop.

"I'm just—"

Gavriela interrupted, in an insinuating singsong tone: "She's thinking about it!"

Kosmas offered Daphne a plate of dry, stale-looking cheese pastries.

"No, thanks," she said. "My aunt stuffs me with cheese pies every morning."

"Just like my mother." Kosmas passed them to the grizzly, cigarette-stinking priest. "I bet you can't stand the sight of them."

"Just about."

The bishop's pot-bellied, mustachioed assistant approached with a hot-water pot in one hand and a steaming teapot in the other. "More tea?" he said in Turkish.

"Thank you," said Daphne. "Very light, please."

The man poured an inch of dark tea and paused before topping up with water. "Is that all right?"

"Perfect. And might I have a glass of water?" said Daphne, with a side-nod.

"Of course."

Kosmas offered the sugar bowl. Daphne placed her hand on her heart in a gesture of polite refusal. "I drink mine plain."

"Your Turkish is superb, Daphne," said Rita Tereza, whose armpits barely reached the table top. Daphne wondered if they ought to bring her a booster seat.

"Indeed," said the bishop. He stabbed a quartered sesame ring with his mini-fork and held it in the air. "But it's not just that. It's the accent, the intonation, the mannerisms . . . all entirely Turkish."

"You heard very little, Your Eminence," said Daphne. "I make loads of mistakes in conversation."

"Grammatical errors are one thing," said Rita Tereza. "Mannerisms and accent are another. You must have spent quite a lot of time with Turks."

"Maybe it's from watching my teachers," said Daphne, avoiding eye contact with the bishop. To parry any more delving into her origins, she asked, "Which reminds me, Your Eminence, could you suggest a chocolate shop? My teacher's birthday is tomorrow."

Kosmas winced. In her haste to change the subject, Daphne had forgotten that he was a pâtissier: asking about a sweet shop other than his had been bad manners on her part.

"Of course," said the bishop. "The Savoy has always been one of the best."

Even worse: the bishop had also forgotten Kosmas's profession.

"It's true," said Rita Tereza. "But the Lily's mille-feuille is superb." She smiled flirtatiously at Kosmas. "My grandmother always said that the secret to a good mille-feuille is freshness. It has to be made and eaten on the same day and left at room temperature."

"Actually," said Kosmas, "there are many secrets to good mille-feuille. But, Rita Tereza, I thought you didn't eat sweets?"

Rita Tereza pushed up her glasses. "I ate them until I was twenty-nine. But it seems there are things I don't know about *you*, too, Kosmaki. You never mentioned you had an American friend."

Dimitris, with his briefcase resting on his lap, grinned boyishly. "So what *are* the secrets to a good mille-feuille, son?"

"The *beurrage*, for example." Kosmas grabbed the pile of napkins at the center of the table and ran his finger along the side. "It's the butter, separating the dough, that creates layers like these, thin as leaves."

"I'd think the assembly would be the most difficult part," said Daphne, trying to figure out what sort of relationship Kosmas had with the Mad Hatter albino. If Rita Tereza was indeed his girlfriend, how could he not know that she used to eat sweets? Perhaps they weren't a couple after all.

"Of course," said Kosmas, straightening his suit jacket. "It takes years to learn how to cut the pastry without a ruler. Mille-feuille is architecture. It must be symmetrical, squared, and level. If anything is off, it will be a failure, like the Leaning Tower of Pisa."

Fanis, whose voice was still a little raspy from chanting, said, "Mille-feuille *is* a princess, but the queen mother was the Balkanik."

"I asked Uncle Mustafa about that pastry," said Kosmas. He picked up Daphne's fallen napkin, gave it to the mustachioed man, and handed Daphne a new one from the stack he had used to demonstrate butter layering. "He described it to me as best he could: the choux pastry, the consistency and flavors of the creams, the unique way in which they were piped. I actually made a first attempt, but it fell short of Uncle Mustafa's memories. You see, making a good chocolate, cardamom, cinnamon, or pistachio cream isn't a big deal, but I haven't been able to figure out how so many flavors can complement each other in one pastry without turning into a discordant mess."

"The recipe was lost," said Fanis. "Anything you make now will be a poor imitation, an impostor Balkanik."

"Somebody must have written it down," said Daphne. "Perhaps we could contact the families of other old pastry chefs."

"Even if the recipe *could* be found," said Gavriela, "you have to remember that the Balkanik was a pastry for parties. Where would you eat it now? With which friends? We used to drink our tea every day at five o'clock. We used to play cards on Tuesdays, do something else on Wednesdays, go dancing on Fridays and Saturdays, to church on Sundays, and to the buffets after church. Every day there was something to do, and there was always a pastry to go with it. Now there's nobody left."

"Excuse me, Gavriela," said Fanis, "but who are *we*? Nobody?"

Without waiting for a reply, Fanis excused himself to the restroom. He could take only so much of that "we're finished" rubbish. Even if he sometimes thought the same things, he didn't want to hear about them in the church tea room. For God's sake, it was the only place where he could almost pretend that they *weren't* near the end.

He climbed the stairs to the hot, rancid lavatory, fumbled for the light switch, and unzipped his pants. At least he could still see his nicely circumcised penis. His uncle had always said that you were in fine form as long you could look down from a standing position and see your pecker. Until the age of seventeen, Fanis had suffered from phimosis. His tight foreskin hadn't bothered him at all until he reached puberty and began to masturbate, and even then it had only caused him a small amount of discomfort. On the day that he fell in love with Kalypso, however, he was obliged to tell his uncle that something was wrong.

It was the afternoon of New Year's Eve, 1952. The entire neighborhood was perfumed with the scents of mastic and *mahleb* baking in Saint Basil cakes. A light, feathery snow was falling, and hordes of children had filled the streets, singing carols and collecting baksheesh. Fanis was seventeen and in the first year of his apprenticeship with Mr. Yorgos, the neighborhood antiques merchant. Kalypso, just fifteen, was one of the carolers. She wore a heavy wool coat and a red beret. A brown braid hung over her shoulder. Her voice—a sweet mezzo soprano—rose above the others and passed straight through Fanis.

That evening, while reimagining Kalypso beneath his thick winter blankets, Fanis had a date with his right hand, which he affectionately called Madame Fist. But his phimosis was so painful that he wasn't able to finish. The next day he told his uncle. On January 4, 1953, Fanis was circumcised at the German Hospital. His penis became a clean, free, handsome acorn, just like those of his Jewish and Muslim friends. He hadn't had any other problems since, except for those few weak erections of late, and now, for the first time in the church lavatory, a reduced flow.

As Fanis was shaking it, he felt a contracting pain in his chest. An image of Kalypso's braid flashed before him. His eyes overflowed with tears. There it was: uncontrolled weeping. Another symptom of vascular dementia. Perhaps he shouldn't have burned those prescriptions.

Fanis rezipped his pants, washed his hands with the bit of dirty soap resting on the edge of the sink, and covered his eyes with wet fingers. Then he noticed the muffled sounds of a radio. They were coming from somewhere outside the church complex.

That was how it had started, with the announcement, at half past four in the afternoon, on September 6, 1955, from the Ankara radio station: Atatürk's birthplace in Thessaloniki had been bombed. Fanis had heard it at Mr. Yorgos's antiques shop while beating out an antique Bergama carpet in the back garden. The news made him go to the front of the shop and look across the way, toward the windows of the mint-green mosque, but he pushed the thought out of his head and returned to his work. At a quarter to five, a boy passed selling the *Istanbul Express*. Fanis bought a copy and beheld the falsified photos of the damage to Atatürk's first house. A few seconds later he heard hateful shouts resounding from the direction of Sıraselviler Avenue: "They destroyed the house of our father! Infidels! Cyprus is Turkish!"

Fanis called out to his boss: "Do you hear?"

Mr. Yorgos emerged from his office. "Lower the shutter," he said.

Mr. Yorgos was a practical man, and he already had a practical solution to whatever little disturbance might occur. He called one of the toughs to whom he regularly gave protection money. They would pass once per month for their allowance, always with the same assurance: "Whatever happens, we're here." It was understood that Mr. Yorgos was buying protection from the thugs themselves rather than from any unknown enemy, but calling them was worth a shot.

To his surprise, Mr. Yorgos was told that two men would be dispatched within the hour. While waiting, he emptied the safe of cash and stuffed half of it into his underpants and the other half into his trouser pocket. He bound some of the more expensive jewelry to his chest and to Fanis's. Then he called a friend in Taksim. "Close up," said the friend. "They're going mad." By six o'clock, the toughs had arrived and, true to their word, they kept the shop safe. Fanis left thinking only of his mother, who had been widowed when he was eleven. It was natural that he should go to her instead of trying to find Kalypso. In any case, Fanis didn't believe that things would get as bad as they did.

Weeping in the stench of the church lavatory and unable to relieve himself, Fanis couldn't justify his lack of thought for Kalypso as he had taken his precautions, gone home, and tipped the doorman of his building with some cash that Mr. Yorgos had stuffed into his pocket "in case of need."

Now he whispered Kalypso's name. He hadn't pronounced it in years. He said it again, more loudly, and again, more loudly still. He couldn't stop. There was a reason he had ended up alone: in a pinch, he always thought of himself instead of others. Even taking care of his mother was just another way of putting himself first.

"Are you all right, Uncle Fanis?" someone asked in Turkish. It had to be Samuel, the bishop's assistant and chauffeur.

Fanis splashed cold water onto his face. "Fine, fine," he said. "I'm coming."

Fanis returned red-eyed and disoriented to the tea room. Everyone was laughing. He wondered if they were making fun of him. "What's going on?" he asked, in Greek.

"Nothing, nothing," said the bishop. "Just a little joke you missed. Ladies and gentlemen, I'm going to change. I wish you all a good afternoon."

Fanis took advantage of the bishop's exit to collect himself. He smoothed his flying curls and took a deep breath.

Gavriela whispered in his ear, "You look like you've seen a ghost."

"I suppose I have," Fanis replied. "But never mind that. Why don't we all go for coffee?"

Gavriela wrapped a few leftover sesame rings in a napkin. "I don't think today's the day. Daphne and I have other plans. But if you ever need to talk, come and see me."

8

The Princess in the Park

DAPHNE WAS RELIEVED TO GET into the shade of Gezi Park after the long walk from the church. She took a deep breath. Instead of the exhaust and hot asphalt of Taksim Square, she smelled grass, rotting leaves, and the sea. A cool breeze was blowing up from the Bosporus and rustling the plane trees, red maples, and low Australian laurels. "Where to, Auntie?" Daphne was surprised by the loudness of her voice. In Taksim, you had to shout to be heard. In the park, anything above a low murmur seemed inappropriate.

"Over there," Gavriela said. "Do you see her?"

Selin waved from the park café that overlooked the Bosporus Bridge, a patch of silver-blue water, and the Asian side of the City. She wore a festive lime-green dress that made Daphne feel drab in her habitual black. They made their way through the tunnel of trees, kissed Selin, and sat down. "Finally I get to speak some Turkish," said Daphne.

"Sorry we're late," said Gavriela, staring disdainfully at the overflowing metal ashtray in the middle of their table. Daphne knew how vile her aunt considered cigarette butts. Strict no-smoking laws were Gavriela's favorite thing about the United States.

"No problem," said Selin. She resettled into her molded plastic chair and pulled her skirt tightly over her legs. Daphne noticed the microscopic white and yellow flower designs on her immaculate red fingernails. She wondered how Selin managed to play the violin and always have such perfectly manicured hands.

"We used to live near a Rum church," Selin continued. "Your liturgies are like Jewish services. They drag on forever."

"Today was even longer than usual," said Gavriela, already cleaning the tabletop's scattered ashes with an antibacterial wipe. "Pentecost Sunday. Fanis chants beautifully, but he's unbelievably slow."

"So he really is a cantor?" said Selin. "I thought he was just showing off."

"Absolutely," said Gavriela. "And he's completely in love with his own voice."

Selin sat back in her chair. "I wonder what he was like when he was younger. He must have been handsome."

"Selin," said Daphne, with a wink, "are you into Mr. Fanis?"

"Not in *that* way. But his appreciation of Hebrew chant impressed me."

Gavriela brushed a fallen leaf out of her bleached, curled, and hairsprayed old-lady do. "Fanis might be a catch for an old lady, Selin, but you need someone with more . . . How shall I say? *Stamina?*"

"I'm forty-three. Even some guys close to my age—including my ex-husband—are losing it. So what's the difference?"

"Then I'm surprised you haven't fixed up with the Frenchman," said Gavriela.

"Are you kidding? It would be like dating an uncle."

Daphne tied the straps of her bag around the chair arm so that it couldn't be snatched. "Well, Selin, if you *have* taken a liking to Mr. Fanis," she joked, "you're going to have to fight me for him."

"*What?*" said Gavriela, so disturbed by the comment that she took a second antibacterial wipe from the packet and began scrubbing the chair arms. "He could be your grandfather!"

"A grandfather with an amazing voice," said Daphne. "But I'm not sure what to think of the Einstein hair. Is it eccentric and debonair? Or does it just need to be chopped off?"

"I'd say debonair," said Selin. "But I never said I fancy Mr. Fanis. I just respect his openness to other traditions."

A waiter passed with a tray of full tea glasses. Selin caught his eye and nodded. "Anyway," she said as the waiter served three teas, "it's been so long since my last boyfriend that anything would be a blessing."

"Tell me about it," said Daphne.

"*What?*" said Gavriela. "Not even *that?*"

Daphne and Paul hadn't made love for two months. Lovemaking was probably the wrong term, anyway. Paul had sex. He didn't *make love*. He had boring bedroom sex. If they did end up splitting, Daphne swore she'd never get into a relationship with a conventional missionary type ever again. "It's just a phase, Auntie," she said. "It'll pass."

Selin leaned forward. "What about Kosmas? He's put you in the eye."

"I doubt it," said Daphne. "He's got a girlfriend. Rita-something."

"Nonsense," said Gavriela. "If he had a girlfriend, his mother would know. And if she knew, I would. Besides, I haven't seen anything on Face."

"Face" was what Gavriela affectionately called Facebook. Although she couldn't use a computer or even email, she was an adept smartphone Facebooker.

"I think your aunt's right," said Selin. "The other day, before you showed up at the tea garden, Kosmas was looking forward to your arrival."

"That's hard to believe," said Daphne. She waved her hand dismissively, as if the information were a swarm of gnats. Secretly, however, she was flattered.

Gavriela grinned. "You should have seen him today, Selin. So attentive. He kept asking Samuel to top up her tea glass. He picked up her napkin when it fell and asked if she was cramped sitting in the corner."

In order to cut her aunt's momentum, Daphne said, "Don't tell me you didn't see the way he raised his eyebrow sarcastically every time he spoke to me."

"He fell off his bicycle when he was six and knocked his forehead. It's a *scar*, not an expression." Gavriela slapped a hand onto her crumpled antibacterial wipe before the wind took it. "And a *gentleman* is always attentive."

"Fine," said Daphne, rueful of her hasty judgment. "But he probably wouldn't consider me a *real* Rum."

"Because you're American?" said Selin.

Daphne had slipped. She remembered her mother's warnings: *Don't tell Gavriela's friends that your father is Turkish. They won't trust you.* For a second she considered telling the truth: after all, Selin was Jewish and wouldn't care that Daphne wasn't a thoroughbred Rum. But then Selin might tell the others, and that would create a strange situation. Gavriela's friends would wonder why Daphne hadn't been up-front from the start.

"*Boş ver,*" said Gavriela, covering for Daphne in her moment of hesitation. Give empty. This was one of her—and Daphne's—favorite Turkish phrases, meaning something like, "Never mind, drop it."

"Well," said Selin. "The Lily makes the very best *baton salé*. And when a man knows what he's doing in the kitchen, he usually knows what he's doing elsewhere. I'd go for Kosmas myself if he were five years older, but I've never been into younger men."

"Did you hear that, little mama?" said Gavriela. "Or are you listening with your ass?"

"Yes, Auntie, I heard. And by the way, you forgot to hide your cross."

Gavriela looked down at her chest and dropped her gold crucifix inside her blouse.

"On second thought," said Selin, "getting involved with

Kosmas would probably be a bad idea. He's never leaving the City, at least not while his mother's alive, and you'd be crazy to leave America and come here."

"Don't be so sure," said Daphne. Seeing her aunt's expression brighten, she clarified: "I didn't mean that in relation to your friend's son, Auntie. I just meant that things aren't as perfect in America as you might think."

"How so?" said Selin.

"For one, I'm a language teacher, and Americans don't care about learning languages."

"All the more reason for you to move here," said Gavriela, raising her voice above the sea-like sound of the wind blowing through the leaves.

"How about some toasted sandwiches?" said Daphne.

"Cheese and sausage?" said Gavriela.

Selin put her hand over her heart in polite refusal. "I'm fine with the tea."

"Cheese only for me," said Daphne.

"No sausage?" said Gavriela.

This again? Why did her aunt refuse to remember that she didn't eat meat?

"Just cheese, please."

Gavriela flagged the waiter, who was already carrying a heavy tray of used glasses and plates. "Three mixed cheese and sausage sandwiches," she said. "With plenty of butter. We don't like them dry."

"Yes, ma'am," said the waiter.

"And could you take this dirty ashtray?"

"I'll be back for it in a minute, ma'am."

Gavriela clicked her tongue in disapproval. "He's going to forget."

Just then a strong burst of wind scattered more dirty ashes over the table. Gavriela took out another wipe.

"What's Miami like?" asked Selin.

"Colorful, fun, and predictable," said Daphne, shielding

her eyes from the sun escaping through the tree leaves. "You can easily make your life there, but there's little history and no decay, no domes and minarets, no craziness, no secrets. In Istanbul you never know what's around the next corner."

"It could be a policeman in riot gear, or a teargas canister, or a bombed synagogue or bank," said Selin.

"At least people aren't walking into primary schools with guns here. Terrorism is everywhere. I don't get why people think Turkey's more dangerous than anywhere else."

"Prejudice," said Selin.

"Still," said Gavriela, "you have to admit that America is easy. Nice roads, automatic bills, systems that work, space, parks, no smoking. Not that I'm trying to convince you to stay."

"Sure it's nice," said Daphne. "But it's lined with cotton wool. I don't know if I want to live in such an insulated place. I don't know if it's the home of my soul."

The wind picked up and rattled the almost empty tea tulips. Selin steadied hers. "Of course, if you're thinking about moving here, you also have to think about how much you value free speech. If you talk about the Armenian matter, for example—"

"Hush, girls!" said Gavriela. "That's not a good subject."

Daphne tried to take a deep breath of the acacia-scented air, but she inhaled a cloud of cigarette smoke instead. She looked to her left: the men at a neighboring table had just lit up. Aunt Gavriela was right about America's no-smoking policies. She turned to Selin and said, "Why did you come back?"

"Because of my parents—I want to be near them during their last years. And because Istanbul's home. The place I grew up. No bombs—"

"Girls!" Gavriela made a zipper motion over her mouth. "Enough of the B-word. Half the people in this park are plainclothes cops. They might think you're terrorists."

Daphne watched her aunt fidget with the pack of bacterial

wipes, opening the sticky flap and closing it again, opening and closing. Everything was always hush-hush with Gavriela. It was as if she were stuck in the oppressive atmosphere of the fifties and sixties.

"This isn't talk for the park." Gavriela nodded toward the children skipping around the stone fountain. "When I was sixteen, we went to the Sunday buffet they used to have just over there. One evening, a young man asked Grandma for permission to dance a waltz with me—"

"Uncle Andonis?"

"No. Kostas. My first husband. I fell in love with him for his dancing."

"Your *first* husband?" Daphne had never heard anything about a Kostas.

"So you're divorced, too?" said Selin.

"Yes, dear," said Gavriela, speaking offhandedly to Selin about a topic that she had kept secret from Daphne for decades. "It's not a pleasant thing to go through, but sometimes you've just got to realize that some clothes are so badly wrinkled they can't be pressed."

Selin nodded in agreement. "I know exactly what you mean."

"Kostas was dashing at first," said Gavriela, "but as soon as we married he stopped taking me out and made me quit my job. And then he continued gallivanting alone. I couldn't get used to being cooped up. So I divorced him."

"Good for you," said Selin. "That's why I don't date guys from here. To them women are nothing but—pardon my English—*fucking machines*."

Gavriela lifted her dark glasses. "What does *fakin mashinz* mean?"

"Baby machines who stay home and take care of the house."

"But they seem so chivalrous," said Daphne. "Then again, when I think of our Cubanos in Miami, it's the same. All roses and *mi reina*, and then one day they just turn off the switch and want their shoes shined so they can go out with their girlfriends."

"Exactly," said Selin. "They're all like that. Except, maybe, for Kosmas. You can tell from the way he takes care of his mother."

"She's a racist," said Daphne.

"Don't talk like that," snapped Gavriela. "You don't understand where Rea's coming from. We've been through a lot."

Daphne's mobile sounded the generic Turkcell ringtone. The caller ID read PAUL. She glanced at the Bosporus, flashing like thousands of little mirrors in the afternoon sun. She wanted to hear his voice, but she didn't want to interrupt the conversation with Selin and Gavriela. *Later*, she thought. She pressed the red button.

"Who was that?" said her aunt.

Daphne put the phone back into her pocket. "You know."

"The mayonnaise has separated," said Gavriela.

"What's that supposed to mean?"

Gavriela shook her finger as if she were scolding a child. "If the mayonnaise separates, you've got to throw it away and start over."

Daphne waved another cloud of smoke from her face. "He's a boyfriend, not a condiment."

The waiter served the toasted sandwiches. Gavriela picked up one with a napkin, examined it, and grumbled, "Dry, just as I feared."

Daphne removed the sausage from her sandwich.

"Little mama," said Gavriela, "what *are* you doing?"

"I'm pescatarian. I don't eat meat."

"Pesca-*what*?" Gavriela hissed, like a snake. "Oh, why didn't you remind me?"

The waiter returned with the second round of tea. "No, no," said Gavriela. "We'll have three medium coffees instead. And could you *please* take this stinky thing?"

The waiter sighed and took the ashtray.

Staring at the pile of round sausage slices on Daphne's plate and at the two bites Selin had taken from her unwanted sandwich, Gavriela said, "You girls need to get married."

"You find a man who understands musical culture and who respects my all-day practices, nighttime performances, and trips—*and* treats me like a queen," said Selin, "and I'm ready."

"I'll work on it," said Gavriela. She put down her toast, raised her palms to the sky, and said, "May I see you both brides, here, in our City, with beautiful dresses, flowers in your hair, and lots of tulle."

"*İnşallah*," said Daphne, using the Turkish phrase for God willing. It was always the easiest answer to bridehood wishes, especially if one wanted to avoid an argument.

"*İnşallah*," Selin repeated. "Minus the tulle."

9

The Long Shadow of Old Sins

THE FOLLOWING FRIDAY, JUST AFTER the midday call to prayer, Fanis entered Neighbor's House, grabbed a home-decorating magazine from the rack, and sat at a table in the indoor area. The magazine issue's theme, unfortunately, was ultra-modern décor, which Fanis found more boring than the hot weather. He tossed the magazine aside and began reminiscing about the Contesse, the tea salon that had occupied the same plot half a century ago. Fanis liked Neighbor's trendy wood and white brick theme, but it was a far cry from the Contesse's rich wainscoting, art-nouveau light fixtures, giant mirrors, and tile portraits of the nine muses.

Kalypso had lied to her parents the first time they met there. Once or twice per week she would pass by Mr. Yorgos's antiques shop. Fanis would wait for her inside his doorway with a rose in hand, present it with a bow, and say, "*Pour vous, mademoiselle.*" After he had given her a few dozen roses, she informed him in a letter that on the coming Thursday, at four o'clock in the afternoon, she would pass by the Contesse, and if she saw him in the window, she would join him. Fanis arrived early on the appointed day and secured a table by the window. True to her word, Kalypso entered at four o'clock sharp, sat down at his table, and adjusted her red saucer hat to prevent her face from being seen from within the pâtisserie's salon. Fanis drew the curtain that screened the lower part of the vitrine. Thus shielded, there wasn't too much danger of Kalypso being recognized and tattled upon.

Fanis could still picture her, down to the last detail: the complexion smooth as a spring leaf, the peep-toe shoes she displayed by crossing her long legs, the nylons that made her calves look smoother than they were, the point at which her knees disappeared beneath her full, red-and-white polka-dot skirt, the matching handbag she placed on the table with the confidence of a princess, the voice with its harmonious range of middle tones that were never too high or too low, and the laughter. Her careless laughter.

They had spoken of movies and food, subjects that Fanis still heard dating couples discussing as they tried to determine whether their tastes were similar or opposed. Then, when Fanis praised her singing, she asked who his favorite was.

"The great Sinatra," he said. "And yours?"

"Roza Eskenazi."

Fanis felt a frisson of synchronicity at hearing the name of the Great Diva, the Queen of Underworld Rembetiko. "I adore Roza. But my mother won't allow any of those popular albums in the house. She says they're *basse classe*."

"Neither will mine," said Kalypso. "So I bring them home secretly and play them when Mother's out."

"Sing something," he said.

Kalypso chose "My Sweet Canary," one of Roza's songs. But she skipped the innocent overture and dove straight into the most provocative verse, begging him to come into her embrace so that she could fill him up with kisses. Although he was two years older than Kalypso, Fanis blushed. It was true that he had wanted a demure bride, and she was far from demure. Moreover, he had never fancied girls who put their elbows on the table, as she did. He had said that a woman should not laugh too much, and Kalypso was always laughing. But he realized on that day that perfection belonged only to angels and he wanted a woman, this enchanting young woman, and not an angel.

When Kalypso decided it was time to leave, she grasped her red saucer hat so that it wouldn't fall, sprang forward, and—so quickly that Fanis didn't have a chance to react—kissed his ear lobe. She was out the door in a second. Fanis was left sitting there, paralyzed by the sensation of her kiss: he hadn't known that the ear was an erogenous zone. Over the months to come, her ear-lobe kisses progressed to nibbles, licks, and bites. Fanis had never before experienced such intense pleasure. After Kalypso's death, he never let another woman touch his ears. That part of his body belonged to Kalypso.

"At your service."

Fanis looked up at the waiter. Then he looked at the other customers. Everyone was dressed badly, which meant, of course, that it was still 2011. "Four cherry-jam-filled surprises and a tea," he said.

"Right away."

Fanis turned his attention to the street and saw a young woman walking so quickly that she was almost skipping. Her long hair bounced against the small of her back. Without thinking, he jumped up and knocked on the glass. She turned and waved. "Come in," he said.

Daphne came over to his table. "I'm meeting Selin," she said, between cheek kisses.

Daphne's outfit lacked the joy of Kalypso's polka dots, but it had an ethnic sort of elegance: an ankle-length black dress and a long necklace with a silver pendant that looked like . . . the hand of Fatima, daughter of the Prophet Muhammad. Did Daphne have tendencies toward *the other side*?

"What's that?" Fanis asked.

Daphne picked up the pendant. "This? My favorite necklace."

"I'm not talking about it as jewelry," said Fanis, "but as a symbol."

"It's Fatimah's Hand for Muslims, Solomon's Hand for Jews, and the Mother of God's Hand for Christians."

"How lovely," said Fanis, relieved. "My favorite Turkish word is *hoşgörü*, which means looking pleasantly upon other people and their ideas. So much better than *tolerans*, isn't it, which really just means that you've decided begrudgingly to put up with others? That hand, as you've explained it, Daphne dear, is a symbol of *hoşgörü*."

"I love that," said Daphne.

"Do you know what *I* love?" said a woman.

Fanis turned and beheld cherry-red fingernails clutching a drawstring duffel. God, he thought, I must start coming to Neighbor's House earlier in the day.

Selin sank into a chair beside Fanis and answered her own question: "I love that Istanbul is the biggest city I've ever lived in. Bigger than Paris, and yet I still manage to run into someone I know almost everywhere I go. Isn't that wonderful?"

"Certainly," said Fanis. "It must be because we're always out."

"Unfortunately we can't stay long," said Selin. "There's something we have to do."

"Something important?" said Fanis.

"Yes." Selin took a Chinese fan from her purse and aired her perspiring face. "A secret."

"You'll have a tea at least."

Daphne hugged her unbleached-canvas schoolbag to her chest. "We have an appointment."

Fanis sighed. Selin shifted an ear toward one of the wall-mounted speakers, exposing the left side of her neck. There it was: the persistent hickey. She definitely had a boyfriend.

"Do you hear that?" said Selin. "It's Ella Fitzgerald's 'It Don't Mean A Thing.' I just love the Stuff Smith violin solo."

Fanis closed his eyes and sang along.

"Your voice is extraordinary," said Daphne.

"That's kind of you to say, dear," said Fanis, "but it's Ella's rhythm that's extraordinary, not my voice."

"I must hear you chant sometime," said Selin.

"I must hear you play sometime," said Fanis.

"Perhaps you will." Selin crossed one meaty leg over the other. "Mr. Fanis, do you mind if I ask an indiscreet question?"

"That's the only kind I like."

"How old are you?"

"How old do you think I am?"

Daphne twisted her beautiful long hair over one shoulder. "Sixty-five."

"Sixty-two," said Selin. "Come on, tell us. And don't lie."

"I don't know how to lie," said Fanis. He removed his identity card from his wallet and displayed the birth date. "March 27, 1935. Seventy-six. Would you have guessed it? And I have no one in the world, neither children nor relatives." He looked Daphne in the eye. "My future wife will inherit everything: my apartment, my antiques, even my illustrious Byzantine surname."

Fanis hoped that this might tempt Daphne, but it was Selin who responded, "Surely, Mr. Fanis, a man like you doesn't need to entice women with an inheritance."

Who was this siren, this enchantress, set on preventing him from marrying one of his own kind? Then again, Fanis reasoned, was not his goal, in a larger sense, to perpetuate old Istanbul, and was not Selin, a Sephardi whose family had lived in the City since 1492, a part of old Istanbul? He couldn't deny it. As lovely as Daphne was, those comfy sandals and untrimmed cuticles might grow tiring. Yet Selin—with her kitten heels, her flawless maquillage, and her artsy spunk—was already overworking his old heart.

"We need to get going," said Daphne.

"But you haven't had tea," Fanis protested.

He didn't even have a chance to stand. Selin leaned over and kissed his cheeks, paralyzing him with the scent of her perfume—Yves Saint Laurent, Cinéma?—and a peek at her dark décolletage. "Goodbye, Mr. Fanis," she said.

"Have fun, girls," he heard himself say, but he was unable to move. As soon as they were out of sight, he glanced downward and noticed, right in front of him on the table, a business card. In white letters on a blue background were the words "Selin Kerido, Violinist" and . . . *her phone number.* Fanis looked left and right, grabbed the card, and stuffed it into his wallet. The waiter delivered the plate of cookies that Fanis had ordered before the girls' arrival. Just the thing to soothe his excited nerves. He wouldn't want to risk an ischemic stroke.

Ten minutes later Fanis left Neighbor's House. With Selin's card in his wallet, he felt as if he was floating rather than walking. Selin Kerido, *querida mia,* he repeated to himself. Not that he planned on giving up Daphne, but it couldn't hurt to have Selin "in reserve," as young Greeks were fond of saying. Fanis descended the hill into Çukurcuma, but he was too excited to return home. So he kept walking, taking the polluted air in deep breaths, and he reached Yeni Çarşı before he realized it. He was so euphoric that he didn't think of the police captain until he had almost stumbled upon one of his chickens. Fanis instinctively took a step backward. Then, buoyed by Selin's attentions, he rounded the corner and entered the alley.

"Good evening," said Fanis, resisting the urge to grab the captain by his shirt and throw him against the lamppost.

"Good evening," returned the man in the Panama hat. "Isn't it a bit hot for that scarf?"

"I don't feel the heat," said Fanis. *But I did feel it on the night of September 6, 1955, when you refused to help my fiancée's father.*

The captain retrieved another stool from his entryway. "Have a seat. I'd enjoy some company."

Was this old-style Turkish hospitality, or had the captain recognized him? Either way, Fanis had no intention of sitting with the man as if they were old friends. "Thank you, but—"

The captain shouted to his wife, "Semiha! Two teas. We have a guest."

Fanis felt his lower legs begin to tremble. "How long have you lived here?" he asked, suspicious about why the captain had returned to the old neighborhood.

"Just a few weeks. We were further down before. We took this place because we had trouble climbing the stairs of the other. You know how it is. And you?"

"I've lived here my whole life. On—" Fanis hesitated. Perhaps it wasn't a good idea to tell the truth. "On Sıraselviler," he said.

"It's not the same place we were born into," said the captain.

Semiha's rubber clogs thumped on the entryway tile. She brought teas "dark as rabbit's blood," as Fanis's mother used to say, as well as a plate of butter cookies. "Welcome," she said.

"Well I find you," said Fanis. "I've put you to trouble, and I really can't stay . . ."

"None at all." Semiha set the tray on the stand beside her husband. "I made these cookies an hour ago. My mother used to say that if you want company, you should bake."

"Wise woman," said Fanis, sitting. "Health to your hands."

Semiha bowed and withdrew inside the house.

"Married?" said the captain.

"No," said Fanis. *Thanks to you.*

The tinkle of spoons hitting the sides of tea tulips echoed through the alley.

"It's not good to be alone," said the captain. "A man needs someone to make his food, someone to say good morning to, someone to drink a tea with, someone to give him medicine when he's sick. Isn't that right?"

Fanis bit his tongue so hard that he could taste blood. He didn't want to lash out right away. He wanted answers first.

"You mentioned that you lived further down," he said. "A friend of mine had a *meyhane* further down. The Petridis Winehouse. Do you remember it?"

"Do I remember it? I was its best customer. Their raki was something else."

"Do you remember the owner as well?" Fanis rasped. His dry mouth stuck to each word.

The captain tossed a handful of seed to his clucking chickens. "How could I not? It's too bad he left, too bad they all left. That was the beginning of the end of our Istanbul."

"I was engaged to that man's daughter," said Fanis. He expected some sort of reaction. The captain had to have heard something about Kalypso. As much as her family had tried to hide it, rumors had eventually spread.

"Were you? I can't say I remember the family. You didn't marry?"

"No," said Fanis. He could feel sweat accumulating on his palms. "The *meyhane* was destroyed and the family dishonored. They picked up and left for Canada."

"Things were better when the Rums were here."

The hypocrisy! Fanis rose to his feet. His tea tulip smashed onto the curb. "How dare you?"

"Friend, what—"

"The worst part of it," said Fanis, trying to control his urge to pummel the man, "do you know the worst part? The worst part was that her father, Tasos Petridis, went to the police station to ask for your help, and *you*—a regular customer who was never allowed to pay!—you kept him waiting for an hour. You said you couldn't spare the men, and then, and then . . ."

The captain also stood. He set his empty glass on the tray. "Friend—"

"No!" Fanis kicked the curb. "I am not your friend!" His whole body was shaking. He wondered if the stroke was coming. He had to hurry. "Tasos Petridis was beaten unconscious as soon as he left the station. That's why he wasn't with his daughter when . . . when *it* happened. That's why they were all alone." Hot tears pooled in Fanis's eyes. Afraid that his voice was about to break, he added, almost in a whisper, "And I have *never* forgiven you."

"Please, brother, have a seat."

Fanis fell back onto the stool. Otherwise he would probably have collapsed and shattered on the cobblestones just like the tea glass.

The captain called to his wife, "Sugar, collect the birds and bring us more tea." As Semiha herded the chickens and the rooster through the entryway and into the back garden, the captain asked, "What's your name?"

"Fanourios Paleologos."

The captain took off his sunglasses. "You sought me out on purpose?"

"No," said Fanis, feeling the resurgent helplessness of that night. "I followed you for years, and then, after I married, I gave up. But the other day I was walking down Yeni Çarşı and saw you feeding the chickens. I recognized you instantly."

"Why did you come back?"

For a second Fanis didn't know. Then he collected himself: "To ask why you didn't help people who treated you so well. To ask how you could stand by and do nothing when your neighbor's shops were being destroyed and their homes invaded. To ask what gives you more of a right to this place than we have. To tell you how I suffered when my fiancée—"

"Murat Aydın," said the man, holding out his hand. "Retired librarian."

"I don't understand," said Fanis. "You're not Tayyip Aydın? You're not the police captain?"

"Tayyip was my brother."

Fanis examined the man's bulging nose, the deep lines in his forehead, the trim mustache, the way he squinted in the afternoon light. It was all Tayyip Aydın. Was he lying?

"Listen, friend," said the man. "I can't answer your questions."

An escapee chicken toddled outside and nudged her owner's pants leg. Murat tossed her a few cookie crumbs. "There was a Rum family in our building," he said. "We played hide-and-seek with their children when we were young. My mother and I hid them in our apartment during the pogrom. We thought that Tayyip would also help our neighbors."

"But why," whispered Fanis, "why didn't he?"

For a few moments, Murat stared at the chic twenty-somethings sipping cappuccinos in the tourist café across the street. Then he straightened his back and said, "When Tayyip was a teenager, he worked as an errand boy for a haberdasher, a Rum with a huge belly. Mr. Takis. Not a bad guy, but he would order meat from a neighboring restaurant every day for lunch, whereas Tayyip ate bread and olives in the back room, like a hungry mouse. That bothered Tayyip. Later he became a policeman and started believing all that propaganda about the Rums being a threat to Turkey. I'm sorry for him, friend. Sorry for all of it."

Fanis had readied himself for a confrontation. He had even thought they might come to blows. The apology, however, refreshed the pain, the betrayal, the disillusion. A sob escaped him. The chicken startled, flapped her wings, and sped back into the building.

"Don't worry about the glass, brother," said Murat. "It's an evil eye broken. Someone must have been jealous of you. Better the glass than your health. Semiha! Bring some cologne!"

Semiha hurried outside and squirted lemon cologne into Fanis's extended hands. He looked at her like a helpless child, unable even to rub his palms together. She poured some cologne onto her own hands and applied it to his forehead and cheeks. Then she grabbed a broom and began sweeping the shattered glass while Murat held a shot of raki to Fanis's lips. Fanis recovered from his stupor after one swallow, which seemed to go in through his mouth and exit through his eyes. Murat set the glass on the doorstep.

"Let it go," he said. "Let it go."

"The captain?" said Fanis.

"He died in a car accident eighteen years ago."

Fanis surprised himself by saying something that he had always thought impossible: "May God have mercy on his soul."

"I don't know if he'll get it, but thank you for saying so." Murat took a sip of raki from Fanis's glass. "You know, I was imprisoned afterwards, when they tried to blame it on the Leftists and rounded us up. I was accused of being one of the rioters. My brother had me released. He wanted me to worship him as a hero for that favor."

"What was he like?" asked Fanis. "I don't mean at his job, or when he went to football games. What was he like *at home*? Forgive me, I know it's impolite to ask, but I've always wondered."

Murat took another sip of raki. "Up until the pogrom, I thought he was a good guy. You know, the kind who'd stick up for you, who wouldn't push you around or blame you for things he shouldn't. He was good for a game of backgammon or for a night out at the *meyhanes*. A quiet type. The change was sudden."

"The change?"

"It happened when he was promoted to captain. Whether he was wearing his uniform or not, he knew that everybody was paying attention to him. He became so arrogant. Even tried to kick me out of the house because I kept company with Communists. He calmed down a bit when he married and had kids, but our Tayyip—the good kid—was gone forever."

Semiha returned with more tea. "Come, Uncle," she coaxed. "Tea heals."

Fanis downed half the steaming glass. It soothed the pain in his throat.

Murat went inside and came out with a scrap of paper. "That's my number," he said, "but you can drop by anytime. We're always here."

Fanis put the paper into his wallet, next to Selin's card, and shook Murat's hand.

10

The Tango

OVER THE PAST FEW DAYS, Kosmas had managed to lock his keys into the house, lose his public-transport card, drop a tea tray on his mother's favorite rug, and fold salt instead of sugar into the batter for Hungarian Dobos torta. Fortunately, Uncle Mustafa was working beside him at the time and caught the mistake. "*Yemek çok tuzlu olursa*," he said in Turkish, "*aşçı aşıktır*." If the food is too salty, the cook is in love.

Kosmas leaned against the giant stainless-steel refrigerator and ran his palm over his forehead. "If things go on like this," he said, "my life is going to fall apart."

The corners of Uncle Mustafa's mustache rose into a smile. "Name?"

"Daphne. Every time I'm near her it's like the whole world fades into darkness. All I can see is her."

Uncle Mustafa continued piping cheese onto the dough rounds that would become mini cheese pies. "I assume you haven't called her."

"Am I that predictable?"

Uncle Mustafa raised his thick black eyebrows and set down the pastry bag. "Son, there's only one remedy. Call her and ask her out. If you don't get over your fear of rejection . . ." Uncle Mustafa didn't finish his sentence, but Kosmas knew how it would end.

Kosmas took his phone from his pocket, scrolled through to Gavriela's number, and pressed the green circle. When

Gavriela answered, he twisted his left index finger in an apron string and said, "Good afternoon, Madame Gavriela. It's Kosmas."

"Kosmaki! What a charming voice you have. Almost like a pilot's. I never noticed until now."

"Thanks. Listen, Madame Gavriela, I want to ask Daphne out to dinner tonight. Could I talk to her?"

"Just a minute."

Kosmas heard a rubbery pulling sound, a tapping, and a muffling that did not serve its purpose. The apron string had cut off his circulation and his index finger was going numb, but he was too nervous to release it. Uncle Mustafa gave him an encouraging nod. Finally, Gavriela said, "She'd love to."

"I'd like to speak to her if I could—"

"What time?"

"Eight?"

"Perfect. Give your mother my regards. See you soon. *Ciao-ciao*-bye-bye."

Kosmas ended the call, grabbed Uncle Mustafa's floury hand, and kissed it.

"That's my boy," said Uncle Mustafa, gently smacking Kosmas's cheek. "By the way, does your sudden interest in the Balkanik have something to do with Lady Daphne?"

"Maybe."

Uncle Mustafa winked. "Okay, son. I'll clean out the storage room as soon as I'm done with these cheese pies. And if it's not there, I'll search every cupboard and drawer in my flat."

"Thanks, Uncle Mustafa."

After work Kosmas went home and locked himself into the bathroom with the Turkish *GQ* magazine that Fanis had absentmindedly left at Neighbor's House. Rea's cleaning lady had scoured the bathroom with bleach that day. The lingering odor would probably give Kosmas a headache, but he needed absolute privacy. He sat on the fuzzy pink toilet lid cover and flipped through the magazine. He noticed that the models wore black shirts and jeans in the photographs that were supposed to represent romantic trysts. Kosmas wouldn't be able to manage the flat abs or sexy biceps, but at least, thanks to Fanis, he could duplicate the outfit. He stuffed the magazine through the swing top of the rubbish bin and turned on the shower.

Rea knocked on the door as soon as she heard the running water. "Take a clean towel from the cabinet," she said. "And dry your head off well so you don't catch cold."

"It's summer, Mother," said Kosmas, stripping.

"Doesn't matter. The worst colds are the summer ones."

He scrubbed himself down in the narrow shower, shampooed twice to get rid of the bakery smell, and put on the Armani shirt and jeans that his mother had washed in lavender-scented soap, ironed, and hung in his closet.

"Where are you going dressed like that?" she said, when he came out of his room.

"To dinner," he said. "With Daphne."

"*Daphne?* But I made lamb shanks today, your favorite, and I never make lamb shanks!"

"It was a last-minute idea, Mama. Besides, you're always saying that I should find a Rum girl and get married. I thought you'd be happy."

"Not about *her*," murmured Rea.

"Mother. We talked about this."

"If you *must* go out, you can't go dressed like a hooligan. Why don't you wear your gray pants and the orange and black shirt I bought for your name day?"

Kosmas had the good sense to disobey, but he didn't want to look like a hooligan. His only other option was the tailor-made brown suit. Rea became so emotional when she saw him in it that she shed tears of joy. "You look just like your father did when we were dating. Where's the camera? I have to take your picture."

"It's not my first day of primary school," said Kosmas.

Rea air-signed a cross to ward off the evil eye. "I don't know how Daphne and I will get along," she said, "but at least she's one of ours."

Kosmas checked to make sure his wallet was in his pocket. Then, noticing that the mold on the living-room wall had crept up the room's corner almost to shoulder height, he said, "Could you call Mr. Ahmet about that? I keep forgetting."

"I'll have someone paint over it."

"You know painting doesn't work. Call Mr. Ahmet, will you?" Kosmas kissed his mother and fled the apartment before Rea had time to object.

After a brisk walk down the hill, he arrived at Gavriela's building and climbed the dark, twisting stairway to the third floor.

Gavriela opened the door. "Kosmaki!" She popped her soapy-smelling mastic gum. "Come on in, my child. Have a seat." She pointed to the leather-upholstered foyer armchair and brought him a glass of water, which he downed in seconds. "I'll go and tell her you're here."

While waiting, Kosmas examined the various evil-eye talismans stuffed behind the water pipe above the door: thistles, horseshoes, holy water, a bunch of wheat, walnut leaves, a ceramic plate with the Arabic word 'Allah,' and a pair of scuffed white baby shoes. Gavriela had no children, which meant that the shoes were probably Daphne's.

"Just a few more minutes," said Gavriela, returning.

"Am I early?" Kosmas looked at his watch. It was ten minutes past eight.

"No. But you know us women. We primp for hours and hours." Gavriela lowered her voice to a whisper: "Especially when we've put the gentleman in the eye."

"Sure, sure," said Kosmas. "Might I have another glass of water?"

As Gavriela bustled about, Kosmas replayed the telephone conversation in his mind. Maybe Daphne hadn't agreed to go out with him at all. Maybe her aunt had said yes for her without even asking. Maybe this was all an imposition. But he couldn't back out now.

"There you go," said Gavriela, handing him the glass. She seemed a bit too cheerful. Something was definitely going on.

But just as Kosmas was finishing the second water, Daphne stepped into the entryway in a sleeveless, low-cut, calf-length black dress that flared at the knees. Her wavy chocolate hair hung loose, like the never-cut tresses of honor that one used to see dangling down the backs of unmarried women. She wore hardly any jewelry—just a thick black bracelet and a turquoise evil-eye anklet. Her makeup was almost invisible. Because Kosmas was used to over-jeweled Istanbul women and over-painted Athenians, he found Daphne's minimalism odd . . . but elegant. He offered silent thanks to Fanis for his fashion tutelage: it would have been a shame to escort a woman like that in a horizontally striped shirt.

"It's a beautiful evening," he said.

"Thank—" Daphne stopped, as if she didn't know how to complete her sentence. "Thank God. It was hot earlier, wasn't it?"

A positive sign, thought Kosmas. She's just as nervous as I am.

The taxi dropped them off at the bottom end of the crowded Balık Pazarı, the former fish market of Pera. They passed fruit stalls, cheap jewelry and trinket stands, and tourist shops with shelves of boxed lokum and Turkish honey. Beneath bulbs hanging like full moons, a few holdout fishmongers sold mackerel and sea bream with gills painted to look fresher than they were. The alleys between the shops were so full of tourists and locals that Kosmas was not sure whether he should let Daphne precede him, which meant they would hardly advance behind the knapsacks of gawking Americans, or whether he should push ahead and risk losing her in the crowds. Before he could decide, they were jostled by a pack of Greek tourists, and she momentarily took his arm. For the first time in his life, Kosmas thanked God for the self-absorption of his Hellenic brothers.

He paid no attention to the young men attempting to harass passersby into looking at their menus. Instead he led Daphne—who kept a disappointing distance as soon as they broke away from the crowd of Greeks—straight to the only restaurant with an owner too proud to beg for clients. A familiar waiter shook Kosmas's hand and ushered them to two free places at a long common table. Kosmas pulled out Daphne's chair and waved to Mr. Spyros, the bald nonagenarian owner, whose bushy brows loomed over his eyes, like the restaurant awnings in the street outside.

The old man rose from his desk, wove through the waiters coming and going from the cold meze case, and approached their table. "It's been ages," he said in Greek. "Why don't you come more often?"

"Daphne," said Kosmas, "this is Mr. Spyros, one of my father's old friends."

A wide smile spread between the old man's flabby ears. "How is it possible that I've not met this beautiful young lady before now?"

"She lives in America," Kosmas replied, hoping he would soon leave them alone.

Spyros pulled up an extra chair. "Do you speak Greek, young lady?"

"Of course," said Kosmas. "She's one of ours."

"Are you going to let her talk for herself? Or are you afraid I might steal her away?"

Daphne shot the old man a sweet smile that almost made Kosmas jealous. "Thanks. Could you tell me where the ladies' room is?"

Spyros pointed to the upper floor. "Top of the stairs, on your right."

Kosmas watched her go. The clothing that she had worn on other occasions had prevented him from fully distinguishing her lines. The slim black dress, however, allowed him to make out her breasts: they reminded him of the first oranges of December. Her bare legs were pale, as if neither the sun nor another man's eyes had seen them in years.

"Always one of the highlights of the evening, isn't it?" said Spyros.

Kosmas pulled himself out of the trance. "Sorry?"

"The moment when a woman goes to the powder room. She must like you. Since she dressed up like that, I mean."

Kosmas realized that Spyros was only trying to be encouraging. "I doubt it," he said.

"You did tell her that she looks beautiful, didn't you?"

"No. I didn't want to overdo it. It's better to be discreet at first, isn't it?"

Spyros shook his head. "Son, you've got to say that every time you go out with a woman, even after you've been married for fifty years, and even if she looks like an old rag. Women don't feel beautiful unless a man says so, and if they don't feel beautiful, you're through."

"Is it too late now?"

"Of course not. But wait until you've had something to drink. You'll know when."

A waiter brought a tray of cold appetizers in rectangular white dishes. Everything was fresh, impeccable, and tastefully decorated with red pepper slices, lemon wedges, olives, and minced parsley. Kosmas wondered what Daphne would like best. He ordered mussels stuffed with cinnamon-flavored rice, smoked eggplant salad, cod roe spread, and salt bonito in oil.

"And after the cold appetizers," he said, "we'll have fried smelt and picarel."

"To drink?" said the waiter.

"A small raki."

"And fried potatoes," said Spyros. "She looks like the kind who likes fried potatoes." When the waiter had gone, Spyros said to Kosmas, "Another thing, son."

"Yes?"

"Give her a little room, let her talk for herself. I've met a lot of European and American women. They like the chivalry. They love it when I get up and help them with their coats, but they can be touchy, too. They don't enjoy being treated like children."

Kosmas determined to make up for his earlier faux pas. "Anything else?"

"Relax. Enjoy yourself and remember that it's all in the hands. If she lets you hold her hand, you're in. If she doesn't, she's not ready or not worth the trouble."

Daphne returned, followed by a trail of lemon cologne. Spyros winked at Kosmas, shot a flirtatious two-eye scrunch at Daphne, and shuffled off to visit other tables. The waiter served the appetizers, a 20-cl bottle of raki, and a little bucket of ice.

"Looks like you ordered," she said.

"We can get something else. Maybe some liver, or lamb ribs, or . . ."

Daphne pushed her hair away from her face. "It's just that . . . I thought we'd look at a menu."

"*A menu?* Those are for tourists."

"Never mind. This looks good."

Kosmas grabbed the ice tongs. "How many?"

"Excuse me?"

"How many ice cubes in your raki?" He picked up a cube with the tongs. "Or would you prefer wine?"

"I don't drink," she said, with a polite smile.

"You can dilute it. Most people do."

"I don't drink," she repeated, this time sounding like a schoolteacher trying to maintain her patience with an insistent first-grader. "Water's fine."

The ice cube slipped and landed in the stuffed mussels. "I'm such an idiot," said Kosmas. He scooped up the ice with his fork and dumped it onto his meze plate. Unsure what to say next, he dropped a fresh cube into his narrow glass, poured the raki over it, and added a few centimeters of water. What fun was a girl who didn't drink? Not that he wanted to see her inebriated, but total abstention was a bore.

"To our health." He grasped the cloudy white glass by the base so that the toast would produce a clear ring. "But you have to clink twice with water, to get rid of the bad luck."

"Bad luck? Says who?"

"My mother." He double-tapped his glass against Daphne's, took a sip of raki, and served her dollops of eggplant salad and cod roe spread, as well as one of the cinnamon-rice-stuffed mussel shells. "Mr. Spyros's cook makes the best mussels. The salt bonito is also one of his specialties, but the flavor's a little strong, so I'd recommend leaving it until last."

"Interesting," said Daphne, with a quizzical nod that he couldn't interpret. "Don't they have music here?"

"Never. Mr. Spyros says it ruins conversation. How are the mussels?"

"Good."

That wasn't what he wanted to hear. He was hoping for amazing, excellent, the best I've ever had. "If you don't like them, we could—"

"No, I do. You have great taste." Finally her voice was warming a little. "Do you cook?"

"Never," he said. "Cooking and pastry-making are entirely different professions, like novelist and poet."

"Do you like poetry?"

"A little Nazim Hikmet. Some Cavafy."

"I spent a semester on Cavafy at college." Daphne added. "We read absolutely everything . . ." She continued speaking, but he lost her words. He heard only the tone of her voice, increasingly soft and feminine. He ate without tasting the food. What importance did it have when he was near her? Was this the moment? Should he tell her she looked beautiful in that dress, with her hair falling over her shoulders? No. Better to start with something small.

"Pretty bracelet," he said. "It suits you."

"It's a watch." She turned the thick black band so that he could see the face. "My boyfriend gave it to me for my birthday."

Kosmas had a sudden urge to cough, but his mouth was full of fried picarel. He grabbed his raki glass and washed it down. "Have you been together long?"

"Four years."

It was all lost. All his dreams, his hope for himself and his community, all swept away by that one word. Boyfriend.

"But we're on a little break right now."

"A *break*?"

"We're taking some time apart."

"Who could ever need time away from you?"

"I'm a very difficult person," said Daphne, resuming her officious, teacherly tone. "I'm critical, I don't eat meat, I can be jealous, I hate shoes indoors, I wash my hands as soon as I come in the house, I have trouble sleeping when he's snoring, I don't give him enough space, et cetera, et cetera."

Lucky I brought her to a fish restaurant, thought Kosmas. "Apart from the meat thing," he said, "it seems to me that you're not difficult at all, just Rum. And *titiza*."

"What?"

"All good Rum women are *titizes*. They're meticulous. They hate dirt. They like things just so."

"*Titiza*," Daphne repeated. She looked up at the miniature Turkish and Greek flags hanging from the ceiling, side by side, like old friends. "Maybe. But I can be aggravating." Her voice was lower now, as if she didn't want to be overheard.

"Is it serious?" he asked.

"After four years, I should hope so."

What would Fanis do now? The old philanderer would take whatever she had said and twist it around to his advantage. That's what he'd do. "You know best. But in my opinion, being *titiza* is a good thing. You deserve a man who appreciates who you are."

A busboy collected their oily meze plates and replaced them with clean ones. "We haven't finished," said Daphne. "Why is he changing our plates?"

"If he doesn't, Mr. Spyros will be all over him. Nobody likes mixed flavors."

A hand reached between them with a plate of fried potatoes. Two plates of tiny fish—fried and salted like popcorn and resting on a bed of arugula—followed.

Daphne pressed her hands together like a happy child. "I love fried things! Especially little fried fish. How did you know?"

"They're my favorite, too," said Kosmas. He was going to beat this boyfriend after all. "Later on, I thought we'd go for dessert—"

"I have a better idea for *after*."

Could it be true that American women were as forward as the four characters on *Sex and the City*?

"A tango lesson," said Daphne. "It's free at a studio not too far from here. I found it on the internet and wrote down the address." She took a scrap of paper from her purse and showed it to him.

Without bothering to look, he said, "I can't dance. I've always wanted to learn, but—"

"Now's your chance."

Kosmas's fork slipped from his hand and landed on the tablecloth with a soft thud. He was terrified of making a clown of himself on their first date. "I'd rather start with something easier, like the waltz, maybe. Tango seems so difficult."

"Please. I really want to go."

Kosmas dished out the fried smelt.

"I can serve myself, you know," said Daphne. She attempted a laugh, but Kosmas could tell she was piqued. It was exactly as Spyros had said: some women could mistake old-world manners for patronization.

Kosmas loosened his tie and looked over at Spyros, who was having his photo taken with a group of loquacious Italian women. "Ready for the main course?" he said.

"And the tango lesson?" said Daphne.

Spyros helped the last Italian woman into her jacket, kissed her goodbye, and returned to his post behind the cash register. Kosmas said, "Mr. Spyros, can I leave Daphne in your hands for a moment?"

"You trust me?"

"Of course. And could we have a grilled gilt-head sea bream?"

Kosmas bounded upstairs and relieved himself. As he hummed the Greek happy-birthday song, with which he always timed his sudsing, he gave himself a pep talk. Relax, you can turn this around. Maybe Gavriela forced her out, and maybe the dance lesson will be a disaster, but look at the other side of things: it will prolong the evening. And the boyfriend? He's on the other side of the world.

Kosmas held out his hands to the attendant, received his squirt of lemon cologne, and rubbed it in while descending the stairs. "Everything okay, Mr. Spyros?" he said.

"More than okay. I've been looking into Daphne's pretty eyes the whole time. Remember that when you get to be my age. No one can stop you looking into a woman's eyes, no matter how old, ugly, or married you are. Bon appétit, kids."

Over the next half-hour, the itinerant vendors provided so much entertainment that Daphne did not reopen the tango subject. First a man came by with a box of butterflies and a microscope. Daphne paid him fifty cents for a peek. After the sea bream was served, a lottery seller wearing a paper crown approached their table. Fortunately his attention was diverted by a news segment on the muted television mounted above Spyros's head. In large red letters at the bottom of the screen was the headline "For a day or forever, everyone needs an escape."

"I'd choose forever," said the vendor. He held up his ticket roll one more time. Kosmas lifted his chin. The vendor moved on.

"Would *you* escape if you could?" Daphne asked Kosmas.

"Maybe. Sometimes I wonder what it would be like to live in a place where nobody cares what my religion is. To go and be a foreigner somewhere for real. What about you?"

"I've done it. For the summer, that is." There it was again, the sweet tone, clear, without the smallest bit of hoarseness. "Could we go to that tango lesson?"

She'd turned him into marzipan paste. No longer able to resist, he said, "All right. But after that we're going for dessert."

The dance studio was a two-minute walk from the restaurant. They climbed six floors through a cigarette-stinking stairwell to the penthouse studio. A small woman—the teacher, it seemed—herded Kosmas, Daphne, and the other prospective students to the room's center. First they learned how to walk by sliding their feet across the floor, brushing one ankle past the other. Easy enough. Kosmas thanked God there was no hip motion, yet he couldn't understand so much insistence on walking.

"Stop!" the teacher shouted. "Time to learn the embrace."

Daphne encircled Kosmas with her left arm and spread her fingers over his back. He had no idea what to do with his right arm, so the instructor assisted by wrapping it around Daphne's back, just beneath the shoulder blades, all the way to the armpit, and ever so close to . . . Don't even think about it, Kosmas told himself.

"Walk in time to the music!"

Kosmas took hesitant steps lest he tread on Daphne's feet. Soon, however, he realized that Daphne was never in his way.

He moved with greater confidence, pushing the body that leaned forward to meet him, and walked straight into a wall. Renewing his efforts, he navigated a corner and experienced a brief fifty seconds of enjoyment, as if he had awakened from a bad dream. He listened to the sound of Daphne's breath in his ear, took in the floral scent of her hair, and glanced at her low *décolletage* as the fabric of her dress shifted over her breasts. *This* must be why men learned to tango.

"Change partners!"

Daphne left Kosmas and approached the next cavalier, a Harrison Ford lookalike who was no beginner at all, but rather the obliging brother of a lady who wanted to try the dance. The music began, but Kosmas couldn't concentrate. Getting his new partner to go anywhere was like trying to push a mountain. Worse yet, Kosmas stepped on her foot twice while trying to catch glimpses of Daphne in a close embrace with the Lothario on the other side of the studio.

"Careful," said the woman.

"Sorry," said Kosmas. "Can you give me a minute?"

He took a short break and observed the other couples. They seemed uncomfortable with the touch of a stranger and held each other at arm's length, but Daphne had closed her eyes and fit her forehead into the valley of her partner's left temple. She was obviously no beginner at all because she responded with precision and sometimes even foot adornments to her partner's seductive directions. Still, despite his jealousy, Kosmas couldn't help being turned on by the way her round behind moved in the tight-fitting dress. The evil-eye charm slid over her shoe strap, catching the candlelight. On turns, her skirt swirled upward, revealing a few centimeters of thigh. But she was in the arms of another man, damn it. Was Argentine tango truly an art form or just some sick kind of sadomasochism invented to torture watching partners? Just when Kosmas thought he could bear it no longer, he heard clapping. The lesson was over.

He needed a drink. While the teacher distributed brochures, Kosmas went to the studio bar, ordered a glass of wine and a bottle of water, and took them to the table where Daphne awaited him. "Having fun?" he said.

"Lots. It's a great venue, don't you think?"

"Definitely." He swilled half the glass of vinegar-tasting wine. "Ready to leave?"

"Dessert?" said Daphne, following him out.

Kosmas pondered where to go. He remembered the new Saryan. The traffic along the coastal road would be terrible at that time of night. Still, it was the only place—outside of his own shop—where he enjoyed eating sweets.

"You'll see when we get there," he said.

They found a taxi in the boulevard behind the studio. For a few minutes Kosmas was pleased with himself for having spared Daphne further walking, but soon a truck cut off the taxi, enraging the smelly driver. He screamed out the open window, "You asshole! I'll shit on your glasses so that you'll see the whole world through nothing but shit!"

"Excuse me, sir, you're completely right," said Kosmas, "but there's a lady present."

The driver slammed his free hand into the steering wheel, like an axe. "Bastard ejected from the asshole of a whore while farting!"

Kosmas looked at Daphne. She was covering her mouth to hide her laughter. "He sounds just like my father," she said.

"Your father cusses like that?"

"Always. But only in the car. Otherwise he's a perfect gentleman."

"In *Turkish?*"

"Of course. He . . . he thinks it's better than Greek for swearing. Turks have as many words for shit as the Inuit have for snow. You never swear?"

Kosmas hesitated. The cabbie's fit had amused Daphne, which made him think that perhaps he should admit to his bad habit. Yet Fanis had given a stern injunction against vulgar speech, and Fanis was rarely wrong about women. "No."

"Such a good boy," said Daphne. "Your mother must be proud."

A mobile phone rang. Kosmas thought it was the cabbie's, but then Daphne opened her clutch and took out a cheap flip phone. At first her replies were curt. Her brow furrowed. Her bottom lip pursed, pushing the top one upward. If the caller was the boyfriend, he didn't have a chance. What had Kosmas been so worried about? This guy was finished.

A few minutes later, however, Daphne's expression softened. Kosmas heard something about beaches, dogs, and tango, but he couldn't understand the meaning of the conversation. He wished he had paid better attention in English class. At the end of the call, he thought he heard her mumble, "Love you too." Goddamn mobiles.

The taxi pulled up to the Saryan just after she snapped the phone shut. Kosmas handed a bill to the driver, exited, and jogged around to Daphne's side in time to open her door. That call, he told himself, never happened.

Halfway up the pâtisserie's staircase, the air changed. A cool mix of air-conditioning and sea breeze rushed downward, carrying the scents of expensive chocolate, ice cream, and freshly ground coffee. Kosmas took a deep breath to clear his memory of the cabbie's onion stench, which had been even more embarrassing than his language. Now that they were at the Saryan—with its elegant chocolate-colored décor and 1960s-style circular lamps—Kosmas could be proud of his City once again.

He led Daphne through the little packs of well-dressed, quietly chatting Bosporus socialites to the balcony that overlooked Bebek Bay. They were lucky enough to find a recently vacated table, from which a waiter was still clearing half-eaten éclairs and coffee cups. Daphne sat facing north, but Kosmas knew she would have a better view from the other side.

"Sit here," he said, pulling the chair opposite her. "That way you'll see Bebek Mosque. It's pretty when it's lit up at night."

Daphne switched chairs. "Looks old."

"Not really," said Kosmas. "Early twentieth-century, Neoclassical style. The newest mosque will be built just over there." He pointed toward a high hill outline on the other side of the Bosporus. "That's Çamlıca, where my parents used take me for picnics on May Day. The prime minister is going to build a big mosque there, a monument to his term, just like the sultans used to do."

"It seems like that's what he's turning into," said Daphne. "In the States, the president has eight years at most and he's out."

"This isn't America." Kosmas moved the prickly cactus centerpiece to the side of the table. Potted cacti—instead of fresh flowers—were the latest fashion in Istanbul.

"But his views on women, contraception, the West, even Twitter . . ." said Daphne, lowering her chin and looking up at him with an expression of disbelief.

Kosmas could see that explaining would be a wasted effort. Daphne had been a full, undisputed, equal citizen of the United States all her life. How could she understand that a politician's ideas about condoms and social media were of secondary importance when that politician respected your long-deprived right to live, work, and be happy? Besides, Kosmas hadn't meant to get into a political conversation when he pointed out Çamlıca Hill.

"All I want is to live in peace," he said. "As long as I have that, I can ignore the rest."

Without waiting for a reply, Kosmas caught the waiter's eye and nodded. The Saryan was an old-style place in every way. Its waiters were never in a hurry to take orders and deliver checks. Only a fixed gaze and a polite nod would to bring them to your table.

"At your service," said the waiter.

"Two teas," said Kosmas. "And a plate of house choco-lates. Two each of *Mon Chéri, Plaisir, Tendresse, Amour, Désir*, and *Passion* . . . and winged hearts, of course."

When the waiter had gone, Kosmas turned back to Daphne, who was watching the passing ships. He listened to the wakes gulping and smacking against the sea wall. Daphne was physically in his territory, but her heart and mind, he could see, were lagging behind.

Come on. She's still here. You can't give up until she rejects you flat out.

The waiter served the teas and the plate of ultra-elegant chocolates.

"Uncle Mustafa and I used to play a game," said Kosmas. "He'd make me guess the flavors. To sharpen my palate. Shall we try?"

Daphne bit into a long, narrow chocolate shaped like a short-order cook hat. "Caramel."

"Bitter coffee and whiskey ganache," he corrected.

"You already knew that."

Kosmas stared at the chocolate clinging to her lips. He wondered what her mouth tasted like and how the flavor of the chocolate would change if it came straight from her lips to his. "I swear I didn't," he said.

"What's your specialty?"

"I have a few. Besides mille-feuille, of course, I like doing apple strudel, Hungarian Dobos torta, profiteroles . . . but the thing I like best is cake decorating. Especially wedding cakes."

"Isn't that a hobby for bored housewives?"

"Not in Istanbul." He stared at her. Could she have meant to be so rude? Had there been some cultural misunderstanding?

"Sorry," she said. "I didn't mean it that way. I was just wondering why wedding cakes would interest you."

Kosmas gazed toward the antique wooden motor launch anchored just a few meters from the sea wall. It bobbed in the current, plunging down abruptly, almost violently, then slowly bobbing up, over and over. "At first it was the aesthetic," he said. "The marriage of architecture and food. Later, when I started baking for real couples, I realized that cakes are also expressions of joy, a manifestation of the couple's love for each other."

"Most wedding cakes I've seen were nothing but generic sugar mounds with tacky plastic dolls on top," said Daphne.

"That's exactly what I don't do. I never start by showing a catalogue. I talk to the couple, look at their invitations, decorations, and outfits. I try to understand who they are, how they met, what their dreams are. I want them to remember not only the appearance, but also the taste of the cake long after the wedding is over. Maybe that memory will help them through future bitterness. Or maybe it will be something they can tell their kids about."

Daphne put her elbows on the table and rested her chin in the hammock of her interlaced fingers. "For example?"

"Yesterday I did a cake for a florist and his assistant. He proposed to her with a bouquet of orange blossoms—the marriage flower. So I did a narrow six-tier with side icing sculpted to look like satin ribbons. Each tier was separated by invisible ten-centimeter columns. I filled the open spaces with fresh purple freesia and orange blossoms. The cake itself was flavored with vanilla bean, but I added orange-blossom water to the icing as a subtle compliment to the groom's proposal. People told me the bride was so happy with the cake that she cried."

Daphne absentmindedly turned the cactus's black pot. "What kind of cake would you make for me?"

Kosmas took another deep breath. Daphne wore no perfume, but he fancied that he caught the natural scent of her skin. He closed his eyes to assemble flavors and images. When the cake had come together in his mind, he said, "For you I'd do five round tiers delicately accented with green cardamom from the Egyptian Bazaar. Butter-cream icing, without coloring, because the natural cream is understated and elegant, like you."

He paused. Car lights flashed from the rim of the bay, lighting up her face. She was smiling and looking directly at him now, as if no one else existed. He shook off the dizziness caused by her gaze and continued: "The decoration will be of the same cream color. Piped like embroidery, not stenciled. You'd never fit into a mold. The motifs will be Ottoman: foliage, tulips, carnations, hyacinths. From top to bottom, in an elegant curve, will stretch one stem of white orchids. The serving tray will be specially made to accommodate the orchid's pot so you can keep the plant alive for the rest of your life."

"*That* doesn't sound like a bored-housewife cake," she said.

Kosmas noticed how thin her fingers were. He wanted to kiss that hand and hold it to his forehead, like a student showing respect to his teacher, and then keep kissing, all the way up to her armpit . . .

"What will your wedding cake look like?" she asked.

"The same."

Now he'd done it. He'd said too much. She would cut the evening short and never go out with him again. He scanned the restaurant, searching for the waiter. Where the hell was he?

"Are you getting tired?" he said. "Shall I ask for the check?"

"Not yet." Daphne looked him in the eye for a second before transferring her attention back to the chocolate plate. She picked up one of the rectangles with swirly decorations ending in hearts and held it to her nose. "Coffee."

"Cappuccino."

She conceded with a coquettish side-nod. "You haven't told me what you thought of the tango lesson."

Would she ever give him a break?

"It was fun. By the way, what would your boyfriend think about you dancing with me?"

"He wouldn't care." Daphne slumped in her chair and folded her arms over her chest. "That's how Paul and I met. Dancing."

"I know it's none of my business, but it seems to me that you and that guy have a strange relationship. What man would be indifferent to seeing you in the arms of other men?"

"Dance is art, not flirtation."

"Come on. When a man and a woman snuggle up together in evening clothes, there's always the possibility of a spark."

"You don't dance," she said, looking like a benevolent schoolteacher again. "You wouldn't know."

"So you feel exactly the same with every partner?"

"No. Sometimes there's more of a connection than other times."

"*Connection?* Please. Does your boyfriend know you're out with me tonight?"

Daphne pulled her hair over one shoulder and twisted it around her hand like a rope. "I told him I went dancing with one of my aunt's friends. He didn't care."

"Because you wouldn't let him dance with other women if you couldn't dance with other men."

"It's called trust." She turned her face toward the Bosporus. "He's a fantastic dancer. I'm not. He's needs to dance with women of his own level."

"You looked good to me."

"That's kind of you to say, but you don't dance, so you really can't tell. I'm not good enough for Paul. With me he's limited. Besides, he needs to dance with women his own height."

"It's seems to me that the dance should be more about the woman you're with than her skill or height. And just how do his partners dress, anyway?"

"In evening wear, skirts, dresses. Quite a few have *les seins à l'air*, as the French say. Breasts in the open air."

Kosmas clicked his tongue. "Wake up, Daphne. Gunpowder and fire don't sit together for long."

Daphne grabbed a napkin from the dispenser. "Can we talk about something else?"

Suddenly he understood why she had turned her face toward the water. "I'm sorry, I didn't mean—"

"Forget about it." She pressed the corners of her eyes with the napkin.

"That's a lovely dress."

Daphne laughed through her tears. "This old thing? It's my aunt's. She got mad at me because I was so caught up in studying that I forgot you were coming."

So she hadn't spent an hour primping, as Gavriela had said, and she hadn't dressed for him, as Mr. Spyros had conjectured. But they were still together. That was what really mattered.

"You look beautiful in it," he said.

Daphne lifted her heavy lids and pressed her mouth into a sad and unbecoming attempt at a smile. "My aunt and I are going to Antigone Island on Sunday. Would you and your mother like to come?"

Kosmas glanced toward the water. The motor launch was nearly still. The Bosporus, undisturbed by ship wakes, lapped gently against the sea wall. "Of course," he said. "I mean, sure. I think we can make it."

11

Ablutions

EMOTIONALLY EXHAUSTED, FANIS RETURNED HOME from Murat Aydın's house on Friday evening and fell asleep on the couch. He didn't awake until the sunset call to prayer ascended the hill from Kılıç Ali Paşa Mosque. A few seconds later, the muezzin of Karabaş Mustafa Ağa Mosque began his call to prayer, and then the loudspeaker of Tomtom Kaptan picked up the chant and finished it, leaving the distant hum from some other mosque, farther away, to carry on the relay. Fanis rolled onto his back and stared at the ceiling until the last traces of the call to prayer had faded and he could hear nothing but street noise and seagulls squawking.

The phone rang. He was so disoriented that he picked up and said hello.

A sinister voice asked, "Who's there?"

Fanis hung up and took the phone off the hook: that was the only way to deal with such callers, unless you wanted to risk involving the police. He turned off the hallway light, sat down in the outward-facing armchair of the oriel, lifted a corner of the heavy velvet curtain, and peered out.

Across the street was a stately, gray–mauve apartment building with new window boxes that had already become coffins for unwatered geraniums. Through the side pane of the first floor glowed a red lamp. The gallery windows of the ground floor were circled by holiday garlands. It was still lit at half past nine in the evening. Suddenly Fanis felt short of breath—not because he suspected that the telephone voice inhabited that house, which was too gentrified and expensive to harbor common criminals but because of a certain fortuity: the lit windows coincided exactly with those of the street's few Muslim apartments on the fateful night of the riots, just as he had seen them when he peered out of his darkened living room. As naïve as the other Rums, he had considered it wise to let the storm pass in darkness. The others, however, had been better informed: they'd been told to leave their lights on so that the pogromists would know that the houses were Muslim.

Fanis poured himself a shot of sour-cherry liqueur and returned to his perch. The next apartment building had a modern, two-tone design of light and dark paint like the braids of candy ribbons. Half a century ago, the ground-floor shop had been occupied by a quiltmaker. On the night of the riots, a watchman had passed through Faik Paşa Street before the mob. He had written *tamam* on the building's door in chalk. *Tamam*: okay. The mob had passed the quiltmaker's shop as if it hadn't even existed.

Fanis heard a loud cry from somewhere nearby. In European or American cities, the noise might have passed without much more than a few raised heads. People might not have interrupted their viewing of the evening news, their phone calls to place dinner takeout orders, or their internet surfing. But in Çukurcuma, curtains were drawn from the side panes of almost every oriel. Fanis dropped his. He thought: everyone had seen; everything had been seen.

Another shout—*gâvur*—resounded not from the street, but from his memory. *Tamam* was the word for some. *Gâvur*, infidel, was the word for others. Fanis fumbled for the lights. He wondered whether that caller kept bothering him because he was old and alone, or because they considered him a *gâvur*. Fanis had cantored in Rum Orthodox churches for decades. While doing his military service, he had prayed in the mosques of Erzurum, where there were no open churches. He wondered if God existed at all and if there would be a hereafter waiting for him when he no longer had the strength to struggle with this life, but, God or no God, he would always be *gâvur*.

He was about to close the curtain when he noticed that the rental sign had been removed from the gray–mauve building's garret window. There was both light and movement inside. Through the fluttering curtains Fanis spied the silhouette of a solid woman with curly dark hair. Could it be?

A few minutes later, the wind blew the curtains high once again, and Fanis imagined that he saw Selin. "Dr. Aydemir was right," he said out loud. "I'm a deluded old man who sees whatever he wants, wherever he wants."

He went to the bedroom and groped through the nightstand drawer. Somewhere there had to be a few remaining sleeping pills, even if they were expired. He knew he shouldn't take them after drinking, but he had to shut out his hallucinations at any cost. He found a half-pill that had loosened from its bubble pack and nestled into a corner of the drawer. He swallowed it with the water that he always kept by the bed, double-checked that the windows and doors were properly locked, then turned on the balcony light and all the lamps in the living room, kitchen, and his late mother's bedroom. He didn't even remember lying down before a drug-induced coma overtook him.

Fanis awoke groggy on Saturday morning. He sat up, rubbed his disheveled head, and restored the phone to operation. Three seconds later, it rang.

"Fanis," said the high-pitched voice. "Fanis, is that you? It's me, Gavriela. I've been trying to reach you all morning. Are you all right?"

"Fine, fine. I was just out running errands."

"Get a mobile phone, will you? Listen, the whole gang's going to Antigone tomorrow. Aliki invited us to her cottage for lunch. We'd like you to come, but I suppose you have to cantor?"

"I can have somebody fill in for me."

"Perfect. Be at the quay, outside the ticket office, at a quarter past eleven."

After uttering the usual string of salutations—"*Ciao-ciao-ye-ia-yeia*-bye-bye"—Fanis hung up and threw himself directly into the shower, but he couldn't wash off the haze caused by longing, sour-cherry liqueur, and the sleeping pill. His transformation back into the mature gentleman known throughout Pera for his dapper appearance would require more than just a shower.

Although Fanis hadn't visited his neighborhood hammam since it raised its prices to the tourist levels of the Old City, he knew that its attendants were some of the only people who could improve his desperate situation. So, he readied a kit of towels, flip-flops, and a boar-bristle exfoliation mitt and left the apartment.

As soon as he was out in the street, he spotted the sixty-something matron who owned the top three apartments of the blue mansion opposite his building. "Good morning, Madame Duygu," he said. "You seem rather busy."

She looked up from the dossier she had been perusing. "Mr. Fanis, what a lovely surprise!"

"*You* are the lovely surprise. Did I see that you rented the garret?"

"Yes, finally. An 'artist' took it, but who cares what they call themselves as long as they pay the rent and don't disturb anyone? Moving in today. That's why I'm here."

Fanis wanted to ask further questions, but it would probably take the fun out of the evening's window-watching, so he plodded up the road to the Galatasaray Hamam, a monument built in 1481, just twenty-eight years after the fall of the City to Mehmet the Conqueror. Fanis paid in the wainscoted entryway and asked the pot-bellied male receptionist if he could have Hüseyin as his attendant.

"Hüseyin?" said the receptionist. "He retired a decade ago and moved to Ankara to live with his daughter."

Fanis grumbled. Now that he had already paid the fee listed in euros, which was exorbitant, despite the significant "local" discount for which he had haggled, he wouldn't even have his old *tellak* to scrub him down. "What about Isa?"

"Today's your lucky day, Uncle. Isa only works on Saturdays."

"Nothing's like it used to be," said Fanis. Then he shocked himself by uttering a vulgar expression: "Everything's gone to shit."

Fanis left his shoes in the vestibule with instructions that they should be polished to a shine while he bathed. He put on his flip-flops with the receptionist's help and took a key to one of the ground-floor cubicles, where he removed his clothing and wrapped his lower half in a woven towel. Then he caught his reflection in the mirror: he looked like one of the swarthy, bulging, wrinkly Rum gnomes who had filled the baths half a century before. It had been at least twenty years since Fanis had been to the hammam. He wondered what he had been thinking when he decided to return. Sleeping pills: they impaired one's judgment.

Fanis took his toiletries in hand, stepped into the cold room, and seated himself on one of the high-backed chairs arranged around the central fountain. Presently a man with an even bigger belly than the receptionist's entered through the heavy wooden bath door. His triangular breasts were as large as a woman's, and his double chin sagged in folds like the rest of him. His chest was covered with gorilla-like hair, but Fanis could see, when he raised his hand to salute, that his underarms were shaved.

"Isa?" said Fanis. "Is that you?"

"Unfortunately so," said a gruff voice that Fanis would have recognized anywhere.

The two men cheek-kissed and laughed at each other's bodies. Fanis patted Isa's belly. Isa rubbed Fanis's balding head.

"I can't believe it," said Isa. "Fanis Paleologos, the comfort of every woman in Pera with an absentee husband. Still getting some?"

"You know I never talk about women. And you?"

"Not for a long, long time, Captain. Sad, isn't it?" Isa offered his arm and led Fanis into the white marble antechamber. "Did you want to do the first rinse-down yourself?"

"No, Isa. I'm not taking any risks with slipping. I have a new—never mind. I'd appreciate it if you'd do it."

"A new pistachio?"

"Please. You know I would never insult a woman by referring to her as a pistachio."

Isa filled the bronze dish and repeatedly doused Fanis as if he were a small child. Fanis surrendered to the warm water and to the carroty scent of the hammam's soap. Sometimes his young acquaintances wondered why anyone would go to a bathhouse. They couldn't understand the pleasure of having one's back, hair, and even the insides of one's ears washed by another human being. Neither could they appreciate the relaxation brought by the maternal care of another, even if that other was a fat and hairy man.

"Well, whatever kind of nut she is," said Isa, "at least you've got her."

"Not yet. That's partly why I'm here. I need to freshen up. The other reason is that I'm confused."

Just then a familiar-looking old man passed through the antechamber on his way to the warm room, followed by two younger men quacking away like ducks. They had to be Americans. The older man greeted Isa in Turkish. *That voice*, thought Fanis. That wobbly gait, so familiar . . . could he possibly be . . . the husband of Sophia Papadopoulou, the nursery-school teacher who, forty-three years prior, had proven the truth of the Turkish saying "*gündüz öğretmen, gece fahişe*," teacher by day, whore by night? People said that Polyvios Papadopoulos, Fanis's former classmate, had flown into a violent rage when he found out about his wife's affair. Luckily for Fanis, the disclosure had occurred in faraway Chicago, and Papadopoulos had been unable to carry out his threat of revenge.

Fanis took a better look at the man through the open door: bump in the back, skinny legs, flaccid dead-chicken skin, disgusting body hair. Did Polyvios have a bump in his back? Fanis thought back to his school days. He remembered Polyvios hunching over his desk and Miss Evyenidou coaxing him to sit up straight. Good God. Fanis's heart was now beating dangerously fast. Would Polyvios attack him? And would Fanis, unable to endure the stress, have the ischemic stroke now, in the hammam, all because of his past sins with Sophia Papadopoulou?

"Go attend to those fellows," Fanis said to Isa. "I'd like to have a good sweat in the hot room. *Alone*, if you can manage it."

"Sure thing, Captain."

Fanis covered his head with a towel, tiptoed through the warm room to the cubicle-like hot room, and lay down on the marble bench. Sweat poured from his forehead, armpits, chest, thighs, and groin. He began to feel dangerously drowsy, but he knew that Isa would fetch him if he stayed too long. He drifted into sleep and felt Sophia Papadopoulou's long black hair, which she hadn't cut after she married. It tickled his face and shoulders. Before their affair began, he had fantasized about how her hair would cover him when they made love. Once things got going, however, Sophia's tresses made Fanis uncomfortably hot. While making love he often had to shout, as he did then in his dream, "Tie it up!"

He swatted at her hair with such energy that he emerged through the layers of sleep and realized that Isa was telling him that it was time for his scrubbing.

"Are they gone?" Fanis asked.

"Taking cold showers before they come in here," Isa replied.

Fanis sat up. "Let's go quickly, then."

"A husband?"

"Probably. What's his name?"

"Poly-something."

"Definitely a husband." They passed into the warm room. "Keep my face covered while you work, will you, Isa? I don't need a thrashing today."

"As you wish, Captain."

Fanis stretched out on the heated platform in the center of the room. He listened to the splashing and running of water, the metal clank of dishes on basins, and the music of the foreign languages spoken by the tourist bathers. He reveled in the boar-bristle-mitt scrubbing of his thighs and back, but when Isa arrived at the right shoulder blade, Fanis squealed.

"Sorry," said Isa. "That side was always numb."

"Things change," said Fanis.

After the scrub down, Isa wrapped Fanis's waist in a dry woven towel, draped a fluffy white towel over his shoulders, and wrapped another around his head.

"Where are they now?" Fanis asked.

"Still in the hot room. Fat Mehmet will take care of them. Let's go have our tea."

Fanis and Isa returned to the cold room. Isa turned two chairs inward toward the fountain.

"Still in the same place?" Fanis asked, easing himself into the chair.

"No. Can't afford Pera anymore. Now I'm living further up, but who knows? They're building there, too. Soon I may have to go somewhere else."

"You're as restless as the Rums. We were driven out of Anatolia. We left the Old City. Soon we'll disappear from the earth altogether. Tell me, Isa, after your wife passed, may she rest in brightness—"

"Amen."

"—did you find another woman?"

"To sleep with, yes. To marry, no. You?"

"The same, but now I want to marry. I'm sick of being alone."

"Got one in mind?"

"That's just the thing." Fanis and Isa took their teas from the attendant's tray and stirred in their sugar cubes. "I'm pursuing a stunning Rum woman who has just come back to the City from America. Pretty, intelligent. A good soul. There's another fellow after her, nice enough, but hardly competition for an old pro like me. My suit is going swimmingly, but a complication has presented itself."

"A complication?"

"A feisty violinist. The problem is that she's not Rum, and please don't misunderstand me, but I was set on finding one of my own. Yesterday, however, she gave me her phone number."

"Good-looking, I assume?"

"Fetching."

"Nice quinces?"

"An entire balcony."

"Age?"

"Forties. Older than I'd like, but—"

"Maybe that's why the feeling's returning to your back. Love healed you."

"No," said Fanis. "That's something else. If I tell you, you'll think I've gone mad or, worse yet, senile. And I've already broken my vow never to discuss women, which shows that I'm not as sharp as I used to be."

"I've always thought you were crazy, so it won't make much of a difference. Tell me."

Fanis reached his hand into the fountain's trickling water and whispered, "It's the god Hermes. He's told her that she must send me on my way."

"*Who?*"

"The nymph Kalypso. I saw it in a dream."

"You're lucky I'm more pagan than Muslim," said Isa.

"And I'm discovering, as the years pass, that I'm just as

pagan as I am Christian, but don't tell anyone: I want to be buried properly, with all the blessings of the Orthodox Church."

"Of course. But can I ask you a question? Why do you care if the violinist is Rum or not?"

"Because I want to feel home again."

Isa took a sip of tea. "Listen. We're lucky to feel anything at our age, so if the violinist does it for you, you ought to go for it. As far as I'm concerned, if a pullet with nice quinces gives me her phone number, I don't care if she's a Turk or a Martian."

"Yes, you have a point. But women aren't interchangeable, Isa. You have to decide which one you can really love, which one will really love you."

Isa patted Fanis on the shoulder. "Good luck with that," he said. "Now get going before your nemesis is ready for his tea, and get your ass back in here before I retire."

Fanis dressed, gave Isa a handsome tip, and exited into the back alleys of Galatasaray. Having retraced his steps down Turnacıbaşı Street, he turned the corner into Ağa Hamamı Street and found Ali the barber, in his habitual white jacket, leaning against the doorjamb of his shop with a glass of tea in hand.

"No customers on a Saturday?" Fanis asked.

"Welcome, Uncle," said Ali. "It's lunchtime. Give 'em fifteen minutes and my shop'll be full again. Where have you been?"

"I was trying to let my hair grow so that it would cover the bald spot better, but it's not working. I'm a mess, and I need you to fix things."

Ali made a half-bow and stood aside so that Fanis could take a seat in the red faux-leather chair.

"By the way," said Fanis, staring at the photos of Atatürk on the wall above the mirror, "I sent a young friend of mine here for a haircut. Tall fellow, Rum. Has he been in?"

Ali swung the polyester cape over Fanis's head. "Stopped by this morning to make an appointment. Was supposed to be in half an hour ago for his cut."

Perfect, thought Fanis. I'll have a chance to find out

exactly what's going on with Daphne.

Bits of hair flew this way and that. Fanis, feeling more and more bald, closed his eyes. When Ali had finished, he opened and beheld the bishop sitting in the waiting chair. He was reading a copy of *GQ* magazine. "Your Eminence," said Fanis, as Ali spread cream on his cheeks with a fine badger brush. "I didn't know that you, too, were a fan of *Gentlemen's Quarterly*. By the way, I love your shirt."

"Hüsnü Mirza made it for me this week. You know, the tailor recommended by Kosmas. You should try him."

Fanis did not respond because his straight-razor shave had already begun, and the slightest move could have resulted in a severed jugular. Finally, after an anointment with perfumed lotion, Fanis said to the bishop, "I can't tell you how glad I am to see one of my own."

"Although we are few, we are infinite," said the bishop.

At that moment Kosmas came through the door, out of breath and yet looking strangely triumphant. "Elder," he said, nodding to the bishop. "Mr. Fanis. Mr. Ali. Good afternoon."

Kosmas sat down beside the bishop and began fanning himself with a newspaper. "Sorry I'm late, Mr. Ali. I was out until three a.m., and then I was a little distracted at the pâtisserie. You know how it is."

Had Kosmas been out with Daphne? That, Fanis supposed, was inevitable. The important thing, however, was not whether they had seen each other, but whether things had gone well.

"Out drinking raki with the boys?" said Fanis, while Ali massaged his shoulders.

"No," said Kosmas, with an uncontrollable smile. "I had a date with Daphne. I'm a little concerned about how it went. She's different, you know, one of us but not entirely like us."

"Yes, I did notice a certain *something*," said the bishop.

"But she's a nice young lady, and nice-looking, and a teacher, which is a calling rather than a profession."

"She has a boyfriend in America," said Kosmas.

"So?" said the bishop.

"You don't see the boyfriend as a problem, Elder?" said Kosmas.

"Of course it's a problem," said Fanis, as soon as Ali had finished trimming his nostril hairs. "You should be respectful of the other man and desist."

The bishop turned toward Fanis and raised his bushy eyebrows. "And *you* would know all about *that*, Fanis, wouldn't you?"

Fanis shot the bishop a playful smirk, then returned his attention to Kosmas. "Did you kiss her?"

Kosmas switched places with Fanis. "No. You told me not to. But something did happen." Kosmas leaned his head into the sink. "I had some chocolates boxed up for her at the Saryan, and when I gave her the package, our fingers got mixed up in the ribbon."

"And then?" said Fanis, sitting bolt upright in the waiting chair.

"That's it. But that finger mix-up was almost as sensual as a kiss, like our hands were making love. I'm pretty sure she felt it too."

"It's best not to jump to conclusions," said Fanis, slouching back into his chair. He needed to disguise both his jealousy and his excitation with a relaxed stance. "Otherwise you get carried away and make hasty moves."

"I'm glad we're onto this subject," said the bishop. "It's something I've wanted to talk to you about for some time, Kosmas. Ever since I was ordained, my absolute favorite thing has been the first presentation of an infant when it is forty days old. I take the baby in my arms and carry it to the front of the church. Most of the time it keeps its eyes on me, except for the moment when I pass beneath the dome. Absolutely every baby I've ever presented shifts its gaze to Christ at that moment, as if it knows it is meeting its maker."

"Thank you for sharing that, Elder," said Kosmas. "But I don't understand what it has to do with me."

"You haven't had children yet. You haven't married. I'd like to present your children before I die."

"I'm working on it," said Kosmas.

"He's not the only one who might have children," Fanis muttered. He stood, put Ali's money on the cashier counter, and made a move for the bishop's hand.

The bishop slapped his wrist and said, "See you tomorrow?"

"Unfortunately not. I'm going on a little outing to Antigone. But I've arranged a substitute."

"So you're coming, too?" said Kosmas, while Ali trimmed his wet hair.

"Excuse me?" said Fanis.

"Daphne invited me last night. But she didn't say anything about you."

Just fabulous, thought Fanis. But perhaps it's for the best. Let Daphne see how we compare.

"How nice," he said. "Oh, and Kosmaki, one last bit of advice. It's my ultra-secret weapon. I've never told anyone, but because I see you as a son, I'm going to share it. You know how I told you not to kiss a woman on the first date? That's only part of it. You really shouldn't kiss her for at least—and I mean *at least*—ten dates. That way, sometime after ten, she'll be so hungry she'll tear your clothes off. You won't have to make the smallest effort to get her into bed."

That is, Fanis said to himself, if she hasn't yet grown bored of you, given up, or decided that you're gay.

Fanis left the shop and walked home at a brisk pace. He was so absorbed by his analysis of the Daphne situation that he forgot all about his new neighbor. He cursed the moving truck blocking his street and stormed straight upstairs. Without even peering across the way to the garret, he put Sinatra's *Swing Easy!* on his 1955 Magnavox Consolette, turned up the volume, and paced the living-room floor. It was always while listening to the Sultan of Swoon that he came up with his best plans and strategies.

12

The Island of Antigone

SEAGULLS SWOOPED AND DOVE ALONGSIDE the ferry, riding the air currents as if they, too, were on their way to the islands. Daphne turned her face into the wind. The air didn't smell like Biscayne Bay. It was less salty. Cleaner. Fishier. And the waves in the Sea of Marmara were more like lake ripples than Florida's swells. Up ahead, a gray church dome rose above the ceramic-tile roofs and white clapboard mansions of Antigone. Speedboats anchored in the island's harbor slid heavily over low waves and wakes. Wooden fishing barks tied to the quay bobbed merrily, pulling on their lines, like dogs straining on leashes.

A gust of wind caught Daphne's straw fedora. Kosmas, sitting beside her, grabbed it just in time. "Hang on to that," he said.

"Time to make our way downstairs," said Gavriela. She put on her ultra-dark, post-cataract-operation sunglasses and held out her hand to Daphne. "Let's go, little mama."

The friends pushed their way through the crowd and down the stairs to the boarding deck. A few impatient daredevils, including a headscarved woman carrying a newborn baby, scorned the rickety gangway and leaped over the gap between ship and shore. Nobody seemed to have any sense of order or lines.

"It's always a mess like this," said Julien, as soon as they had made it across to the quay. "*Kimin siki kimin götünde.*"

"Professeur!" snapped Gavriela.

"What? *You can't tell whose dick is in whose ass* is a perfectly good Turkish saying. Part of the culture."

Gavriela clicked her tongue in disapproval. "Come along. Let's not keep Aliki waiting."

As they walked, Daphne took in the resin scent of the pine trees. She noticed cats sleeping on the steps of Italianate villas, behind metal dumpsters, and on café chairs. There wasn't a car or bus in sight. Stray dogs lazed wherever they wished, even in the middle of the street, and moved only at the sound of oncoming hooves. Instead of automobile horns, one heard the harmonious ringing of phaeton bells. It was hard to believe that the island was, administratively at least, part of Istanbul. No longer afraid of pickpockets, Daphne lifted her bag from its tiresome crossbody position and let it dangle from her shoulder. She tore a jasmine tendril from a plant spilling over a picket fence, inhaled its sweet perfume, and asked, "Are we going to have a chance to see the rest of the island?"

Kosmas stopped walking. Suddenly decisive, like a ship's captain announcing a change of course, he said to the old-sters, "Daphne and I will see you all later. We're going on a phaeton ride."

Fanis clapped his hands. "Just what I had in mind."

"Perfect," said Rea. "I love phaetons."

"Don't get too excited," said Kosmas. "Daphne and I are going alone."

Rea leaned heavily on her sparkly pink cane. "But I can't walk to Aliki's without you."

Dimitris stepped between Kosmas and his mother. "Don't worry, Ritsa. I'll take care of you."

Kosmas winked at Dimitris. "You see, Mama. True men have solutions for any problem. Mr. Dimitris, you're a star."

Kosmas flagged down a passing carriage. As it slowed to a stop, Daphne noticed the odd contrast that Kosmas's small triangular rear made with his thicker middle. She couldn't help comparing it to Paul's ideal proportions. Kosmas had turned out to be a nice guy, but Daphne still didn't feel an overwhelming physical attraction.

"How much for the big tour?" Kosmas asked the driver.

With one hand resting on the brake wheel and the other clutching the whip and reins, the shabbily dressed driver replied, "Forty lira."

Kosmas nodded to Daphne. Impressed that Kosmas hadn't even tried to bargain, she climbed beneath the phaeton's tasseled roof. As soon as she had settled onto the soft cushion of the basket, however, she realized that the phaeton was more attractive from afar than from inside, especially in the summer heat: not that she expected the horses to be fragrant, but their stench was overwhelming, as if they hadn't been bathed or cared for in years. Kosmas jumped in with her. The driver made a clucking sound to the horses, and they left the oldsters behind.

Daphne tried to forget the excrement smell by focusing her attention on the landscape, the houses, and their oriel windows. Her grandmother's wooden house, as she had seen it in a photo, had boasted an oriel supported by corbels. As a little girl, Daphne would look at that picture and imagine herself sitting in its window, watching the street below or reading a book.

"Do you see that old lady up there?" she said, nodding toward a woman with an arm dangling over her oriel sill.

"Probably Rum," said Kosmas. "She'd have to be Rum— or Jewish—to have an old house like that. That's what I love about Antigone in the summer. You can even hear Greek and Ladino coming from open windows. It's like smelling the rich aroma of *tsoureki* bread wafting out of bakeries at Easter time."

Kosmas lowered his arm onto the back of the basket. Daphne felt the heat of his skin through the wicker. His fingers bumped against her bare shoulder. For a second, she almost wished he would put his arm around her instead of the basket. And then she heard three loud, squeaky vibrations.

"What was that?" she asked.

"An expression of the horses' appreciation of their master," said Kosmas. The warm gas reached their nostrils. Daphne covered her face. Kosmas gave her shoulder a quick squeeze. "If *you* couldn't talk," he said, "how else would you get back at a bastard sitting behind you?"

Daphne laughed as the carriage merged into the sea road. Kosmas pointed out a blue and white church surrounded by olive trees. "Saint George Karypi," he said in a tour-guide tone. "It's been through fires and earthquakes. Even served as an asylum for White Russians. According to Mr. Dimitris, a Russian princess lived there for a year, but I've never found that mentioned in any history books."

Daphne transferred her attention from the church to Kosmas. "You read history?"

"All the time. Ancient, Byzantine, Ottoman. Everything I find about the City. My favorite is Edmondo de Amici's 1877 travelogue *Constantinople*. After raving about the beauty of the City from afar, de Amici begins his second chapter by describing Constantinople—in which he had, by that time, spent five hours—as a monstrous confusion of civilization and barbarism. Which is exactly what Istanbul remains to this day."

Daphne stared at Kosmas. He was obviously not just a casual reader.

"I read de Amici every night while I was studying in Vienna," he said. "That's how much I missed the City. Do you miss Miami?"

Daphne looked out over the blue Marmara toward the tall buildings of Istanbul's Asian side. "Not yet. Eventually I suppose I'd miss my parents, my students, the public-library system, the salsa bands, the tango community. . . . No, strike that last item. Although I'd miss the dance itself, I would definitely not miss the tango tramps and showoffs."

"Are you thinking of moving here?"

They slowed for a turn. A derelict cottage of dry boards caught Daphne's eye. Through its glassless windows and tattered lace curtains, she glimpsed dusty, abandoned wicker furniture and a paper icon tacked to the wall. She wondered why the cottage's owners had left without even collecting the furniture and curtains. Had they been deported in 1964? Had they been unable to endure the nationalistic pressures of the seventies?

"Maybe," said Daphne. "But then I hear people talking about the pogrom and the deportations, and I'm not sure anymore."

"Things are better now. It's not like when our parents were young."

"But you don't know about tomorrow. My mother says Turkey is the land of surprises and contradictions."

Kosmas leaned closer. "Perhaps Istanbul will surprise you in a good way."

Daphne flinched when the driver swatted one of the horses with his whip. She said, "I'm not sure if I'll fit in here."

"Nobody does. That's partly why we like it." Kosmas's face was embroidered with the shifting lights and shadows passing through the artificial flowers sewn to the carriage roof. His eyes rested on her lips for a few seconds, then darted off. "But maybe your boyfriend won't let you move here."

The driver took a quick turn. The carriage jolted, and Kosmas's arm slid—partly at least—onto Daphne's shoulders. His hand remained on the basket rim, but she could feel his skin and bristly arm hair brushing her upper back. Daphne wanted to lean into his arm, rest her head against his shoulder. But she also didn't want to lead him on. "My boyfriend wants to come for a visit," she said.

Kosmas tapped the driver's arm. "Can you drop us here and wait a few minutes?"

The driver made a blowing sound with loose lips. The horses slowed to a stop.

"I thought we'd have a quick walk down to the beach," said Kosmas.

They descended the uneven, rocky path, which was flanked by bushes, scrub, and all sorts of beach garbage: half-liter water bottles, discarded wet wipes, melon rinds, seed husks, chocolate wrappers, and even a used condom. When they arrived at the pebble beach, Daphne took a deep breath of the seaweed- and sunscreen-scented air. She looked at the water flashing between the mossy rocks. The heads of a few swimmers bobbed in the open sea. A fat old woman and a shirtless man lounged on beach chairs, sipping Coca-Cola from glass bottles and reading newspapers that still had not tired of discussing the prime minister's victory in the elections of the preceding Sunday.

Daphne's long black skirt felt hot against her legs. Her hair was sweaty and sticking to her neck and shoulders. "I'd give half my kingdom for a dive in the sea," she said.

"Impossible," said Kosmas, squinting in the bright sun. "As much as I'd like half your kingdom. We don't have bathing suits."

"What if we took a dip in our underwear? Over there, behind those rocks. Nobody would see."

Daphne could hear her mother already: *Put it out of your head, missy. You're in Istanbul. Everybody's watching, all the time.* But Daphne didn't care. She wanted to get into that water, let it close around her, let it filter out the sunlight and the tango bullshit that had caused her so much upset during the past year.

"What color?" said Kosmas.

"What *color*?"

"Your underwear. If it's black, then maybe . . ."

"Beige."

Kosmas's eyes widened. "We'd better not. The driver's waiting for us. We'll come again another time."

160

"Even the fat old lady over there is close to naked," said Daphne.

"Who cares about the fat old lady? But if you go swimming in beige underwear, believe me, there will be an audience." In four large strides, Kosmas returned to the path.

Daphne ran across the pebbles, sinking into them with each step. "Wait," she shouted.

Kosmas stopped beneath a cypress tree and wiped his brow with an old-fashioned cotton handkerchief. "I'm sorry," he said, raising his voice above his usual, aristocratically polite museum tone. "I know I'm just a friend. But I'm not a tango dancer, and I'm not American, and I don't like to share."

Kosmas continued up to the road, leaving Daphne to the metallic buzzing of the cicadas. Paul didn't care if she danced with other men; Kosmas blushed at the thought of her being seen in wet underwear by probably no one. Paul didn't care if she traveled across the world by herself, yet Kosmas had accompanied her to the lavatory on the ferry and waited outside the door until she was finished. Daphne remembered having felt flattered by Paul's trust at the beginning of their relationship, but over the past year, she had begun to wonder if he was just indifferent. Kosmas's protectiveness might eventually grow tiring—perhaps even stifling—but for now it felt like sitting in the sun after a bout of cold and dreary weather.

The driver dropped them off just outside Aliki's white clapboard cottage. Kosmas pressed the doorbell. It tweeted like a happy bird, but no one answered. "They probably can't hear," he said.

He led Daphne around the cottage, through a jungle-like alleyway that hosted a fig tree, a bright purple bougainvillea bush, a deserted fishing bark covered with torn netting, and a few renegade New Guinea impatiens. Just before they reached the gate, Daphne overheard Aliki saying: "—on the beach maybe, or beneath the pine trees, or in the phaeton?"

"Absolutely not," said Rea. "He would have asked my permission first. And his grandparents' rings are still in the safety-deposit box."

"Who needs rings?" said Julien. "I proposed to my wife the night I met her. It wasn't even a date, just a Bastille Day party, and there was no diamond, although I bought her one later. I was drunk, but never mind that."

Daphne couldn't believe her ears.

Kosmas called out: "We're back!"

"We were just wondering when you'd be along," said Julien, innocently.

Embarrassed, Daphne followed Kosmas through a maze of lavender, geranium, marigold, and hydrangea pots—some flourishing and some dried out, all with prickly weeds growing in between—to a white plastic tea table beneath a grapevine trellis.

"You must be starving," said Aliki. She lifted mosquito tents from plates of sauced summer vegetables, fresh bread, feta cheese, cucumber salad, stuffed vine leaves, and celery root with lemon and dill.

While Aliki served, Julien asked, "How was *the ride*?"

"We did the whole tour," said Daphne, "all the way to the end. We even went down to the beach and—"

"You had a *good time*," said Julien.

"Yes, Professeur," said Daphne. "A very good time."

"I'm surprised you like phaetons, Daphne dear," said Fanis. "Just last week there was another newspaper article about a horse that collapsed from exhaustion. And everybody knows that the drivers leave the sick ones to die in the forests."

Daphne set down her fork. Her unwitting contribution to animal abuse had cut her appetite.

Fanis continued: "Some drivers even drown their old horses in the s—"

"Didn't you say just an hour ago," interrupted Julien, "how much you loved phaetons?"

"I do," said Fanis. "But I know which drivers are good to their horses, and the one that Kosmas chose certainly isn't." Fanis turned to Daphne. "Next weekend, dear, we'll go to Prinkipos Island and take a phaeton with a very good and humane driver. Then we'll eat grilled lamb at the monastery restaurant."

Aliki frowned. "She's vegetarian. And, besides, you said you'd help me with the sale of my antiques next weekend."

Had Aliki put Fanis in the eye? Daphne looked to Kosmas, wondering if he was thinking the same thing. But Kosmas wasn't paying any attention to Aliki and Fanis: he was staring at Daphne's waist and hair as she leaned forward to eat. Daphne felt a tingling in her chest, as if she had overdosed on caffeine.

"The antiques aren't going anywhere," said Fanis. "They've been in your family for over a century. Couldn't they wait another few weeks?"

Aliki clicked her tongue. No.

Julien tugged on the open flaps of his fishing vest. "I'd be happy to help."

Aliki clicked a second time. "Thanks, Teacher, but the antiques aren't musical instruments. I need Fanis's expertise."

"Daphne, have you noticed the view?" Dimitris pointed a split yellow fingernail toward the corrugated polycarbonate roof panels upon which cats were taking their afternoon siesta. Just beyond them, Daphne could distinguish the green contours of another island, as well as the blond rocks at its base, disappearing into the sea. "The Halki Theological School is just there," said Dimitris, "at the top of the hill. It's mostly hidden by trees, but you can make out the roof."

"She probably doesn't know what the Halki Seminary is," said Rea. "Maybe you should explain, Dimitraki."

"Actually," said Daphne, "I did a lesson on the Halki Seminary with my sixth-graders a couple of months ago. They wrote letters to the prime minister asking for its reopening."

"*İnşallah* that will happen soon," said Gavriela.

The word *inşallah* relayed around the table.

"*That*'s where we'll go next weekend," said Fanis. "Now, how about some music?"

He went inside the cottage. A few minutes later, the first piano chords of Louis Armstrong's "Dancing Cheek To Cheek" sailed out. Fanis floated back down the stairs, stepping with the lightness of Fred Astaire and singing along. Daphne was surprised that, despite his not speaking English, Fanis knew all the words. In fact, his smooth bass was just as suited to American jazz as it was to Byzantine hymns. He stopped in front of Daphne. "Care to dance?"

Daphne stood and took Fanis's hand. He danced well, with good time, agility, clear direction, and consideration. He didn't hold Daphne too tightly, as Metin had on Friday night. He didn't get frustrated if she didn't follow a step or perform high *boleos*, as Paul did. And he wasn't distracted by her proximity, as Kosmas had been at the lesson. After the final piano flourish, Fanis kissed Daphne's hand. She kissed his cheek and took in a last breath of his citrusy cologne. Everyone applauded.

"Time for the children's coffee," Aliki said. She reached behind her for the blue camp burner sitting at the base of a dried-out date palm.

With a sudden desire to show off her new coffee-making skills, Daphne said, "Madame Aliki, you went to so much trouble over the food. Please allow me."

"Don't be silly," said Aliki. "This is the first time you've been to my house."

"I insist," said Daphne. She placed the camp burner and copper pot before her on the plastic table. Julien handed her the coffee and sugar jars. Kosmas passed the cups, saucers, and spoons. As Daphne took the water pitcher from him, their fingers brushed, just as they had when he had given her the chocolate box on Friday night. This time, however, instead of an urge to get away, she felt a dangerous flutter.

"Medium for me," said Kosmas.

"I'll take another," said Rea.

Daphne stirred the coffee and water gently, just until the sugar melted. She removed the pot from the burner as soon as the coffee started to swell, filled the cups halfway, and then returned the pot to the flame in order to create a perfect foam. After the coffee had bubbled again, she let it rest a moment before topping up.

Kosmas took a sip. "The best I've ever had. Health to your hands."

"Bravo, my doll," said Rea, smiling at Daphne, "but a little too sweet. A medium should be—"

"Time for my biscuit terrine!" Aliki interrupted.

Daphne and Kosmas finished their coffees while Aliki cut and served slices of her semi-frozen cream and biscuit log. After the first bite, Rea said, "The perfect amount of sweetness!"

Of course, thought Daphne. *Because Aliki made it, not me.*

"I'd hire you any day," said Kosmas.

Aliki blushed.

"Aliki's an old-style City woman," said Fanis, after he had scooped the last bit of melted chocolate cream from his plate. "She has golden hands."

Gavriela tossed a shredded napkin onto the table and grabbed Kosmas's overturned coffee cup, but it was glued fast by the sandy dregs. "You'll get your wish," she said. "Look how hard I'm pulling."

"Of course he will," grumbled Julien.

Gavriela twisted the cup loose and peered inside. "I see a circle and a house: marriage and family happiness."

"I do hope the lucky girl will take proper care of him." Rea sighed.

"Amateur," said Fanis, taking the cup. "You're selling fairy-tales, Gavriela. Your circle is an upside-down head, which means that he isn't going to. . . . Oh, never mind. Have it your way."

Daphne looked at Kosmas. His face had turned the color of sour-cherry liqueur. A tiny dot of saliva had collected in the right corner of his lips. He was dying of embarrassment.

Gavriela clicked her tongue at Fanis, set Kosmas's cup aside, and lifted Daphne's. "You'll have a child sooner than you expect."

"Sorry, Auntie," said Daphne, wondering if her face was now turning the same color as Kosmas's. "No babies in my plans. At least, not for another five years."

"I do hope you'll be strict with your children," said Rea. "Today's mothers are too lenient."

"*My niece*," said Gavriela, "will be an ideal mother."

"Were there any pillows?" Julien tapped a teaspoon against the tabletop. "My first mistress used to say that pillows were the sign of a good sex life."

Aliki swung her chin from side to side like a pendulum. "Then we obviously will not be seeing any pillows in *your* grinds."

Rea reached for the cup. "I see a mask, just there! That means secrets and deception. Either someone is deceiving *you*, Daphne, or there is something you aren't telling *us*."

"Mama, enough," said Kosmas.

It was the first time that Daphne had heard him use so stern a tone with his mother. Still, Daphne was capable of defending herself. "Look, Madame Rea, I don't have anything to hide. *My father*—"

The call to prayer sounded from the local mosque. "It's getting late!" said Dimitris. He winked conspiratorially at Daphne, although she couldn't understand why, and then continued: "Our lovely Ritsa needs plenty of time to get down to the quay."

Aliki leaned toward Fanis. "You look tired. You know, I have an extra room if you'd like to stay the night."

Julien dropped the teaspoon he'd been tapping. "You want *him* to stay the night?"

166

"Tired," said Fanis. "It's like saying, 'We will be visiting you in the cemetery soon.'"

Aliki fluttered her blue-powdered eyelids. "I didn't mean it that way. I just thought you might like to take a little break."

Julien looked importunately at Aliki. "*I* would *love* a rest."

"Another time, Professeur. I've only got one guest room."

"Come on, Prof," said Kosmas, patting Julien's shoulder. "The ride back will be boring without you. Besides, we have to remember what they say about the one who leaves, don't we? And the other ten who come to take her place?"

"You can't sell Father's gifts back to Father," Julien grumbled.

Kosmas shook his head, crossed to the other side of the table, and helped Julien to his feet. As he did so, Daphne took another look at his little posterior. It was almost cute.

Taking advantage of the commotion, Dimitris whispered in Daphne's ear: "All things in their time, my girl, all things in their time!"

13

Sweet Nymph and Old Hag

AFTER THE OTHERS HAD GONE, Fanis helped carry the tea and coffee things into the kitchen. An hour later, while he was enjoying his last tea on the patio and admiring the vinca vines, which were turning a glowing orange-green in the pre-sunset light, Aliki appeared in the doorway with her purse in hand.

"Let's go have some fun," she said.

"How?" asked Fanis.

"We can take a phaeton to the promontory, have lamb ribs for dinner, and get drunk."

"I'm in," said Fanis.

They locked up the house and walked arm in arm to one of the streets where phaetons queued for customers. The first in line was a red carriage with turquoise seats. Fanis haggled for his usual senior discount, then said to Aliki, "When ascending stairs or entering carriages, in the interests of propriety, men should always precede women."

With that he climbed inside and offered both hands to Aliki. But even with his help, she couldn't manage to take more than one foot off the ground. The driver tossed aside his whip and offered to help by giving a boost from behind. After some strategic planning and a coordinated effort, Aliki finally landed on the carriage seat with a jolt that startled the horses. Fanis straightened his sweater vest. The driver wiped his brow, threw away the cigarette that had been hanging from his mouth, hopped onto his bench, and snapped the reins.

It wasn't exactly the ride with Daphne that Fanis had planned while listening to the great Sinatra after his visit to the barbershop, but it was pleasant enough. At the open-air restaurant, Aliki chose a table beside the pine trees that had once sheltered impromptu dances, and in the course of the evening they ate more grilled lamb ribs and drank more house wine than their doctors would have approved. Just after the waiter had cleared the table, Aliki looked over the blackness of the sea, toward the glowing lights on the Thracian shore, and said, "I'm so glad you stayed. Sometimes I get a little lonely."

"I'm glad you invited me," said Fanis, smiling as convincingly as he could. The truth, however, was that he couldn't stop obsessing about how things had gone with Daphne. He had certainly scored points with the dance number, but he couldn't shake the feeling that she preferred his rival. She had faced Kosmas squarely whenever he spoke, carelessly—and somewhat rudely—turning her back to others in the process. That wasn't a good sign.

Aliki took out her pink pill box, opened the Sunday Evening compartment, and swallowed its contents with a gulp of water. "You don't take anything?" she said.

Fanis recalled the embers of Dr. Aydemir's prescriptions hovering above the sink, like fireflies. Thank God he had burned those nasty threats of living decomposition. He should never have accepted them in the first place. The box of blue pills dispensed by Pharmacist Sözbir, on the other hand, had been a pleasure from the moment Fanis's fingers had touched the precious cardboard. He had placed it like a trophy on its own private shelf in the medicine cabinet, confident that, with its help, he would be able to beget a son to carry on the Paleologos name.

"What would I need pills for?" said Fanis. He took a sip of the deep red wine and held it in his mouth for a moment, savoring the hints of dried fruit, fig, and oak. "Illness can't get you if you refuse to acknowledge its existence. Just the other day I read something about a goiter sufferer who was doing just fine until they made him do a biopsy. He died three days after seeing the C-word on paper. They said his body had dealt with the cancer for years and years, but the mind couldn't handle it for more than a few hours. So I say to Hell with doctors."

"But you wouldn't ignore symptoms, would you? If you had them?"

"Of course I would. Most of them are in our heads anyway."

Aliki met his gaze. Their table's only lighting was a string of holiday bulbs woven into the vine trellis above their heads, but Fanis saw well enough to recognize the worry in her fading blue eyes. "Is there something you're not telling us?" she said.

"No," said Fanis. It wasn't a lie. It was a Greek Truth: something that had to be said to avoid problems.

"That's a relief," said Aliki. "Anyway, you're still a fabulous dancer. Do you remember the rumba we danced here?"

Fanis fumbled: "Eh . . . sure." He had danced so many cha-chas, waltzes, and rumbas with so many girls. It was, of course, probable that she had been one of them.

"You were the best dancer back then. All the girls wanted a turn with you. How could you remember us all?"

"*Of course* I remember," said Fanis. He took a deep breath of the sea air. "You had on that dress . . ."

Aliki grinned. "The pink organza! You *do* remember. God, could you wiggle those hips. That's why we loved dancing with you so much."

"You were quite good yourself," said Fanis. "Good timing, soft hands."

"Afterwards," said Aliki, "you went straight back to your fiancée. I was jealous of Kalypso because she was such a good dancer. I was even a bit jealous of Daphne this afternoon. I wish I could still move about like I used to."

"Ka—" said Fanis, but he couldn't complete the name. It choked him. Although they had been taking tea together for at least a decade, neither Aliki nor Rea had ever tried to dig up the past by mentioning Kalypso. He had always been grateful for their tact.

Fanis remained silent for a while. Aliki praised Kalypso's beautiful dancing, her singing, and her intricate embroidery, which Aliki had never been able to match, try as she might. She reminded him that his fiancée had once broken a heel after failing to follow one of Fanis's fancy moves. As a result, both Fanis and Kalypso had fallen onto the pine needles.

"I miss those days," said Aliki. "I miss Kalypso, as well as my parents, my husband, and all who have gone. Do you miss your wife?"

It must have been the wine that made Fanis reply, without any of his usual artifice, "Not at all."

"Do you miss Kalypso?"

"Terribly. It's as if I've gone through life without my right arm."

He finished his wine. He felt that she was near. He could hear her laughter, the laughter of all those nights on the island, the laughter of all those young men and women. He tasted the saltiness of Kalypso's skin after she had lain on the beach, baking like a lobster. He felt her lips brushing the tip of his ear. He heard her singing one of Roza's songs. It was a party tune, playful and upbeat, but the voice was lachrymose and dark. It whispered in his ear, "Let's go home."

Fanis echoed her: "Let's go home."

"All right," said Aliki.

The response startled Fanis. He hadn't realized that he was speaking out loud. Damned vascular dementia. Now he was talking to himself. He wondered if Aliki could feel Kalypso's presence, but he didn't dare ask. Instead, he thanked her for the evening and asked for the bill.

"But you're my guest," said Aliki.

"Impossible," said Fanis.

"Always such a gentleman."

"Someday we'll all be dancing again," he said, picking at a piece of honeydew melon to avoid meeting Aliki's gaze. "You'll see. When we finally cross over to the other side, there will be plenty of rumbas."

On the way home Aliki placed her hand on his. Fanis thought it was a friendly gesture, or perhaps even one of pity, so he squeezed it and held on until the phaeton pulled up at her doorstep. She, too, missed Kalypso, he reminded himself, and his mourning had been delayed far too long.

Aliki showed Fanis to the guest room. The sheets were freshly ironed and smelled of rosewater. The inlaid tables were polished and covered with starched doilies. The curtains, he could tell, had recently been washed and rehung, and the hardwood floor was waxed to a shine. Either Aliki was one of the best house-widows on the island or she had been preparing for him for over a week. Perhaps her invitation to spend the night had not been as impromptu as it had seemed. After a few minutes, she brought him a pair of her dead husband's pajamas, wished him a pleasant dawn, and withdrew. Fanis felt immense relief. They were just good friends after all.

The tinny pulse of the crickets soon carried him off to a June evening half a century before. He smelled the fatty smoke of roasting meat and saw the gnarly pines twisting into dark shapes before the broad wall of the sea as he sat joking with his friends, a few meters away from the little clearing that served as a dance floor. Despite the money his mother had spent on lessons, Fanis had been too shy to ask Kalypso to a rumba. He had watched her sing and laugh with her cousins on the other side of the restaurant, but he hadn't been able to push himself past the devastation that he knew he would feel if she said no. It wasn't until the end of the evening, when somebody announced the last dance, that Kalypso had skipped over to him and said, "Are we *ever* going to cha-cha?" She was fifteen then, and ten times braver than he.

Fanis felt her homemade blue gingham dress beneath his sweaty palms. He saw her open-mouth smile, felt the whip of her ponytail. As sleep overcame him, the memory morphed into a dream: they rose into the sky, still dancing, and flew to the other side of the island, where the tall trees grew. "Set to," she whispered, pulling an axe and an adze from behind her full skirt. "Make your sailing bark." Then she disappeared, leaving him alone and at a loss, for he had no idea how to use an axe and adze.

Fanis awoke. He tried to make sense of the shapes and shadows to which he had opened his eyes but, like a disoriented traveler in a foreign land, he recognized nothing. A light shone under the door. He groped his way to it and shuffled down the hallway to a bright bedroom perfumed by pink garden roses peeking out of an eighteenth-century Persian Qajar vase. Inside, Aliki was sitting on her sofa in an off-the-shoulder lace nightgown that seemed overly elegant for a regular night's sleep.

"I had a dream," said Fanis.

Aliki patted the brocade sofa cushion. "Come. Have a seat."

Still confused, Fanis entered, sat down beside her, and asked, "What are you doing?"

"Waiting for you."

Fanis was taken aback. "How did you know I'd have a strange dream?"

"I didn't. But I knew you'd come." Aliki pointed at the steaming porcelain teapot on a Chippendale piecrust table. "Look, I already made you a chamomile tea."

"*Chamomile?* Men never drink chamomile. Not good for the . . . you know."

"Guess it's not for *you*, then," she said with a smile. "What about mint?"

Her effort was touching. Nobody had taken care of him like that since his mother died. "Maybe in a little while," he said. He leaned his head on Aliki's soft, sloping shoulder, breathed in the weedy scent of the chamomile tea, and took a peek at the current state of affairs: sagging wineskins. They couldn't compare to Daphne's lemons, but he also couldn't imagine Daphne taking care of him like that. And Selin? He couldn't afford to think of her right now.

Fanis yawned. He was feeling drowsy again, but he didn't want to leave. A few seconds later, he felt Aliki's hand on his knee. Was she mothering him? Or . . . ? He lifted his head to ask about the mint tea. At the same moment, Aliki leaned forward to plant a kiss on his forehead. Their lips met by accident. Fanis jumped to his feet and murmured something about feeling better and not needing the tea.

"It's no trouble," said Aliki, fiddling with the top button of her nightgown. She scanned his face as if she were searching for some sort of go-ahead. "I've been dreaming of this moment my whole life."

Fanis tried to let her down softly. "I think there's been a misunderstanding. You see, I could never get involved with one of Kalypso's friends. It would be disrespectful to her memory."

Aliki grabbed her satin robe from the back of the sofa and drew it over her shoulders. "Kalypso's been dead for over half a century."

"I know, and . . . you're lovely, Aliki, but . . ."

"Sit, Fanis," said Aliki, in a quieter tone. "Let's talk about this."

He obeyed but perched himself on the opposite end of the sofa, his fingers buried between his thighs and his knees glued together.

"Fanis," said Aliki. "I've been in love with you since I was twelve. Sure, I married somebody else, but I never stopped imagining your face on the heroes of the romance novels I used to read with a flashlight while my husband slept. And now that we've both been widowed, it's like life gave us a second chance, don't you think?"

"Certainly, but—"

"No buts," said Aliki, inching closer to him. She put her finger to his lips.

Fanis felt panic flood his body. In a few seconds he was on his feet and out the door, calling over his shoulder, "We'll talk in the morning."

He stumbled back to his room, locked the door behind him, and spat out the open window. After crawling back into bed and pulling the covers over his head, like a shy virgin, he said aloud, "She tried to take advantage of me!"

Early the next morning, Fanis grabbed a towel from the dresser and crept down the hallway to the bathroom. Thank God, he made it without being heard. He cranked the shower lever to its hottest setting, stripped, and stepped inside for a good think session. While letting the hot water run over his face, he decided the Kalypso thing wasn't going to be enough. He had to come up with a better excuse. As soon as his chest was fully sudsed, he recalled Julien's crush on Aliki. Although the *professeur* flirted outrageously with women young enough to be his granddaughters, he still hadn't made a move on Aliki because he was afraid of ruining the friendship. Fanis hated to betray Julien's trust, but ultimately he would be doing a good turn to both his friends by setting them up.

Fifteen minutes later Fanis entered the kitchen fully dressed, his belt drawn more tightly than usual. Spread before him were savory pastries, garden tomatoes, plates dressed with cheeses, tiny ceramic bowls with homemade jams, and a freshly brewed pot of black Turkish tea. Fanis sighed. He tasted a small portion from each plate, just as he used to dance one song with every girl, but he was as distant as he would have been with a beauty he had pursued and possessed the night before. After his second cup of tea, which he drank scalding hot, he declared that the breakfast had been "nectar and ambrosia" and announced that he had to be off to catch the ten-thirty boat because his godson was arriving that afternoon for a two-day visit—his standard getaway excuse.

"At least eat your breakfast," said Aliki.

Fanis glanced at his watch. "I had a wonderful time yesterday, a thousand thanks, but the ferry—"

"You said we'd talk in the morning."

"Yes, I did, didn't I?" Fanis noticed a smudge of blue eye shadow on Aliki's cheek. Apparently she'd missed the mark. He finished his tea. "Listen, Aliki, you're a lovely woman, inside and out, but, you see, it's . . . the *professeur*."

"Julien?"

"Yes. He's in love with you. Has been for years."

Aliki threw down her napkin. "Please. He tells me I'm too fat for the chairs at Neighbor's House."

"It's an odd way to flirt, I admit. But Julien has a thing for full-figured women. You see, he confessed his feelings, and from that point on, it becomes a matter of honor for me to step aside."

Aliki squinted. "Fanis Paleologos, are you lying to me?"

Fanis leaned toward her, looked directly into her eyes, and said, "I would *never* do such a thing."

"This is nonsense," Aliki snapped. "If the *professeur* likes a woman, even remotely, he doesn't hesitate."

"He doesn't hesitate when he's joking, but when he's serious it's a different thing altogether."

"Then why hasn't he spoken to me?"

"Perhaps for the same reason that you never said anything to me. When you've been friends for a long time, it's awkward."

Aliki's cheek began to twitch. "But I never caught even a hint, not for a second. . . . Are you *sure*?"

"What can I say, Aliki? You've stolen some hearts yourself, though you're too humble to notice."

She sat back in her chair, dazed. "Even if it is true . . . that doesn't mean I'm suddenly going to be sighing *aman, aman* for him. I mean, I can't just cancel my feelings for—"

"Shh!" Fanis put a finger to her lips. "All I'm saying is think about it. For me. Now"—he tapped his watch—"I had a fabulous time. A thousand thanks for everything, but I must be going or I'll miss the boat."

"Are we still on for next Saturday? You know . . . the antiques?"

He air-kissed her forehead and said, "I'll call you."

14

An Unexpected Suitor

"How was the trip to the island?" asked Uncle Mustafa, entering the Lily's kitchen on Monday morning with a tablecloth-swaddled package.

"Couldn't have been better," said Kosmas.

Mustafa extended the bundle. "I think I found something. Under my bed."

Kosmas unwrapped it: inside were three heavy old books. Kosmas opened the first. The edges of the moldy-smelling leather binding were worn. The title page read, in the old Ottoman script that was unintelligible to most modern Turks: *Recipes of Hamdi the Pastry Chef.* Kosmas thanked God that he had taken those Ottoman classes four years ago.

"Your grandfather's?" said Kosmas.

Uncle Mustafa winked. "Yep. Second pâtissier of the last sultan. Some of his colleagues were Rum, so it's possible that he learned to make the Balkanik from them."

Kosmas looked at the date beneath the title: 1320. He added a round six hundred to the Islamic Hijri date, which placed the book in the early 1900s, the last years of the Ottoman Empire, exactly as Uncle Mustafa had said.

"I can't read a word of it," said Mustafa, "so I don't know if the Balkanik is actually in there. Good luck."

Kosmas hugged Mustafa, rewrapped the books—they were far too precious to be left around the kitchen—and placed them in the pâtisserie's safe.

"Now get going," said Uncle Mustafa.

Kosmas looked at his watch. It was already half past nine and he had a cake consultation at ten. He hurried up the hill to the Maison Café, an upscale Grand Avenue restaurant that his mother's friends considered pretentious and ridiculously expensive. Kosmas rather liked the Maison's stylish blend of retro floor tiles, pine tables, potted ferns, exposed industrial ceilings, and whimsical chandeliers. He admitted that the food prices were only appropriate for Istanbul's elite, but as long as his clients stuck to tea and coffee, he could happily spend a few hours in the place.

On that day, however, the happy couple—a bald, chain-smoking, phone-obsessing middle-aged attorney and his seemingly career-less twenty-year-old socialite fiancée—had ordered a full Turkish breakfast, detox juices, and cappuccinos, from which they took no more than a few sips. Apparently, they had fired the pâtissier who was supposed to make the cake for their wedding, which was to take place on the Saturday of that same week. Kosmas had tried to turn them down politely, but the bride had mentioned that she was a good friend of the Lily's landlord. As Kosmas wanted to expand the pâtisserie by renting the adjacent shop space, he decided to make a special effort.

Still, he had trouble paying attention during the twenty-minute conversation, which was regularly interrupted by phone calls from the groom's work, as well as by photo-taking and Facebook-posting on the part of the bride. Moreover, Kosmas couldn't stop thinking how much he'd rather be doing something meaningful, like reading Hamdi's books and experimenting with the Balkanik. Perhaps he'd even translate the volumes into modern Turkish so that the work of Uncle Mustafa's grandfather would be preserved for future generations.

"So what do you think?" said the bride.

Kosmas pulled himself out of his reverie and made a creative pitch based more on the couple's appearance than on what they had said: "From what I've gathered, you're bold, no-nonsense, future-oriented people. So I'd like to propose five square tiers: square is more edgy than round. I'm thinking all white, with each tier sealed by black sugar ribbons. Calla lilies at the base and crown."

"Mmm," said the fiancée. She slurped the rest of her detox juice through the straw.

Just as the attorney was about to give his opinion, Kosmas's phone rang. He glanced at the screen: it was Mr. Dimitris, who very rarely called. Could something have happened to Rea? A fall? A sudden illness?

"Excuse me," said Kosmas. "It might be an emergency." He raised the phone to his ear. "Mr. Dimitris? Is everything okay?"

"Of course. I was just wondering if you could come by and help me change a few light bulbs."

"*Light bulbs?*"

Mr. Dimitris had never asked him over before. In fact, nobody, not even Kosmas's mother, had ever set foot in the old journalist's apartment. People said he must have someone buried in there. Kosmas bit his lip and looked at his watch. He had at least ten minutes to go with this couple—maybe more—and another consultation in one hour. He'd be cutting it close. Then again, some exercise would probably help him burn off the excess energy he was feeling after that glorious Sunday outing with Daphne, and Dimitris's building wasn't far away.

"I'll try," he said.

He ended the call and refocused his attention on the attorney. "I'm terribly sorry. Now, getting back to the cake—"

The attorney ostentatiously rattled his Rolex. "How much?"

Kosmas was about to give his standard price, but a sudden instinct told him to double it. "Four thousand six hundred liras."

"Rather expensive," said the attorney.

"He's one of the best," said the fiancée.

"A little discount would help," said the attorney.

"I don't usually do this," said Kosmas, "especially for something on short notice, but you're such a charming couple. I'll take off fifteen percent."

"Thanks." The attorney stood, shook Kosmas's hand, and nodded to his fiancée, who picked up her Hermès purse and toddled off. As soon as the couple was out of sight, Kosmas paid the bill, dashed across the Grand Avenue, and cut through an old arcade, whose Christian and Jewish haberdasheries had been replaced by liberal booksellers, lingerie shops, and coffeehouses. He glanced at the long-haired students playing backgammon, smoking, discussing, snacking, checking text messages, and flirting. Thank God Daphne wasn't one of those. Kosmas loved how she had given him her full attention the day before, both in the phaeton and then on the ferry trip back from the island. Daphne had an old-fashioned calmness about her. Kosmas hoped it was because she was falling in love.

As he ducked beneath a dingy archway, hurried past the British consulate, and crossed a busy avenue into Tarlabaşı, he scrolled through his phone calendar. He'd left things open with Daphne when they said goodbye on Kabataş Quay, saying he'd call her on Monday. Now he realized just how busy he was that week: five more consultations, one anniversary, two circumcisions, an Armenian baptism, and four weddings, in addition to his everyday duties. But he would call. That evening, at the latest.

Upon arrival at Dimitris's ramshackle building, Kosmas rang the bell and was buzzed inside.

"Let's do the bedroom first, son," said Dimitris, standing in his apartment doorway. "And then we'll have a lemonade."

Kosmas was obliged to duck beneath the hand-washed boxer shorts and undershirts drying in the long corridor, which was decorated with faded prints of pashas and harem girls. He passed a small, windowless dining room containing a child's bed, eight Empire-style chairs, and a formal mahogany table covered with newspapers, dirty coffee cups, and leftovers from last night's dinner.

"Mr. Dimitris," he said, "I thought you'd never been married. If you don't mind me asking, why do you have a child's bed in here?"

"Mine, of course." Dimitris ushered him into the bedroom and opened the balcony door.

In the daylight Kosmas saw that the bedroom, too, was filled beyond capacity with furniture. On the walls were icons, a wooden cross, and a framed photo of a 1950s football team. By the balcony door, Dimitris's suitcase lay half unpacked.

"Planning a trip?" said Kosmas.

"Oh, no," said Dimitris, waving his hand dismissively. "Just haven't unpacked since my last jaunt to Athens to see my sister."

"When was that?"

"About six months ago."

Kosmas loosened his collar. "That big carved bed doesn't seem your style."

"Mother's," said Dimitris. "Haven't changed a thing since she left us."

For a second Kosmas wondered if he, too, would end up living in a time-warped pigpen after his mother died. His heart began to race. He had a choking sensation in his throat. *İdare*, he told himself. *Management. Control.* It was his favorite Turkish word, the one he had whispered during the Pfeifenberger competition. He still repeated it whenever he was building a difficult cake on deadline and afraid that the creation wouldn't hold. *İdare.*

"Are you all right?" asked Dimitris.

Without waiting for a reply, he pushed Kosmas out onto the iron balcony, where more lines of laundry hung above a neighboring gypsy's garden. Kosmas took a few deep breaths and attempted to release his fears of becoming a lonely old man. Things are going well with Daphne, he assured himself. This apartment is not your destiny.

He returned inside to change the light bulb that Dimitris could not reach. Tall as he was, Kosmas didn't even have to stretch. "Mr. Dimitris," he said, "how have you been changing your bulbs all these years? Don't you have a stepstool?"

"Broke yesterday," said Dimitris. "I suppose I could've run out for a new one, but . . . I've been wanting to talk to you."

Great, thought Kosmas. Another get-married-fast pep talk.

After they had replaced the bulb in the blue glass fixture of the living room, Dimitris cleared the old bills and other papers from the round table at the room's center and brought a tray laden with bowls of chocolate ice cream and bottled lemonade.

"Listen, Kosmaki," he said, "I've always boasted that I would remain a lifetime bachelor. Over the past year, however . . ."

"Yes?"

"You might have noticed yesterday at Antigone, or on other days . . ."

"*What?*"

Dimitris took a deep breath. "My feelings for a certain lady have blossomed. I think my time has finally come. How would you feel about your mother remarrying?"

"*My* mother?"

Kosmas had never maintained any silly notions about widows' virtue. He teased his mother about her flirtation with their cobbler, and he had once suggested that Dimitris would make a nice boyfriend for her, but she had dismissed his idea. After fidgeting for a moment with the bottle cap, Kosmas said to Dimitris, "Well, you could ask, but you might be disappointed. Not that she doesn't consider you a very good friend. It's just that . . . it's a big step, and I doubt she'd—"

"Are you sure? Because I thought that maybe, felt that maybe . . . I mean, when I come to your house for dinner, I have the impression that . . ."

Kosmas stood. "I'm really sorry, Mr. Dimitris, but I have a cake consultation in ten minutes. I've got to go."

"Of course, of course. I didn't mean to keep you from work. A thousand thanks for your help. Just forget what I said."

Kosmas felt his head spinning. He said a hasty goodbye and was soon traversing the underpass that led out of Tarlabaşı and back to the Grand Avenue. He hardly noticed the urine stench, which usually made him want to vomit, for he was trying to understand how these old folks with one foot in the grave could have so much more courage than he did.

15

A Friend at the Door

At about the same time that Kosmas was leaving Tarlabaşı, Fanis skipped onto Kabataş Quay with the exhilaration of a prisoner just escaped from an island fortress. He felt bad for Aliki. Her attentions had been both flattering and sweet, but she wasn't for him. At least he'd put fleas in her ears about Julien, however: now they'd be whispering to her day and night, tempting her with the possibility of romance with the *professeur*. Fanis hoped things would work out. Both deserved a companion.

After a five-minute taxi ride and a two-hundred-meter walk up a one-way street, Fanis turned into Faik Paşa, looked up, and saw that the windows of the blue mansion's garret apartment were wide open. Sheer curtains were blowing through the empty frames and waving over the street in a subtle invitation. This was going to make for some delightful window watching.

"Fanis, is that you?"

He lowered his gaze to ground level. Beside him stood a man in a Panama hat and mirrored sunglasses. "Murat," he said. "Good morning."

"I'm on my way back from the greengrocer's." Murat raised a blue plastic bag of vegetables.

"Perfect timing," said Fanis. "I've just returned from Antigone, and I've got cherry liqueur and cheese pies. Made by a friend of mine on the island. Come on up."

"Sounds delicious, but I don't want to put you to trouble."

"Don't be silly."

As they climbed the four flights of stairs, Fanis tried to remember in what sort of state he had left the place. He always made his best effort to keep bachelor laziness from encroaching upon the feminine elegance with which his wife and his mother had graced the apartment, but every so often something escaped him. Upon opening the door, he darted inside and glanced around. Not too bad. He turned on the air-conditioning with one of the remotes from the bonbon bowl and pulled down the *Elle Décoration* calendar that he had taped to the kitchen door. There wasn't time for anything else.

"The house is a little untidy," he said, ushering Murat into the living room. "Please excuse me. Have a seat here and I'll get us a glass of water."

Like a good host, Fanis went into the kitchen, put a paper doily on his mother's best silver tray, and loaded it with two glasses of water, napkins, the bottle of liqueur, and the cheese pies, properly arranged on a Kütahya plate. He returned to the living room, wished his guest *afiyet olsun*, good digestion, and took two silver liqueur goblets from the display cabinet that still housed his mother's crystal. After pouring the liqueur, he begged his friend to take one of the Pavlidis chocolates whose gold foil wrapping bore the portrait of a sad Mona Lisa. "*Yeia mas*," he said, in Greek, clicking his goblet against Murat's.

"*Şerife*," replied Murat, in Turkish. "I've always thought that one can learn the most important values of any culture through its toasts and salutations. You say *to health*, we say *to honor*. You sign letters *with appreciation*, whereas we sign them *with respect*."

"Interesting," said Fanis. "But ultimately no culture can get very far without all four."

"True," said Murat. "Magnificent liqueur, by the way."

Fanis took a sip and swished it around his mouth. "She uses peppercorns. A sly one, that Aliki."

"Excuse me?"

"My mother always said that women who put pepper-corns in their liqueur are looking for something."

"Has she found it?"

"Not in me," said Fanis. "But she's a good soul. I wish I could reciprocate, but it's not possible. I want crazy love. Do you know what I mean?"

"At *our* age?"

"Absolutely. I don't understand why everybody thinks that after seventy you should curl up with a warm blanket and wait to die."

"What about friends and family?"

"I don't have any family. I love my friends dearly, but I live for Eros. As Philostratus of Lemnos said, 'Love is not illness, but rather not-loving.' I want to be in love. Not just hold somebody's hand."

Murat shrugged his shoulders. Fanis saw that it was useless to try to convince him.

"Anyway," said Fanis, "have a cheese pie. They're absolutely delicious. Shall I make coffee?"

"No. There's nothing better than sour-cherry liqueur."

Fanis looked at Murat sitting on the sofa beneath the fading and chipping blue and ochre wall. "Listen, friend," he said. "I want to apologize for the other day."

"Don't mention it. I'm glad we had a chance to clear things up."

Fanis topped up their goblets. "You're kind."

"I hope you don't mind me asking," said Murat, "but do you have a picture of your fiancée? I haven't been able to stop thinking about what you told me."

Fanis paused for a second, then sucked down the whole goblet of liqueur. He hadn't looked at a picture of Kalypso for more than thirty years, not since he had hidden them away on the night before his wedding. On many occasions he had been tempted to take them out, but he had always resisted. "Well," said Fanis, trying to buy himself some time. He almost felt as if he were protecting Kalypso by keeping her photographs hidden.

"I wondered if I knew her," said Murat. "And I wanted to understand a bit better."

Wasn't that what Fanis had been searching for all these years? Some understanding? Some empathy? Some regret? And here was Murat, offering exactly those. Fanis had an obligation to show him the pictures, however upsetting it might be.

He emptied the sideboard drawer, pulled it out from the slides, and turned it over: to the bottom was taped an envelope that he had wanted his wife never to find. He opened it, removed two photographs, and showed them to Murat. One was a stiff portrait of Kalypso and Fanis, taken in a photography studio after their official engagement. Kalypso wore her hair in a high chignon with a satin headband that Fanis had stolen as soon as the photo session was over. She had scolded him for messing her hair, so he did it again when the lights dimmed in the movie theater to which they went afterwards. How he had loved it when she scolded him.

The other photo was a Polaroid snapshot of a tanned Kalypso sitting on a stone wall beneath the pine trees of Saint George Karypi, with the sea behind her. Fanis had taken it himself on Antigone, just a few weeks before the riots. That night, they had sneaked away from a party and made love for the first time, in a horse barn. He remembered nuzzling her breast, just beneath the collar bone. He remembered her tentative kisses, her chapped lips, their tongues mixed up, the lovely smell of her hair, and his fingers around her neck. He was sure that barns and straw were made only and exactly for moments like that.

Fanis handed the photos to his guest.

"She was beautiful," said Murat. "But I don't remember her. If I may ask, what exactly happened?"

"Suicide," Fanis said. "Dishonored during the pogrom. Jumped from the rooftop two days later."

"How terrible. I can't even imagine how great her shame must have been, to do that . . ."

"I never saw her after the pogrom, you know," said Fanis. "My mother told me to give her some time, let her mother and grandmother take care of her for a while, and then . . ." Fanis choked up. He tried to blink away his tears.

"No need to say more, friend." Murat rubbed Fanis's upper arm and handed him a tissue. "But you ought to keep the photos out. Confrontation is the only way to exorcize ghosts."

Fanis took the pictures from Murat and looked at them again. Perhaps his friend was right. He set them on the table with the photographs of his parents and wife, unsure whether he would be able to bear the sight of them every day, but certain that they could no longer hide in that envelope, taped to the bottom of the drawer.

16

The Vespa and the Maenad

ON MONDAY AFTERNOON, FIFTEEN MINUTES before the end of her Turkish class, Daphne received a text from Kosmas: "Stop by if you have time. Sıraselviler Avenue, next to the German Hospital."

She entered the Lily while the midday call to prayer was sounding from the loudspeaker of the local mosque. Vanilla-scented air, blown by the fan above the door, refreshed her sweaty forehead. Through the half-open door to a back room, she spied a mustachioed old man performing the *namaz* prayers. A few feet away from her, a shy twenty-something employee was quietly manning the cash register. At the opposite counter, a middle-aged fellow with a brush-cut attended to customers and wrapped their orders in white boxes with lavender ribbons. Both the cashier and the server wore black ties and white lab coats, as if the sticky summer weather had no business entering the Lily.

While patiently waiting her turn, Daphne peered into the glass cases full of crescent-shaped cheese pies, golden *batons salés*, French viennoiseries with tempting bits of chocolate peeking through their seams, trays of mille-feuille, and a variety of delicate cakes and tarts decorated, she supposed, by Kosmas himself.

"Can I help you, Madame?" The mustachioed old Turk was standing squarely in front of her, wearing a white paper hat instead of the knit prayer cap in which she had seen him earlier.

"*Allah kabul etsin*," she said, in Turkish. May God accept your prayer.

"Amen," he replied. "How could God refuse the wish of such a beautiful lady?"

Daphne wondered if non-flirtatious Turkish men existed. Her dad had charmed every woman in Little Havana, including their toothless ninety-three-year-old neighbor Josefina and her tattooed lesbian great-granddaughter.

"Is Kosmas here?" Daphne asked.

The old man winked playfully, passed halfway into the kitchen, and called, "Lady wants you."

Through the swinging door, Daphne glimpsed Kosmas whipping something by hand in a wooden bowl. He looked up from his work and said a few words to the old man, who then returned to the shop floor, allowing the door to swing back into place. "He needs a minute to finish up. I'm Mustafa, by the way. Taught him everything he knows. Correction. Everything he knew before he went off to Vienna and became a hotshot."

"He speaks of you fondly."

"None of my kids is interested in pastry-making," said Mustafa. "It's a passion I share only with Kosmas, which makes him like a son to me."

Daphne reached over the counter. "I'm—"

"Daphne." Mustafa shook her hand. "A pleasure to finally meet you. Now go out the door, turn right, and follow the building around to the kitchen entrance."

Kosmas was waiting out back, wearing his white chef's coat with the sleeves rolled up to the elbows. "June's always like this," he said. "Super-busy." He held out a small box with an elaborate gold and lavender bow. "I made you something."

Daphne stepped into the shade beneath the door's awning. "It looks too pretty to open."

"Don't, then. Until you get home."

"What are you making in there?"

"Uncle Mustafa finally found his grandfather's book, but I haven't had time yet to read through the minuscule Ottoman script. So right now I'm experimenting with Uncle Mustafa's help."

"Can I taste?" Daphne reached for the doorknob, wondering what this mystical Ottoman creation would look like. But she didn't have a chance to see anything before Kosmas pulled the door shut.

"Sorry, but I'm as superstitious as a bride about her dress."

"Not even a peek?"

"I've only been trying out different creams, which I'm going to pipe into a regular wedding cake. In any case, the cake is half finished, and I don't let anyone but Uncle Mustafa see my stuff before delivery—"

"Please."

Kosmas sighed. "Not one woman has ever been in the back room. . . . It might be bad luck to start now."

"So it's a sexist thing?"

"Not at all. Just the way it's always been."

"A little taste, then?"

Kosmas brushed Daphne's cheek with cinnamon-scented fingers. "You've already got it. In that box."

She closed her eyes and leaned her head into his hand. It was the first time he had really touched her.

"Can I take you out tomorrow tonight?" he asked. "Nine o'clock?"

She looked into his eyes, then at the endearing scar above his brow. "Perfect," she said.

Later that afternoon, while Aunt Gavriela made tea, Daphne opened the box and found a small, snail-shaped pastry crowned by a single orchid. Her heart fluttered. She had never before seen such an artistic outpouring of love. She carefully lifted Kosmas's creation from the box, cut it down the middle, and gave half to her aunt. The pastry was soft, fresh, and buttery. The creams were smooth and rich. The cardamom, cinnamon, and rose flavors transported Daphne to the Egyptian Bazaar as she imagined it would have been a hundred years before. This was the taste of Ottoman Istanbul.

"Lucky girl," said Gavriela.

"You mean he got it?" said Daphne.

"No. It's not what I remember. But he's trying so hard. *That*'s what makes you a lucky girl."

While finishing a wedding cake, Kosmas thought about where he would take Daphne the following night, whether they should go in a taxi or on his scooter, and how he could bring things to some sort of favorable conclusion before her scheduled departure on Sunday. He wanted to pick her up with his new Vespa, but he wouldn't be able to wear a suit if he took the bike. Then he remembered how much his teenage sweetheart had loved their rides, and how he had felt so much less inhibited as he sped through Istanbul's back streets and boulevards with her arms wrapped around him. So he dressed casually and rode the Vespa Super Sport over to Gavriela's at half past eight on Tuesday evening.

Naphthalene-scented air wafted out of the apartment when Madame Gavriela opened the door. She was wearing an old-lady housedress and flat slippers that took away three inches of what Kosmas remembered as her natural height.

"Kosmaki," she said. "What *are* you wearing?"

He looked down at his suede athletic shoes, his jeans, and the black shirt with double breast pockets that made him look as if he had been working out in the gym. "Is it so terrible?"

"No, not *terrible*." Gavriela picked a piece of lint from his collar, pulled the flap straight, and brushed at something imaginary just above his heart. "But the suit was something else."

"Is Daphne dressed?"

"Not yet."

"Could you tell her to wear pants?"

Gavriela put her fists on her hips. "On a *date*?"

"We're going on the Vespa."

"Where?"

"Madame Kyveli's. In Tatavla."

Gavriela herded Kosmas toward the open living-room door. "Don't stay on your feet. We need to talk."

While making his way between the marble-topped sideboard, the Chippendale chairs, and the shelves covered with handmade lace, artificial flower arrangements, snow globes, plastic butterflies, and ceramic elephants, Kosmas knocked his shin on the coffee-table.

"I'll bring ice," Gavriela whispered, trying not to wake her husband, who was napping in his American-style recliner. Mr. Andonis's snoring stopped, but he didn't open his eyes.

Kosmas sat on the sofa and rubbed the sting in his shin. "Don't worry. It's nothing."

"Sure?" said Gavriela.

Kosmas nodded.

"Listen, then." Gavriela sat beside Kosmas. "It's nice of you to want to take her to my old neighborhood. But on dates, ladies prefer—"

"Leave him alone," said Andonis. "Don't listen to a word she says, son."

"But Tatavla is dangerous," said Gavriela.

"Not really," said Kosmas.

"It's full of transsexual prostitutes, drug dealers, and—"

"*Sus*, woman!" said Andonis.

The recliner's footrest released with a popping noise that startled Kosmas. Andonis struggled to his feet, hobbled down the hall with his hand on his lower back, and rapped on Daphne's door. "Put on a pair of pants, girl. You're going to have an adventure tonight." Returning to the living room, he said to his wife, "Now let's have some tea while the boy and I watch the game."

"Evil hour," murmured Gavriela. She huffed off to the kitchen.

"Women." Andonis winked at Kosmas and made a patting motion in the air, as if to say, 'Don't worry, it's all settled now.'

Kosmas nodded in thanks and tried to make himself comfortable, but he was sinking deeper and deeper into the little cavern between the back of the sofa and the seat. Soon Gavriela returned with the tea. Daphne followed, wearing a broad American smile and a pair of tight-fitting jeans. She leaned on the doorjamb, lifted one foot as if she were practicing yoga, and strapped on a three-inch-heeled silver sandal—significantly sexier than the black pumps she'd worn on the first date. While she buckled, Kosmas noticed something turquoise on her ankle. She must have guessed his foot fetish.

Gavriela set the tea tray on the rust-stained lace of the central coffee-table. "Do you at least have a helmet for her?"

"Don't worry, Madame Gavriela," said Kosmas, threading his way out of the furniture maze. "I'll bring her back safely."

"But you haven't had your tea!"

"Another time."

The Vespa was waiting for them on the sidewalk outside Gavriela's door. Daphne ran her fingers over the front grille slots, the white piping on the leather saddle, and the dark, satiny finish of the delivery compartment at the rear. She imagined her legs straddling Kosmas, the rumble of the motor, Kosmas stopping in some deserted back alley. . . . He handed her an immaculately cleaned and polished vintage helmet and helped fit the chin strap through the buckle. "We're going to Tatavla," he said, as he climbed onto the bike.

"Really? I asked my aunt to take me, but she always says it's ruined and not worth a visit."

"Tatavla isn't as picturesque as Antigone," said Kosmas, "but since it's where your mom grew up, it's at least worth a visit." With both feet on the ground, he rocked the heavy bike backward to gain momentum, then forward to retract the kick stand. They threaded through the tight two-lane traffic of Sıraselviler Avenue, emerged into the madness of Taksim, and whizzed past exhaust-spewing buses, taxis, and trucks. The sudden swerves and a near collision with another motorcycle terrified Daphne, yet left her wanting more. She wrapped her arms all the way around Kosmas, resting her chest against his back. She knew this wasn't the way he usually drove. She'd seen him motor by Neighbor's House on the Vespa two or three times that summer, driving as carefully as if he had a baby on board. Now he was accelerating quickly, braking abruptly, and taking risks.

"How are the pegs with your heels?" he asked, after stopping at a traffic light. He picked up her right foot, adjusted its position on the peg, and playfully spun the charm on her anklet. "Nice."

Daphne had worn that anklet at least a dozen times without Paul's ever having said a word. But nothing escaped Kosmas. "Thanks," she said.

The light changed. They turned off into a neighborhood where laundry lines of ghostlike sheets drooped between rotting oriels. With expert skill Kosmas dodged automobiles, piles of rubbish set out for the nightly collection, formidable gangs of young men, and herds of girls dressed for Carnivale. Was this really the same Kosmas who fulfilled his mother's every wish? The same meticulous chef who had won the Pfeifenberger competition?

They climbed a steep hill and came to a stop before a low, dreary white shack with a corrugated aluminum roof— the restaurant, apparently. Daphne took off the helmet. "That was better than a rollercoaster."

"Glad you enjoyed it." Kosmas carefully chained the Vespa to one of the posts supporting the building's brown awning. Daphne sighed. Although his driving skills indicated that he might have hidden talents, only a conventional type would tuck his scooter in like that. "Ready," he said, taking the helmet from her.

They followed the host into a courtyard where ivy dangled between the branches of whitewashed citrus, mulberry, and black poplar trees. At the oilcloth-covered tables sat a few couples, two large men-only parties, and a pack of gabby ladies. The street view was completely blocked by a red wall, but at the far end of the restaurant, the opening between a wooden sun shelter and waist-high shrubbery allowed a glimpse of ceramic roofs and navy blue sky.

The host indicated a table that was marked as reserved with an empty wine bottle. He pulled a chair over the dull blue and yellow floor tiles, offered it to Daphne, and wished them good digestion. A few seconds later, a waiter set plates of honeydew melon and feta cheese on their table. "To drink?" he asked.

"Water," said Kosmas. He placed the Vespa's helmet on an empty chair beside him.

"No raki?" said the waiter.

"No, thanks. We're not drinking tonight."

When the waiter had gone, Daphne said, "You don't have to do that."

"It's okay. I'm afraid it might throw me off course later on." Kosmas paused and flashed Daphne a playful smile. "I'm driving the Vespa, remember?"

She rested her chin on her hands and wobbled her head mischievously. "Just how far off course can one go with a Vespa?"

Kosmas, who seemed surprised that she had both caught his wordplay and matched it, remained silent. Daphne let him savor the momentary awkwardness before she asked, "So what's this place called?"

"Madame Kyveli's."

The name sounded like something straight out of her mother's stories. "I think my dad used to bring Mom here. He'd request a special song, something like . . ." Daphne shut her eyes and breathed in the faint scent of musty wood, but she couldn't recall the title of the song her father used to sing.

"What about the tune?" said Kosmas.

She closed her eyes again and hummed, but only a few words came. She sang out loud: "*Dance ... fairytales ...*" She felt his hand on hers. *Finally.* She opened her eyes and turned her palm to meet his. It was softer than she had expected, given his profession. Holding it both excited her and gave her a feeling of security, as if nothing could go wrong while he was nearby. If only she could hold on forever. . . .

"I know which one you mean," he said.

The host leaned the meze tray against their table. The portions were bigger than they had been at the first restaurant, and they included something that looked like—and was soon confirmed to be—calf brain. After naming each plate, the waiter looked to Kosmas.

"It's the lady's choice tonight."

"But you know the restaurant," said Daphne.

Kosmas squeezed her hand and let go. "When men decide, you eat to bursting."

"And when women decide, you go hungry," said Daphne.

"Let's decide together, then."

They chose stuffed grape leaves, salted mackerel, fried eggplant mixed with garlic and yogurt, and broad beans in a tomato, carrot, and celery-leaf sauce. The waiter took their selections directly from the tray and set them on the table. Unlike the Balık Pazarı restaurant, the meze at Madame Kyveli's was not plastic-wrap-covered samples, but ready-to-go appetizers.

"And a plate of *muska* cheese pies," said Kosmas.

The waiter nodded and left them.

Kosmas served Daphne a heaping portion of broad beans. "Try this first. It's the house specialty. I hope you like fried cheese pies? The triangular ones?"

"Anything fried is good with me."

"They're called *muska* because they resemble the Muslim prayer amulets of the same name."

Daphne smiled at Kosmas. "I'm crazy about cultural details like that."

Kosmas's cheeks dimpled. "Eat so that you'll grow up strong!"

The beans were soft but not mushy. The tomato-and-onion sauce was lightly seasoned with fresh garlic, clove, and celery. "Just like my mom's," said Daphne.

"Home-cooked food without the mothers," said Kosmas. "That's why I like it here."

"So . . . your mother gets on your nerves sometimes?"

"*Gets on my nerves?* Busts my balls is more like it."

Daphne giggled. This was a new side of Kosmas. "Speaking of your mom," she said, "I ran into Mr. Dimitris in the street today."

Kosmas took a sip of water. "What did he have to say?"

The time had come. Just as Daphne had suspected, Dimitris did indeed remember Ilyas Badem. As they walked in the Grand Avenue, the old journalist had promised that the secret was safe with him. But that, in fact, was the problem: Daphne didn't want to keep any secrets.

"He said you helped him change a few light bulbs yesterday," she said.

Kosmas cleared his throat loudly, as if trying to suppress a cough.

"Are you okay?" she asked.

"Fine, fine. Something went down the wrong way."

A group of musicians filed in, sat down beneath the ivy tendrils swaying in the evening breeze, and began tuning their instruments.

"Mr. Dimitris also said he never forgets a name." Daphne scanned Kosmas's face. He had stopped chewing. His jaw was clenched and his torso was stiff, as if he were wearing a corset. She said, "He remembered my father. Did he talk to you about that?"

"I don't know. It's a bit of a blur."

"What is?"

Kosmas wiped his mouth. "Mr. Dimitris asked permission to marry my mother."

"How romantic! I thought something was going on with those two. They're always smiling at each other."

The musicians began playing "Reverberating Melodies," a lively Zeki Müren song that always made Daphne's father weep. Kosmas stabbed one of the *muska* pies just delivered by the waiter. "The problem," he said, "is that my mother has no intention of getting married."

"She said so?"

"No, but I know her."

"How would *you* feel about her remarrying?"

"Mr. Dimitris is part of the family." Kosmas chased a slippery broad bean with his fork. "But I think it would be uncomfortable if he were actually living with us. And it would be strange to see someone in my father's place."

"They couldn't move into his apartment?"

"You'd need a bulldozer to clean it out. My mother would faint if she saw it. That's probably why he doesn't invite her."

"You've never had a place of your own?"

"Only in Vienna."

"It might be good for you, too, if your mother got married. It's about time you weaned, don't you think?"

"I'm there for *her*. Not for *me*."

"Typical Mediterranean son."

"Typical Freudian bullshit," said Kosmas, with an impish smirk. He swirled the water in his glass, staring at it as if he wished it were something else. "I guess I couldn't ask a woman to consider moving in with us. Living with a mother-in-law is awful, isn't it?"

Daphne put down her fork and turned her attention to the musicians. "Hell would probably be a better word for it."

*

Kosmas raised his hand to a passing waiter. "A grilled sea bass, please!" He couldn't believe that Daphne would say such a thing about his mother. *Hell?* He was offended. Rea wasn't perfect, but she wasn't a demon.

By that time the musicians had stirred up the restaurant. A couple of male customers were singing along. A tipsy party of women were seductively turning their wrists to the melody. At a break between songs, Kosmas put a bill into the *baǧlama* player's pocket and asked for "Bournovalia," the optimistic Smyrniot dancing song that he'd recognized instantly when Daphne had sung a few words. As soon as the rocking rhythm began, she said, "That's it! The one my father used to request for my mother."

With the satisfaction of a knight who had managed to ride his horse a few meters closer to the castle, Kosmas said, "It's always been one of my favorites."

She coquettishly pushed one shoulder forward. "Mom danced it for Baba. On their twentieth wedding anniversary. I never saw him so happy."

Daphne looked toward the musicians. Kosmas noticed the violinist glancing furtively at her. The *baǧlama* player was practically drooling. The accordion player was transfixed by her breasts. The guitarist-singer had turned his back to Kosmas, as if he didn't even exist. It was just like the words of the song: a thousand eyes were piercing her.

Suddenly Daphne stood and drew the backs of her hands along her chin and into her hair, raising it so that he could see her neck. Was she actually going to dance, here, in front of everyone? She moved to an open area between the tables. Her torso undulated to the 2/4 rhythm. She looked neither at the musicians, nor at the other customers: her eyes were fixed directly on Kosmas. There was no vulgarity in her *tsifteteli*, as there was in the tremors and jolts of professional belly dancers. Yet Daphne was certainly not an amateur. Her fingers separated like the plumes of exotic birds, flitted around her torso, and nested in her long hair. Her chest and abdomen slithered and snaked. This was the real thing: refined, sensual *tsifteteli*. The other customers watched, but not one woman dared get up and dance beside Daphne.

At the end of the song, the musicians applauded Daphne's accompaniment and reluctantly moved on to another table. One of the drunk ladies cheered, "Lucky man!" That was when Kosmas realized that his erection might be visible. He quickly moved his legs back under the table and squeezed his knees together. With a woman who could dance *tsifteteli* like that, he would never have any need for prescription stimulants, not even at ninety.

"I'm rusty," said Daphne. "It's been four years since I danced *tsifteteli*, since before I met Paul."

"You didn't dance for him?"

"Once, for about ten seconds in his living room, and then he waved for me to stop. I think he found it embarrassing."

"You're an easterner, Daphne, one of ours. Frankish men aren't for you." Kosmas served her a helping of eggplant and yogurt. "By the way, what's your father's name? My mother wondered if she knew him."

Daphne wiped the corners of her mouth with her napkin. "Badem."

How could her father have a Turkish name? Then Kosmas remembered how often Rum names were misspelled, mangled, or outright changed by the registry office employees. "What was it before?" he asked.

"They didn't have one before. They chose it in the twenties, when everyone was required to take a surname."

"But the Rums already had family names."

Daphne flagged the waiter. "A single raki, please!"

Something had gone wrong. The drunk-on-love expression that Daphne had worn while dancing had disappeared. "I thought you didn't drink," said Kosmas.

"I don't." Daphne conjured an uneasy smile. "Half an hour ago, you passed on the raki in order to stay on course. Now a bit of deviation is necessary."

The word *deviation* titillated Kosmas, but something told him that this would not be the kind he liked. He asked, "Are you okay?"

The waiter delivered a small ice bucket and a tall glass with two inches of clear alcohol at the bottom. Daphne dropped two ice cubes into the glass and said, "Drink so you'll grow up strong." As soon as he'd taken a sip, she opened her purse, took out her student card, and slid it across the oilcloth.

Kosmas read her full name on the card: Daphne Zeynep Badem. "What's this? Why the Islamic middle name Zeynep?"

"My father is Ottoman," said Daphne, replacing the student card in her wallet.

Kosmas froze. He'd fallen for Daphne believing she was one of his own. Now he wasn't sure what she was. She didn't drink. Her middle name was Zeynep. Her surname was Turkish. She liked the call to prayer. Kosmas swallowed half of the straight raki. Feeling short of breath, he raised his hand to loosen his collar, only to find that the top of his shirt was already open. He unfastened a button and slid his hand over his quickly beating heart. "Under Turkish law," he said, "you're Muslim."

The space between Daphne's black brows narrowed. "I think *I'm* the one who decides that," she said.

"And the name Zeynep?"

"It was my grandmother's."

"I also noticed that . . ."

"*What?*"

"You take your shoes off in the house."

Her mouth pursed like a wrinkly apple. "I don't like dirt."

"And the alcohol? And the pork?"

"*What pork?* I don't eat meat. And why do you care so much about my father's religion, anyway?"

"I didn't mean to be rude, it's just that . . . if you get involved with somebody, you get involved with the parents as well."

"If I'd thought about it that way . . ."

"Why didn't you tell me sooner?"

"This is ridiculous," she said, tossing her napkin onto the table.

Kosmas took a sip of water and pushed his chair back. "Excuse me for a second. I have to check on the Vespa."

He crossed the courtyard in two large strides, stopped in the entryway, and rubbed his eyes. Come on, he said to himself. Mother will get over the Ottoman-father thing, won't she? It might take years, decades even, but in the end she'll get over it. Then again, she's seventy-two. She doesn't have decades. Maybe it will even kill her. And maybe she's right in the end. Daphne deceived us both. Who knows what else she could be hiding?

Kosmas opened his eyes. What was his destiny? To marry Daphne and have his mother fall over dead before the wedding? To reject Daphne and regret it for the rest of his life? To end up like Mr. Dimitris, alone in a rat hole? Kosmas leaned against a wall. It's all right, he said to himself. Daphne's leaving on Sunday. We'll just have this little fling. Enjoy ourselves a bit. We don't have to get married or even get serious. There isn't time for that anyway. And if she ever returns . . . we'll think about it then. He went outside for some fresh air. There was the Vespa, still chained to the overhang post. And Daphne was still inside, waiting for him, if he could just get control of himself.

Kosmas returned to the courtyard. The musicians were already on the other side of the restaurant, serenading someone else. Daphne's eyes were glassy. He crouched at her feet and took her hand. "I've been a beast, upsetting you like that," he said. "I'm so sorry. I don't care that your father's Ottoman. So is Uncle Mustafa, and he's been like a father to me since mine died."

"And your mother?"

"Let me handle that."

"You don't look so sure."

"It won't be a problem. I'm really sorry."

"It's partly my fault, I guess," said Daphne. "I should have told you from the start. I wanted to, but it just seemed awkward."

So she hadn't meant to deceive him. He rose to standing. Half the restaurant was staring at him. The drunk women applauded. He bowed, took his chair, and said, "How about I take you to the Lily for dessert?"

The pâtisserie kitchen was more stylish than Daphne had expected: it had old-fashioned cement tile flooring, yellow cabinetry, ceramic brick backsplashes, and baroque molding framing a daring black ceiling.

"It's the only place where I really feel at home," said Kosmas, cracking a high window. "We redid the kitchen just a few months ago. Uncle Mustafa gave me carte blanche." He scrubbed his hands, lit the oven, donned his double-breasted chef coat, and rolled up his sleeves. "What will it be?"

"Something from Vienna."

"Apple strudel?"

She nodded.

Like a soldier under orders, he piled ingredients onto the central steel table: flour, apples, butter, sugar, lemons, oil, cinnamon, rum, breadcrumbs, an egg, and finally raisins. Daphne sat on a high stool and watched while he combined the dough ingredients by hand, transferred the ball to the floured countertop, and worked it with firm, rhythmic movements. He roasted the breadcrumbs in butter, cored and sliced the apples with speed and precision, and mixed them with lemon juice, a shot of rum, and a few spoonfuls of sugar and cinnamon. An hour before, Daphne hadn't been sure if she wanted the relationship to go any further. But watching him now, she couldn't help thinking that he was rather dexterous.

He floured a tea towel, opened the dough with a rolling pin, picked it up, and stretched it over his fists. When the circle had reached a transparent, leaf-like thinness, he transferred it to the tea towel, trimmed the rough edges with scissors, and spread the apple mixture on top. After folding a pastry edge over the filling with the care of a father covering his sleeping infant, Kosmas lifted the tea towel, causing the pastry to roll. For a second Daphne wondered if he would care for his children—perhaps *their* children—with similar tenderness. Then she reminded herself that this was the same guy who had just flipped out about her father's religion.

Slow down, she said silently.

Kosmas buttered the seam, twisted, cut, and tucked the ends. Finally he transferred his creation, still swaddled in its tea-towel hammock, to a baking sheet and set it in the oven. Selin was right. Kosmas knew what he was doing in the kitchen.

"May I?" said Daphne. She amassed the trimmings into a ball and began rolling out the dough, just as their neighbor Josefina had always done with leftover bits. Kosmas leaned against the refrigerator, crossed his arms over his chest, and fixed his gaze on . . . her breasts? Or her dough rolling? She asked, "What are you looking at?"

"You'll blush like the apples if I tell you."

Daphne leaned even further. Kosmas's gaze deepened, leaving no doubt. She sprinkled the dough with cinnamon and sugar, rolled it, cut it into slices, and said, "That's what our Cuban neighbor used to make with the scraps."

Kosmas transferred each pinwheel from the counter to a buttered baking tray, which he placed in the oven, on the shelf above the strudel. Then he slipped behind Daphne and turned off the industrial fluorescent lights, leaving the kitchen dark except for the warm orange glow of the oven. A moment later Daphne felt his hands on her hips. They caressed her lightly, almost imperceptibly, slowly rose over her back to her shoulders and neck, and finally descended to her breasts. She turned within his embrace. He entwined his hands in her hair, kissed her, and bit her bottom lip. She took a deep breath of the sweet apple-and-cinnamon steam as he pulled her blouse over her head. He lifted her onto the steel counter, beside the hot oven, and stood back to observe her. His eyes traveled over her bare chest. It was more arousing even than touch, as if he was already making love to her in his mind. He kissed her on the mouth, inhaled the scent of her neck, and kissed her mouth again. She wrapped her legs around him, locked her ankles behind his waist, and pulled him toward her.

17

The Song of the Siren

ON WEDNESDAY EVENING, FANIS OPENED a window to let the place air while he was at tea. Just as he was about to draw the sheer curtain, however, he heard a great tumbling of plastic. He looked across the way to the garret. So far the new tenant had kept well hidden behind half-closed shutters, but now there she was, bustling about the apartment with her hair tied up in a red bandana like a West African queen. She was shouting all sorts of profanities in a language that seemed familiar, but which Fanis could not make out.

Could it be?

Fanis remembered Selin's card. He had not yet called because he always allowed at least seven days to pass between receiving a phone number and using it. How many days had it been? Four? Five? Six at most. She would undoubtedly think he was hungry if he called her now, and a woman must never think that. And then there was the distasteful possibility that she only liked him in a daughterly way. But what if it *was* her? And what if he missed the opportunity to help her settle in? Fanis decided to make a small exception to the rules of the chase. He would call. She didn't have his number, anyway. If he heard a mobile phone ringing across the way, or if he suddenly saw the new neighbor search for something, he would stay on the line. If not, he would hang up and try again on Thursday.

He settled into the street-facing armchair in the oriel, dialed, and waited. He heard the ringing on his end, but not on hers. Steady, he told himself. The connection might take a few seconds. And then, suddenly, faintly, but surely: a custom ringtone that was devilishly familiar—*Witchcraft*.

The beauty grabbed her phone. "*Allo?*"

Fanis said in Turkish, "Selin, my princess, why didn't you tell me we were going to be neighbors?"

"Who is this?"

"Look across the way."

Selin stuck her red-kerchiefed head into the sunlight. "Fanis?"

The informal use of his name—without the respectful "Mr."—thrilled him. "What would you say if I brought over a snack?" he said.

"It's a mess here right now, so I'd rather—"

"Perfect. I'll be over in an hour."

While brushing his teeth, Fanis thought about his telephone conversation with Gavriela earlier that afternoon. In colorful Istanbul–Greek idiom, Gavriela had conjectured that, on their date the previous night, Kosmas and Daphne had finally *eaten it*. "Good digestion, then," Fanis had replied, hardly able to conceal his jealousy. After hanging up, he had devoured an entire box of bitter almond cookies as a consolation. But now, as he rinsed his mouth with saltwater and anticipated spending time with Selin, he was significantly less bothered by the defeat.

Once outside, Fanis took a deep breath of Istanbul's polluted air and skipped off to the meatball shop, where he ordered two portions of meatballs and potatoes, and a tomato salad with plenty of parsley and absolutely no onion. He took his time climbing Selin's stairs, for he wanted to be neither out of breath nor sweating when he knocked on her door. Selin opened in a short, strappy yellow dress, without the kerchief, and with her hair doing its crazy dance in the air current.

Fanis had always enjoyed the range of expression allowed by a simple cheek kiss. There was the air kiss, which was nothing more than a chicken-like motion of the neck; there was the perfunctory cheek tap for people you semi-liked; the full cheek press for your good friends, beloved family members, and people you hadn't seen in a long time; and finally the true kiss with lips planted firmly on both cheeks. When Selin performed the last—and when Fanis simultaneously understood that her seductive perfume of almond-tree blossom, vanilla, and jasmine had been recently applied—he suddenly felt so lightheaded that he had to lean against the doorjamb for support.

Selin welcomed him inside. "Excuse the mess."

"Shall we eat while it's warm?" said Fanis, pretending not to notice the pile of scattered CD cases at the foot of a red art-deco armchair.

"Absolutely. But I'll have to move some stuff."

She was about to pick up the large box on the dining table when he said, "Don't, my soul. Let me get it." He sucked in his abs, took a deep breath, and made a tremendous effort not to show any sign of strain while transferring the box to a coffee table made from a piece of polished driftwood. He made a show of protest when Selin followed with the second box, but inwardly he thanked her for sparing him another show of prowess.

"Let me clean up the table," said Selin, bustling off to the bathroom. "I'm so sorry, but I can't find any of my hand-embroidered tablecloths, and I have such a nice collection . . ."

She was in a flutter over his arrival. Just a few weeks ago, her demeanor might have made him feel smug about his ability to seduce women. But now that Daphne had shown a preference for Kosmas, Fanis was feeling insecure.

Selin returned with a wet cloth and began wiping down the table. As she did so, her dress rose over the backs of her tanned thighs. Fanis lost his appetite for food. He tried to distract himself by looking at the pile of spilled CDs, but there, on top of various violin albums, was *Songs for Swingin' Lovers!* He picked up the CD case. "My dear," he said, "I heard the ringtone, but I thought it was a fluke. Are you truly a fan of the great Voice?"

"Of course." Selin switched on the player and put in the CD. Fanis recognized his moment. He pulled out Selin's chair, wished her good digestion, and, standing in the center of the living room, gave her a dinnertime serenade. He clapped his hands to the opening notes of the first track, just like he'd seen Frankie do in a televised concert, and then, playfully bouncing his shoulders, he sang "You Make Me Feel So Young."

A schoolgirl smile overcame Selin's house-moving fatigue and puckered her cheeks with dimples. She was so amused that she snapped her fingers to the beat. At a break between stanzas, Fanis had to scold her, "Eat! Eat!"

"Your voice is incredible," she said, when the song had finished. "It's as if Frankie's come to visit."

"You're kind." Fanis bit into a fried potato. "But it's not difficult to sing well when one has inspiration."

Selin flushed red. "Thanks for bringing dinner. I haven't properly cleaned the kitchen yet, and—"

"Do you have an apron?"

"What for?"

"I'm going to tackle that kitchen while you eat, dear. I'm as *titiz* as any old Rum housewife. I disinfect everything."

"You can't be serious."

Fanis stood, took off his navy linen jacket and watch, and rolled up the sleeves of his favorite sky-blue shirt. "Perfectly serious."

"I can't let you do it."

"You eat and have a little nap," said Fanis. "I'll do the kitchen, and then we'll finish the rest of the house together."

"You're an angel," she said.

The word was balm. He felt his cleaning wings sprouting already. He resisted the temptation to kiss her and slipped away. While she ate and rested, he scrubbed the little kitchen so thoroughly that even his obsessive-compulsive mother would have approved. By the time Selin woke from the long nap that she had insisted she would not take, Fanis had washed and put away all the dishes and pans that he'd found in the kitchen boxes. Hearing Selin stirring, he lit a burner, roasted a cup of Mehmet Efendi coffee, and, still wearing a pink apron over his off-white linen pants, served it to her on the modernist driftwood coffee-table.

"I've never met anyone like you, Fanis," she said. "You sing, you clean, you make coffee."

"I also cook," he proudly announced. "I make a mean chickpea pilaf."

Selin rubbed her eyes like a child, unwittingly causing her mascara to flake. "All day I was wondering how I was going to have the strength to perform Friday night. But after that little rest, and with all your help, life seems manageable again. How can I thank you?"

Fanis sat on the sofa beside her. "Since the day we met, I've been waiting for you to invite me to a concert."

"Friday, then, at Lütfi Kırdar. There will be a ticket for you at the box office. But that's hardly enough to repay you for all you've done."

"Maybe you're right. How about a backstage visit as well, after the performance?"

"It would be my pleasure."

"Go inspect the kitchen, then, and I'll tackle that pile of CDs. I'm dying to see what you've got."

Fanis spent the rest of the evening—as well as the following day—serving as Selin's special helper. He sorted CDs, cleaned the bathroom extractor fan, drilled holes in the wall for hooks, ironed and hung curtains, brought breakfast, fixed the almost-broken hinges on the bedroom cupboards, and unplugged the bathroom sink with a plumbing snake. By Thursday evening, he was as exhausted as a corpse and had to take two aspirins for his aching head and put himself to bed at nine o'clock, but Selin was well worth the trouble. On

Friday morning, he took his old tuxedo out of the closet and was surprised to find that it still fit him. He knew he would be overdressed, but he also knew that Selin would be in an evening gown, and he wanted to be worthy of her, even if it was only from afar.

Fanis had planned on arriving at Lütfi Kırdar early but, as he walked up Sıraselviler Avenue, he realized that he ought to buy a bouquet. So he took a shortcut down Meşelik Street, past the headquarters of the stately neoclassical building that housed the Constantinopolitan Society of Cantors, of which he was a proud member. He hurried on, but when he came to the student entrance of the Zappeion Lycée, he paused and gazed for a moment at the blackened stone gate. That was where Kalypso had gone to school. The Zappeion's pupils were now so few that a separate student entrance was considered superfluous. The door was locked and chained. Such a shame. Fanis remembered how Kalypso would come sauntering through that gate at the end of the school day. He remembered how, after their engagement, he would often bring her a single flower: a rose, a lilac branch, a sprig of orange blossom, which she'd stick under her headband or in her ponytail. Once, during their walk home, she had pulled him into an alley and kissed him passionately. He'd given her daisies that day. They had caused him to sneeze as they kissed. So embarrassing.

And then, just as quickly as he had slipped into his reverie, he pulled himself out. He didn't want to be late for the performance. He hurried past Holy Trinity Church, hung a right into Taksim Square, and headed toward the tents of the gypsy women who sold flowers by the Ottoman-era reservoir. When he finally settled on unconventional orange snapdragons, the fat gypsy in saggy *shalwar* pants tried to charge him fifteen liras for the flowers and an extra two for gift wrapping.

"Is that the tuxedo price?" Fanis snapped. "Or perhaps you've forgotten that your neighbors sell exactly the same flowers you do."

The next gypsy, having noted the failure of the first, said twelve liras. The last, a pretty young lady with a baby strapped to her chest, asked for ten. Fanis nodded. As he scurried away with the bouquet, the pretty gypsy called out, "Hope Grandma likes them!" Fanis made a mental note never to buy anything from her ever again.

While waiting at the bus stop at the foot of Gezi Park, he glanced at his watch. He'd still make the performance, but there wouldn't be time to use the men's room. He concentrated on his bladder for a moment. Nothing there. That was a relief. Ten long minutes later, the bus arrived, and Fanis stepped up for his daily dose of humiliation. As soon as he swiped his retiree bus pass, an automated male voice said over the loudspeaker, "We thank you for giving priority to our elderly and handicapped passengers." A young fellow—whose tight nipples were vulgarly showing through his thin T-shirt—immediately offered his seat. Fanis turned up his nose, proceeded to the middle doors, and remained standing to prove that he was not in the least bit elderly.

He arrived at Lütfi Kırdar just a few minutes before the start of the performance, collected his ticket, and made his way through the shiny granite entry hall.

"Your seat number, sir?" said an usher.

"I have no idea," said Fanis. "It was a gift."

The young man took his ticket and winked. "Somebody loves you then, Uncle. Follow me."

The usher escorted Fanis to a center seat in the front row. What a treat, he thought, although he would probably come out with a stiff neck. He simpered at the middle-aged couple next to him and ignored their top-to-toe scan of his tuxedo. He had only a minute to glance at the program before the lights dimmed: the first piece was to be Mendelssohn's Violin Concerto in E minor. He strained to catch a glimpse of Selin as the string players filed in. Alas, in the front row, all that one could really hope to see was the conductor's ass.

Just when Fanis had given up hope, Selin entered, wearing a flowing white gown instead of the black worn by the other female musicians. She stood—rather than sat—to the left of the conductor.

There was no orchestral introduction. There was only Selin, jumping straight into a virtuosic passage with a discreet accompaniment from her peers. Half of her black curls were pinned to the crown of her head; the rest bounced and snapped with every movement. During a brief orchestral section, she let her violin and bow float down to her sides while she stared up at the ceiling, as if making some sort of tortured supplication to the gods. Then the piece became more playful, more tentative, and Fanis wondered if she was trying to tease him. Fireworks seemed to spring from the violin, and for a second Selin raised her head like a warrior. Fanis lost himself in the relentless exchange between light-hearted passages and savage intensity, and he realized, as Selin performed the finale, that he had hardly known anything about her until that evening. Selin Kerido was not just any line violinist, but a highly talented soloist. Fanis felt a swell of pride before a strong undercurrent of self-doubt nearly drowned him: she had to have dozens of admirers, which meant that she was even less attainable than he had thought.

After the concert, Fanis waited for her at the stage door with the bouquet of orange snapdragons. When she came to meet him, he said, "Mendelssohn's Violin Concerto in E minor has just become my favorite piece of Romantic period music. You were majestic."

She kissed him on the cheek, complimented his tuxedo and his original choice of flowers, and led him into the wings. There she introduced Fanis to a tall, fifty-something bassoonist with a full head of salt-and-pepper hair. "Fanis," she said, "I'd like you to meet my dear friend Orhan."

Dear? Was *this* the guy who was giving her the hickeys?

The bassoonist, who had obviously not heard Selin well, said, "Pleased to meet you, sir. I absolutely adore your daughter."

Selin cleared her voice. "He's not my dad—"

"Oh, *Uncle*, excuse me," said Orhan. "My ears are still ringing from the concert!"

Orhan patted Fanis on the back, held an imaginary phone to his ear—whatever *that* meant—sent Selin an air kiss, and rushed off. Other introductions followed. Like Orhan, the rest of Selin's colleagues treated Fanis like a harmless old man, who could never aspire to possessing such a goddess. But he was proud just to be called a friend.

"Come," said Selin to Fanis, at a pause in the tide of musicians. "I want to show you something."

She led him onto the empty stage. The lights were still so bright and blinding that the seating areas of the theater disappeared into semi-darkness. Fanis had the impression, even though the place was probably still a quarter full, that he and Selin were alone.

She took him to the left side of the stage. "That's my regular chair," she said. "Yours for now."

"Concertmaster?"

Selin gave one short, downward nod. "A guest soloist usually does the concertos, but I got a lucky break when the scheduled soloist cancelled."

"I love a successful woman." Fanis loosened his collar and dabbed his forehead with a handkerchief. Those damn lights were hot. Or was it the cerebral arteriosclerosis that was causing him to sweat?

"Now tell me all about that piece you just played," he said.

"Only you would say that," said Selin, her face illuminating from within. First she spoke of the piece's cyclic form and the various plagiaries that ensued after its success. Then she lightly tapped his knee and said, "But I'm getting ahead of myself. Well before he began to compose, Mendelssohn wrote that a violin concerto was running through his head and that the beginning of it 'gave him no peace.'"

"Sounds like vascular dementia," said Fanis.

"Excuse me?"

How could he have let that slip?

"A bad joke," he said. "A friend of mine has the disease. What I meant was that the concerto overwhelms, almost like an illness. I was completely absorbed while you were playing, but in an interior way, like I was traveling inside myself."

Fanis snuck a peek at the hickey on Selin's neck. It was as prominent as ever, perhaps even a little redder. Surely the bassoonist was the perpetrator. Annoyed, he said, "You must be exhausted. Let's get you home."

They took a taxi back to their neighborhood. When they finally pulled into Faik Paşa Street, Fanis stuffed a bill into the driver's hand and trotted around to Selin's side to open the door. Seeing the embarrassed expression on her face, he offered his hand in a brotherly manner and said—*before* she had a chance to tell him that she would invite him up if it weren't for such-and-such—"Goodnight, dear girl. You were marvelous this evening."

He rushed inside his building without a backward glance, leaned breathless against the painting of the goddess Athena, and said to Hermes, "You see? I finally have an attractive female friend. Not that I'd say no to her becoming more but . . . friendship is a big step for me. I hope you're proud."

18

Recognitions and a Tower

JUST BEFORE DAWN ON WEDNESDAY morning, Kosmas delivered his beloved and her package of apple strudel to Gavriela's door. After looking up and down the street to make sure that no one was watching, Kosmas backed Daphne against the building wall, grabbed her bottom, and lifted her to his height. He caressed her lips with his, nibbled her, and pulled her tongue into his mouth. It was almost as if they were making love again. But he knew he couldn't keep her there for long. Indiscreet eyes were numerous, and even if they couldn't cause a scandal in a secular neighborhood like Cihangir, gossip was never pleasant.

"I've got to go," said Daphne. "If my aunt's neighbors see . . ."

"Tomorrow night?"

She nodded yes and pulled away.

Kosmas returned to the Lily, where he found Uncle Mustafa sweeping white buttons and other debris from the kitchen floor. Not once in his life had Kosmas left the kitchen in disorder. He started to apologize, but Uncle Mustafa patted his shoulder and said, "All my life I dreamed of getting Madame Bahar onto this countertop. You know, the one who comes for strawberry tart on Saturdays. Now I'd break my back if I tried. I'm glad somebody finally put this kitchen to good use."

"I might be falling in love," said Kosmas.

"Are congratulations in order?"

Kosmas hesitated. "Not yet."

"Let me guess." Uncle Mustafa leaned the broom against the counter and poured their morning tea into tulip glasses. "Rea can't stand Daphne."

"It's more complicated than that. I'm ashamed to admit it . . ."

"Take the fava bean out of your mouth, son."

"Her father's Muslim. You know my mother's not prejudiced, but if things got serious with Daphne, it would be a problem."

"Of course," said Uncle Mustafa. "And if it weren't that, it would be that Daphne's feet were too big or too small, or her hair too blond or too black."

Kosmas stared at Uncle Mustafa: his expression was blank, as if he were discussing a supply order. But he had to be joking. Rea wasn't *that* bad.

"The problem isn't Mom," said Kosmas. "Daphne's got a fiancé in America, and she's leaving on Sunday. So this is probably a temporary summer thing."

Uncle Mustafa took a sip of tea. "Either that," he said, "or you'd better get to work."

"Meaning?"

"I mean that maybe you shouldn't let this chance slip by."

"The thing is . . . I always thought I'd marry a Rum, to keep our community and traditions alive."

"That's understandable, son. Anyway, it's not always easy for a Muslim girl to marry a Christian boy. Just because it's legally possible doesn't mean that getting her family to accept you will be easy."

"She's Christian. Or at least so she says."

"I see." Uncle Mustafa switched into Greek, which he spoke reasonably well when he wanted to: "*To vrikes, to thes kai ksyrismeno.*" You've finally found a pussy and now you want it shaved.

"Excuse me?"

Uncle Mustafa reverted to Turkish: "Your father's favorite saying. You got what you wanted, but now it's not perfect enough."

Kosmas was speechless. Such hard talk wasn't like subtle Uncle Mustafa. And Kosmas had certainly never heard his father say *that*.

"Anyway"—Uncle Mustafa glanced at the apron still lying on the floor—"you'd better tie ribbons to the back door. In case I come to work early."

"Good idea," said Kosmas.

On Saturday morning, after yet another night of lovemaking at the Lily, Daphne snatched a few hours of sleep and awoke to the characteristic message alert of her Turkish cell phone. It had to be from Kosmas. Not yet ready to open her eyes, she pressed her face into the starched pillow and thought about the past three nights. On Wednesday, Kosmas had taken her on a Vespa ride to Rumelifeneri, a village on the shores of the Bosporus and the Black Sea; they had picnicked on fresh tomatoes, goat cheese, boiled eggs, and olives in the arch of a Byzantine castle while waves rushed against the rocks beneath them. On Thursday evening, they had gone for coffee at a chic café in Teşvikiye and lounged on couches while drinking latte macchiato, talking about their childhoods, and admiring the rose bushes surrounding the illuminated mosque. On Friday, they had gone to a *rembetiko* club, which led to Daphne's second *tsifteteli* performance. The scene that had followed at the Lily was the reason she was having such a hard time getting out of bed now.

She reached over to the nightstand, grabbed her phone, and rubbed the sleepies out of her eyes. The message, however, was not from Kosmas. It was from Lidia, an Argentine friend in Miami. "*Mira tu email, nena.*" Check your email, girl.

Daphne pushed herself to a sitting position, slid her feet into her flip-flops, and stumbled into the kitchen, where her aunt was already busy peeling potatoes. "Coffee," she said.

"Not yet," said Gavriela. "You've been out with him until four a.m. every night since Tuesday. I want to know: is he that good?"

Daphne scrunched both eyes shut for a second and smiled.

Gavriela paused mid-peel and grinned mischievously. "Who'd have guessed?"

"I'm thinking about breaking up with Paul. I can't keep cheating on him like this. I feel guilty."

"Paul's been cheating on you for months, little mama, if not years."

"I don't know if that's true. He dances with other women, and he's told a few lies, but I doubt he's actually *slept* with any of them."

Gavriela raised her eyebrows and resumed her potato peeling. "You know best."

Daphne cut a piece from the *tsoureki* bread Kosmas had baked on Wednesday. "I'm going to break up with him as soon as I get back."

"Better late than never," said Gavriela.

Daphne kissed her aunt's cheek. "I'd do it now, but telephone breakups are insensitive."

Back in her room, Daphne sat down at her little desk. While waiting for her laptop to start up, she took a bite of *tsoureki*: in its perfumy mastic and *mahleb* flavors hid memories of a midnight picnic—and endless kisses—at Rumelifeneri. Daphne had never expected that a mama's-boy pâtissier would kiss so well.

She found Lidia's email with the title *Lo siento mucho*: "Nena, forgive me for being the bearer of bad news, but you always said you'd want to know. Paul was with Luciana at La Rosa Negra last night, snuggling in a corner. Cristina says they're sleeping together. I'm so sorry. That tramp isn't worth the heels of your shoes."

Daphne pulled up Luciana's public Facebook page, which identified her as an actress-model-dancer-singer-songwriter. At the very top of the timeline were two photos of Luciana and Paul in a close embrace, as well as a video of them dancing together. She clicked through to Luciana's website and skimmed the online CV. The first professional qualification was Luciana's bust size: 42. The second was her waist: 25. The third her hips: 38. It seemed that she was the Dolly Parton of tango. Daphne then scrolled through the photos of Luciana's modeling days, over ten years before: there were topless shots, bare rear shots, open-mouthed come-hither poses. What kind of woman put photos like that on the internet, published her cell-phone number to the world, and listed her measurements as if they were diplomas?

The initial adrenaline rush and shock had blocked Daphne's emotions, but now tears of wounded pride slithered down her cheeks. Her relationship with Paul was a lie. She was just a cover, the good girl he presented at work and to parents while escorts and prostitutes fulfilled his real desires. Aunt Gavriela had been right.

"Here's your coffee, little mama," said Gavriela, startling Daphne. Her aunt had entered silently and now stood behind her, staring at the photos of Luciana. "Now there's an artiste if I ever saw one."

"Paul's new girlfriend."

Gavriela hissed like a snake. "I hope you told him to eat shit?"

Daphne picked up her cell phone. "Right now."

"That's my girl. Send him to the devil and then come out for more *tsoureki*. It's absolutely divine."

As soon as Gavriela had left the room, Daphne called Paul. Despite his being a tango night owl, he hadn't been answering late calls for the past week. So Daphne was surprised when he picked up after only three rings. Juan d'Arienzo's "El rey del compás" was playing in the background.

"Where are you?" said Daphne.

"The Biltmore."

That was where they had met. At a tango lesson Lidia had dragged her to. Daphne remembered how courteous Paul had been in comparison with the other tango leches. She recalled the wainscoted walls, the portable dance floor that kept coming apart; Paul had carefully led her away from the gaps so that she wouldn't trip.

"Do you have something to tell me?" she asked, after the long pause.

"I don't know what you're talking about," said Paul.

"Luciana."

"That again? She's just somebody to dance with."

"Is that what you were doing at La Rosa Negra?"

"Nothing happened."

"Do you know she posted photos of you on Facebook?"

"Yes."

"Do you know that she has her bust size on her site?"

"*Yeeees.*"

"And that she's done soft porn?"

"She's a dance partner, for Christ's sake!"

"I'm not that stupid, Paul."

Silence.

Daphne said, "If you want someone else, fine. But why the lies? Couldn't you at least have had the respect to—"

"We've become so different. And you're not so into tango anymore."

"So you got yourself a whore?"

"A dance partner."

"I'm not even going to ask if she was the first."

A woman shouted in the background: "Paulito! Is that you over there?"

Daphne wanted to throw the phone out the window. "Go make your date for the evening before somebody else reserves her. I'll send my dad for my stuff." She hung up, closed her laptop, and went to find her aunt.

Gavriela was sitting in a living-room armchair with her pudgy legs crossed. She took a sip of coffee from a gold-rimmed demitasse cup, turned her face into the bright light streaming through the sheer curtains, and said, "Did you shit on him well, little mama?"

Daphne collapsed onto the footstool beside Gavriela. "Yes."

"Enjoyed it?"

"Not at all, Auntie." Daphne whimpered. "I knew it was over, but now it's like it was all a lie from the very—"

Gavriela set her coffee on the side table. "Stop it right now. You've been with Kosmas all week."

"I know, but that woman . . ."

"Would you have preferred a man?"

"If she's what he really wanted—a porn star with fake boobs—then why was he ever with me? It's my self-image."

"Ay, *siktir*," Gabriella hissed. Like most Rums, she preferred the Turkish phrase for *fuck* to the Greek. "This is ridiculous. Your self-image comes from *yourself*, little mama, not from any Paul, nor any Kosmas. Who cares whom that monoglot American is doing? You gave him the road, now shut the door and move on. A man with such bad taste is not worth any woman's tears. So stop that sniveling, make yourself pretty, and go see Kosmas. He's the perfect cream for your sunburn."

That same afternoon, Kosmas took a short break while waiting for Mr. and Mrs. iPhone's icing to set in the refrigerator. He made himself a double Turkish coffee, took the first volume of *Recipes of Hamdi the Pastry Chef* from the safe, and set it on the office desk to peruse while he sipped his coffee, but he soon found himself lost in a labyrinth of recipes without any sort of organization. Some of the titles and directions were blotted out by liquid and food marks, and what Kosmas could make out was so interesting that he couldn't resist taking notes. Losing track of time, he studied the recipes of mysterious confections such as a thirteenth-century quince *murabba* preserve and a Crimean *kaysefe* made from fresh apple boiled in water and butter along with dried white mulberries, figs, raisins, and cinnamon. Kosmas was completely taken in by a recipe for *memuniyye*: fried dumplings made from shredded chicken, almonds, rosewater, rice flour, and honey. Mehmet the Conqueror had so enjoyed *memuniyye* that they had become a standard dish at Topkapı Palace and the crowning delight of a banquet given in honor of the Venetian ambassador, Andrea Badoero, in 1574.

"How's it going?" asked Uncle Mustafa, poking his head into the office.

Kosmas jumped to his feet. "What time is it?"

"Twenty past four."

"Damn it. I'm going to be late with that cake."

Kosmas wheeled the cake trolley out of the freezer, drove lollipop sticks into the fourth tier, settled the fifth on top, and gave the cake a slight jiggle to test its structural integrity.

"Finding that recipe is going to take a while," said Kosmas to Uncle Mustafa. "It's almost impossible to skim Hamdi's books because you might miss something, so you have to really read, and his writing is so fascinating that you get swallowed up by the palace history and completely forget what you're looking for."

"All things in good time," said Uncle Mustafa. "Except that cake. If you're late with that, we're in big trouble. Because we want to expand, remember?"

Kosmas nodded and began sticking prepared lilies into the dowel-enforced green florist foam at the base of Mr. and Mrs. iPhone's cake. He nestled some flowers close to the foam while allowing others to extend slightly over the black-rimmed plate. Another masterpiece. He was going to get that next-door shop space. And he was going to find the Balkanik as well. It was simply a matter of perseverance.

Kosmas folded the protective box flaps up and over the cake and suddenly realized he hadn't given any thought to where he would take Daphne that evening. It had to be something special. Things were going well, better than he could have expected, but every time he hinted that Daphne should stay past Sunday, she changed the subject. He loaded the cake into the refrigerated delivery truck, returned to the kitchen, and picked up his cell phone. Just as he was about to push the call button, he heard a knock at the back door. He opened and found Daphne wearing dark sunglasses even though the sun had already slipped behind the buildings of Sıraselviler Avenue. He wrapped his hands around the base of her neck and pulled her toward him. "This is a pleasant surprise," he said.

"I gave Paul the road, as my aunt says. We broke up."

"Are you okay?"

Daphne took off her dark sunglasses. Her eyelids were swollen. "I'm fine. I was just a bit shocked when I found out that he'd taken up with somebody else. A *putana*. Literally."

Kosmas felt as if his chest were being wrung out, like a towel. What was wrong with him? This was what he wanted, but . . . *Plan B*. That was it. He wanted Daphne, but not if he was her second choice now things hadn't worked out with the American.

"My aunt said I shouldn't tell you because it would lower me in your eyes," said Daphne, "but I can't help it."

"Nothing would ever lower you in my eyes," said Kosmas. He bit his bottom lip. There was no longer a rival, he repeated to himself. This was no longer a fling. But she'd been crying for another man. He felt a burning sensation in his stomach. He released Daphne and grasped the counter.

"Are you okay?" she asked.

"It's probably just indigestion . . ."

"I'll get you a glass of water."

And to think that today he'd been going to tell her he loved her.

She grabbed a glass and filled it from the demijohn. "Here," she said, handing it to him.

He set the glass on the counter without even taking a sip. "I don't want to be your Plan B."

"What's that supposed to mean? I was going to break up with him anyway. I'm upset because my pride was hurt, not because he broke my heart."

Kosmas stepped backward. They had to leave that kitchen, breathe some fresh air, get some perspective. Otherwise he might say something he'd regret. "Wait here," he said.

He hurried into the lavatory and put on the blue dress shirt his mother had ironed for him that morning, after he told her he would be going out on his last date with Daphne directly after work. Upon hearing the word "last," Rea had recovered from the knee pain that had prevented her from ironing that week. She had gone straight to her board, ironed a blue shirt with perfect arm creases, and said, "Tell Daphne I wish her a wonderful trip!"

Returning to the kitchen, Kosmas took Daphne's hand. "Come on. I want to show you something." They rode the Vespa to Galata and parked outside a tourist shop that sold hammam towels, soap, and evil-eye charms. He led her through the tower square, which was frustratingly crowded. Western tourists and bohemian Turks sat in the cafés, loitered on benches, took photos, and smoked profusely. They rounded the corner of the old Genoese wall and found themselves at the foot of the nine-story, cone-capped tower whose solidity had always impressed Kosmas. He hadn't been inside it in years, but he remembered the feeling of pride and certainty that its view had given him as a schoolboy. Up there, he knew that the City belonged to him just as much as he belonged to it. He could look down on the place where his ancestors had lived for centuries and know that, whatever obstacles stood in his path, he could always rise to the occasion. Perhaps Daphne might feel the same way.

They climbed the outer steps, bought their tickets, and took the elevator to the fifth floor, from which they climbed another two flights up a narrow medieval staircase. Kosmas led Daphne along the narrow and crowded observation deck to the side facing the Old City. From there one could observe the Golden Horn, the low tourist boats sliding under the Galata Bridge, the Ottoman palace of Topkapı nestled in the trees of the Byzantine peninsula, the dome of Hagia Sophia, the Blue Mosque with its six minarets, and the sun descending through the pollution haze. Seagulls swooped, dove, and squawked. Horns honked on the busy streets of Lower Galata. The wind, now salty, clean, and unmixed with cigarette smoke, lifted and tangled Daphne's hair.

She pointed toward a row of old Ottoman houses at the foot of the tower. "Look at all those beautiful oriel windows. I wonder if I'll ever get mine."

"You will if you move here," said Kosmas, embracing her from behind so that the tourists wouldn't jostle her. He wouldn't say how much he wanted her to remain in Istanbul. That was her decision now. She had to make it without his help.

Daphne remained silent. An especially strong gust rushed up from the Bosporus. A seagull on its way past the tower hovered before them, unable to advance despite the energetic flapping of its wings. "I'm in love with the City," said Daphne.

"Love isn't a little of this and a little of that," said Kosmas.

"What are you talking about?"

Kosmas felt the burning in his stomach again. "It's total and complete, Daphne, no bullshit. Solve your problem with this guy, then decide what you want."

She reached behind her, took his cheeks in her hands, pulled his head down, and kissed the scar above his brow. "I'm in love with *you*," she said.

"That's not the impression you gave an hour ago."

"I'm sorry, I didn't mean—"

Kosmas realized that his jealousy was ruining the moment. He had to get control of himself. "I love you, too, Daphne. But our love has to be steadfast. Like this tower."

She returned her gaze to the minarets of Hagia Sophia. "I'm thinking of coming back here to stay."

Kosmas squeezed her more tightly. He didn't want to let her go, not then, not ever. But he needed to know that she was just as sure. "Moving here requires decision and determination," he said.

"I know. And my parents are against it. Would you visit me in Miami? If they met you, then maybe . . ."

Kosmas felt his throat contract. "I'm booked for weddings through Christmas."

"January, then."

Daphne had the stubbornness of a camel. Which meant that she was Istanbul Rum through and through. Kosmas yielded: "In January."

19

The Nightingale and the Seagulls

THE SECOND WEEK IN SEPTEMBER, Selin finally said that she was coming to the Panagia to hear Fanis chant. She promised to arrive shortly after the start of vespers. Twenty minutes into the service, however, she was nowhere to be seen. Fanis gave up hope: Selin had to have been delayed at rehearsal. But then, just after the bishop descended from his throne in a tizzy because no one was helping him with his robes, Fanis turned to his left and saw the top of Selin's curly head. She might even have been standing there the whole time, shielded by the throne.

After the service, Selin waited in her place until the parishioners had withdrawn for tea. Then she picked up her violin case and approached the cantor's stand. "Outside we have the nightingales," she said to Fanis. "Inside we have you."

Fanis felt his cheeks flush. "So you liked it?" he said, fishing for more.

"Your voice exudes optimism."

Her glassy-eyed wonder made him feel like a sultan. He stepped down from the cantor's stand.

"Really," she said. "It's sexy."

Now that was the best compliment anyone had ever paid him. Even better than the nightingales and optimism. But Fanis didn't allow his imagination to scamper about like a five-year-old on a sugar buzz: just because she found *his voice* sexy didn't mean that she actually found *him* sexy.

"And that hat," she whispered, shaking her hand playfully, as if she had burned it. "Wow. Slightly fez-like, but black velvet. Orhan would love it."

She always had to spoil things by mentioning Orhan. Never mind. It helped keep Fanis grounded. He would have liked to introduce her to everyone in the church tea room, but he decided that he ought to protect her reputation. So he said, "Hungry?"

"I made leek fritters last night," she said. "Why don't you come by my place and try them?"

"Perfect," said Fanis. "I made stuffed grape leaves this morning. I'll bring them over."

He hung up his robe and stuck his cantor's hat into a boutique bag to take home for some spot cleaning. They hurried out, around the far side of the church so that they wouldn't be seen and called back. Just before they reached the gate, Fanis reached for her violin case. "Let me take that," he said.

"Please. I carry it all the time. It's very light."

"You shouldn't," said Fanis, taking the handle.

"Thanks," she said. "I guess I was getting a little tired."

"I know what I'm talking about," said Fanis. "A famous soloist like you shouldn't have to serve as a hamal."

They plodded through the tunnel of towering houses whose edges were made smooth by the coal smoke coming from the poorer apartments. The cold had set in early that autumn, making heating necessary in the evenings. The damp, soot-stained pavement outside the greengrocer's shop was littered with scallions and lettuce. Fanis and Selin rounded the bend to their part of the street and found it completely dark: the electricity had gone out.

Fanis climbed his stairs with the aid of his key-chain flashlight and grabbed the stuffed grape leaves, a paper-wrapped package of garlicky beef *pastırma*, and a jar of his favorite pickles. Once over at Selin's place, he insisted that she sit down at the kitchen table and relax with a glass of Cappadocian

Chardonnay while he, by the light of Selin's super-bright kitchen flashlight, made a lettuce, mint, carrot, and walnut salad, drizzled it with pomegranate concentrate and olive oil, and warmed the fritters on the gas stove.

"Ach," said Selin, putting her feet up on a stool. "This is just what I needed."

You're just what *I* needed, thought Fanis. But then he remembered his resolution: friends. He tasted a leek fritter and said, "Magnificent . . . the dill, the subtle white cheese, so well combined with the egg—" Just then there was an angry outburst of seagull screeching. "Poor things," he said. "When I was young, they feasted on fish in the Bosporus and squawked peacefully. Now they have to pick at garbage dumps. They're as angry as the rest of us."

"There must be a new nest up there," said Selin. "Things were quiet when I moved in, but now I hear them going at it morning and night."

Fanis stuck wooden spoons in the salad and transferred the fritters to a serving plate. "I bet they're saying, 'This isn't the Istanbul of our ancestors. The City is ruined, polluted. We used to live the dolce vita here. Now everything has gone to the devil.'"

Selin laughed. If Fanis were trying to seduce her that would have meant he'd reached a milestone. Fanis picked up the salad and the plate of fritters. "It's ready. Just grab the stuffed vine leaves for me, dear, will you?"

Over a candlelit dinner, they talked about her work. The Mendelssohn concerto had been so well received that the orchestra's conductor wanted Selin to prepare for a January performance of the Tchaikovsky Violin Concerto in D Major.

"Which is wonderful," she said. "It's sentimental, but very uncomfortable. Both Monsieur Julien and my boss say that it never gets easier, no matter how much you practice."

Fanis looked up at the ceiling corner onto which Selin's shadow was projected by the candlelight. He took a sip of wine, savoring its hints of honey, orange, and vanilla. "During my first years of cantoring," he said, "I found that the most beautiful hymns really strained my voice. But with time, I began to feel the sound pass through me, like it didn't even come from me. I was just a vessel, a channel. Perhaps that might happen with you as well."

Selin looked into his eyes and smiled with admiration. "It's so good to talk to someone who understands."

Just then the windows across the street illuminated, the television clicked, and the refrigerator resumed its humming. Fanis reached for the light switch, but Selin said, "Leave it off. It's nice like this."

Fanis crossed the room and took a CD from the case, but in the dim light he couldn't tell what it was. He turned on the player, inserted the CD, and tried to think of something banal to say: "I forgot to serve the *pastırma* and pickles! Let me go get them."

"Just *sit*," said Selin. "We don't need anything else."

Fanis returned to the table. The first piano notes of "The Delicate Rose Of My Thought," a classical Turkish love song, sounded through the chilly September evening. The strings joined the piano, and Selin began singing along with Sema Moritz about the nightingale of her heart.

"I'm enchanted," said Fanis, when it had finished.

"It's always been one of my favorites. But my voice is nothing in comparison with yours."

"Don't be silly. You sing very nicely."

"What we really need is a voice and violin duet," she said. And then, as if she had remembered something, she took out her J.S. Phillips violin and played the first notes of a piece that Fanis recognized instantly: Özdemir Erdoğan's "Teacher Love," a bittersweet duet between a young violinist and her much older instructor. Fanis dutifully sang his part about counting the days until their lessons. Then, on a sudden impulse, he replaced the *twenty years* of the original lyrics with the number of his and Selin's gap: *thirty-three*.

Selin's eyes darted from her violin to his face as soon as he said it. She had definitely noticed. As soon as the song was over, he turned on the lights and said, "I'll just do the dishes before I head home."

Selin replaced her violin in its case, took a liqueur set from a cabinet beside the black leather sofa, and said, "Leave the dishes. Let's have some of Mom's strawberry brew."

The friendship experiment was in jeopardy. If they went on like this, he would undoubtedly make a move, Orhan or no Orhan. So he said, "Another time, dear. I've got to get up early for . . . for . . . a doctor's appointment."

He hastily kissed Selin goodbye and tiptoed down the stairs. He had hoped to slip out of the building discreetly, but he met Madame Duygu, Selin's landlady, on the raised ground-floor landing.

"Mr. Fanis," she said. "What are you doing here?"

"What are *you* doing here?" he returned. "Especially at this hour."

"The people under the garret complained about the *artiste*. She was playing loud music and, apparently, she has an animal. A tomcat that makes all sorts of noise. I specifically said I don't allow pets."

"I don't know what they heard, Madame Duygu," Fanis said, "but I can assure you that the lady has no cat."

"And the sounds?"

"It must have been the seagulls."

"*The seagulls?*"

"They don't just squawk, my dear Madame Duygu. They have a language all of their own. Sometimes it's like a dog barking, sometimes a cat howling, and sometimes even like construction hammering or a monkey laughing. I study them in my spare time."

"Are you all right, Mr. Fanis?" Duygu looked him over and sniffed the air. "You smell like . . . women's perfume."

"Please, Madame Duygu," said Fanis, tickled that she might think him capable of seducing Selin. "I'm seventy-six." He smiled, bowed, and skipped down the last few stairs.

20

The Test of the Package

KOSMAS SPENT ALL HIS NON-WORKING hours that autumn at his office desk. Not only was he determined to find the Balkanik, but he also wanted to translate the recipes for use at the Lily and perhaps even publish them. For, Kosmas reasoned, even if Hamdi hadn't recorded the Balkanik, his other culinary treasures had to be preserved for posterity.

Finally, on a cold night in early January—when Kosmas was about three-quarters through the last volume—he came upon something that resembled the famed pastry. The handwriting was minuscule but clear, running right to left in boxy little figures, but the page was not in good shape. There was a brown stain in the lower right-hand corner. The ingredient measurements had been hastily crossed out and annotated more than once, and wormholes pierced the assembly directions. Kosmas stuck his nose to the brown stain and inhaled: the mold overlay was strong, but he was sure that beneath it he smelled chocolate. And then he saw a scribble in the margin: Balkanik. Kosmas felt the sudden joy of discovery, the sensation that everything would fall into place.

He rubbed his stinging eyes, stuck a marker between the pages, returned the book to the safe, and walked home, hardly feeling the chill. It was three days before he was to leave for Miami: just enough time to transform the recipe into something functional so that he could continue his experiments in Daphne's kitchen.

He opened the apartment door and found his mother seated in her favorite armchair. An unopened package rested in her lap. She was unusually calm. That worried Kosmas.

"I went to the bank today," said Rea.

The previous evening, during a commercial break in *Magnificent Century*, Kosmas had announced his intention to propose to Daphne. Rea had stared at the television screen without comment. Perhaps her hearing was going. Kosmas had raised his voice: "Would you mind going with Mr. Dimitris tomorrow to get Grandma and Grandpa's rings from the safe-deposit box?" Instead of replying to his request, Rea had complained about Hürrem Sultan's bad makeup job. "I guess I'll have to do it myself," Kosmas had said.

Now, however, Kosmas was surprised to see that his mother had actually done what he had asked. "Thanks, Mama," he said. "It means a lot to me." He kissed her wrinkly, baby-powder-scented forehead.

Usually she grinned like a little girl when he did that, but this time her expression remained blank. "The whole time I was in the bank," she said, "I was thinking it's far too early for you to propose. Has Daphne said she wants to get married?"

Just the week before Daphne had said "I don't want a city that was built for me. I want one that was born for me. *You* are my city." Kosmas had therefore supposed that she would say yes to his proposal.

And yet, now that his mother had asked . . . Daphne did always shy away from the topic of marriage. "No," Kosmas said to Rea. He peeled off his damp Puffa jacket. "I want it to be a surprise."

"But it's too soon. You could scare—"

"Where are they?"

"There."

Kosmas looked around the living room. In October, his mother had brought in a painter. Not Mr. Ahmet the mold specialist, but a cheap laborer recommended by Aliki. The

240

man had repainted the wall behind the television, but the mold had returned, just as Kosmas had said it would, and now it was blossoming in gardens of pinkish-orange circles. Kosmas would have to call Mr. Ahmet.

"Where?" said Kosmas.

"On the sideboard. Near the Christmas tree."

The arrangement that Rea called a "tree" was a vase filled with holly branches and Christmas ornaments. Beside the vase was a small silver tray lined with one of Kosmas's grandmother's crocheted doilies and crowned by a thick silver wedding band and a thinner gold one. His grandparents had maintained the old Byzantine ring tradition: women wore gold because it represented purity, beauty, elegance, and rarity; men wore silver, the symbol of strength. He picked up his grandfather's silver ring and slipped it onto his left ring finger, where it would be worn during the engagement. Then he tried it on the right, to which it would be transferred after marriage. The fit was slightly big.

"It needs to be resized," he said. "I know an Armenian goldsmith in the Grand Bazaar, a friend from the army. I'll take it to him tomorrow." He looked up at his mother. She was staring at him with both hands flat on the package. "What's that?"

"Something from Daphne. Addressed to me."

"Why don't you open it?"

"I'd like you to read the return address label first."

Kosmas looked at the sticker. In the left-hand corner was a picture of a dog with three legs. Probably from one of those animal-protection organizations to which Daphne belonged. "It says Humane Society, Mama. Maybe that's a dog she helped save."

"That's not what I meant," said Rea. "I mean *her name*. Daphne Zeynep Badem. Would you explain that, please?"

Kosmas sat down on the sofa and wiped his hand over his tired eyes. "Her father is Ottoman."

Rea leaned forward. The package slipped from her knees and landed with a crackly thud on the floor. "How could you have kept this from me?"

"I didn't keep it from you. I just don't see why it matters."

"Why it *matters*? I've been called an infidel my whole life. Even the most modern and cultured among them always have the word *infidel* on their lips. The second they think we're not listening, that's what they call us."

"What about Uncle Mustafa?" said Kosmas. "He took care of us after Father died. You never lacked anything while I was in Vienna. Did he ever call you an infidel? And what about your friend the cobbler, or Madame Vildan, who brings you the newspaper every morning?"

"I'm not saying they aren't good people. Just that they never forget we're different. And neither should we." Rea slipped her hand inside her blouse, over her heart, and looked furtively around the room, as if she were worried that they weren't alone.

"Mama, are you okay?"

She kneaded her chest beneath the collar bone. "My aunt used to pretend we were all the same. Her door was always open to Ottoman women. But in fifty-five, when the rioters broke into her house, destroyed everything in sight, and smashed her pearls with a hammer, one by one, neither those women nor their husbands made any attempt to intervene. My aunt never invited anyone into her home ever again. She had learned her lesson."

Kosmas knelt at his mother's side and put his hand on her knee. "But Daphne's mother is Rum, and so is Daphne."

"That's not what her identity card will say. They'll register her as Muslim. You'll see."

"And even if they do, so what?"

"If you have children—"

"They'll be Christian, Mama."

"And if she divorces you and marries a Muslim? Have you thought of that? Have you thought of how your children will be raised?"

"I'm not even engaged and you want me to think about divorce?"

"You have to think about everything before you marry!"

"Mama, she's an Orthodox Christian, period." Kosmas scratched his head with the aggression of a flea-bitten dog. "Even if her identity card says otherwise, that's what she is. Who cares about the government's stupid categories?"

Rea fumbled for her cane and inadvertently knocked it onto the parquet floor. Kosmas snatched it up and handed it to her. "*Please*, Mama."

Their eyes locked. It seemed to Kosmas that the fine lines running down and outward from beneath Rea's lower lids had both increased and deepened. Her upper lids drooped like elephant skin. Behind her clear brown pupils, however, Kosmas saw a scared little girl. "Mama?"

Rea lifted her chin in silent reply: *No*.

Kosmas slid the ring off his finger, returned it to the tray on the sideboard, and locked himself into the bathroom. He turned on the shower to its hottest setting and vented his frustration—with Rea's doubts and his own—by scrubbing himself raw with an exfoliation mitt and a bar of carrot-smelling soap. It was three days before he was to leave for Miami. As soon as he got back, he would find an apartment and move out.

When he had worked out the details of his plan, he got out of the shower and threw on a robe. Steam poured out of the bathroom as he opened the door. "Mother!" he shouted. She didn't reply. "Where are you?"

He went into the living room. The package, still unopened, rested at the foot of the armchair. He went to the kitchen. First he saw the soil spilled all over the floor, then the African violet, and then his mother crumpled beside it. Her eyes were open.

243

"Mama! Mama, are you okay?"

She tried to pull her housedress down over her swollen legs, as if she were embarrassed to be showing so much skin. "I don't know," she whispered.

The hospital doctors said she'd fainted from hypotension caused by mild bradycardia, which was common in older patients. Fortunately, she hadn't suffered any fractures or head injuries: just a few nasty bruises. The emergency-room intern hung a Holter monitor around her neck, stuck its five sky-blue electrodes to her chest, and explained to Kosmas that his mother had to be monitored to determine if she needed a pacemaker.

"A pacemaker?" whispered Kosmas. He and the intern were standing in the stark hallway. Rea was still hooked up to a saline IV in the examination room, but the door was open. "Is this serious?"

"It doesn't look so at the moment," the intern said. "The ECG was fine. She doesn't have a temperature. But at her age, it's best to be careful. Put a bit more salt in her food, keep her well hydrated, increase her intake of red meat. Her blood tests showed low iron levels. Anemia, that is. She could lose a little weight. She's not diabetic yet, but she's headed in that direction. You have to keep a good eye on her."

"For how long?"

"Until we can determine what's going on. We may need to keep her on the Holter for a couple of weeks."

"I'm supposed to go to America in three days." Kosmas glanced at the wall clock. It was past midnight. He corrected himself: "Two days."

"Is there anyone else who can take care of her? Your father? A sibling?"

Kosmas thought of Mr. Dimitris. He wouldn't refuse, but the situation would be awkward for Rea. And Kosmas would also be guilty of encouraging Mr. Dimitris in a hopeless suit. Better not to involve him.

"No one," said Kosmas.

The intern stuck his ballpoint pen into his shirt pocket. "Perhaps you could postpone."

Kosmas felt like a child whose ice cream had fallen off its cone onto the dirty pavement.

After taking his mother home and putting her to bed with a cup of chamomile tea, he took his airplane ticket from his dresser drawer, sat down at the narrow kitchen table, and stared at the mess left in the wake of his mother's fainting episode: the black soil spilled on the floor, the hot red pepper flakes scattered across the table. Then he read every word and abbreviation on his red and white Turkish Airlines ticket. His chest tightened. He had to talk to Daphne right away.

She answered his call immediately, but instead of greeting him, she said, "Only three days left until we're together again!"

Kosmas heard traffic noise and happy Latin music that seemed entirely out of place as he stared at his mother's jumbled bottles of olive oil and vinegar. "About that," he said, trying to remember what day and time it was for Daphne. "Where are you?"

"At dinner with a friend. Is something wrong?"

"It's Mother. She fainted and had to be taken to the hospital. They have to monitor her heart for a couple of weeks. She might need a pacemaker."

"Is she still there? In the hospital?"

With his ticket, he swept the table of hot pepper flakes—called *acı* in Turkish, the same word for pain. "No," he said. "She's here, napping."

"Is she going to be okay?"

"Hopefully, it's just . . ."

Again Kosmas heard electric steel strings. The Spanish lyrics that accompanied the music, although unintelligible, seemed to express his longing and disappointment.

"You're not coming," said Daphne.

Kosmas felt a rush of relief. The tightness in his chest eased: she'd made the decision for him. "I'm just not sure if it's the right thing to do," he said.

Daphne was silent.

For a moment Kosmas heard nothing but the ripping of wind. Daphne had moved away from the music.

"Did she receive my birthday gift?"

"Today—no, yesterday. But she hasn't opened it yet."

"I guess she didn't have a chance. Why don't you give it to her now, to cheer her up? It's a Pantone coffee maker from the Pérez Art Museum. Pink, her favorite color. "

Kosmas was too tired for concealment. "Before she fainted, we had our talk. I told her your father is Muslim."

"I thought you already did that."

Kosmas lowered his foot over the potless violet and squashed it into the floor tile. Now he had a second crisis on his hands: Daphne had learned that he'd lied to her a month ago about the talk with his mother.

"And?" said Daphne, her voice frighteningly quiet. "Does this change things for us?"

Kosmas thought of calling Mr. Dimitris whether Rea liked it or not. He could get on that airplane after all. He could talk this out with Daphne, face to face. But that wouldn't be right. It was his filial duty to stay. He ripped his ticket in half and threw it onto the soil and *acı* pepper at his feet. "Nothing's changed," he said. "I love you just as much as ever. But I have to look after her now. I'm all she has."

21

The Moon and the Star

On January 8, the day Kosmas should have arrived, Daphne invited her parents to dinner at Versailles, a Cuban restaurant with chandeliers and mirrors reminiscent of those in old Istanbul pastry shops. Ilyas Badem ordered his favorite fried green plantain chips, three portions of shredded chicken and rice, a Cuban beer for his wife, and guava juice for himself and his daughter. The family spoke, as always, in a strange mix of English and Istanbul Greek with a spicy sprinkling of Turkish and Spanish.

Out of respect for her father, Daphne waited until the waiter had left their table to say: "No soup, Baba? What kind of Turk are you?"

"The soup!" said Ilyas, slapping his cheek. "How could I have forgotten?" He called the waiter back and ordered three bowls of cream of *malanga*. Then he looked into the wall mirror. His sweep hairstyle had been upset by the strong winds. He rearranged his strands so that they properly covered his bald spot and then, pointing at the parking lot palms whipping about in a sudden gust, said, "This hurricane's going to be a bad one."

"This *storm*," said Sultana, rolling her eyes. "Hurricane season is over, for God's sake."

"In January of 1952," said Ilyas while the waiter served the beer and guava juices "A tropical storm passed over southern Florida quite near Miami. And in late December of 1984, Hurricane Lili hit Hispaniola. So you never know."

"You're obsessed," said Sultana. "Why don't you learn to play golf?"

Ilyas shook his head at his wife and leaned toward Daphne. "So why didn't he come? Out with it."

"His mother's ill," said Daphne. She hadn't allowed herself to complain to anyone, but she couldn't keep from wondering whether Rea had faked the fainting episode to prevent Kosmas from traveling. "She might have to get a pacemaker."

"What else?" said Ilyas.

"Nothing," said Daphne, twisting her napkin beneath the table.

Sultana adjusted her rhinestone barrette. Although she hadn't been to Istanbul in thirty-four years, her excessive jewelry, bright nail polish, and girlish hair accessories made her look as if she had been beamed into Miami from 1960s Turkey. "I hope you've given up that silly idea of moving there," she said.

The waiter served the steaming *malanga* soup, Daphne's favorite. She took in the nutty, garlicky vapors that reminded her of their neighbor Josefina's kitchen, but she still had no desire to eat. Her appetite had vanished the day of Rea's accident.

As soon as the waiter had gone, Daphne asked, "Why did you two really leave?"

Over the years, she had heard various answers to that question, the most common being that her father had received an excellent job offer that he couldn't pass up. But she knew this wasn't the truth: after all, Ilyas Badem had been assistant manager of the Istanbul Hilton, and he had started at the newly built Hilton Miami Downtown as a night manager.

"I don't want to dig up the past," said Ilyas. He pushed back his chair.

"Baba," said Daphne. "I need to know. Will you sit down and talk to me for once?"

"*Buen provecho*," said Sultana. She puckered her lips and drank a steaming spoonful of *malanga* soup. "Daphne, why aren't you eating? You've lost weight, you know."

"Baba?"

Ilyas took a sip of sweet guava juice. "I don't see why we have to discuss this."

"Baba, I'm thinking about moving there. I want to know why you left."

"Talk to her, my love," said Sultana. "Maybe she'll get some sense in her."

Ilyas looked out the window at the overcast sky. "We shouldn't even be here. The hurricane could hit anytime."

"Are you going to tell her?"

Ilyas remained silent.

"Fine," said Sultana. "*I* will. My people—not my family, but my friends and the community—rejected me. They said I'd gone over to the other side. First I lost my job in a hat maker's shop. Then one of my best girlfriends didn't invite me to her wedding. Of course she said it was an oversight and apologized, but I knew the truth."

For emphasis, Sultana gave her spoon a single shake in the air as if it were a maraca. "The other side didn't want me either. Once I went to a *mevlit* prayer service with your father's relatives. I told his cousin Ayşe how beautiful I thought the reading was. She fawned over me and said, 'We love you so much that you should become Muslim.' I said, 'Let Muslims remain Muslims and Christians Christians.' Ayşe and the other women didn't speak to me for the rest of the evening. So you see why we came to America. It's a place that was—*and is*—full of people like us. People who are neither here nor there."

"And you were unhappy here," said Daphne.

"Of course we were at first. Still, I don't regret coming. We got used to it and had a life here that we couldn't have had there. Here nobody cares that my husband is Turkish. But America doesn't have that . . . that . . . *Byzantine salt*."

Daphne turned to her father. "Baba, why didn't Grandma Zeynep ever come to visit us? And why didn't we go to visit her?"

Ilyas flipped his spoon from one side to the other, looking around the restaurant. Then, addressing the palms swaying in the parking lot instead of Daphne, he said in English, "We had issues."

Sultana took her husband's hand, held it to her lips, and kissed it. "Jealousy issues."

"Now you know," said Ilyas, standing. "With your permission, ladies." He made for the men's room before Daphne could object.

As soon as the door had closed behind him, Daphne said to her mother, "Why did you name me after Grandma Zeynep?"

"It was an attempt to appease her."

"Did it work?"

"Are you kidding? Listen"—Sultana lowered her voice— "we're not talking about normal jealousy. We're talking about an illness. When we were first married, I brought Zeynep gifts, put cream on her itchy back, painted her nails . . . there wasn't anything I didn't do for her. But the things she said every time she got me alone! Once it was, 'Why is it that you didn't find a Rum groom? Was it because word got out that you don't know how to keep house?' Another time, after I'd cooked all day and prepared a feast for her, she said, 'It doesn't matter that you don't know how to cook, Sultana dear, you'll learn eventually.' And another time I walked into her living room and found her crying. When I asked why, she said, 'For my son. He would have been so much happier if he had married Nur Yılmaz instead of you!' And when she found out about your name"—Sultana dropped her spoon into the soup—"do you know what that woman said? She said, 'I wonder if the girl will amount to anything.' Can you believe that? A grandmother about her own grandchild!"

"Sounds like a real bitch."

"That's just the thing. She wasn't a bitch with anybody else. Only with me."

"You could've moved to another part of the City."

Sultana snorted. "The other side of the Bosporus wasn't enough, my love. We needed an ocean."

"Kosmas's mother isn't like that. Or . . . at least she's not that bad."

"Don't kid yourself. All Istanbul mothers-in-law are demons in heels."

"Why couldn't we have talked about this before?"

"It's too painful for your father. Do you think he can bear to hear his mother's words repeated? Especially what she said about you? We wanted to protect you. From conflict, confusion. A double identity."

"I have all that anyway."

"At least we tried."

Ilyas returned, straightened his blazer, and sat down to eat his soup. Daphne swallowed a few spoonfuls and said, "Baba, there's something else. His mother fainted when she found out you're Muslim. That's how she ended up at the hospital."

"Oh, *a fainter*," said Sultana.

"How are things with him now?" asked Ilyas, his eyes fixed on the fried green plantain chips just delivered by the waiter.

"We talk every day. And although I'm not crazy about his mother, I admire Kosmas's commitment to her."

Ilyas dabbed his short mustache with his napkin. "I understand what he's going through."

"So do I," said Sultana. "But whether this guy is Rum, Turk, American, Cuban, or Chinese, if he had any sense in him, he'd find someone to care for his mother and get over here. So erase him from your head, my girl. He's not for you."

"Mom, I know this is hard for you, but—"

"*Geçti Bor'un Pazarı sür eşeğini Niğde'ye!*" said Sultana, raising her voice.

Daphne understood the Turkish words—*The Bor Bazaar is over, take your donkey to Niğde*—but she had no idea what they meant. "Pardon?" she said.

"She means," said Ilyas, "that it's time to move on."

Sultana nervously pulled her sky-blue cardigan over her shoulders to protect them from the air-conditioning. "This is all Gavriela's doing," she said. "My little girl would never have thought of leaving me if Gavriela hadn't interfered."

"This has nothing to do with Aunt Gavriela," said Daphne. "*I'm* the one who wants to live in Istanbul."

"*Excuse me?*"

A boy opened the restaurant door for his six-member family. A burst of hot, damp wind rushed into Versailles. Even if the storm didn't hit land, they would still have good rain.

"I've applied to PhD programs in oral history at Boğaziçi, Bilgi, and Istanbul universities," said Daphne.

"And you kept this a secret from me?" said Sultana.

"It's not a secret, Mom. I just didn't tell you."

"As if there weren't any good PhD programs in the States! Do they even know what oral history is over there?"

Daphne took a deep breath, held it for a few seconds, and exhaled. "I'm also applying for Turkish citizenship."

"You're *what*?"

"I got most of the papers together, but I need copies of your Turkish and American passports."

"Studying there is one thing, Daphne, but *citizenship* . . . They won't recognize your American citizenship, you know. If you get into trouble—"

"I've made my decision, Mom," said Daphne, trying to sound certain. "Can't you understand how at home I felt there? I love the afternoon tea, the way total strangers help you out, the sense of adventure, the warmth, the deepness of the friendships. Here everybody's in such a hurry. Americans meet you for coffee and ditch you forty minutes later, but over there, you sit with your friends for hours. They know how to live."

"*If* the government *lets* them live," said Sultana.

"It's a democracy, Mom."

"The twilight of a democracy," Sultana corrected.

"Whatever. Home is home."

"And Miami isn't home?"

"It is, Mom, but it doesn't have Istanbul's history. *Our* history. The Byzantine and Ottoman salt."

Sultana sucked in her lips as if she were fighting back tears. Ilyas took her hand.

"I already gave my notice at the school," said Daphne.

"You're insane." Sultana picked up her beer, but she was so agitated that she spilled the foam onto the table. She set it back down and said, "You're making a sentimental decision without giving any thought to anything, not even the political situation. It's like moving to Germany in thirty-nine."

"Don't you think you're exaggerating a little, Sultana?" said Ilyas, mopping up the beer puddle with his napkin.

Both Sultana and Daphne stared at him. He rarely took sides in their arguments, and he never called Sultana by her given name. In fact, Daphne couldn't remember ever hearing her father address her mother as anything but *hayatım*—my life.

"Daphne," he said, "you have a good life here. We worked hard to give you that. What's missing? A man? We'll find you a better one in Miami."

"That's not it, Baba." Daphne picked up a plantain chip, but it was still burning hot. She dropped it back onto the plate. "It's the feeling when you wake up in the morning in Istanbul. Every day, you know that anything can happen. I don't want my life to be a routine of work, gym, and shopping in generic strip malls."

Ilyas took a long look at Daphne as if he had only just noticed that she had grown up. "It's your choice. We don't agree, but I'll get the passports." He rubbed Daphne's back and added, "But your mother's right about one thing. You *have* lost weight. Now finish that soup before it gets cold."

*

On a February Saturday, just before Daphne left to teach an afternoon of private lessons, she opened her mailbox, grabbed the contents, and shuffled through them at the kitchen table. She tossed a dentist advertisement in the trash, set her bank statement and electric bill aside for later, and arrived at an envelope from the Turkish Consulate General in New York. Inside was a letter saying that her application for citizenship had been approved.

On Monday she called the consulate, hoping to arrange to have her passport sent, but a polite female employee informed her that she would have to come to New York in person to complete the process.

"There isn't any way for me to do it from here?" said Daphne.

"I'm sorry," said the employee. "There's been talk of a consulate opening in Miami, but it probably won't happen for a year or two."

Daphne called her father and asked if he knew someone who could pull a few strings. He laughed. "Welcome to Turkey, my girl. If you don't like bureaucracy, you ought to stay here."

This only made Daphne more stubborn about her decision. She took two personal days to go to New York. As soon as she stepped into the warm consulate from the cold, dirty, slush-covered street, her anxiety eased: the consulate smelled of lemon cologne, bleach, and naphthalene—the scents of home.

A guard accompanied Daphne to the desk of Arzu Çetinkaya, the officer with whom she had spoken on the phone. Mrs. Çetinkaya took a pile of yellow, plastic-wrapped packages from her desk drawer and flipped through them. "Strange," she said. "I could have sworn it was here."

"Is something wrong?" Daphne asked.

Without reply, Mrs. Çetinkaya went to a cabinet on the other side of the room, pulled out a plastic crate, scooped up half of its plastic packs, and gave them to Daphne. Taking the rest for herself, she said, "You do those, I'll do these."

Daphne stared down at the pile: they resembled thin packets of Kraft singles. "And I'm looking for . . . ?"

"Your passport, dear!"

Hardly able to believe that a consulate employee was engaging her help in sorting through other people's passports, Daphne mechanically flipped through the packets. But she didn't find her own. Neither did Mrs. Çetinkaya. Could a previous new citizen have been ordered to look for his passport in this mess and taken hers by mistake?

"It *has* to be here somewhere," said Mrs. Çetinkaya, but her pinched mouth betrayed her worry. She swept the passports back into the crate, replaced them in the cabinet, took another crate, and again divided the packets between herself and Daphne. The anxiety that Daphne had experienced on the early-morning flight returned. She didn't have any more personal days to spend on this passport business.

"Here it is!" said Mrs. Çetinkaya, holding up the passport as if it were a Cracker Jack prize.

Daphne took a deep breath and released. *"Allah'a şükür."* Thank God.

She peeled back the plastic, revealing a burgundy Turkish passport with its gold crescent moon and single star. As an American, Daphne had a birthright to fifty stars, but she suddenly felt that the only one that truly mattered was now beneath her fingers. She opened the passport, stuck her nose into it, and breathed in its aroma of fresh ink. It smelled just like new money, like promise. Memories of oriel windows and Bosporus views flashed through her mind.

"Ahem!" Mrs. Çetinkaya cleared her voice, folded her hands on top of Daphne's file, and said, "For the identity card, you'll find an application in the corridor. Kindly fill it out and take it to the Citizen Services Hall."

"Thank you," said Daphne.

The lady smiled and scrunched her eyes. Daphne proceeded into the hallway and called her father: "Already did my passport, Baba. Couldn't have been easier. In a few minutes I'll be done with everything."

Ilyas chuckled.

"Fine," said Daphne. "I'll call back in ten minutes and laugh at *you*."

She took the identity-card application from a wall file and took a seat on one of the plastic student chairs in the Citizen Services Hall. Leaning over the uncomfortably small tablet arm, she filled in and ticked away, her sense of victory increasing with each completed section. And then she came to the religion choice. On an identity card? It seemed so backward, so 1940s. She couldn't remember *ever* officially disclosing her religion in the US. She completed the rest of the form, signed, and waited another thirty minutes for her number to be called. Were they really going to mark her, officially, on her ID, as one thing or the other? But hopefully she wouldn't have to choose. Hopefully she could just leave it blank without taking sides.

When her number appeared in red on the display, Daphne proceeded to her assigned window. A fit, middle-aged clerk with a military-style buzz-cut stood flagpole straight behind it.

"Good day, sir," she said. "*Kolay gelsin.*" May it come easily. She hoped this standard Turkish wish for a good workday might soften the clerk from the start.

"At your service," he said.

"If I may make a request"—another courtesy formula—"might I leave this box blank?"

The clerk took off his glasses and wiped them with a microfiber cloth. "You used to be able to. But not anymore."

"Please. I don't want to choose."

He put his glasses back on and made a jumpy move. It seemed to Daphne that he might actually have heel-clicked. "I'm afraid the current government considers it obligatory."

Daphne set the form on the mahogany counter. Which was more important: interest or identity? An easier life or a man who might not be willing to displease his mother in order to be with her? If she wrote Muslim, she'd be accepted as a full Turk rather than an infidel foreigner. But if there was any hope that things would work with Kosmas, she *had* to write Christian. Daphne hastily scrawled the second and slid the form beneath the glass partition. The clerk read her choice and sighed. He took her file from the stack on his counter, shuffled through, and said, "This is a mistake. Your father is Muslim. That makes you Muslim, too."

"My mother and I are Christian."

"But it's the father who counts."

"Forgive me, sir. *I* am the one who counts."

"Why do you want to do this to yourself?"

"Do *what*?"

"Things will be better for you as a Muslim. Don't you want to be *really* Turkish, not just a Turkish citizen?"

"Of course I do."

"Then go to church if you want, but write Muslim."

At that moment, Daphne realized that her choice wasn't only for Kosmas. It was also for herself. She pulled out her gold baptismal cross from beneath her shirt and said, "I am really Turkish. *And* I'm Christian."

The clerk sighed. "Have a seat."

While waiting, Daphne recalled Kosmas's mini-meltdown in Madame Kyveli's restaurant. She imagined Rea staring at a return label with a tiny photo of a rescued dog and a name that brought back memories of hiding in woodsheds and fear of rape and pillage. Maybe Rea wasn't so awful after all. Maybe she was just afraid. Daphne shifted her weight in the hard plastic seat. She thought of her own mother sitting in Versailles restaurant and saying that they were neither here nor there.

"Ms. Badem!" called the clerk. "Take this to Station Three, please, down that way."

Daphne looked at the form still lying in the deal box. Right in the middle was the red approval stamp of the Turkish Republic: a moon and star underlined with the year "1923." Officially, Daphne had become an Orthodox Christian thirty-one years before, when she was baptized at Saint Sophia's Cathedral in Miami. But it was only now, after completing a Turkish bureaucratic procedure, that she felt she had truly earned the word *Christian*.

22

Discovery

On a Wednesday morning in January, Fanis awoke to a city dressed in white. He went to the kitchen to make his coffee and omelet, but he was so excited by the flakes falling past his window that he forgot all about breakfast, called Selin, and said, "Look out the window. Faik Paşa is sprinkled with powdered sugar like a tray of mille-feuille."

As they gazed at the winter wonderland from opposite windows, Fanis remembered he was to receive his retirement stipend from the Greek Consulate that day. He and Selin had planned to go together and then have a coffee in the Grand Avenue before she took a bus up to Lütfi Kırdar. Seeing the snow, however, Fanis had second thoughts about their plan. "The streets will be dangerously slippery," he said to Selin. "I don't think you ought to go to work. And I guess I can wait and collect a double stipend next month."

"I have no choice," she said. "Today's the final rehearsal for the Tchaikovsky concerto."

"Right." Fanis pulled his plaid robe more tightly around his shoulders. "We'll walk over to the consulate together and take a taxi up to the concert hall. I'll stay until you've finished."

"You'll be bored."

"Bored at the Borusan? Are you out of your mind? Besides, there's no question of you coming home by yourself. The weather could get worse, and the doctor said you have to be careful of colds."

Three-quarters of an hour later, they met in the street. A thick layer of snow had already settled over everything. "See?" said Fanis. "You couldn't get a taxi to come to your door even if you phoned."

They plodded up to the sky-blue, neoclassical consulate and entered the unusually short queue on the opposite side of the street. While waiting, Fanis noticed Selin shivering. He wrapped his arm around her shoulders.

A second later, wearing a homemade pompom beanie, Aliki came hobbling out of the consulate. "Fanis? *Selin?*"

Fanis tried to let his arm slide slowly and discreetly down Selin's back, but it was too late. Aliki's eyes darted back and forth between them. Her head twitched as if she had a tic. She licked her lips repeatedly. Had Fanis not known her better, he would have thought that she was suffering from mental illness.

"But," Aliki stammered, "I thought it was only because of Julien . . . and since he never said anything, never made a move . . . and when you and I went for soup, I thought that maybe . . . "

Fanis realized his mistake. Two weeks before he had helped Aliki sell the antiques that had lain in boxes since the summer. He had obtained such a good price that she had insisted on treating him to tripe soup and saffron pudding, and they had passed a pleasant afternoon reminiscing and telling jokes. Aliki had obviously mistaken his mirth—whose source was his friendship with Selin—as interest in *her*.

Aliki continued mumbling incoherently and glaring at Selin as if she had sprouted two heads: "Are you two *really.* . . . How long?"

Fanis spotted a taxi slowly approaching through the lane cleared by the plow. He raised his hand to the driver, took Aliki's arm, and said, "How lucky you are, dear. Hardly any taxis out now. You'd better take it." As soon as the vehicle had come to a stop, he helped Aliki inside. Just before shutting the door, he winked and said, "We'll talk this afternoon, at

Neighbor's House." Aliki continued staring through the foggy window as the taxi pulled off through the slush. Poor thing.

"Did she really think that . . . *we* . . . ?" said Selin.

Fanis threw his head back dismissively. "I'll go straighten things out this afternoon."

"She has a thing for you, doesn't she?"

"Perhaps. But it's not mutual. Come on. It's our turn to go inside."

After collecting his stipend, Fanis helped Selin up the steep byway to Sıraselviler Avenue, hailed a taxi, and delivered her to the concert hall. He then spent a delightful day listening to Tchaikovsky's concerto. He was taken in by its gentle and unassuming beginning, its promise of a long journey to an unknown destination, and its dark and lyrical second movement. He closed his eyes to experience the full power of the explosive third movement. What he liked best, however, was the bittersweet energy of the finale, which seemed to signal that the end was not the end at all. Fanis tried to catch glimpses of Orhan the bassoonist, sitting stiffly in his chair. Sure, Orhan was handsome enough, but Fanis couldn't believe that a man who played such a clumsy and confined instrument could possibly be the kind of lover who would satisfy Selin.

When Fanis was not spying on Orhan, he fixed his gaze on Selin and the sweat that had collected on her forehead like a diadem. He questioned if such intense playing could harm her recently operated-on heart. At one point she broke so many bow hairs that she had to stop playing and take up a fresh bow. Fanis wondered what the surgical scar on her chest looked like: would it be an ugly jagged thing or a well-healed seam? It would have to be a red line, he decided, delicate and thin. He felt his tongue run along the ridge. . . .

Selin's voice recalled Fanis to the reality of Lütfi Kırdar: "That's it for today." She was standing before him and holding two steaming paper cups, one of which she held out to him. He hadn't even noticed that the practice was over.

He took the hot cup in both his hands and said, "You were marvelous."

"You're kind," she said.

"Selin . . . do you remember that thing you said about the next man who entered your heart? Last June, at the tea garden? You said that before men came and went through the hole, but that the next one was going to have to stay. Would that be Orhan?"

Selin looked at him with the sassy expression that one usually saw only on the faces of teenagers. "Orhan?"

"Yes. Maybe it's none of my business, but sometimes, from my window, I see him come and go from your place. I didn't want to be indiscreet and ask questions, but. . . . Where is he now, anyway?"

She sat beside him. "Gone already, but he sends his regards. He has a date with Ahmet, his boyfriend."

Fanis flopped back into the velveteen seat. "He's gay?"

"Are you okay, Fanis? You look a bit pale."

Fanis put a hand over his heart. It was still beating. "Of course," he said. "But what about that hickey?"

"*What* hickey?"

He pointed to the discoloration beneath her jaw line.

"And you call yourself a musician? That's fiddler's neck. A hazard of the profession."

"So . . . there's no boyfriend *at all?*"

"Unfortunately not. What about you? It seemed like you were interested in Daphne."

"Oh, come on. Daphne's all right, but I prefer a woman with a better sense of style, an ear for music, and a fuller figure."

"That's good. Because Kosmas is planning on proposing. As soon as his mother is better, that is. I didn't want to tell you because I thought you might be upset."

Fanis finished his tea and crumpled his cup. "Good for Kosmas," he said. He didn't mention that he had sent Daphne a

Christmas card, just to keep things open on the off-chance that she changed her mind. "I always thought they'd make a nice couple. Listen, there's something I want to talk to you about."

Selin gave him a sidelong glance. "What?"

"Did you ever want children?" That wasn't what he'd planned to say. But still, now that he knew she was single, it was an important question.

"Of course I did. But the years passed and now I'm forty-three with a heart condition."

He squeezed her hand. "Another thing we've got in common."

"How so?"

She was being honest with him. He had to man up and do the same. "It's difficult for me to admit this, but . . . I have cerebral arteriosclerosis and early vascular dementia. I could have a stroke at any time."

"Are you taking medication?"

"I burned the prescriptions in the kitchen sink."

"That's a relief."

"Not really. The doctor promised imminent death if I didn't start taking them right away. For a while I put the diagnosis out of my mind, but Rea's fainting scared me a bit."

"*If* she fainted." Selin took his cup from him and stuffed it inside her own. "Don't let her issues scare you, Fanis."

"But Dr. Aydemir is a good doctor. I just wanted you to know because you're my closest neighbor, perhaps even my best friend—"

"Your *best friend?*" Selin tilted her head to one side. "Really?"

"Yes, you are. I always said that friendship between opposite sexes was impossible but, look, we're doing it."

"I'm honored." Selin put her hand on his forearm. Her shimmery black-painted fingernails stood out against his tan cashmere sweater, like beads of licorice. "Listen, Fanis," she said. "Do you feel ill?"

"No." What was he saying? Wasn't he confessing so that she would be prepared for the inevitable? "Well, sometimes," he said. "But not very often."

"If you don't feel ill, then you aren't. But I'm here if you need me. That's what best friends are for."

Fanis sighed at those words: *best friends*. They were as bittersweet as Tchaikovsky's concerto. But in his condition, could he possibly hope for more?

He took Selin home in a taxi, then trudged through the snow to Neighbor's House. Upon arrival, he passed straight into the heated, mirror-walled back area, which his friends used almost as if it were their own private living room. Julien and Gavriela were sitting by the window overlooking the dim snow-covered garden where they took tea in summer.

Julien stood, as he always did out of good breeding. Yet there was something aggressive in his bearing as he pulled out an empty chair for Fanis. "So what's this I hear about you and my kid?"

Apparently Aliki had recovered her ability to speak and put her telephone to use.

"Your kid?" said Fanis, taking his seat.

Julien crossed his arms over his fishing vest. "She may not be my biological child, but she certainly is a scholastic one."

Gavriela raised her sweater neck a little higher, so that it covered the bottom half of her chin. "Selin's hardly a kid."

Julien sat. "I taught Selin for three years at the Lycée," he said, rapping the wooden table with his index finger. "I gave her private lessons for five years before that. I wrote her recommendation for the Conservatoire de Paris. I went to her first professional concert in Lyon. And I got a phone call every time some bastard made her cry. That makes her *my kid*, damn it. And then *you*, Fanis . . . you're old enough to be her grandfather—"

"Not exactly," said Gavriela.

"Please—" said Fanis.

"But he's a womanizer!" said Julien.

All heads in the tea garden turned toward Julien. Gavriela raised her penciled eyebrows and expressed everyone's thoughts with an old Greek proverb: "*Eipe o gaidaros ton peteino kefala.*" And the ass called the cock a bighead.

"Evil-hour!" spat Julien. "Have you got a mouth, Gavriela! Fanis has a right to his fun, but not with my kid. I don't want any more teary phone calls."

"Listen," said Fanis, "we—"

"Emine," said Gavriela, "another round of tea, if you please."

Gavriela extended a loaded plate of butter cookies to Fanis. He took one to calm his nerves, but it was sour and malty, as if the butter had gone bad. Emine returned with the teas. In order to wash away the cookie taste, Fanis took a sip, but the tea was stale. It had obviously been sitting for hours.

"What I think the *professeur* means to say, Fanis," Gavriela resumed, "is that, although you may be in love with Selin, you do need to think about what you have to offer her."

"*Offer* her?" said Fanis. "We're good friends."

Julien rolled his eyes. "As if *you* could be friends with an attractive young woman. Look here, old man, you're not fooling anybody."

"I swear I haven't tried to seduce her," said Fanis.

"Cut it," said Julien. "You've been with her for months. That's why you've been so scarce. And why I haven't heard about any new boyfriends."

Gavriela hissed in disapproval. "In a few years, you'll be a burden to her. Do you really want to weigh her down with your care?"

There it was again: Dr. Aydemir's horrid little prediction in the form of friendly meddling. Why did Fanis have to give in to old age and illness? Why couldn't he just have fun?

But instead of saying any of these things, Fanis shook his head, rose slowly to his feet, and walked out, paying no attention to Julien's attempts to call him back. The bakery door closed behind him with a rude jangling that unleashed the tears he had felt welling in his eyes from the moment Gavriela had said the word "burden."

23

In Winter and in Love

AFTER KOSMAS HAD DISCOURAGED DIMITRIS'S marriage proposal to Rea, the old journalist had had second thoughts.
He had feared that Kosmas was right: perhaps Rea saw him
only as a friend. The seventies are the age of platonic friendship, he told himself. He had already missed the love and
marriage window.

Dimitris put Kosmas's sourness out of mind and took refuge in his old refrain about freedom: "I'm single. That's the
way I like it. Free, without any Madame to give me trouble at
home." As the winter holidays approached, however, he wondered if Kosmas might have been wrong.

In December, Rea told Dimitris to start coming to tea earlier, before Kosmas returned from work, so that he could read
the newspaper to her. She said that her eyes were going, but
Dimitris suspected that this was a lie because one afternoon,
when Rea was worried about the side effects of her statin
medication, she put on her bifocals and read the minuscule
print on the crinkly paper insert without any difficulty at all.

In January, when Rea fainted, Dimitris was her first visitor.
He rushed over on the morning after the episode—just forty
minutes after Kosmas had called him—with a pile of newspapers, a bag of salted pistachios, and two kilos of oranges.

"The nurse has arrived," he called as he entered, bran-
dishing the newspapers over his head like a trophy. Seeing
Kosmas, Dimitris stopped abruptly: the boy's eyelids were

swollen and his face unshaven. "Time for you to take a break, kid," Dimitris said.

"I can't. The doctor said I have to keep an eye on her—"

"He didn't say that *you* had to," Dimitris replied. "He said that *somebody* had to."

"Thanks. But I don't want to impose. Besides, she never lets anybody see her without makeup."

"At least tell her I'm here."

Kosmas nodded and withdrew. Dimitris set the bag of oranges on the kitchen counter, rummaged in Rea's drawers for the small plastic press he had seen her use dozens of times, and set to work. By the time he'd filled a tall glass with orange juice and emptied the pistachios into a chipped porcelain dish, Kosmas reopened the door to Rea's bedroom and called, "She's ready."

Dimitris carried the tray as steadily as he could into the only room in the house he had never seen: Rea's sunny boudoir. She was sitting up in her bed. Her hair was freshly brushed and loosely held by a headband. She had put on powder, fuchsia lipstick, and rouge. "You're as beautiful as ever," said Dimitris, kissing her perfumed cheeks. "It's like nothing happened at all."

That was a lie, of course. He glimpsed an electrode peeking out from beneath Rea's nightshirt. He saw the small, V-shaped gash on her cheek, the bruise on her arm, the under-eye circles that were accentuated rather than covered by the powder, as well as the embarrassment in her expression. The important thing, however, was to make her *feel* beautiful.

Rea stopped the trembling in Dimitris's right hand by clasping it within her own. "I'm glad you came."

Dimitris surrendered to the loose silkiness of her hand. He felt a thrill in his chest and a stirring in his groin—not a full erection, of which he was no longer capable, but a fluttering, an "I'm still alive." He wanted to kiss Rea there and then. Yet Kosmas was sitting opposite him, on the other side of Rea's double bed.

Dimitris said, "You've been missing some important discussions." He grabbed an orange-juice-spattered newspaper from the tray and read the headline: "'The Prime Minister says Syria is headed for a war that could pose a threat to Turkey.'"

"Isn't there any happy news?" said Kosmas "That sort of thing might upset—"

"Nonsense." Rea took a sip of orange juice. "I want to know what's going on in the world. It helps take my mind off my own problems."

Dimitris read: "'At a press conference yesterday in Ankara, the Prime Minister expressed fears that Syria's multi-ethnic and multi-religious population of twenty-two million could disintegrate.'"

Rea clicked her tongue. "Such a shame."

"Kosmaki, really, why don't you go get some rest?" said Dimitris. "And . . . I know you said you weren't going to Miami, but if you did want to go, I'd be happy to sleep on the couch and take care of your mother."

Rea took a short breath.

Kosmas reached for her. "Are you all right, Mama?"

"Fine," she said. "But Kosmas can't go anywhere. It's out of the question. Not that I wouldn't be thrilled to have you, Dimitraki, but people would call me a loose woman if we slept in the same house without any formalities."

"At our age?" said Dimitris.

Rea placed her soft, age-spotted hand on his. "*Especially* at our age,"

"Thanks for offering, Mr. Dimitris." Kosmas looked back and forth between Dimitris and Rea. "But I've already cancelled my ticket. If you could come during the day so that I could go to work for a few hours, I'd really appreciate it."

"Of course!" Dimitris picked up the newspaper to hide his enthusiasm. "Let's see, for the Eurovision Song Contest representative, they've chosen—"

"I guess I'll be going now," said Kosmas, standing.

"Get some rest, son," said Rea. "Or go to work if you need to. The orange juice did wonders for me."

Kosmas paused in the doorway. "Remember when I changed the light bulbs last summer, Mr. Dimitris?" he said.

"Of course," said Dimitris. He could never forget *that* day, one of the worst of his life.

"We don't always understand the people closest to us, Mr. Dimitris. Especially their silence. In other words, cancel whatever shit I said back then."

"Kosmas!" said Rea. "Watch your mouth."

Dimitris felt a surge of hope. He nodded to Kosmas and said, "The problems created by silence can be solved with love."

"What are you two talking about?" said Rea.

"Guy stuff," said Kosmas. "I'll leave you two alone now."

The following day Dimitris bought a diamond ring, just like they did in American movies. It was nothing imaginative: a 4.1mm round solitaire with an 18-carat gold band, but he felt like a millionaire while picking it out. He decided to wait a few weeks to give it to Rea because he didn't want to put any more strain on her overtaxed heart. And then, when the Holter monitor finally showed that Rea didn't need a pacemaker, he decided it would be most romantic to wait until Lover's Day.

On the morning of February 14, he ironed a lime-green shirt, buttoned it all the way to the top, tied a green and pink floral necktie beneath the collar, put on a pair of brown wool pants, and pulled a sweater vest over the shirt. He donned his winter galoshes, his flannel-lined gabardine, and a herringbone newsboy cap. Then he picked up his briefcase, which was empty except for his cell phone and the brown-paper envelope that served as his wallet, and set out on a mission: to say goodbye to his freedom.

He walked to his favorite candy shop in the Balık Pazarı, where he was greeted by his old friend Muharrem, who had been wearing a white lab coat and working in the minty vapors of his father's candy shop ever since he had graduated from the prestigious Galatasaray Lycée fifty-three years before. Muharrem was not only the best-known candy-maker in Pera, but also the most thoughtful: he still phoned Rum neighbors who had immigrated to Athens whenever he read about earthquakes or floods in Greece, just to make sure that they were all right.

"Monsieur," said Dimitris, using a French title because Muharrem spoke that language as if he had grown up in France, "I am saying goodbye to my freedom today."

Muharrem adjusted the lid of a great copper urn, whose handwritten label read *Rose Preserve*. Then he clasped his hands behind his back and said, "*Votre liberté?*"

"I'm proposing to Rea Xenidou."

"Excellent choice," said Muharrem in Turkish. "I always admired her gait when she promenaded in the Grand Avenue with her mother. So graceful."

"She has a cane now," said Dimitris.

"But I'm sure she hasn't lost her poise."

"Certainly not. What sweets should I take her?"

"In winter and in love," said Muharrem, like a doctor giving a prescription, "cinnamon lokum is the best choice."

"A box of cinnamon lokum, then. Perhaps I should offer her some chocolates as well?"

Muharrem put his index finger to his chin. He scanned first the chocolate case and then the glass jars with satiny candies of every flavor—ginger, mint, sesame, cinnamon, quince, fig, sour cherry. "No," he said. "Anything else will ruin the taste of the cinnamon lokum."

Dimitris conceded: "You're the expert."

"When will the wedding be?" asked Muharrem, while filling a half-kilo box with powdery lokum cubes.

"Soon, *inşallah.*"

"*Inşallah,*" Muharrem repeated. "Will I be invited?"

"Of course. How could I get married and not invite you?"

With his package of cinnamon lokum smartly wrapped in cream paper with gold moons, Dimitris set out for Rea's neighborhood. He bought a dozen red roses on the way and was soon sitting in Rea's living room, beside the barred window that she despised. Through it, they could see the park and its trees dusted with snow, as well as children attempting to build miniature snowmen. With that view, over coffee and cinnamon lokum, Dimitris said, "Rea, I need to speak with you."

"About what?"

Dimitris felt a sense of panic. He had focused so much on working up the courage *to* ask that he hadn't thought of *how* he would ask. "Do you think that getting married in one's seventies makes one a laughing stock?" he said. Where had that come from? Dimitris mentally pinched himself.

"Sometimes." Rea stuck a lokum into her mouth and took a sip of coffee to melt it. That was always the way she ate candy. Otherwise the sugar bothered her teeth.

Dimitris continued: "So, if you were giving advice to a widow friend, you'd tell her not to remarry? Out of fear of what people would say?"

"I might have a few years ago. But then I heard something interesting: you shouldn't let your actions be controlled by what others say, because they will say it no matter what you do. And I heard on a talk show that it's never too late to change your life. Not even at seventy."

"That's modern."

"Just like me," said Rea.

It was time. Dimitris pushed himself off the sofa, knelt on his good knee, and took the black velveteen box from his pocket. "Will you be my wife?"

Rea covered her mouth with her hand. Her eyes glassed. She looked out the window, toward the children who were now sticking carrots in the faces of the snowmen. "I . . . I . . . "

He had misjudged. She didn't want to marry after all. He had upset her. "Don't worry, Rea, I didn't really think—"

"I thought you'd never ask," she said. "Of course I will."

She leaned down to him, cupped his cheeks in her palms, and gave him the open-mouth kiss of which he had been dreaming for years. When his knee began to ache, he sat beside her on the sofa and asked the even bigger question: "But will Kosmas give his permission?"

"Why in the good world would I need his permission?" said Rea. "I'm over seventy. Can't I make my own decisions?"

"And your widow's honor?"

"To hell with widow's honor," she said.

24

Intervention

"BETTER," SAID PERIHAN, THE TANGO instructor. She was so short that she didn't even reach Kosmas's chest. "An improvement, *but* . . . "

This was the part of the Sunday lesson that Kosmas hated most. Every Tuesday evening he participated in a group tango lesson, and every Sunday evening he did a private with Perihan. Both took place in the penthouse dance studio at which Kosmas had attended his first *milonga* with Daphne. So far, he had mastered the walk, the embrace, turns, and basic pivots. At the end of each private session, Perihan would choose one of her favorite songs and order Kosmas to lead her. A thorough critique followed.

They were standing in the middle of the dance floor. Perihan slid her pointy tortoiseshell glasses up her nose and said, "That *sacado* was nice the first time. Beautifully executed. But then you did it three more times. You see, tango is like dating."

Kosmas had already learned to expect outrageous statements from Perihan.

She put her hands on her hips. "When a man does something once, it's nice. But four times? *Boring!*"

He protested: "But you said I had to dance to the end of the song. I'm just a beginner. I don't know enough moves not to be repetitious."

"I guess we need to keep working," said Perihan.

Kosmas changed out of his new suede dance shoes, thanked Perihan, and hurried down the stairwell. Before he reached the door, his phone began ringing with a Skype tone. Daphne appeared on his little screen. He could tell that she had just washed and styled her hair: it shone in the sunlight of her balcony. "Congratulations," she said. "They make the perfect couple."

"You know already?"

"My aunt just called. Apparently the news is a few days old. I'm surprised you didn't tell me yourself."

She was right. He should have told her. But he had been avoiding any thought of his mother's engagement. "It's been a little overwhelming. I haven't really digested the whole thing."

"You're not happy for her?"

"Of course I am. Dimitris is a good guy. But I'm even happier that you called. How are the Valentine roses? Holding up?"

"Still beautiful. Thanks again." Daphne took a sip from a big American mug. "My aunt also said that Mr. Fanis is having a fling with Selin."

"Mr. Fanis does have a certain reputation," said Kosmas.

"That's Istanbul gossip for you. Selin says he's been a perfect gentleman. He hasn't even tried to flirt with her. She's almost starting to feel unattractive."

"How about you? Do you miss flirting?"

The screen froze. Damned Skype. It always chose the worst moments to malfunction. "There is a problem with the call," the message said. "Hang on while we try to get it back." The little white dots bubbled, and then Daphne reappeared, holding up her passport. "I'm a Turkish citizen now."

The stress and exhaustion brought on by the lesson, as well as the sudden good news, overwhelmed Kosmas. He sank onto the stairs. "That's so exciting. Congratulations."

"Thanks. How's the Balkanik coming along?"

Between caring for his mother and working, Kosmas had managed to translate the recipe into something he could use.

He now understood the general construction: the Balkanik was a long hollow pastry with a consistency that fell somewhere between that of an éclair and a sponge cake. It was filled with lightly flavored creams: chocolate, vanilla, cardamom, rose, pistachio, saffron, mastic gum, orchid root. The creams were piped one beside another, but not mixed. Finally, the filled pastry was glazed, carefully coiled into a snail-shell shape, and reglazed. The replication, however, was not easy. The wheat of the early 1900s was not the wheat of 2011, as Fanis often said. Hamdi's measurements were inexact, his cooking times nonexistent, and a few terms escaped Kosmas's comprehension. Even so, Kosmas was getting close.

"Super," he said, trying to sound confident. "I'm sure I'll have it perfected soon. And I've got more good news. After Easter we're taking over the next-door shop space. We're going to double the Lily's size."

"*Hayırlısı*," said Daphne. May it turn out for the best. Then she added, "What about Easter? Are you finally going to use your ticket?"

"I'm trying, my love. I'm even interviewing assistants, but I haven't found anyone yet."

"You know, I was thinking about something you said when we were at the Galata Tower. You said our love had to be steadfast, and you were completely right. I was an idiot for crying over Paul. But now I'm wondering if the issue is more than work. Perhaps it's still your mother."

How could she have hit that back at him?

"Absolutely not," said Kosmas. "Believe me, I'm trying hard to find another pâtissier to help out. It's just that my standards are high. You know that."

"*Tamam*." She blew him a kiss and waited. Kosmas also waited. Daphne hadn't said it first in a week, but he desperately wanted to hear it: the *first* "I love you," not just the reply.

"Have a good night, then," she said. "We'll talk in the morning."

He started to say "I love you," but she had already hung up.

On February 25, Kosmas readied a box of macaroons, asked one of Fanis's neighbors to allow him in when the doorbell went unanswered, climbed Fanis's four flights of stairs, and knocked at the apartment door.

"Who's there?" Fanis asked.

"It's me, Kosmas."

Fanis opened. He wore an old-fashioned navy smoking jacket belted at his waist. "Ah, Kosmaki . . . come in. What are you doing here?"

Kosmas held out the box of pastries. "I thought you might like a visit."

"Perfect! I just made a pot of tea. Have a seat!"

While Fanis bustled about in the kitchen, Kosmas noticed a men's corset that had been carelessly thrown onto a side table. Well, well. Apparently Fanis hadn't shared all his beauty tricks.

Kosmas sat down in the oriel just before Fanis returned with the tea. "Aren't you engaged yet?" Fanis asked.

"Excuse me?"

Fanis poured the tea into gold-rimmed porcelain cups. "I'm a gracious loser."

"Selin seems more your type, anyway," said Kosmas, glancing at the corset.

"Selin is a *friend*."

"Sure, Mr. Fanis. Whatever you say."

Fanis sighed and shook his head. "How's the *professeur*?"

"Still a bit angry, but he'll get over it."

"And the ladies?"

"Aliki will probably need some time."

"Tell me about Daphne, then."

Kosmas cracked his thumb. "Things have cooled down a little . . . because of my mother." He took a tissue from his man bag and wiped the sweat on his forehead. Ever since Rea's crisis, Kosmas had been having more and more of these moments. His heart raced. He sweated excessively. For a few minutes, he would feel like he had entirely lost control of his life, and then, slowly, he would regain his perspective, but the fear of losing Daphne never left him.

"I'd do anything for her, Mr. Fanis," he said. "Anything. I've even been taking Argentine tango lessons so I can surprise her, and I'm looking for an apartment, but still, if she and my mother can't get along, none of it will help."

Fanis sighed. "Mothers." His eyes wandered over his eclectic antique furniture and settled on the corset. He sprang to his feet and threw it into the sideboard cabinet. "Excuse my untidiness," he said.

Pretending not to have noticed, Kosmas said, "Did Selin tell you that Daphne's father is Ottoman? It doesn't bother me, but my mother—I'm worried."

Fanis reassumed both his seat and his philosopher's expression. "You get over your mother, and she'll get over the Ottoman father. I know what I'm talking about. You see, I was in love with a girl once. At a crucial moment, my mother convinced me not to go see her. I think my mother's motives were good, but of course I shouldn't have listened. That mistake cost me dearly."

Kosmas downed half his tea, almost as if it were raki, and made a second confession: "Mr. Dimitris is moving in next week."

"You see? Rea gets over you quite quickly when she wants to. Bravery and brass: that's what life requires, son. You've got to stand up to your mama, no matter how much she faints." Fanis leaned over the arm of his chair. "Listen. I'll tell you a little secret, even though I swore not to tell anyone. Daphne is coming for Easter. She's arriving on her name day."

"Palm Sunday?" Kosmas stood. "But just last week she was asking if I'd go to Miami."

"Perhaps she gave up on you. Anyway, her father bought her a ticket so that she could visit again and see how she feels before she gives up everything there. Selin said I wasn't to tell anyone, but I've never been very good at keeping secrets. Of that nature, at least. Now drink your tea and let's talk about something else, like your tango lessons. Maybe I'll give it a try."

"Don't," said Kosmas. He retook his seat, but his right foot began tapping nervously. "It's absolutely excruciating. It takes hours and hours just to learn the tiniest thing. The couples argue, and the singles are all looking for dates or at least a cheap feel—"

"Really?" said Fanis, widening his eyes. "Even the women?"

"Even the women."

Fanis bit his lower lip and raised his shoulders. "So it's like wife-swapping, but with your clothes on?"

"I guess you could put it that way."

"Sounds like great fun."

"No, Mr. Fanis. It's like wearing a starched shirt—stiff and annoying as hell. I'm doing it for Daphne."

"There's only one thing that you need to do for her."

"Thanks for the tea. With your permission . . . I've got to talk to my mother."

"With my *blessings*," said Fanis.

Kosmas rushed home. As he was chaining the Vespa to a lamppost opposite his mother's barred window, he heard a familiar voice say in Greek, "Just in time for tea!"

Kosmas looked up. Dimitris was standing on his doorstep with a bag of groceries. "What's up, son?" he said. "You look like you've been hit by a storm."

Kosmas tried to swallow, but his throat was too dry. "Has my mother said anything to you about . . . Daphne's father?"

Dimitris placed his hand on Kosmas's forearm. "What? That he's Ottoman? Son, I'm a journalist. It's my job never to forget a name or a face. I've known all along, and I can tell you that Ilyas Badem is a fine man."

"You *knew?*" Kosmas couldn't believe it. And yet . . . hadn't Daphne said something about Dimitris and her father when they were at Madame Kyveli's?

Dimitris winked. "I usually try to stay out of this stuff, but—if you'd like—I'll put in a good word."

"*Yeia sto stoma sas*, Mr. Dimitris." Health to your mouth.

Kosmas followed him inside the apartment. In the kitchen, they found Rea already mixing coffee and water in a copper pot. A plate of chocolates sat in the middle of the two-seater linoleum table: she had obviously been expecting her fiancé. "Mama, I need to talk to you," said Kosmas, nervously snatching a chocolate. "About Daphne."

Rea turned to Kosmas while stirring the coffee briskly with a metal spoon. Kosmas could almost hear the damage to the pot's tin lining.

"I thought we'd settled this," she said.

Kosmas put the chocolate in his mouth and mumbled, "She's coming for Easter."

Rea tossed the spoon into the sink. Behind her, the already lit gas burner hissed. "I thought you didn't eat sweets at home," she said.

"*Tatlı yiyelim, tatlı konuşalım*," said Kosmas, in an effort to lighten the mood. It was one of his mother's favorite Turkish expressions: Let's eat sweets and speak sweetly.

"Is that even possible?" said Rea, staring hard at Kosmas. "With *this* subject?"

Dimitris pushed past Kosmas, forcing him back to the doorway. There wasn't enough room in that kitchen for three. Dimitris kissed Rea's cheek with a loud smack, just as one did to make babies laugh. The kiss had a similar effect on Rea: she smiled despite her annoyance.

"Love of my life," said Dimitris, "you know I don't like squeezing into your relationship with Kosmas, but there's something you should know. Have a seat."

Rea set the coffee pot on the burner, pulled a creaky kitchen chair all the way to the door, and sat. Kosmas had to take a step into the hallway so that he wasn't hovering directly above his mother.

Dimitris continued: "In 1963, when I was a young reporter and things were heating up in Cyprus, I used to go to the Hilton regularly for tea. Ilyas Badem always took care of us. One evening some nationalist bastard—who had obviously been drinking—walked into the tea room, grabbed me by the collar, and called me a filthy Rum instigator. I hadn't even been covering Cyprus then. So you see how ridiculous the whole thing was." Dimitris glanced at the coffee. "Anyway, Ilyas called two of his doormen and threw the guy out. He gave instructions never to let the man into the Hilton again, and later he apologized to me."

Dimitris served Rea and Kosmas their coffee and began mixing a third for himself. "What I'm saying," he said, "is that you should be proud your son is in love with the daughter of Ilyas Badem."

Rea lifted her cup from the saucer and mopped up the coffee that had spilled on the way from the counter to the table.

"I know it's hard," said Dimitris, "but sometimes you've just got to let go. Now, if you'll excuse me, I have to use the bathroom. Kosmaki, you'll mind my coffee, won't you?"

As soon as Dimitris had gone, Kosmas set his coffee on the table and sat in the empty chair opposite his mother. "Mama," he said, "I congratulated you when you got engaged."

Rea ran her fingers over the leaves of the new African violet that Kosmas had bought her as a get-well gift. It was almost as if she was seeking solace in their softness. She said, "It's not the same thing."

"Mama, please."

Rea looked up at Kosmas. Her eyes were full of tears. Kosmas understood the battle going on inside her, the struggle between identity and humanity. Knowing that he was the cause of that turmoil broke his heart.

"I don't know," she said. "I don't know."

25

Bride Unwedded

FOR A FEW WEEKS AFTER their falling-out, Fanis did not see or speak with Julien or Aliki, and his communication with Gavriela was confined to brief small talk at the supermarket or in the Panagia's narthex. When Gavriela called one morning in early March and asked if she could accompany him to the Salutations to the All-Holy Mother—the first of the five Lenten services—Fanis decided it was time to forgive. After all, how would he take Holy Communion at the Easter Resurrection service if he were still angry with his friends?

The following Friday afternoon, as Gavriela and Fanis climbed Yeni Çarşı Street, it began to drizzle. "Good heavens," said Fanis. "The weather report said nothing of rain."

"And I just had my hair done," said Gavriela. She pulled a plastic rain bonnet from her purse and tied it around her chin.

On the corner of Yeni Çarşı Street and the Grand Avenue, boys holding buckets of clear plastic umbrellas shouted, "Umbrella, umbrella! Ladies and gentlemen, come on over!"

Fanis bought one and held it over Gavriela. Then he remembered that he wanted to buy a box of cinnamon lokum. He'd been feeling dizzy lately, and sugar always seemed to help. He looked at his watch: four thirty-five. Since his trainee would be at the church, however, it wouldn't matter if they were a few minutes late. "Let's stop quickly at Muharrem's," he said. "On the way, you can catch me up on Kosmas and Daphne."

"That crosspatch Rea is trying to break them up," said Gavriela. "It's not that I don't understand her point of view. I wasn't happy when my sister married an Ottoman. But this is different. It isn't about religion at all. Rea just wants Kosmas all to herself."

"I can't say I haven't suspected the same thing."

"Daphne's like a daughter to me, Fanis." Gavriela made her characteristic hissing sound. "I had such high hopes that she might come home. But Rea's going to ruin it for all of us."

"Come, come," said Fanis, as they hurried past fish tables and shop fronts illumined by single bulbs dangling into the gray Istanbul evening. "Don't see everything black. She's coming for Easter at least."

"That's just a visit," said Gavriela, with her eyes on the cobblestones. "Only eight days. I want forever."

They stopped beneath the awning of Muharrem's sweet shop. With her eyes fixed now on the baklava trays in the display case, Gavriela said, "Listen, Fanis, I'm sorry about what I said at Neighbor's House. It was such a shock for us."

"Never mind," said Fanis. "It's flattering, really, that you supposed us to be a couple."

"We're all sorry, especially Julien. He told me to tell you so."

"Why doesn't he tell me himself?"

"He's embarrassed. Especially given his record with women. But he wanted you to come to Neighbor's House after the Salutations. He said he'd call and invite Selin."

Fanis glanced at his watch: a quarter to five. He put his hand on the damp shoulder of Gavriela's wool coat. "Past and forgotten. Come, let's say hello to Muharrem and pick up the lokum. Otherwise we'll be late to church."

The Akathist was Fanis's favorite service. He was overwhelmed by its melancholy exultation, its literary beauty, and its use of rhyme, assonance, bold simile, and alliteration.

Upon arrival at the church, he quickly slipped on his scratchy black polyester robe—a good protection against the church's damp, chilly air—and joined his young trainee, Pandelis, at the cantor's stand. At the end of the priest's apolytikion, Fanis swung the music stand toward the boy and said, "Yours, son."

Pandelis chanted the initial troparion alone while Fanis held a drone note to enrich the celebratory melody: "*I shall open my mouth and it shall be filled with the Spirit . . .*"

Pandelis's voice was sweet, but Fanis immediately understood why the Patriarchate had sent him: he was an acrobat afraid to fall. A cantor had to be a swimmer, not a trapeze artist; he had to immerse himself and swim in the notes, not jump from one to the next.

Fanis whispered to the boy, "Instead of trying to hit the right notes, settle deep within yourself and let the chant flow out."

Apart from being Fanis's favorite service, the Akathist was also one of the rare hymns to which the women parishioners chanted along with the cantors. And yet Fanis did not hear Gavriela joining in. He discreetly peered over the back of the stand and saw her sniffling and dabbing her eyes. Was she weeping? She had seemed fine on their walk through the Fish Bazaar. Fanis nodded to Pandelis and approached Gavriela. "What's wrong?" he asked.

"Daphne called today," said Gavriela. "I didn't want to say anything, but . . . she was rejected by Istanbul and Boğaziçi universities. And since Kosmas hasn't rescheduled his trip, I'm afraid she might be reconsidering her decision to move here."

The priest finished the first set of Salutations. Pandelis chanted, "*Rejoice, Bride unwedded.*" His voice was more optimistic. A definite improvement.

Fanis put his hand on Gavriela's shoulder. "But she applied to Bilgi, too, didn't she? And things could change with Kosmas. Listen, we'll talk later, I have to—"

"What if none of our young people return?" Gavriela sobbed. "Is this the end of our community?"

Fanis had to think of something to calm her down. "The Patriarch says we should believe in renewal. Not just hope for it, but *believe* in it."

"My husband says that the Patriarch sells fairytales," returned Gavriela. She blew her nose. "But I *want* to believe."

Fanis squeezed her shoulder. "It'll all work out, Gavriela. For Daphne, for all of us. We must have faith."

The rain had started coming down even harder while they were inside the church. In the Grand Avenue and Yeni Çarşı Street, Gavriela and Fanis had managed to walk single-file beneath shop awnings, but, upon entering Çukurcuma, they were forced to huddle beneath the umbrella. "Aliki's playing bridge with her girlfriends today," said Gavriela, as they climbed the steps leading to Neighbor's House.

"Didn't want to see me, I suppose?"

"She will. Eventually."

"And Rea?"

"She'll come later with Dimitris. Aliki said they went to Holy Trinity today. To see the bishop. Not to avoid you, of course."

They hurried past the budding acacia trees of the mosque's square and turned the corner to Neighbor's House. As Fanis held the door for Gavriela, the half-comforting, half-nauseating odor of the tea garden's factory-prepared cookies wafted out into the damp evening. Wiping his feet on the mat, Fanis realized that the piano music he heard—"La Vie en rose"— was live. Normally they played soft jazz in the indoor space, while the outdoor area was pleasantly quiet, apart from the traffic in Sıraselviler Avenue.

Fanis dropped his umbrella into the holder by the entrance and followed Gavriela to the back room. Near the door to the toilets, they found Julien playing an upright piano. Selin, wearing a red beret, was sitting on the piano bench beside him and singing along to Edith Piaf's "La Vie en rose."

Seeing her, Fanis felt at once blessed to have Selin as a friend and jealous of her attachment to Julien. To hide the latter, he said in Turkish, "Since when did Neighbor's House become a concert hall?"

Gavriela carefully peeled off her rain hat. "The new manager bought the piano last week," she said. "The *professeur* thinks his playing charms the ladies."

Julien brought the piece to an early finish, stood, and held out his hand to Fanis. "Finally remembered us?"

Fanis pulled Julien close for a double cheek kiss. His friend's skin exuded the sweet, rotting odor of whiskey. "I never forgot you," Fanis said.

"You swear you and my kid are just friends?"

This, Fanis surmised, was Julien's attempt at reconciliation. "I give you my word."

They made for the tables by the window overlooking the garden, hung their coats on the wall hooks, and settled in. "On the way over here," said Fanis, switching into Turkish for Selin, "I was thinking that we need to help poor Kosmas with that mother of his."

"That's gallant of you," said Julien.

"I want Kosmas to be happy. Still, I can't figure out what to do with Rea."

"She needs an education," said Selin.

"*An education?*" said Fanis.

A chilly draft blew into the back room. Fanis shivered: his shoes and socks were wet. He hoped he wouldn't catch a cold. Seeing him quiver, Selin took off her wool scarf, wrapped it twice around Fanis's neck, and said, "Rea needs to learn something about genetics. The various peoples of Turkey are not so different. Genetically, anyway."

"Where did you hear *that?*" said Gavriela.

"I read a study about it on the internet."

Fanis opened an unbleached paper tube of brown sugar and dumped it into the tea just delivered by Emine. "You can't believe everything you see on a computer screen," he said.

"This was a serious university study," said Selin. She took her iPad from her handbag and handed it to Fanis. With Julien and Gavriela crowding toward him, he skimmed the text, swept his finger over the screen, and came to a map of Europe dotted with pie charts. Greece and Turkey had almost identical DNA frequencies: balanced pinwheels of orange, green, red, black, and yellow.

"And?" he said.

"Look at the key," said Selin, pointing. "The light green represents the Minoan Greek gene. The Greeks have the same amount of that as the Turks. The black is Caucasian and Greco-Anatolian. The dark green is Arab and Jewish, the yellow Mycenaean Greek. The orange is also Mediterranean, and the red represents Hittite and Armenian."

Fanis set the iPad on the table. "Do you mean to say . . . that the Turks are almost as indigenous as we are?"

"Yes," said Selin.

"Nonsense," said Gavriela. "I don't believe a word."

Fanis stirred his tea, took a sip of its hot, sugary bitterness, and said, "Neither do I."

Julien took the iPad and looked at the charts through his bifocals. "So the Turks aren't Turks?"

"Depends," said Selin. "If you define Modern Turks as the people of Turkey, then of course Turks are Turks. But that doesn't mean everyone is a thoroughbred descendant of Central Asian nomads."

Fanis heard a tremolo of glass and porcelain and turned to see Dimitris approaching with two teas, a third of which had already spilled onto the tray.

"Where's Rea?" said Julien.

"Right behind me." Dimitris set down the tray and shooed the cat from a chair.

Fanis noticed that Dimitris's formerly yellow claws had healed into clear, neat nails—perhaps as a result of the apple-cider-vinegar treatment that Rea had imposed. Love was working miracles.

A cane snapped on the laminate floor, heralding Rea's appearance in the passageway. Fanis was surprised by how youthful Rea looked. He almost wondered if she was doing those poisonous injections called something like *buttocks*.

"How's your health, Rea?" said Julien.

Rea hung her cane on the back of the chair that Dimitris held for her at the head of the joined tables. Fanis glanced at Gavriela: she was looking out the window at the flooded garden, as if even the sight of Rea was unbearable.

"*O gegonen gegonen*," said Rea, using an Ancient Greek expression. "What happened happened. But it's not likely to happen again. The doctors say I'm not even anemic anymore, with all the liver and onions that my fiancé fries for me."

Fanis and Selin exchanged a glance. "Thank God," said Fanis.

"And the wedding?" said Selin.

"No rush." Rea's new peacock-feather barrette—miraculously untouched by the rain—bobbed as she spoke.

Selin pronounced the standard Turkish wish: "*Allah bir yastıkta kocatsın.*" May you grow old on the same pillow.

"I'm all for the same pillow," said Julien. "But old . . . who wants it?"

"Speak for yourself," said Rea. "If you could take the physical problems away—the bad knees, the swollen ankles, the illness—I've never been happier. I like making my own decisions. I never did that before my husband died."

Emine delivered a plate of almond cookies on the house. Fanis smiled at her, graciously took a cookie, and said to Rea, "I went by the Lily yesterday. Kosmas said he rented an apartment. That must give you some peace of mind, Rea, knowing he's settled, but nearby?"

Rea turned abruptly toward Fanis. Dimitris explained in a whisper, "Rea is traditional. She doesn't think her son should move out until he's married."

Fanis looked to Selin, who always knew how to remedy a difficult situation. She winked at Fanis, fingered the edge of the white-work collar peeking out from beneath Rea's cardigan, and said, "I adore your blouse."

"It's broderie anglaise," said Rea. "They say I do an excellent satin stitch."

"You did it yourself?"

Rea took a deep breath through her nose and nodded. The peacock feather bowed like a graceful ballerina. Now that a little flattery had put Rea in better spirits, Fanis slid the iPad over the table. He said, "We've been doing some reading about genetics."

"Genetics?"

Fanis showed Rea the multicolored pie charts of haplotype distributions across Europe and Turkey. "It's a little disconcerting, but . . . look at the colors. What do you notice if you compare the Greek and Turkish charts?"

The vein on Rea's neck throbbed. "What would I know about reading charts?" she said.

"Look, dear," said Fanis. "Just compare them as if they were cakes."

"They're almost the same," said Rea.

"Exactly," said Selin. "See the green and black? That's Ancient Greek. The Turks have almost as much of it as the Greeks."

"The sliver of yellow is the Central Asian element," said Julien, raising his eyebrows as if he didn't believe his own words. "Apparently they don't have too much of it."

"Your point is?" said Rea.

"The point," said Selin, "is that, genetically speaking, nobody is any one thing."

Rea set the iPad down. "Of course," she said. "The Ottomans forced so many Christians to convert. That's how they got our genes."

"In fact," said Selin, "many Christians and Jews converted willingly. Out of interest."

"It's true," said Dimitris. "The historians say there were more Rums fighting for the Ottomans outside the City walls than there were defending it from the inside in 1453. When you get right down to it, all our conflicts and wars are really just the same sort of infighting that has been occurring since Homeric times."

"Where are you going with this?" Rea asked.

"It's unsettling," said Fanis, "but it seems that when we call them 'Ottomans,' we're not really talking about an entirely different race. Just a different religion."

"But that different religion makes all the difference in the world in their eyes, Fanis. *You* of all people should know that."

Fanis ignored Rea's reference to Kalypso. He had to stay focused. "And if the religion doesn't differ at all?" he asked.

Gavriela, who had, until then, followed the conversation with her lips pressed tightly together, now snapped her gloves on her lap and said, "And if the religion is the same? What's the problem *then*, Rea?"

"The problem," said Rea, her whole body trembling like Dimitris's hands, "is that we're second-class citizens. I don't know where you found those charts Fanis, but you can't wipe away all that's happened to us!"

"I understand your feelings, Madame Rea," said Selin. "During World War Two one of my great uncles was hit hard by the Capitol Tax against non-Muslims and sent to a labor camp in the east. He got very sick and almost died. It's not easy for my parents to forget that."

"They shouldn't," said Rea.

"But," said Selin, "nobody under sixty participated in that stuff—neither the Capitol Tax, nor the pogrom of 'fifty-five, nor even in the expulsions and nationalistic pressures of the sixties and seventies. And not everybody over sixty participated, either. Many of them supported us."

"She's right," said Fanis. "What it really comes down to is this, dear Rea. Daphne's father had nothing to do with what happened. He wouldn't have married a Rum if he had. So why are you holding Daphne responsible?"

"Please. Stop," Rea pleaded. "I don't want to lose my son."

Fanis put his hand on her shoulder and said, "If you keep going like this, you will."

26

The Tomb of a Goddess

A WEEK BEFORE DAPHNE'S ARRIVAL, Fanis realized he was out
of drinking water. He placed an order, but he knew that the
service could take all day, so he put on his coat and went down
to the minimart. Its Anatolian proprietress was sitting on her
doorstep with her chin in her palm, probably waiting for her
grandchildren, who came every afternoon to play with the
balls kept in a net pinned to the shop's exterior wall.

"Welcome, Uncle," she said.

Fanis gritted his teeth at the respectful title, mumbled a
"Well we find you," and scanned the crates of onions, tomatoes, lemons, and potatoes lying on the sidewalk. He asked for
a half-liter bottle of water.

After finishing his errand, he should have gone straight
home. Instead he moved on toward the inevitable. He
looked frequently over his shoulder to make sure that the
next truck did not flatten him like roadkill. He turned
into Ağa Hamamı Street and continued walking until he
arrived at the dreaded cul-de-sac. For years his heart had
been breaking whenever he unwittingly caught sight of the
satellite dishes, crumbling stairs, corrugated plastic sheets
installed as awnings, and other signs that the mansions of
Kalypso's street had become poor tenements. On that day,
however, he received an even greater shock: the exterior
of the wooden house where she had lived had been completely renovated. Its front stairs had been redone with new

marble, its corroding door replaced with a steel security door painted bright green, and its shingles varnished to a shine he had not seen in over fifty years. Fanis ascended the alley. Two little girls sitting in the doorway of another house giggled. They were probably laughing at him, a short old man turning in circles and looking up at those houses as if he were lost not in space, but in time.

Fanis returned home and went straight to his mother's room, which he maintained exactly as it had been during her lifetime. He sat down on the violet-embroidered coverlet that his mother had made before she was married. Above the headboard, in a heavy, gold-painted frame was a vista of the Bosporus lined with pine trees. On the nightstand was his parents' wedding photograph, taken on the steps of the Panagia. He knew that if he looked into the armoire, he would find all his mother's clothes protected by prodigious amounts of naphthalene and lavender. Since her death he had not dared open it even once.

He did not pull back the lace curtains that shielded his view of the street. Instead, he imagined his neighborhood of vines hanging from wires between the houses. He saw Ağa Hamamı Street torn up for repaving, as it had been the previous summer. He envisioned the men who had set up their plastic chairs to watch the bulldozers as if they were at a sporting event. He saw his mother and wife step out of a beauty parlor that had closed decades ago. They were whispering as they walked, and he was sure that they were talking about him.

"Mother," he said out loud. "Why did you tell me not to go?"

Fanis took off the two wedding bands he had worn on the same finger since his wife's death. He placed them on his mother's pillow, took Kalypso's photo from the side table on which he had left it after Murat's visit, and exited the building. He climbed Turnacıbaşı Street, merged into the pedestrian traffic in the Grand Avenue, and turned off into the byway leading to the Panagia church. There he found the bishop half asleep in an office chair.

Fanis cleared his voice to wake him gently. When that didn't work, he said, "Your Eminence."

"Leave off with the fancy title,'" said the bishop, pulling himself up straight. "You know I'm not fond of protocol."

Fanis stuck his nose into the narcissus flowers on the bishop's desk and inhaled spring. "Do you remember, Elder," he said, "when we were not alone?"

"Of course," said the bishop.

"And do you remember when Pera was full of churches?"

"It still is. But more than all that, I remember when Pera was full of pastry shops. A step and a pastry shop. Another step and another pastry shop. Those were the days. Now tell me, what brings you here?"

"Confession," said Fanis.

"You haven't confessed for as long as I've been a cleric."

"Then it's about time, isn't it?"

The bishop removed his tie and jacket, donned his vestments and pectoral cross, and said a prayer. Then he sat down across from Fanis, in one of the armchairs in front of the desk. "Behold, my child," he said. "Christ stands here and hears your confession."

"I have been licentious my whole life," said Fanis. "I was unfaithful to my wife countless times . . ."

"Why don't you tell me something I don't already know?"

Fanis took the photo of Kalypso from his breast pocket, kissed it, and handed it to the bishop. "It was the name day of my fiancée's grandmother," he began. "I was supposed to close the shop at six and go to dinner at her grandmother's house in the Old City. Instead, when the troubles started, I saw to the shop and my mother. My fiancée's father went to protect the family business. My fiancée, her mother, grandmother, and siblings were left alone."

"There is no sin in looking after one's mother," said the bishop, quietly passing the photo back to Fanis.

"Perhaps there isn't, but while I was looking after my mother, my fiancée was . . . raped on the steps of her grandmother's house. People saw. When those things occur behind closed doors or in secret places, the girls can attempt to face the world as if nothing has happened, as if the shame doesn't hover between them and their family, friends, and neighborhood. They aren't forever known as one of the girls dishonored on the night of the pogrom. But Kalypso—"

"Still, it wasn't your fault."

"It's not just that, Elder. My real sin—the weight I have been carrying all these years—is that I didn't go to visit her immediately afterwards. I thought there was time. I didn't want to cause her any more distress. My mother said it was better to let a couple days pass, let her womenfolk attend to her, and I was so angry at those men I didn't know . . . I wasn't sure if I could control myself, or if I could listen to details if she chose to tell me—"

"Fanis, caring for a loved one who has survived trauma is difficult, to say the least. You need to be a bit gentler with yourself. You didn't know what to do. That's all."

"But, Elder, that has to be why she killed herself."

"How do you know?"

"I feel it. She thought I'd abandoned her."

The bishop sighed. "The secrecy of the mystery of penance is indisputable," he said, staring up at the yellow watermarks on the ceiling. "But"—he lowered his gaze—"when the penitent has already passed to the other side, and when one of those in this life can be helped, perhaps a disclosure is in order . . ."

"Elder?"

"The girl's father came to me before the family's sudden departure for Canada. He, too, blamed himself for the suicide. Apparently, despite what happened, the girl didn't want to leave the City. Whether it was for you or because she didn't want to leave her home, or both, I don't know, but Petridis insisted on taking her away from here, shouted in his frustration even. A few hours later, after the others had gone to bed, she did what she did, God rest her soul."

"It wasn't that she knew I knew? That I didn't tell her it was all right, that it didn't matter, that it made no difference to me? It wasn't *any* of that?"

"Fanis, what happened was terrible, but it certainly wasn't your fault. Or her father's. You were both traumatized. Secondary survivors."

"What does *that* mean?" said Fanis, annoyed that the bishop would choose a time like this to show off his English.

"My niece—the smart one who did her PhD in Boston—taught me the term. It's what American psychologists call the family of trauma victims. In a way, you, too, are—indirectly, of course—a rape survivor. And survivors must never blame themselves."

Secondary survivor? Fanis had never thought of himself in that way. If he had called himself secondary anything, it would have been secondary criminal. Or secondary murderer. Certainly not secondary survivor. Tears came to his eyes.

The bishop ran his fingers along the edge of the embroidered stole. "What brought you here *today*, Fanis? After all these years?"

Fanis glanced down at the sunburned girl sitting on the church wall. "I need to say goodbye to her, Elder. I . . . even if what you say is true . . . I feel I need to erase the old notebook, as they say. I don't want to live with ghosts anymore. And . . . I never visited her grave. I just couldn't. I guess I thought that maybe, if I didn't see her grave, then it didn't exist. So, you see, I abandoned her in death as well."

The bishop cleared his throat. "Listen, Fanis. It's true that, as Orthodox Christians, we have no past and no dead. Our past is always present, and the dead are always with us while we are in church. Still, the dead should not be a part of our daily life. Put your hand to the plow. Stop looking back. And take a good look around you: *now* is quite different from *then*."

"Yes, Elder." Fanis crossed his arms over his chest and bowed at the waist.

The bishop covered Fanis's head with his stole and gave the absolution: "Whatever you have said to my humble person, and whatever you have failed to say, whether through ignorance or forgetfulness, whatever it may be, may God forgive you in this world and the next."

The bishop whistled—the same piercing whistle with which he had frightened girls when he was a teenager. "Get the car ready," he called to Samuel, his assistant. Then, to Fanis, "I'm on my way to Şişli Cemetery for a Trisagion. Would you like to come? We'll say a memorial for Kalypso as well."

"So you remember her name?"

"Of course I do. You're the only one who pretends to have forgotten her. Now, are you coming or not?"

Fanis sat in the back of the bishop's black Opel Astra with nervous anticipation. At the cemetery gate, the bishop gave him an affectionate shoulder shake and went off with Samuel to read the first Trisagion. Fanis asked the Antiochian caretaker to look up the location of Kalypso's family tomb. Both her death and her funeral had been kept quiet by her family. Fanis hadn't learned of either until she was already in the grave. He had thought of buying poison and going by night to join her, like Romeo unable to live without his Juliet, but he knew that his mother would never have been able to bear it. So he had never gone.

The caretaker spent a few minutes searching for the record of Kalypso's burial in a dusty leather-bound book. Finally he put his finger on a listing: "There she is." He turned to the cemetery map and pointed to the rear left corner.

Fanis was surprised. One of his friends was buried close by, yet he had never noticed Kalypso there. Then he realized that he had brought nothing—no flowers, no potted plants, no whirligigs, votives, or incense. In a childlike manner, he stated his predicament.

The caretaker grabbed a pocket knife, exited, and returned with three hydrangea mopheads. "We have plenty of these, Uncle. I don't normally cut them, but never mind."

"Brother," corrected Fanis.

"Excuse me?"

"Brother," Fanis repeated. "I prefer that you call me 'Brother' instead of 'Uncle.'"

The caretaker patted him on the back.

They picked their way over the slippery mud, and cobbles still wet with the previous night's rain. At one point Fanis nearly fell. The gardener caught him and offered to carry the hydrangeas so that Fanis could hold onto his arm with both hands. Ten minutes later, they came upon a bare metal cross.

"There must be a mistake," said Fanis. He had always imagined that Kalypso's tomb would be covered with a marble slab and crowned by more marble, oval photos, and carved lilies.

"No, we're in the right place, Brother. That's Kalypso Petridou's grave. Says so right there."

Fanis examined the marker more closely. Circling the four points of the cross was a metal wreath on which her name and years had been engraved and blackened. Then he remembered the state that the cemetery had been in at the time. The family tomb had probably been destroyed.

The caretaker stepped away to smoke a cigarette beneath the cypress trees. Fanis threaded the hydrangea stems through the metal wreath and knelt on the damp earth. He ran his fingers over the letters etched in black. The moisture on the ground seeped through his pants and made wet circles on his knees. Kalypso probably hadn't had a visit since her funeral.

"Are you all right?" said the caretaker.

"Fine." Fanis could hear the clinking of Samuel's censor and the light shuffling footsteps of the bishop.

"Is that your wife buried there?" asked the caretaker.

Fanis ran his fingers over the first letters of her name. "No," he said. "It is the tomb of a goddess."

He heard the sweeping of cloth on the dry leaves and then the chant, "Blessed is our God always, both now and ever, and to the ages of ages." He rose to his feet and crossed himself. He tried to concentrate on the prayers, but instead he heard Kalypso humming their song. He closed his eyes.

Kalypso slipped her hand into his and led him down Faik Paşa Street. Through shop windows that had existed decades ago, Fanis saw the quilt maker kneeling on a piece of pink satin and covering it with down. The maid of the stately gray–mauve building finished watering the window-box geraniums and brought out a bucket and mop to scrub her employer's front step. The dusty silk crocuses in Fanis's next-door neighbor's window boxes came to life.

Fanis's street became a beach. Kalypso in her white summer dress, laughing her careless laughter, conjured a warm land breeze. Just before stepping into a sailboat, she threw her arms around his neck, licked his outer ear, and nibbled his lobe with a tender ferocity that made him moan with pleasure. She said nothing. There was nothing to say. They both knew that the way she had gone no longer mattered.

Kalypso cast off the stern hawsers by herself. Fanis, recovering from the ear treatment, pushed the sailboat into the moonlight. She leaned on the oar, keeping the Great Bear and Orion to her left, and sang "My Sweet Canary."

Fanis took a deep breath and opened his eyes to the swaying of the cypresses in the spring breeze.

The bishop chanted: "*Establish the soul of His servant Kalypso, departed from us, in the tentings of the Just; give her rest in the bosom of Abraham; and number her among the Just, through His goodness and compassion as our merciful God.*"

Fanis crossed himself again and said out loud, "Farewell."

27

A Recipe Resurrected

EXHAUSTED AFTER CARRYING BOXES UP three flights of stairs, Kosmas made himself a Nescafé and collapsed onto the padded bench of his oriel window. Boiling-hot coffee spilled onto his jeans. "*Siktir*," he said, feeling the coffee burn his leg. Fuck it.

He set the mug on a box, took off his pants, and threw them onto the floor. Then he examined the pink mark on his thigh: after twenty years of assessing his own burns in the pâtisserie, he could tell it wasn't serious. He settled back down on the oriel bench and took a sip of the remaining coffee.

"*Ach*," he said aloud.

He hated instant coffee, but it was better than nothing. He had only moved into his apartment the day before, and he still didn't have a proper coffee pot. He looked out the window, over the Bosporus. A fast boat on its way to Bostancı left a trail of white in the Sea of Marmara. Üsküdar, on the opposite shore, was lit up bronze and gold in the last strong rays of sunset. Its windows looked as if they were on fire. Kosmas had chosen the apartment for Daphne, who loved oriels. The kitchen was narrow, the floorboards creaked, and the rent was ridiculous, but the building was a beautiful example of late Ottoman architecture. It had high ceilings, floral carton-pierre wall decoration, original flooring and tiles, and richly carved woodwork. Kosmas could already imagine Daphne sitting on the window bench, drinking Turkish coffee with him, watching the Bosporus traffic, or studying some history book—perhaps Edmondo de Amici's *Constantinople*. They were going to be happy here . . . *if* he could convince her to give him another chance.

Kosmas picked up his phone to call her. He selected her number, but instead of pushing the button, he just stared at her name. According to Fanis and Selin, Daphne was due back in Istanbul in one week. But it would only be a flash Holy Week and Easter visit—eight days in total. Kosmas wondered if her secrecy about the upcoming visit stemmed from her desire to surprise him or from second thoughts about their relationship. Perhaps he should call, tell her about the apartment, and convince her to stay with him. But begging probably wasn't going to help anything. He decided to wait until she arrived to tell her about the apartment. He would walk her in—blindfolded—and present her with a fully furnished place, empty dresser drawers for her clothes, and bathroom shelves that awaited women's creams and powders. He'd even buy a pair of slippers and place them by the door, ready for her bare feet. Size 37.

Kosmas dropped the phone back onto the oriel cushion, set the empty mug on the box beside him, and closed his eyes. His moving day had not gone well. He had expected that Rea would give him a few household things, cook and package a couple of days of food, perhaps even accompany him to the furniture store. But since Dimitris had moved in, Rea had been distracted. She had stopped making cheese pies for Kosmas's afternoon snack, and she no longer cared whether he watched their favorite TV shows with her. She'd spent his moving morning at the hairdresser's. Later she had called to apologize for her forgetfulness and offer to bring Kosmas dinner, but when she learned that the apartment was a sixth-floor walk-up, she sighed and said, "Why don't you come here instead?"

Kosmas was too tired to descend the stairs at that point, but he couldn't complain: one of the main reasons he'd chosen the flat was that it was entirely inaccessible to his mother. He sat up, transferred his empty mug to the herringbone parquet, and picked up his pocketknife to open the small package beside him. It wasn't one of the boxes from his mother's house, but rather something that Uncle Mustafa had sent over with the delivery truck. Kosmas cut through the tape, opened the flaps, and found Hamdi's three volumes of recipes. It had to be some sort of mistake. Kosmas called Mustafa. "Uncle?" he said. "Your grandfather's books were delivered to me."

"Of course they were."

"But shouldn't they be kept in the Lily's safe? Until you find a better place than beneath your bed, at least?"

"They're my housewarming gift," said Uncle Mustafa.

Kosmas felt his throat constrict. "But these are family heirlooms . . ."

"Correct," said Uncle Mustafa. "You're family, and they're yours."

Kosmas stared at the books, caressed the smooth leather binding. They had an entirely new charm now that they were his.

"But there's a condition," said Uncle Mustafa. "You're not going to let them sit on a shelf like museum pieces. I want them to smell of cinnamon until your dying day."

"Not just cinnamon," said Kosmas, his voice wobbly with emotion, "but also nutmeg, chocolate, *mahleb*, vanilla, and every other sweet thing in my kitchen. I promise."

The gift helped Kosmas to refocus. Despite the moving mess, he had to perfect the Balkanik for Palm Sunday, Daphne's name day. Although he'd been experimenting since January, the variously flavored creams still didn't complement each other as they should. For that reason, he had hesitated to add orchid-root cream, even though Hamdi's recipe contained it as a flavor option. To Kosmas, the addition of orchid root would be a cacophonous overload. Furthermore, *Orchis mascula* and *Orchis militaris* roots, grown only in Turkey's

Kahramanmaraş region, were now so rare that their export had been banned. Even within Turkey, genuine, unadulterated *Orchis* tuber powder was a precious commodity. But it was the only thing that Kosmas hadn't yet tried.

He remembered that Muharrem, the septuagenarian owner of the famous candy shop in the Balık Pazarı, sold a very expensive orchid-root drink called *sahlep* in the winter months. Muharrem was too much of a traditionalist to use anything but the purest ingredients in his sweet, warm, rosewater-flavored *sahlep*. So Kosmas called the shop and explained that he was using a recipe that demanded pure *Orchis* tuber powder of the finest quality.

"Odd flavoring for a wedding cake," said Muharrem.

"It's not for a wedding cake," Kosmas replied. "It's for something personal, an old recipe called the Balkanik."

"Haaa," said Muharrem. "It was divine. But not everybody used *Orchis* tuber, you know. The creams must have different flavors, but it's up to you to choose."

"I'd greatly appreciate it if you could get me some. I need it for—"

"A lady. Understood. How much do you need?"

"A kilo."

"I'll give it to you at cost, Kosmas. But you know, it's almost as expensive as gold . . . "

"How much?"

"590 lira per kilo."

A week's rent, thought Kosmas. But he'd need at least a kilo for his experiments. "No problem."

"I'll send it over now."

Half an hour later, a delivery boy brought a packet wrapped in white tissue paper with gold stars. Inside was a plastic bag of starchy white powder. Destiny was doing all it could to help.

On Monday evening, after completing his cake orders and regular tasks, Kosmas experimented with variations of the light choux pastry dough, different-flavored creams, and fondant icings. By Wednesday, he had gone through so much butter, flour, and chocolate, so many eggs and nuts, that Uncle Mustafa feared they would have to place special orders so that the bakery would have enough supplies to finish the month. On Thursday at teatime, Uncle Mustafa and his friends gathered to critique the day's experiments: "Good, but not like it was," they said. "Pretty, but not like it was. Almost, but not quite." Kosmas repeated his mantra to himself: *İdare*. You can manage this.

He passed Thursday and Friday nights at work, struggling not only with Hamdi's Ottoman script, but also with the challenge of achieving a taste that he had only heard about and never experienced. All the while, memories of Daphne—the smoothness of her skin on the inside of her thighs, the way her hands fit completely inside his, and the lovemaking that had occurred atop the very table on which he worked—kept breaking his concentration and causing his hands to tremble. On the night before Daphne's expected arrival, Kosmas was so tired that he could hardly stand up. He had to pull a stool to the counter in order to pipe the last creams. Sometime past ten, he stepped outside to calm his nerves with a shot of raki. As he sat in the alley, listening to the scratching of the crickets in the sidewalk weeds and the angry yakking of the seagulls that nested on the building's roof, Uncle Mustafa opened his bedroom window and called, "Shall I come down?"

"Don't trouble yourself," said Kosmas. "I probably didn't get it this time either."

"I'll be there in a few minutes."

Uncle Mustafa descended in black loafers and pajamas, cut the pastry with the care of a contest judge, and inhaled. "A delicate balance of discreet flavors," he said. "Firm but thin pastry. From the scent I'd say you used the organic flour, didn't you?" He took a small bite, closed his eyes, moved it around his mouth, and pronounced his verdict with a blind smile: "*This* takes me back in time."

Kosmas grabbed Uncle Mustafa's shoulders, kissed his waxy forehead, and stepped out into the alleyway. He stretched his hands up to the navy blue sky. "Thank you," he whispered, turning in circles.

Uncle Mustafa called Muharrem the candy-maker. He also rang the doorbells at the nearby apartment blocks where his brother and backgammon partner lived. Then he put the teapot on the stove for their expected visitors and made a strong double coffee for Kosmas, whose hands were shaking from fatigue and over-excitement. Only with an immense effort did Kosmas manage to sip the coffee without spilling too much of it into the saucer.

Ten minutes later, Muharrem arrived, wearing his white lab coat. His expression was inquisitive and serious, like that of a doctor making a bedside visit to an ailing patient.

"Thanks so much for coming," said Kosmas. "I'm so sorry for the late—"

Muharrem held up his hand to quiet Kosmas and said in French, "*Que'est-ce qu'il y a?*" What's the matter?

Uncle Mustafa served him a slice of the pastry. "Your opinion, Master," he said.

Muharrem's white mustache prevented Kosmas from seeing whether he smiled or not, but his eyes brightened. He washed his hands, like a surgeon preparing for a procedure, carefully picked up a clean fork from the steel counter, and swirled it in the creams. "Excellent consistency." He took a bite. "And it seems to me—from the cardamom, which adds a hint of supplication—that you're not just trying to win the lady, but to win her *back*?"

"Yes," said Kosmas. "But I was only following the recipe, so I can't claim that I actually intended—"

"Even *following* is a creative process," said Muharrem, decisively.

"Did I get it right?"

Muharrem took another bite. "From a historical standpoint, yes. This is a very nice version. From a romantic standpoint . . . why don't you ask these fellows?"

Two pajama-clad old men filed inside. They rubbed their eyes and gratefully took the teas that Uncle Mustafa passed out. A few minutes later, after the caffeine and fluorescent lights had awakened them from their television-watching stupor, they tasted the Balkanik.

Uncle Mustafa's backgammon partner—a withered man in a white prayer cap—leaned dreamily back against the refrigerator and said, "This reminds me of Eleni, my first love. We kissed in the boiler room while playing hide-and-seek."

Uncle Mustafa's fat brother sat down on a box of almond flour, causing Kosmas and Uncle Mustafa to exchange fearful glances about the fate of the box's contents. He said, "It reminds me of my neighbor, Janet Benchimol. She broke my heart when she packed off to Israel."

Uncle Mustafa said, "It's everything we lost."

Kosmas slid his hands into his hair, pulling at its roots until it hurt. The pain meant that this was real, that he hadn't fallen asleep and dreamed his success.

"The most important opinion, however," said Muharrem, "will be hers."

Eleven hours later, only four and a half of which were spent in fitful sleep, Kosmas stepped into Neighbor's House, said good morning to the young employees setting up behind the counter, and proceeded to the patio, where Julien sat at the only table ready for customers. Kosmas carefully set a fresh, boxed-up Balkanik on the table and collapsed into one of the canvas patio chairs.

"What's that?" asked Julien.

"A treat I made this morning," said Kosmas. "For Daphne's name day."

Julien opened the flap of his wool overcoat and revealed the jacket of a double-breasted suit. "I put on my Sunday best for the occasion, and I looked so good that I got nostalgic for a Catholic mass. But San Antonio smelled like a goddamn funeral, and the dull hymns almost put me to sleep. I didn't feel any of the sanctity I remember from my childhood. So I came straight to Neighbor's House to keep company with the bones." Julien nodded toward the cemetery, where renegade tea-garden napkins waved like flags on last year's dead stems. Over the winter, discarded water bottles had collected in the cemetery's corners. Kosmas remembered Daphne's Facebook pictures of Miami's spotless, manicured parks. He was embarrassed by Istanbul's litter. Fortunately, red tulips were pushing up between the rubbish and crooked Ottoman obelisks. They were a small consolation, at least.

A cool wind blew into the tea garden, ruffling the branches budding over their heads. Julien shivered. "What's that smell?" he said, sniffing.

"Do I stink?" said Kosmas.

"Not exactly. Kind of like *mahleb* bread baking in a wood oven."

"You mean I smell like a pâtisserie."

"It's not bad. Really."

"I showered and changed, but sometimes the Lily sticks to me."

"Calm down. You're dressed like a *GQ* fashion plate but still you're a wreck. Why don't you run down to the pharmacy for some eye drops?"

"I already tried some," said Kosmas. "They didn't help."

"If I'd been in your place—" Julien began.

"But you weren't," said Kosmas. "So it doesn't matter."

"I don't care whether it matters. You listen to me. It's time to stop jerking off and get the girl, do you hear? Otherwise you'll end up a sorry old man like me, drinking *café-au-whiskey* for breakfast." Julien stood. His chair scraped across the flagstones as he pushed it back. "Here they come," he said.

Kosmas looked up the street. There was Daphne, walking arm-in-arm with her aunt Gavriela, who seemed to be lecturing her about something. Kosmas's eyes traveled over the face he had seen only through a computer screen for the past nine months, the hair that had grown at least ten centimeters since he had last seen it, and the body he remembered better by touch than by sight. Daphne wore a red, unbuttoned gabardine coat and clean, pressed gray pants, the hems of which were "cleaning the pavement," as his mother would say. She had clearly lost weight. Kosmas was struck by how small she was, how delicate. Inside the Skype screen, everything seemed so big.

Kosmas stood but remained rooted to the slate pavement. Julien crossed the patio and embraced Daphne. "I wish you many years, my girl! May you have all that you desire, and in your bed, fire!"

Daphne laughed.

"Health and happiness!" said Kosmas.

Daphne approached him with a sleepy smile. She raised her hands to his shoulders, but as he embraced her, her arms somehow got in the way. He couldn't tell if it had been an awkward move on the part of an exhausted woman, or if it was an effort to push him away. He kissed her cheeks, disappointed that she had shown more enthusiasm for Julien.

"Looks like we need tea," said Gavriela. "Dark as rabbit's blood."

But Kosmas couldn't wait for the tea. He said, "I need to show Daphne something."

Gavriela pulled her dark glasses down her nose and glared at Kosmas over the top of the lenses. "I don't think—"

Kosmas interrupted: "We won't be long. I promise."

He took Daphne's hand in his. Skype could keep a relationship breathing, but it couldn't give you touch. How he had missed her warm hand. As soon as they turned the corner onto Akarsu Yokuşu Street, he pulled her close. She turned her face slightly to the side, so that her chin dug into his chest. Her forehead smelled of jet fuel and cheap airplane soap.

"You came straight here, didn't you?" He squeezed her, as if he were trying to push her body into his, to make it part of him so that she could never leave again.

She took a step backward, forcing him to loosen his embrace. He noticed a wrinkle between her ribbon-like brows. Her mouth was tightly closed. She caressed his cheek, but her expression remained troubled. "We need to talk," she said.

"Let me show you something first."

They started down a sloping street that led to the terrace overlooking Nusretiye Mosque. Because it was early, the tables of the tea garden at the edge of the terrace were still empty. A few faces could be seen in the windows of the apartment buildings above, but there were no passersby. Kosmas looked out to sea. A red ship trailing white foam was sailing between the mosque's two baroque minarets. He leaned on the terrace railing, facing Daphne. "I'm really sorry. My mother's troubles took me by surprise. I overreacted. And then there was just so much to do at the pâtisserie. . . . I should have come, even if it was only for a little while."

The wind blew Daphne's hair into her eyes. She peeled the strands from her face, twisted them, and stuffed the coil into the back of her loose coat. "I'm torn," she said. "I like that you take such good care of your mother, but her prejudices are . . . strong, to say the least. She doesn't want me anywhere near you."

"She doesn't want anybody near her son. She's jealous. Your father is just an excuse. But she'll come around, I promise."

"Even if she does, I'd never be able to live in the same apartment with her."

"Look up there," said Kosmas. He spun Daphne around and pointed to a grand white apartment block with stacked oriels on every floor from the first to the sixth.

"Built in 1897," he said. "See the oriel on the sixth floor? That's mine. I moved out of my mother's place over a week ago. I wanted to surprise you with a furnished place, but I haven't had time to buy anything but a bed. It's still a mess."

Daphne stared upward. The blue sky and a few wispy cirrus clouds reflected on the windowpanes. The wind whistled in the corbels of the first floor. She said, "The oriel must have some view."

"It's yours."

Daphne continued gazing at the building with an expression of wonder. "Your mother?"

"Busy with Dimitris. And you don't have to worry about her visiting us. It's a walk-up. You'll see the whole City from up there without ever setting eyes on her."

Daphne smiled. "It sounds perfect. But what does she think about me moving here?"

Kosmas reached for the railing. "You decided?"

"I got into Bilgi. On a full grant. They want more people working on oral minority history."

Kosmas's heart beat more quickly. That piece of news opened the way to a life together—in the City. "You couldn't do better," he said. "Congratulations."

He slipped his fingers through the hair at the nape of her neck and kissed her. It was a long, energetic kiss, like those of their nights at the Lily: tongues, teeth, lips, all mixed up in a passionate struggle. Kosmas lost himself in her so completely that it took him a few moments to remember where they were—in public, where everyone could see. He pushed the baby hairs back from her forehead. "I missed you."

"I missed you, too. But you didn't answer my question. What will your mother think about me moving here?"

"She knows you've come for a visit. She didn't say anything negative."

"Lack of negative isn't necessarily positive, just an improvement." Daphne drew her fingertips over the scar on his forehead.

"I'm so sorry I upset you," he said.

She placed her hands on his sides, where his love handles used to be. "Would you come to Miami if things didn't work out here? After I'm done with the PhD?"

He looked past Daphne into the unofficial park below, where a few poor migrants were cooking their Saturday lunches on grills forbidden by the municipality. A vendor was circulating with a round tray of fresh mussels and lemon wedges. Kosmas inhaled the scent of the park's pine trees. He couldn't bear the thought of leaving his city, but losing Daphne would be even more painful. "I know we can work things out here," he said. "But if not, I'll do whatever it takes."

She nuzzled her face into his chest. "It's good to be back."

"There's something else," he said. "I've been learning to tango."

"That's sweet of you, but . . . tango caused a lot of problems in my last relationship."

Kosmas felt as if he were sinking into the pavement. He had tried so hard to please her.

"If you get into tango," she said, "you'll want to dance with other women."

"Never. I only want to dance with *you*. I only want to be good enough for *you*. Do you want to see what I've learned?" He stood tall and waited. As Daphne fit her hand into his, he felt like laughing and weeping at the same time. He encircled her back. She wrapped her arm around his shoulder blade. Kosmas led Daphne in a simple tango, without any other music than that which he heard in his heart. She felt different in his arms now. It was as if their bodies were conversing, inviting and replying, giving and receiving, yet moving as one.

And Daphne, instead of wearing a mask of patience, was now relaxed, smiling even, enjoying herself.

They danced the length of the sidewalk at the edge of the ridge, avoiding its potholes, the curb, and a stunted tree that pushed up from a little square of earth in the middle of it. Daphne added adornments: foot taps and circles, as well as tiny caresses of his shin with the tips of her shoes. They ended on one axis, leaning into each other, supporting each other. The tension of Kosmas's lessons with Perihan had dissipated. Joy and ease had taken its place.

"*Maşallah!*" someone called. It was the Arabic expression of joy at events willed by God. Kosmas looked up. A kerchiefed old woman was leaning out of her window. "You dance beautifully!" she added.

Kosmas waved in appreciation, then looked into Daphne's eyes. Her arms slid from the dance position into a true embrace. "There's still something I don't get," she said.

"What?"

"You've done so much to please me. You moved out, you learned tango, you're trying to find that recipe. Wouldn't it have been easier just to get on a plane and come to Florida?"

Kosmas sat on the cliff railing—perhaps an imprudent thing to do in Istanbul, where everything was always breaking—and said "Everything I told you is true. My mother's health issues, work. And I would have come to Miami if it weren't for those things. But if I'm really honest . . . when I was in Vienna . . . or any time I've been outside the City . . . I didn't feel like myself anymore."

She settled into his arms. "I know what you mean."

More than anything Daphne wanted to see his new place—*their* place—but if they went up now, she was sure they wouldn't come out until the following day. She inhaled the sweet, woody pâtisserie aroma of Kosmas's skin, gave him a final kiss, and said, "We'd better go. My aunt asked Selin and Fanis to meet us at Neighbor's House. We shouldn't keep them waiting."

Warmed by the dance and Kosmas's embrace, Daphne took off her coat.

"I'll take that," said Kosmas. "Ladies shouldn't have to carry anything."

How she had missed his chivalry. And how she had missed the City. On the airplane she'd worried whether she had made the wrong decision; whether her mother was right in her comparison of Turkey to Germany in 'thirty-nine; whether she had just thrown her life away for a man who hadn't quite committed to her. But now that she was here, she knew that both Istanbul and Kosmas were home.

They reclimbed the street to Sıraselviler Avenue and approached the patio garden of Neighbor's House, where their friends had gathered beneath the linden tree. Their table was strewn with boxwood branches, which, Aunt Gavriela had explained in the taxi from the airport, was the Istanbul substitute for palms and laurels. Evidently Fanis and the others had come directly from the Palm Sunday liturgy.

Rea, with her head cranked toward the street, spotted her son before anyone else and shouted, "Kosmaki, stay right there! I want to talk to the young lady." She fumbled for her sparkly pink cane and pushed herself to her feet with Dimitris's help.

"Mama, please," said Kosmas.

"Stay right there!"

"*Siktir*," whispered Kosmas, shaking his head.

Daphne giggled at his profanity. "You're sexy when you curse."

Rea's cane made a tinny snapping noise each time it hit the slate pavement: a leitmotif of impending menace . . . *tink* . . . *tink* . . . *tink* . . . like the incessant dripping of Chinese water torture. Daphne's mirth turned to fear. She inadvertently seized Kosmas's forearm.

Rea's brow contracted. Her fuchsia lips hardened, then curled into a smile. "We wish you many years, Daphne," she said, in her most delicate salon voice, "and a very happy name day."

Daphne leaned toward Rea to give her a hug, but the older woman responded with a perfunctory kiss and pulled away.

Fanis brushed a crumb off the wedding shirt that Hüsnü Mirza had made for him last summer. He straightened the silk scarf that he had tied at his neck. "*Maşallah*," he said tentatively. Fanis had said it to convince himself that he was happy for Kosmas, and he found, as he let the word settle, that he truly was. At least somebody was going to get married and perpetuate their race. He transferred his gaze to Aliki, who sat at the head of the table, nervously blinking her blue-powdered lids. It was the first time he had seen her since their encounter outside the Greek Consulate, and he was eager to show that he harbored no resentment. "Aliki," he whispered, "do you think that Rea's really going to come round?"

Aliki stuck the knuckle of her index finger to the bottom of her nose and said, "The countryside is always beautiful before the storm."

"*Daha dur bakalım*," said Gavriela, in Turkish. Let's wait and see.

"*Yaaaa*," said Julien, with a doubtful eyebrow-raise.

Kosmas took off his leather jacket and held up his finger to Emine, who was passing by. "Would you mind bringing a knife and plates, please?" He peeled back the flaps of the pastry box resting at the center of the table and revealed a large, glistening, snail-shell-like pastry. Fanis took a deep breath of baked butter: this was the real thing, just like the butter Kalypso's mother had used in her homemade *bâtons salés*.

"Is that . . . ?" said Daphne.

From behind, Kosmas pulled her long hair over her shoulders to the nape of her neck. "The Balkanik," he said.

Daphne grabbed his hands, brought them to her face, and kissed them. "You did it."

Kosmas whispered something in her ear. She smiled and nuzzled her shoulders into his chest. That was it, thought Fanis. The boy had her. Even if he didn't know it yet.

"*Nobody* remembers how to make the Balkanik," said Gavriela.

"Uncle Mustafa had some old Ottoman books written by his grandfather, who had a Rum business partner. I found the recipe in one of them."

Fanis looked down at the plate. If the Balkanik pastry could be resurrected, then perhaps there was hope for their community. "Bravo," he said.

"I'm proud of you, son," said Rea. She took the knife from Emine, symbolically crossed the pastry thrice, and cut it into slices. The inside was exactly as it always had been: filled with different-colored and -flavored creams.

"Each cream represents one of the Ottoman Balkan peoples," Kosmas explained. "Bulgarians, Romanians, Albanians, Greeks, Serbs, Croats, Jews, and Turks."

Fanis stood and bustled around the table, serving each of the plates from the left, like a seasoned waiter. This little trick, he had learned long ago, made him appear caring and helpful in women's eyes while simultaneously affording him peeks at their *décolletage*. Although the older ladies had nothing worth seeing and Daphne's lemons were well covered by a conservative top, the lotus-flower tattoo on Selin's left breast showed clearly beneath the edge of her white cotton blouse. Fanis paused for a second, staring at the flower. Purity that rose from the mud. Perhaps he should get a tattoo like that.

Julien clicked his tongue in disapproval and murmured, "*Ayıp,*" the Turkish word for "shame." Selin made a half-hearted attempt to pull her blouse closer to her chest and shot Fanis a coy smile. Rea handed Fanis the last piece. He withdrew his eyes from Selin's and lifted his plate to his nose.

The aromas were delicate: vanilla, chocolate, cardamom, pistachio, and a few that he couldn't distinguish. He sank his fork through the pastry and chewed deliberately while looking up at the bright new leaves of the linden tree. Strangely, no memories came to him. Not even of Kalypso. Instead of reliving his past experiences of the Balkanik, he was anchored to the present, to the flittering sun and shade beneath the linden tree, to the sounds of pleasure his friends made, to the way the Bosporus breeze ruffled Selin's curls, to the honking of horns in Sıraselviler Avenue, to the scent of the cemetery lilacs. He was just here. Now. At Neighbor's House. With the hole in his heart finally filled.

Julien pronounced the standard wish: "And next year with health."

"Forever health!" the friends replied in chorus.

"God willing," said Fanis. "But this day, this moment, is more than enough."

Acknowledgments

I OWE AN ENORMOUS DEBT of gratitude to four women brilliant women: Nadine El-Hadi, my editor at Hoopoe Fiction and the best editor I could have hoped for; Alexandra Shelley, my writing teacher, who taught me so much that I still feel her sitting on my shoulder and whispering advice, even when I write in Greek; Alison Jean Lester, author of *Lillian on Life*, who read, encouraged, and critiqued; Rana Haddad, author of *The Unexpected Love Objects of Dunya Noor*, who believed in the novel and introduced me to Nadine.

Many thanks to all at The American University in Cairo Press for their professional excellence.

I dedicate this novel to my husband, Michail.

Although some settings in this novel are drawn from life, the characters and the plot are entirely fictional.

SELECTED HOOPOE TITLES

My First and Only Love
by Sahar Khalifeh, translated by Aida Bamia

The Girl with Braided Hair
by Rasha Adly, translated by Sarah Enany

The Magnificent Conman of Cairo
by Adel Kamel, translated by Waleed Almusharaf

*

hoopoe is an imprint for engaged, open-minded readers hungry for outstanding fiction that challenges headlines, re-imagines histories, and celebrates original storytelling. Through elegant paperback and digital editions, **hoopoe** champions bold, contemporary writers from across the Middle East alongside some of the finest, groundbreaking authors of earlier generations.

At hoopoefiction.com, curious and adventurous readers from around the world will find new writing, interviews, and criticism from our authors, translators, and editors.